A Painter's Camp

Philip Gilbert Hamerton

Contents

A PAINTER'S CAMP

BY

Philip Gilbert Hamerton

PREFACE TO THE SECOND EDITION.

IN the first edition of *A Painters Camp in the Highlands and Thoughts about Art,* the chapters relating to the Camp were merely intended as a vessel to float the Essays into circulation. The plan was successful, and the Author attained, by a combination which seemed to many critics inexplicable, the kind of position he aimed at Now, however, there is no longer any reason for keeping the Camp and the Essays together, and they will henceforth exist as separate books. In its first form the work was very indulgently received; but a few critics saw faults of style and taste which, in his subsequent writings, the author has done his best to correct. The chief of these faults were an appearance of egotism, and an unnecessary diffuseness, from which the present edition will be found, it is hoped, more free than its predecessor.

PREFACE TO THE FIRST EDITION.

IT is known to all who are acquainted with the present condition of the fine arts in England that landscape-painters rely less on memory and invention than formerly, and that their work from nature is much more laborious than it used to be.

Having studied principally in the northern districts, I had to contend against great difficulties of climate. These difficulties I have entirely overcome, having painted from nature on the most exposed moors of Lancashire and the Scottish Highlands in the worst possible weather, and in all seasons of the year.

With no more than such ordinary powers of physical strength and endurance as are to be found amongst average English gentlemen, I have worked from nature **on the spot** seven or eight hours a day, in the wildest situations, and in the most merciless storms of winter. I have carried through the most delicate processes in colour, hour after hour, when shepherds refused to wander on the hills and sheep were lost in the drifted snow.

If anybody cares to know how this was accomplished, this book will tell him. If the reader happens to be a painter by profession, he will appreciate the utility of the expedients I found it to my advantage to adopt.

The expeditions here narrated were not undertaken in the spirit of whim or freak, or from a love of adventure, as persons unacquainted with the objects of a landscape-painter will in all probability suppose. They were not undertaken in any way for pleasure, but as seriously as any other human labour; and had no other motive than that strong desire which every real artist must feel—to get the utmost amount of attainable truth into my work.

It seems necessary to say this at the outset, because, amongst all the difficulties I have ever encountered, the most insuperable has always been an ignorant misunderstanding of motives; and if the reader happened to share this, the whole scope and purpose of the book would be utterly unintelligible to him.

All persons are not artists, and cannot, therefore, be expected to understand, without a little explanation, that artistic labour is an exceedingly delicate affair, and requires for its successful performance some degree of protection from rain, hail, snow, and wind.

But any one, especially if he happens to be a man of business, may, if he chooses, ascertain practically the desirableness of shelter when one has careful work to do. Let him take his papers out of doors some wild winter's day, with nothing in the way of furniture but a portable three-legged stool and a portfolio. Let him carry this apparatus into the middle of some exposed field, and then apply himself as he best may, without shelter, in the rain and wind, to the prosecution of his business.

There is not a clerk nor an attorney in England who would work under such conditions. Men of business are always far too shrewd—understand the laws of work far too well—not to perceive the immense advantage to the workman of having his body at ease, that he may give his undivided attention to the labour in hand. So their offices and counting-houses are comfortably furnished, and are full of all sorts of contrivances for the orderly arrangement of their materials. And does the reader suppose that delicate drawing does not require at least as tranquil a nerve as the addition of a column of figures, or the composition of a letter? It is just as rational for a landscape-painter to take a tent with him to shelter him whilst he works from nature, as it is for a lawyer to rent chambers, or a cotton manufacturer to build himself a counting-house.

Notwithstanding these very obvious considerations, the author has usually found certain invincible misconceptions in most people who are not professed landscape-painters.

Firstly, everybody fancied that I took to tent life because I preferred a tent to a house. This idea was constantly expressed in some such observation as this: "Well, upon my word, I can't see what you like so much in a tent. *I* prefer a good strong stone house with a well-slated roof."

Secondly, a few thought it was from dislike to inns, and argued that the inns were very comfortable, &c.

I did not take to encamping because I preferred a tent to a house ***as a habitation,*** but simply because I found it considerably more portable. My largest tent weighs about one hundredweight—a comfortable house weighs above a thousand tons. It takes about twenty minutes to pitch the most elaborate of all my tents—a good house cannot be built and made ready for habitation in less than twenty months. My best tent cost me a little over twenty pounds—a comfortable house would cost at least a thousand. To have a house of this kind built on every spot where I have pitched my tent would have cost hundreds of thousands of pounds.

I am certainly not very fond of inns; but that is not the reason why I prefer my tent to them. The real reason is, because it is necessary for me to pitch my tent *exactly* (that is, to a few inches) in such a position that I may see a good natural composition through my plate-glass window without stirring from my seat. Now, after considerable experience of Highland inns, I may be permitted to state that as a rule they are not provided with plate-glass windows—that, in fact, at this moment I remember no instance of a plate-glass window in any inn or hotel north of the Clyde—and common glass distorts objects; and, therefore, it is of no use trying to see through it, for any purpose of art.

And there is yet another objection. So far as my memory serves me, Highland inns are somewhat heavy tabernacles, weighing, I should say, a good many tons each; and, being usually built on the earth, and not erected on wheels, it is exceedingly difficult to stir one of them without pulling it down. So when the view visible from one's bedroom window (in the height of the season, usually a garret) does not happen to be quite suitable as a composition, what is to be done, if it should happen to rain?—and rain is a natural phenomenon which not unfrequently occurs in the Highlands of Scotland. What painters residing at inns usually *do* in wet weather is no great mystery. They read the newest **Glasgow Herald** they can lay hold of, or study **Black's Guide,** or smoke tobacco, or drink whisky, or talk to the landlady— all very praiseworthy and profitable occupations, no doubt, only they don't paint from nature.

The light sketching tents sold by the colourmen are good things in their way for summer, but of little use in winter. It is impossible to work long in the snow without a fire as well as shelter. In my tent I work just as well in winter as in summer, having a little stove to heat it. The season of the year is, in fact, a matter of absolute indifference to me, so far as it concerns my work, except that in winter the days are shorter.

HOW THE NOTION OF ENCAMPING DEVELOPED ITSELF.

First form of the idea. Something to shelter a painter from the wind and rain, and yet enable him to see. This led to the devising of a hut for shelter, with plate-glass windows to see through.

Second form of the idea. Suppose the hut erected, somebody must sleep in it to guard it at night. It was a long way from home, if I slept in it myself I should be spared a long walk at each end of the day. This led to sleeping in the hut

Third form. The small troubles of life reminded me that servants are useful people. Accommodation for a servant was wanted. I devised a combination of tent and hut for him. This led to a transition from huts to tents; and now, 1866, my camp is all of canvas—two ordinary tents and a studio tent

Lastly, I may as well confess that having tried camp life I took a great liking for it, and to this day enjoy nothing so much, unless it be sailing.

A PAINTER'S CAMP.
BOOK I.—IN ENGLAND.

CHAPTER I.
A WALK ON THE LANCASHIRE MOORS.

I HAD a wild walk yesterday. I have a notion of encamping on the Boulsworth moors to study heather; and heartily tired of being caged up here in my library, with nothing to see but wet garden-walks and dripping yew trees, and a sun-dial whereon no shadow had fallen the livelong day, I determined, in spite of the rain, to be off to the moors to choose a site for my encampment. Not very far from this house still dwells an old servant of my uncle's, with whom I am on the friendliest terms. So I called upon this neighbour on my way and asked him if he would take a walk with me to the hills. Jamie stared a little and remarked that "it ur feefil weet," but accompanied me nevertheless, and a very pleasant walk we had of it.

By climbing over innumerable stone-walls, and following here and there the course of a narrow sloppy lane for a few hundred yards, we got at last on the wild heath. I think no scenery in England could be sadder or wilder than such scenery as that in such weather. Fancy a vast bleak range of hills partitioned into fields by leagues upon leagues of stone-walls, with here and there a dreary village where the quarrymen live who work in the stone-quarries on the hills, and one or two desolate mansions of the Elizabethan age standing forlorn on the bare hills, their fair parks cut up into pastures, their oak-woods felled long ago, their wainscoted chambers empty and cold, and their lofty gables rent and tottering. These, with the uncouth manners of the peasantry, and the harshness of their northern dialect, recall vividly that wonderful flight of Jane Eyre from the house of Mr. Rochester. Those passages of landscape-description which every one has admired in that marvellous novel were studied by the young woman who wrote it from this very country I am trying to describe now. We passed one or two little out-of-the-way houses that answered exactly to the description of that where Jane Eyre found shelter and friends, and any painter who would illustrate that part of the novel should come here for his backgrounds.

Having found a wild mountain-road, we followed it till we came to the real heather region. I examined very carefully every spot which appeared favourable for camp-work, but have not yet decided which to choose finally. We had crossed the border of Yorkshire before we turned to come home, and I found a very fine wild valley, with one side of it covered with magnificent stones, as big as Highland cottages, scattered about like pebbles on the sea-shore. After spending some time amongst these stones seeking for natural compositions, I was forced to return homewards by another route, as night was coming on, and the moors were misty, and we were very likely to be lost.

And lost we were, and that utterly, for when we got out upon the great broad summit of the moor, night had come on, and I could not see my hand. Jamie was about a hundred yards from me when he began to get confused, and cried out,

"Mestur Gilburd, Mestur Gilburd, con yau tell me where Worsthorn lies?"

"Yes, certainly," I answered, in the most perfect confidence; "it lies down there in the west, where the wind comes from."

"Nay, nay," said Jamie; "I know naut abaat it mysen, but I dunnot think yau'll find it, sur, if yau go thither."

"Well, which way must we go, then?"

"I connot tell."

So I told Jamie to wait till we got together, and then I said we had better walk on till we came to a wall which I knew crossed the moor near some recent enclosures. And we kept together in the darkness, stumbling and falling over the boggy ground, through the pelting rain, as we best could, till I fell into a ditch, and in stretching forth my hands felt what seemed to be a rock immediately in front of me, and then by touching its surface, as a blind man reads an embossed book, discovered that it was of rude masonry and not rock, and then called out in triumph that I had found the wall. On this rose a difference between us as to the direction in which we ought to follow our newly-found guide; but, happily for both of us, I yielded the point and followed Jamie along the wall-side for what seemed an interminable distance, till we came suddenly against another wall that ran at right angles to the first, and then we knew that the road lay there on the other side.

Our anxieties over, I wanted to have a cigar, but my pockets were wet and matches spoiled. So we marched quickly along the road, which was just visible, and mile after mile of the black moorland passed away to the rear unperceived.

At last we came to a village, and seeing, by the glimmering light from a window, a crooked branch of oak, without bark or leaf, suspended over an open door, I knew that we were at the sign of the Crooked Billet in Worsthorn, and entered therein and lighted my long-deferred cigar, and refreshed myself and Jamie with hot ale and the contemplation of a brightly-blazing fire, and then we came home.

Barbarous is the artistic design of the old carved bed I slept in here last night, and slender are its claims to a sculptor's admiration, but as I lay meditating in it after a luxurious bath, and watched the firelight glance unsteadily on grim visages carved deep in the dark panels, and on the absurd old pillars rashly built to outrage all the laws of construction and common sense, with their huge carved blocks of timber, held together by weak and slender shafts—and on the great oak tester these pillars painfully carried century after century, they themselves trembling at every sound under their ponderous burden—I forgave for once all these picturesque barbarisms, and thought myself happy to lie once more under that threatening old tester rather than out on the wet moor with the cold low rain-cloud for a canopy.

CHAPTER II.

THE AUTHOR INVENTS A NEW HUT.

I AM quite determined to encamp to study heather; there is none of it near enough to go to every day, and I must have a few careful studies of it, no matter what trouble and inconvenience they cost me. These green fields and pleasant pastures are all very well in their way, but no preparation for the Highland foregrounds: I hate prim hedges and smooth meadows, belted with plantations. The only valuable bit of study near at hand is a little sandstone stream; but one cannot long work at the same kind of subject without getting contracted ideas.

If I go and live a month on the moor, I think it will be long enough to produce a satisfactory oil study of foreground detail. Then, if I find that camp life suits me, I intend to follow out the plan in the Highlands of Scotland for some months every year.

I have been very busily occupied with the invention of a new hut, which is at last finished, and which appears to promise every accommodation I require in a wonderfully small space. The hut is erected in the garden here, where it excites a good deal of curiosity. It consists entirely of panels, of which the largest are two feet six inches square: these panels can be carried separately on packhorses, or even on men's backs, and then united together by iron bolts into a strong little building. Four of the largest panels serve as windows, being each of them filled with a large pane of excellent plate-glass. When erected, the walls present a perfectly smooth surface outside, and a panelled interior; the floor being formed in exactly the same manner, with the panelled or coffered side turned towards the earth, and the smooth surface uppermost. By this arrangement, all the wall-bolts are inside, and those of the floor underneath it, which protects them not only from the weather but from theft, an iron bolt being a great temptation to country people on account of its convenience and utility. The walls are bolted to the floor, which gives great strength to the whole structure, and the panels are carefully ordered, like the stones in a well-built wall, so that the joints of the lower course of panels do not fall below those of the upper. The roof is arched, and covered with waterproof canvas. I have been careful to provide a current of fresh air, by placing ventilators at each end of the arch, which insures a current without inconvenience to the occupant

This hut is a perfect master-piece of joiner's work, and I have no doubt will completely answer my purpose. It would have been a great treasure in the Crimea, but the design is too expensive and too elaborate for military purposes. For the study of snow in windy weather, when the drifts are most beautiful, it will be a most precious addition to my artistic apparatus, for I shall be able to sit comfortably inside, and still see my subject through the plate-glass just as well as without it, and yet be perfectly protected from the wind. I have described this little hut in detail, because I think some such invention might be of real service to our modem school of naturalistic landscape-painters, whose work from nature is of so exceedingly arduous a character that it ought to have every facility that human ingenuity can contrive for it. I hope, ultimately, to ascertain experimentally how far inventions of this kind may assist artists in their endeavours after truth, and to publish for their benefit any results I may arrive at.

Since the hut was set up in the garden, many of our friends have seen it. One young lady thought it would make a good kennel for my big Newfoundland dog; but an old lady of rank would not hear of any such disparaging comments upon it, and declared very positively that she considered the hut a bit of most refined luxury, adding that she could live in it herself very happily indeed, if necessary.

I have invited one of my most intimate friends, and we have inaugurated the hut with a small banquet, at which we two only were present. The house being at no great distance, everything passed off satisfactorily enough, but I look forward with some anxiety to the difficulties of the culinary department when I am alone on the hill, with no friendly kitchen within call.

CHAPTER III.

UNDER CANVAS—THE WEATHER UNPROPITIOUS.

I AM in camp at last, on the frontier line between Lancashire and Yorkshire, on a vast moor which extends far in every direction. We carted the hut over the hills, and have erected it in a very convenient position. The road led us over ground so treacherous that we were often axle-deep in the morass; but we arrived here safely after all, and built the hut in its place before nightfall, when the men left me.

The rain pelted furiously in the evening, and I was fortunate in getting my house built during the fine hours of the afternoon. The wind, too, rose at night, and howled wofully enough over the moor; but the hut seemed wonderfully snug and cosy when I lighted my pipe and made myself a cup of tea.

When the pipe was finished, I slung my hammock and fell asleep; but during the night there came a storm of wind and rain that made the hut tremble and quake before it. I awoke suddenly, and when restored to a full consciousness of my position, found myself alone, in a sailor's hammock in a slight little wooden cabin, on the stormy heights of a northern moor.

My first sensation was that of imminent danger at sea. I thought the spray beat against the window of my cabin, but it was only the furious rain; I thought the sails flapped above me in the storm, but it was only the canvas roof; I expected the cabin to pitch and roll, but it remained steadfast, though trembling in every fibre.

Then, at last, I became aware that I was not at sea, but only alone on the hills, a thousand feet above it; and I turned in my hammock with an ineffable sensation of profound comfort and satisfaction.

On awaking the next morning, I felt so warm and comfortable, that the idea of getting up was exceedingly repugnant to me; but, having reflected that I had no servants to prepare my breakfast, I came to the wise conclusion that I had better bestir myself and get forward with my work. I had done very little towards effecting a convenient arrangement of all my things when a boy arrived with milk, and offered to fetch me water and show me the nearest spring.

Whoever would realize my position here, should read *Jane Eyre* over again, and pay particular attention to her descriptions of the moor country. I am at the highest point of the mountain-road from Burnley to Heptonstall, about two hundred yards from the border line of Lancashire. I enjoy my rambles on the moor exceedingly. I like the long lines of these hills, with their endless variety and sweet subtlety of curve. They are not mountains, nor have they any pretension to the energetic character of the true mountain-form; but they have a certain calm beauty, and a sublime expression of gigantic power *in repose,* that we do not find in the loftier ranges. If I were not determined to study in the Highlands of Scotland, I could find work enough in these Lancashire and Yorkshire highlands to last my life. They are deficient, however, in the grand element of *water;* and that is a sufficient reason why I have no business to remain here very long, when thousands of noble effects are passing every day from the great northern lakes unobserved and unrecorded.

I am down in a little dell, for shelter, and because the foreground here suits me; but I have only to walk a few yards to see Pendle and all the blue Craven hills, which, from this elevation, look exceedingly grand; a few hundred feet lower, the base of Pendle shuts out all the others. There is a perfectly delightful little dell close at hand, that is completely hidden from the road, and I half repent I did not establish myself there instead of here, where my hut is visible to the passers-by, which will probably cause me some annoyance. As to the other hollow, I found it out by accident, and too late. It is a sweet natural lawn of short soft grass, surrounded by a gigantic wall of ponderous rocks, all crowned and tufted with purple-flowering heather. A tiny stream of crystalline purity winds through this exquisite hollow; and one cannot help imagining that the fairies dance by moonlight on its delicate grass, and revel by its little stream.

I mentioned in the first chapter what a noble valley there is near here, and what magnificent stones. For studies of massive individual **stones,** the Flask Moor is as good as a Highland glen. Blocks equal in size to a good dining-room are strewn about with such colossal energy as almost to revive in one the infantine conception of Divine operation, and to lead one to imagine that a giant-god of mighty muscle and sinew had hurled them about in the sportiveness of supernatural strength.

There are a few farm-houses in these wilds, some of them old, but for the most part not picturesque, and especially deficient in colour. The stone-walls, that cut up the country into thousands of parallelograms and trapeziums, do not carry their geometry over the great heights of Boulsworth; but wherever land is enclosed in this region, it is always by these dull brownish-gray stone lines, hateful alike to the hunter and the artist.

The weather has been exceedingly rough since I took up my residence here. The first night was wet, as I said above, but the second a storm came on at dusk, and during the whole night a hurricane blew from the east, catching one end of my hut, and making it tremble and vibrate all night long. I had some fears for the gables, which are not so well supported as the other panels. However, they stood perfectly staunch; but often during the night violent squalls shook my frail habitation and rattled its contents loudly. My tin salt-box rattled the whole night, or at least was busy rattling every time I awoke. A gust of extraordinary violence would come at intervals, flapping the canvas, so that it gave loud reports, as a ship's sails do in a tempest. The driven rain whipped the window, pans danced and jingled on their shelves, the boards of the hut shrieked in the storm's path, and the canvas flapped with sharp reports like pistol-shots. I determined quietly what I would do if the wind tore the roof off; and having arranged all the details to my satisfaction in a sort of programme, turned over and fell asleep; and though sometimes awaking afterwards to find myself in the dark, with such a confusion of noises about me as might almost have frightened me, I always immediately recollected where I was, turned over quietly, and fell asleep again. Sometimes the flapping of the canvas sounded unpleasantly like the efforts of some robber to break into the hut; but I did not think a thief would have the sense to choose a confusing night. My dog was well off the wind, as his kennel is to the west. In the morning I made an unpleasant discovery. Before the hut was bolted together, I wished to grease the joints with tallow; but the joiner who made it, being very proud of his workmanship, had persuaded me that the joints were so exquisitely fitted that there was no occasion for tallow at all; so I omitted that precaution, and the water gets in. I tried to tallow the joints inside, but could not keep the wet out.

The morning was terrific, and it rained incessantly all day; still I worked very steadily at my foreground. I drew the ground with perfect ease in all its detail, as deliberately as if I had been copying a picture in the Louvre. The subject I intend to paint here is an admirable study of foreground, rich in every variety of moorland vegetation, and I shall stay here until I have every leaf and blade of it on canvas. The season is already too far advanced for the finest purple of the heather-bloom; but what remains of it is still precious, and an infinite variety of colour lies half-hidden under the blasted stems of the burnt heath. Delicate little ferns of the purest green lie close to spots of scarlet as bright as the plumage of tropical birds. Then there are those exquisite oases, where the grass is shorter and softer and greener than palace-lawns, and where, when you go near enough, you may see that a spring, pure and abundant, washes continually every blade with its sweet waters.

The evening did not promise much comfort: it was excessively stormy, and I did not lay my carpet down, on account of the wet. I did contrive, however, to give some appearance of comfort to matters, and drank my cup of tea in peace; after which I got a pipe and a book. I set pans to catch the water, which now dropped at many places, and having hung my hammock in the middle, instead of at one side of the hut as usual, and unscrewed the legs from my table to get it out of the way, got into bed and fell asleep directly, in the midst of a thousand noises.

The storm went on, I suppose, during the night with its old fury, for this morning it seems not at all abated. The wind, however, has veered to the north-east, and so I am better sheltered than yesterday. I am getting a little tired of hearing the water drop into my pans and beat against my house, but so accustomed to it that it is beginning to seem quite the normal state of things, and an odd sort of feeling begins to gain upon me, that I am alone in a dreary land, where it raineth for ever and for ever.

CHAPTER IV.

THE AUTHOR HIS OWN HOUSEKEEPER AND COOK.

WHILST writing a letter this evening to a friend at a distance, it occurred to me to give him a detailed history of one day, as the most likely way to make him understand the sort of life I am leading here. Before sealing the letter, I will copy out that passage for my portfolio.

A. M.

6.0.—Awake, and feel far too comfortable to get up, especially on wet mornings, so turn over on the other side and go to sleep again.

6.45.—Begin to think seriously of getting up.

7.0.—The absolute necessity of getting up presents itself to my mind with terrible distinctness. Begin to feel hungry, and remember that there is nobody here to care whether I am hungry or not, and that if I don't want to perish of sheer famine, I had better get up without further hesitation and make myself some breakfast.

7.10.—Rise vigorously and make my bed. This operation is performed as follows:—I fold the blankets and sheets together till they assume the dimensions of a cushion, about three feet six by one foot three inches. This cushion, decently inclosed in a railway rug, forms a truly decorous and even luxurious protection from the hard oak military chest I sit upon during the day. The hammock being rolled up into the compass of a cylinder two feet six inches long, by four inches in diameter, is strapped well out of the way against one wall of the hut.

7.15.—Make my toilet out of doors in all weathers, often in a neighbouring stream. Brush my clothes, oil my boots, and dress. Having trimmed and lighted my spirit-lamp, and set the pan on with water in it for porridge, rewash my hands and make a large mess of porridge, one half of which I commonly consume myself, whilst the other is destined for the dog, who is the *gentleman* of the establishment in the vulgar sense of the title, as he does nothing whatever for his living.

8.0.—Milk-boy arrives punctually. I eat my porridge with new milk. After this the inevitable toils of washing-up.

8.30.—Go out for half an hour, and walk a mile on the moor with my dog.

9.0.—Set to work at my painting. Paint four hours.

P. M.

1.0.—Lunch, and take another ramble with the dog.

2.0.—Resume painting.

5.0.—Cease painting for the day. Clean brushes, then set about cooking, and generally produce dishes of great novelty, entirely different from anything I intend. The totally unexpected character of these results lends great zest to my experiments in culinary science. Dine. After dinner the woful drudgery of washing-up! At this period of the day, am seized with a vague desire to espouse a scullery-maid, it being impossible to accommodate one in the hut without scandal, unless in the holy state of matrimony: hope no scullery-maid will pass the hut when I am engaged in washing-up, as I should be sure to make her an offer.

7.30.—On fine moonlight evenings take a walk on the moors, on wet ones stay in-doors. The hut is delightful at night, when my curtains are drawn and candles lighted. The wilder the night the better. When the storm-wind sweeps the desolate moors, I only feel that extreme sensation of comfort that one experiences in the snug cabin of a nobleman's yacht far away on the dark seas. Fancy a miniature interior, wainscoted with white panels like those in old country houses that some Vandal has whitened in Queen Anne's classic time; fancy this interior arched over with a roof of emerald green, with little curtains of the same colour before its windows, and a dark red carpet on its tight wooden floor; the walls hung with choice little engravings, a book or two on the table, a cup of tea, and the kettle singing over a spirit-lamp. Then, with a cigar, or perhaps a long, grave-looking meerschaum, and a favourite author, I recline luxuriously in this miniature palace, and chuckle inwardly as I think of certain friends who fancy me shivering with cold and half frozen in the long dark nights. My great dog, too, lies stretched on the warm carpet till the time comes to break up this pretty picture of repose, and then he goes to his canvas kennel, where he has plenty of clean straw to lie in and a big bone to play with.

11.0.—Sling my hammock. Put a loaded revolver on the table, then spread on the stretched hammock a sack of white counterpane containing two inner sacks, one of blanketing and the other of sheets, cunningly sewn together according to a plan of my own, whereby the chief inconvenience of a narrow bed—namely, the certainty that the clothes will be all on the ground before morning—is happily overcome. So I enter with much circumspection the narrow neck of this treble sack, and having fairly bagged myself, extinguish the candles and thus conclude the day.

If ever again I spend a few months in France, I shall certainly apprentice myself to a cook. Every one who has the most remote chance of being thrown on his own resources, should study cookery as a science. Here am I in the wilderness, incapable of preparing the plainest English dinner without some inevitable catastrophe! Any handy little French soldier would live here like a prince.

There is but one thing I can cook tolerably, and that is porridge. I always make porridge for breakfast, and eat it with new milk. The advantages of hot porridge over coffee and eggs are numerous, chiefly on account of economy of time. Porridge, however, requires salt, which, of course, I continually forget to put in, as, if there is any possibility of making a mistake, I am sure to make it. One does not recognize any saline taste in good cookery, but when the salt is omitted, there is an unpleasant insipidity.

My dinner to-day was rather ambitious, being an attempt to imitate the Parisian côtelette de mouton aux pommes de terre. The potatoes are cut into thin slips, and the cutlets fried; but I entirely failed to obtain that dry, yellow crispness that the French cooks give to their potatoes, and I cannot conceive how they manage it. [Notes *: I ought to have used more grease. The French cooks fry potatoes in great quantities of melted lard, so as to immerse them in a sea of boiling oil. Thus they may be sufficiently cooked without losing that artistic gold colour I was trying for. It is very well, however, that I knew no better. If I had suspected that plenty of lard was all that was wanted, I should infallibly have set fire to my habitation.] I cannot say much for my cooking apparatus. It consists of two spirit-lamps, one under the other. With one alone the heat is insufficient. With both it is so excessive as to spoil not only the viands, but the apparatus itself, which is only soldered, and solder is easily fusible. My stove is all in pieces, and now my frying-pan is ruined, for the tin lining has melted, though there was plenty of grease, and I turned the cutlet continually. I must have a little iron frying-pan.

The result of these annoyances is, that I mean to get as much provision as I can eat whilst it is good, by a weekly messenger from home, and to confine my cookery to porridge, coffee and tea, eggs, and a cutlet occasionally. I expect Jamie here one of these days with a basketful of roast beef, roast grouse, potted partridge, and other provisions; in the meantime, I have nothing but raw meat in a safe outside the hut, and must struggle bravely against adversity. Oh for the skill of a Soyer!—and materials to exercise it upon.

But what I hate most is the washing-up. I tried it once with cold water, but it would not do; the fat stuck faster than ever to the plates. I know better now, and heat the water, which melts the fat, and so I get my plates tolerably clean. How I do admire and respect all scullery-maids! What skill and industry do they not all exhibit! these young ladies whose profession, in this wise country of ours (as Thackeray said of painting), is scarcely looked upon as liberal.

How pleasant it would be if one could live upon the incense of cigars! A cigar needeth not to be cooked, and it entaileth not the subsequent troubles of washing-up. A cigar will keep for years; it is light and portable; it is a very miracle of convenience! It yieldeth its sweet smoke in a moment, and wearieth not the patience of him who desireth its consolations. Oh how happy would that painter be who could dwell for weeks upon the lonely hills, with no other provision than the contents of a little pink-edged box of cedar-wood, decorated with outlandish heraldries, and an inscription in the Spanish tongue!

CHAPTER V.

ADVANTAGES OF THE HUT.

HERE am I, painting from nature on a Lancashire moor twelve hundred feet high, in the month of October, in a storm of wind and rain, with my colour-box on a table by my side, and every convenience and comfort about me. Any one who doubts the utility of this hut may come and do without it what I have done to-day. For six hours I have calmly studied the heather tuft by tuft, and the grass blade by blade, and the green mosses and delicate small fern, when you would not have turned a dog out of doors, and the shepherds themselves refuse to wander on the hills. On such a day what painter could work outside in the wind? I can scarcely conceive the results to my success in art that may follow from this contrivance. My winter studies will be as perfect as my summer ones.

The weather is of little consequence now, as far as work is concerned. I shall keep steadily to my painting, however wet it may be, unless the wind should cover my plate glass with rain-drops, which will only happen when it is in the west, and even then I could study out of another of my four windows. An exceedingly heavy fog would also interrupt even foreground study, but from mere wind and cold I have nothing to fear. Every morning I awake close to my work, and, as the place is lonely enough, may reasonably hope to pursue it in peace. The bitterest gale that ever stiffened the morass would not benumb my hand, and I could copy the storm-sculptured curves and azure shadows of the snowdrift as deliberately as the purple heaths of autumn or the tender flowers of spring.

Yes, the hut is a success! Greater space with greater portability might perhaps be desirable, and in some future embodiment of the same idea not difficult to realize. Still, the plan has succeeded to the full I can study nature now in winter as well as in summer. I have gained six months a year for my art. Ten years of life are as good to me now as twenty were before! There will be no limit to my progress in the knowledge of nature but the limits of life itself. I shall not have to shut myself up and fret my heart out in a studio every wet day. In the Highlands I shall not lose sixty or seventy per cent of daylight hours on account of the climate.

I begin to see already how this idea may be expanded into still greater usefulness. The heat and glare of summer are almost as troublesome to a painter as rain and cold. I perceive that this hut, which protects me well enough against cold, would be no protection whatever against heat; it is not lofty enough, nor large enough. But no mere inconvenience of climate ought to conquer a painter who is really anxious to study, and at the same time both ingenious in devising expedients and determined in the application of them.

The study of nature having been hitherto the smallest and most neglected part of the labours of the landscape painter, instead of the great enjoyment and aim of his existence, it is not wonderful that an age so fertile in other useful inventions should have been able to hit upon no better contrivance to shelter a painter during his hours of study than a white cotton umbrella, or a little tent with one end open.

The truth is, nobody has cared enough about the matter to be thoroughly in earnest. Turner's work, and Stanfield's too, and all the work of the minor painters who aim at the same results, is essentially a matter of memory and invention—memory as to effect, invention as to sub ordinate detail and arrangement of subject. To paint well on these principles requires colossal powers; and even granting him such genius as occurs perhaps once in several centuries, the painter who works on such principles is liable to frequent failures, and failures precisely of that kind which a fastidious public is less and less disposed to tolerate in every successive Academy exhibition. But since in the study of nature there are two distinct classes of difficulties, the intellectual difficulties, which affect only the mind of the artist, and the physical difficulties, which affect first his body, yet necessarily the mind also through the body, it is evident that whoever will entirely eliminate even one class only of these difficulties will have rendered an inestimable service to art. By relieving the painter from all physical inconvenience you also assist him in his intellectual labour, and that to a degree scarcely conceivable by any one not practically an artist. For the unrecorded tortures of burning sun, and bitter wind, and biting frost, and penetrating rain, the Egyptian plagues of flies, the Russian plagues of hail and snow—all hard enough to be borne even by strong soldiers in constant exercise—are terrible trials to a refined artist, delicately organized, who has to support them with the quiet patience of a martyr.

Nobody knows what it is, who has not tried, to sit from morning till night before an easel in the open air, exposed to every caprice of the weather, with a pulse not quickened to resistance by vigorous exercise, but languidly yielding to the gradual mastery of the cruel cold. The policeman and the sentinel may march about, the disengaged cabman may beat his blood into something like circulation by throwing his arms across his breast, but the painter is employed on work so delicate, that, as he lays on his tenderest touches, he cannot even breathe, respiration itself being too disturbing a movement, and the only chance of stirring he can hope for is in deserting his post altogether from time to time. Then the rain comes to dabble his drawing, and he puts it hastily by, and waits perhaps half a day for a chance of returning to his work. So his precious time for study slips out of his hands, and leaves no complete or perfect result, but only unfinished fragments, discouragement, and vexation.

Does not the intellectual labour of the artist provide trials enough for the saint-liest patience, without joining to its inevitable difficulties the simultaneous suffer-ings of the body? We painters have no particular vocation for voluntary martyrdom. The mortification of our bodies will not make our pictures perfect, but the reverse. It is not amongst our duties to injure or destroy the delicate machinery with which we produce our results, but rather to protect it from every adverse influence, and preserve it in the highest attainable state of efficiency.

CHAPTER VI.

WHAT THE PEOPLE THINK.

"WHAT I must do is all that concerns me, not what the people think. This rule," says Emerson, "equally arduous in actual and in intellectual life, may serve for the whole distinction between greatness and meanness."

When art shall be better understood, its followers will have less occasion for the spirit of self-reliance, but in our day the only philosophy for the painter is the Emersonian doctrine of individualism. It is, however, very unpleasant to have to as-sume this ungracious attitude of resistance and opposition. It is especially distasteful to persons who, like myself, have a keen relish for friendship, and to whom the so-ciety of cultivated persons is a necessary of life. And yet there is no help for it. I find it quite impossible to make people understand what I am here for; all explanation is useless. There is nothing left to me but quiet persistence and the patient endeavour to keep my temper, with God's help.

With one or two honourable exceptions, the good folks here, whenever they hear of a painter, think it is a sort of artizan whose trade it is to draw their horses and dogs; and they cannot comprehend, for the life of them, what I can find to paint in such an out-of-the-way place as this. People who are not only no judges of landscape-painting, but not even aware of its existence as a living and progressive art in England, are of course astonished when they hear me assign as a reason for my hermit life on this hill that I am painting a study of heather. [Notes *: The son of a Lancashire country gentleman once observed to the author, "There is no painting now; we never hear of any painters." He did not know that there was a Royal Academy in England; he had never heard anybody mention modern painters. The father of this youth declared to the author that he would not give ten pounds for the finest picture in the world, unless to sell it at a profit; and these were people of property, and belonging to a family whose descent was not merely ancient, but illustrious.] They have a dim notion about painters that they go to Rome when they can afford it, and copy Claude, but as for painting on a moor, why, moors were made to be shot over. Rich people often suppose the end of art to be the direct adoration of Wealth; either by painting its portrait, or its wife's portrait, or its horse, or its dog, or its dwelling-house, or anything that is its. This is quite a country gentleman's conception of art, and we ought to regard it leniently, for it requires much education to enable a man of property to comprehend that objects of little value in themselves may be inestimably precious to an artist, and that even the squire's big house, and his well-groomed hunters, and rich, neatly-fenced fields, may not be worth so much, artistically valued, as a poor cottage on the mountains, with a goat grazing at the door, and a half-wild fawn crouching in the heather, that the children feed, for it is motherless.

It would be exceedingly weak and silly to allow oneself to be angry with kind friends on this account, especially since it is quite clear that their comments proceed less from ill-nature than honest, unaffected astonishment; still, to be frank, I am getting somewhat weary of the polite expressions of wonder that have reached me from every quarter for some time now. The marvel is a month old, at least, and nine days is the extreme degree of longevity to which any marvel, even a provincial one, ought legitimately to attain.

I do not think this little enterprise has much affected my standing with the upper classes. I have a convenient reputation for eccentricity, which allows me to do whatever I will. After the first wonderment about my hut-life has exhausted itself,

I should think it probable that it will be remembered only as a mere whim or freak. It may perhaps excite a little hostility amongst the more ignorant sort of gentry, but they will be too polite to trouble me very much with their impressions, and I don't care what they say behind my back.

But I have certainly lost caste in the popular estimate. I am even beginning to feel that I am not respectable, and to lose the relish for respect. If any one were to treat me as a gentleman now, I should be very much astonished, and hardly know how to support the dignity.

In what consists this subtle element, this etherial emanation, this transient halo of glory that shines on high caste? In modern society what *is* caste?

That it is easily lost is evident. Mine evaporated in an hour over the heat of Soyer's magic stove. The first time I cooked my own dinner all my forefathers disowned me.

The popular notion of a gentleman is that he has plenty of money and nothing to do. If you are not utterly helpless, you are no gentleman. If you would be respected, be lazy. Beware of the sin of self-reliance. It is very well for great men like the Czar Peter, the Emperor Napoleon, and the Duke of Wellington to be active and self-reliant; we of the middle class must be lazier than they, if we would inspire awe in the bosoms of our inferiors.

I knew an Oriental Envoy once at the Hôtel du Louvre, at Paris; we studied French together for some weeks. The waiters called him "the Prince"—he was no prince at all, but only a rich private gentleman. A brother of one of the kings of Europe was staying in the same hotel at the same time, but my friend outshone the genuine blood-royal, and remained **the Prince** during our stay there, though he refused the title twenty times a day. At last he asked me why the people would persist in making him a prince against his will. "My good fellow," said I, "it's because you are so royally lazy. These people have a graduated scale by which they measure a man's rank. 'Man,' they argue, 'is naturally an idle animal; only when poor he is forced to do everything for himself. Therefore, the less a man can do for himself, the richer he is likely to be. Now, this Eastern gentleman is absolutely helpless—as helpless as a baby a month old, he cannot even put on his slippers without assistance—and therefore, of course, he is somebody very great indeed. He is a prince, at least, that is certain!' "

The peasants on these outlandish moors argue precisely like the Parisian waiters. "A real gentleman is as helpless as a child; but this man can cook for himself, and seems quite independent of assistance, *therefore,* he is no gentleman." There is no danger of *my* being in convenienced by princely honours. On my arrival here I found that a gruff gamekeeper looked upon me as a possible poacher, farmers asked me what I hawked, and drovers thought I kept a dram-shop. Women came to have their fortunes told, and children to see a show.

Since I neither poached game, nor sold spoons, nor retailed gin, nor told fortunes, nor exhibited wild beasts, these several hypotheses are by the most part abandoned. I am still, however, so far from being respected, that of the thousand questions put to me by curious peasants who flock from all parts of the country to see me, not ten per cent, are without insolence, at least of manner.

I never before thoroughly understood the contempt the English have for poverty. A gentleman who fancied his inferiors very civil and polite, would learn to distinguish between the deference yielded to his money and the true politeness which is universal as the sunshine, by abandoning for a week or two the external advantages of his position, as I have done here.

The notions of the peasantry on the subject of the art itself are, as is to be expected, even less elevated than the ideas of the upper class. The country people always suppose landscape-painting to be land-surveying; a mistake likely to be universal throughout England, since the Ordnance surveys. I was painting an oil study of an oak tree some time ago, and a gamekeeper in going his rounds came every day to see how I got on. A quiet expression of contempt, mingled with pity, and tempered with a lively sense of the ludicrous, illuminated his intellectual physiognomy as he watched me at work. He evidently did not think such a valueless old tree worth "mappin' " at all, and, as my study advanced towards its conclusion, asked every day with something of impatience, when I "should a' done mappin' th' oud tree?"

Droves of pack-horses cross these hills frequently with lime. I know the owners of them tolerably well, having sometimes had occasion for their ponies. Meeting one of these drovers the other day, I recognized in the driver an old friend of mine, who always keeps up the acquaintance with much polite assiduity, having ultimate views to pints of ale. The following conversation on the fine arts then took place between us.

DROVER.—Eh, why, Mestur Amerton, is tat yau?

THE AUTHOR.—Yes; you did not expect to find me here?

DROVER.—Why, noah, it's sich a lonesome sort of a place, loike.

THE AUTHOR.—Well, but I live here now; I'm not far from my new house,—you must come and look at it, and have a drop of whisky.

DROVER.—Thank ye, sir, thank ye; but I'n never yerd tell o' yau biggin' a new ayus; I allus thout yau're livin' at th' Ollins.

THE AUTHOR.—Oh, I've built a wonderful house—about the size of a hencote; it's only a wooden one, you must know.

DROVER.—Why, an' what are ye livin' up 'ere for, i' sich a mooryet place? Are ye shootin', loike, Mestur Amerton?

THE AUTHOR.—No; I have not killed a grouse since I came here. I came here to paint a picture.

DROVER.—A *picthur!*—why, an' what's tat?

THE AUTHOR—(*adopting the drover's dialect to be better understood*). It's one o' them things as rich folks 'angs up i' their 'ouses i' goold frames, yau knaw, to make their walls look fine. Yau'n sin picthurs wi' shaps o' Prince Alburd an' th' Queen, an' th' Duke o' Wellinton, an' sich loike, i' o' colours. Them's picthurs; naah yau knaw, dunnut ye? [Notes *: For the convenience of Southrons I translate the above learned definition of a picture. "It's one of those things that rich people hang up in their houses, in gold frames, you know, to make their walls look fine. You've seen pictures with shapes (likenesses) of Prince Albert and the Queen, and the Duke of Wellington, and such like, and all colours. Those are pictures; now you know, don't you?"]

Then glimmering visions of cottage art arose before the soul of the drover, dim recollections of saints and soldiers in gorgeous hues, and his old eye brightened with a beam of intelligence. We had now arrived at the hut. Gratitude for the whisky, and perhaps also the pleasing influences of the cordial itself, gave my poor friend such sudden power of criticism that he expressed his appreciation in the warmest manner, and as politely, in his way, as the most complimentary after-dinner connoisseur.

It being universally settled and decided for me all the country over that I am land-surveying, it is no use contradicting the good folks any longer. Why not accept the position?

I am, however, considered a very slow surveyor. There are men in the neighbouring towns who could survey the whole mountain in a week, and here am I, wasting a month over a few square yards of it. The people say that I am the slowest and most incapable bungler that ever measured an acre of land.

There are two exceptions to the general impression that I am engaged in surveying land. But the estimate which these two superior persons have formed of my capacity for art is not flattering. It is true that neither of them has seen my picture, but that is as unnecessary for these rustic judges as for a London journalist. My country critics ground their argument simply upon the length of time which I bestow upon the work. One of them has proved to the satisfaction of all his friends that I am a great fool to come here and spend whole weeks on the production of a picture, when I might buy one equally good at Colne fair, with frame, glass, and all, for sixpence. The other has heard that my canvas is only three feet square, and has demonstrated from arithmetical data that I am the slowest workman in Lancashire, as there are plenty of painters who could paint all the wood-work in a farm-house in less than a week.

CHAPTER VII.

TROUBLESOME VISITORS.

AS I lay in my hammock in the dark—I know not at what hour of the night or early morning—I heard a horrible yell. It was close to the door of my hut; so close that it seemed to proceed from some idiot, or wild beast, or fiend, that had already penetrated to the interior. I was startled out of my sleep, and grasped my revolver before I had any clear notion of the kind of attack I had to apprehend. A minute afterwards, wide awake, I sat listening to the most virulent abuse imaginable; holding all the while the loaded revolver, and watching the door noiselessly; ready, on the first attempt against it, to send a bullet or two through its thin wooden panels. A large stone through the window seemed more to be expected than an attack upon the door; but, unless the stone disabled me, I felt sure of wounding the besieger in any case, and so reserved my five barrels for the last extremity.

I cannot repeat, in a paper intended for future publication, the particular phrases of invective directed against me by my visitor; and it is impossible, without such repetition, to give a true idea of their bitterness. It is enough to say that he exhausted every term of reproach, and every expression of hatred, which is to be found in such English as they speak in this desert; that he poured upon me the whole vocabulary of foulness, and that the delicately-chosen theme of his discourse was the death of my own mother.

It was a genuine commination—a denouncing of God's wrath—a worse than priestly anathema—a great and mighty cursing! The theological hatreds of centuries have not produced a more powerful formula than the simple improvisation of this man's anger.

Now, I reasoned with myself, "This fellow may attack me, and I have certainly a good chance of preventing him, for the deal door is no impediment whatever to a bullet; still, though his talk is irritating enough, I have clearly no right to shoot him merely because he calls me hard names. So I will be as quiet as I can till he attacks me with some other member than his tongue only." Wherefore I sat up in bed as calmly as my now increasing irritation would allow, and directed my revolver to the door or the window as the voice changed in direction.

It was a queer position, certainly. "What if this fellow is only vexing me," I thought, "so as to make me open the door of the hut to him and his accomplices?" He called out continually, "Shoot! shoot, man, shoot!" which might mean that he wanted me to discharge any firearms I had before he attempted to break in upon me. This was a proof that the fellow knew I was armed, but there was nothing remarkable in that circumstance, as I had taken especial care to make my means of defence generally known by practising often with my pistol So I thought the wisest plan would be to sit still for the present and do nothing, as it would be an embarrassing position for me if the country people found a dead man at my door next morning, with a bullet in him, and a little hole through the door, indicating whence the bullet had come. "There is no telling how stupid a jury may be," thought I; "and, besides, if I shoot this fellow, I shall be served up by ten thousand penny-a-liners in all the newspapers in England, and a pretty affair they will make of my camp life here, and the reasons for it"

Suddenly the commination came to a close, the torrent of anathemas was arrested, the horrible howls, the demoniac laughter, and the piercing yells, which had succeeded each other now for many minutes, ceased altogether, a wild shriek or two came from the moor, fainter and fainter, as if retiring in the distance, then all was still.

A little suspicious at first of this sudden stillness, I listened attentively for some sound that might indicate a less noisy but more dangerous attack, but I was soon tired of listening, and so laid my revolver in its case, which I left open, and then fell asleep.

Again I was roused suddenly by the same voice, but this time it was in daylight. The cursing was renewed in all its old vigour, but as I now felt sure that the fellow, though noisy enough, was a thorough coward, and dared not attack me till I had first discharged my revolver; I paid no attention, but got a book and tried to read. When the man left me, the heathcocks crowed, and the early sun shone through the green curtains, and it was time to get up. So the affair ended in nothing after all.

During the whole time my big dog never even growled. He is quite worthless.

They call the poachers here, "the Night Hunters." I expect a visit from them every night, and queer visitors they are likely to be. I have a revolver and dog, but the revolver has only five barrels, and the dog is the most amiable and hospitable creature imaginable, and would receive a fellow that came to murder me as politely as my most intimate friend. If the Night Hunters do me the honour to call upon me, I mean to pursue a peace policy. For the present I keep within doors at night, when these banded outlaws range the moors.

The Night Hunters in this neighbourhood are as determined a set of black-guards as ever leagued themselves together for a lawless enterprise. Fancy thirty or forty of them in a gang, well-armed, and with blackened faces. On one occasion a company of sixty set out on a shooting excursion, some of them dressed in women's clothes, others as devils with straw tails, and all of them in the wildest masquerade, and not to be recognized by the sharpest of detectives. The keepers would as soon have thought of attacking a French army as this gang of desperadoes. If they take it into their heads to upset my box when I'm inside it, that will be pleasant! Nothing could be more likely to afford the fellows congenial amusement; and then perhaps they may set fire to it, and the pitched canvas of the roof would burn delightfully on a dry night! Then it would be quite a clever and facetious practical joke to send a charge of shot through the window, a witticism all the pleasanter that the modest author of it could so easily remain anonymous.

Some years ago these merry forresters took it into their heads to have a day's shooting on the cultivated lands nearer the valley. They made a descent on three estates belonging to friends or relations of mine. It was quite a Highland raid. The Night Hunters brought with them people to beat the covers, and others to carry the game, and, in spite of landlords and gamekeepers, bagged a rich booty of hares and pheasants, with which they returned unmolested to their mountains.

The proprietor of the best moor in this neighbourhood is organizing a little regiment of rustics for the protection of his grouse. They say that each man will have half-a-crown and his supper every time he goes on duty. This will be too expensive to be continued long, and therefore the protection will be only temporary, whereas, to be effective, it must necessarily be permanent. All systems of defence are useless which have only an intermittent character, when the danger to be apprehended is constant.

As for the poachers themselves, they are partly actuated by the love of adventure; partly by the hunter's instinct, which they share with their betters; and partly by a rude but half-chivalrous desire to avenge such friends of theirs as have found their way to the penal settlements in consequence of similar irregularities.

The Night Hunters have left me unmolested. No excursion of theirs has hitherto extended so far as this place. Still I have plenty of visitors, and instead of being weary of the loneliness of this place, as all my friends think I must of necessity be by this time, I am constantly wishing it were much lonelier.

I am the centre of attraction to all the country people within a circle fourteen miles in diameter. Immense numbers of women and children come to see the hut; the male visitors are less numerous, but more troublesome and impertinent. If my dog were worth anything I could keep these people at a respectful distance, but I have no means whatever of doing so on my own responsibility. Without being bloodthirsty, I confess it would give me much pleasure to shoot a few spectators occasionally, by way of teaching them to be civil; but prudence compels me to keep the revolver in its box, and put as good a countenance on the matter as my feelings of irritation will permit.

I can fully understand the refined tortures of a monkey of modest disposition exhibited in a menagerie. I am like one of Wombwell's animals, shown daily, without either pleasure or profit to himself, to a pitiless crowd at a village fair; but I have the peculiar disadvantage of understanding the language in which the various commentaries on my person are expressed.

My plate-glass windows are exceedingly convenient, since they allow the public to inspect the animal at its usual occupations; most interesting observations in natural history being thus rendered possible, as in the case of the glass beehives at the French Universal Exhibition. From frequent observations of this kind, made with the utmost care by several eminent zoologists, it appears that I, the animal in question, am not of a gregarious disposition, that I eat the flesh of birds and other animals, but not in a raw state; and that I am remarkable for my industry, being continually occupied with a kind of labour whose object and utility are still the subject of various learned conjectures. The important question whether I am acquainted with the use of fire is not as yet satisfactorily settled, but there are reasons for supposing that I am, since the flesh I devour has evidently been subjected to the action of heat; still this question remains somewhat obscure, no trace whatever of fuel having been discovered in my cell, nor any orifice for the escape of smoke.

Years hence, when this is printed, the reader will think these passages exaggerated; he will not believe that I am stared at like a wild beast. I tell him that the manners of a set of villagers to an itinerant brown bear are pleasanter and more courteous, and in every way less intolerable, than the manners of these Lancashire and Yorkshire clowns are to me.

Take last Sunday as an example. I was walking on the moor, with my dog, and rested on the hill whence I could see the hut. Groups began to collect about it soon, and when it was time to lunch, I had to make my way through a little crowd of forty spectators, who did not seem in the least disposed to abdicate the seats they had taken possession of when the principal attraction came upon the scene. Any properly-disposed dog would have resented this impudence, but mine walked pleasantly up to the forty spectators, and wagged a canine welcome. As for me, being hungry, I got into my hut as quickly as possible, shut the door, and put up the little green curtains. I could hear very plainly all the lively talk outside, and was soon aware that the crowd was increasing fast. I had a cold grouse or a partridge to lunch, I forget which; but I remember it was unfortunately necessary to get it from the meat-safe outside, and the innumerable observations that this simple action gave rise to, were really wonderful in their variety and interest. But to be so near the animal at feeding-time, and not to see it feed, was a bitter disappointment! Fifty or sixty of the spectators (their numbers had now immensely increased) attempted, therefore, to obtain a view through the four windows, but without much success, on account of the curtains. One man, however, effected the discovery that, through a crevice between the curtain and the window-frame a portion of my neck was visible, and forthwith there were twenty candidates for his advantageous position. Having finished luncheon, I determined to remove the curtains one by one, long enough to stimulate, without satisfying, the curiosity of the spectators outside. As I lifted each curtain, I found the pane pressed by a dozen noses; then rose a sudden shout, followed by an intensely eager enumeration of whatever peculiarity each had observed; so that, although the time I allowed was scarcely long enough for the wet collodion process, the combination pf many observers, with retinæ more highly excited than any film of collodion, realized a tolerably characteristic portrait.

In short, the hut is a fashionable lounge. Girls come here to see their sweethearts, and young men to see the girls. On Sunday came a great bevy of bright-eyed damsels out of Yorkshire, led by a fine young Yorkshireman, and escorted by others. The leader of this fair procession silenced me by a very cleverly turned compliment.

I said, "Well, you're a lucky fellow to have so many fine girls with you!" whereupon he replied, on behalf of his companions, "Why, sir, you see they've heard tell, where they come fro', 'at there's a feefil [Notes *: ***Feefil*** is an old Saxon word which now answers to the English ***very.*** I do not remember whether its meaning has changed since the Norman Invasion.] 'ansome young chap 'at's corned a livin' 'ere fur a bit, an' they couldn't 'old fro' comin' to see 'im." One old woman came seven miles to see me, so I asked her in, and explained to her my cooking apparatus and hammock. She went away delighted with what she had seen, and rewarded for her pilgrimage. With strangers I always feign total ignorance of English, answering them only in French, to cut short the else inevitable string of questions. These questions are rather imperative than interrogative, and I have commonly remarked that certain classes of people, in asking the most ordinary question of any one whose appearance does not altogether command their respect, have the air of demanding information rather than requesting it. It was by accident that I happened to think of this expedient of answering in French. One afternoon I was singing one of Frédéric Bérat's delightful songs when a gruff Yorkshireman presented himself suddenly before the window I was looking through as I sat at work, and, naturally enough, my thoughts being at the moment far across the Channel, I told him in French to get away from between me and my subject. He stared very oddly, I thought, and then I remembered that I was by no means in the country of Frédéric Bérat, but in the land of the Lancashire dialect; yet, seeing that the happiest results followed from my mistake, I have since put it into common practice. It was fatiguing to have to explain twenty times a day that I didn't hawk anything, but was there to study landscape, and that landscape-painting was not land-surveying, and that I cooked with a spirit-lamp, and that my Newfoundland dog was young, and that the hut was easily taken to pieces, and that it came in a cart, and so on.

I have a mad friend who comes and sits in the hut whilst I paint, and sings psalms. He dreams dreams, and has the gift of prophecy. He predicted the erection of a house in this place, and regards me with a peculiar affection, as the fulfiller of his sayings. He is civil and attentive in his way, and always calls for letters when he goes to the town in the valley. This crazed creature has many good qualities. He lives in a farm-house near here, where no woman is kept, and does all the work of a farmer's wife and woman-servant: they say, too, that he does this unmasculine work very well indeed, being exceedingly cleanly and industrious. He is a good workman, too, in his masculine capacity, and very strong, physically. His mental ailment produces great wildness of manner, varying in intensity from time to time, but he is not dangerous to anybody who is kind to him, as I am. The enthusiasm of this poor fanatic adds to the wild character of the place. I can fancy myself on the moors above Wuthering Heights, and certainly, if Southern critics had lived here, they would be better able to understand the power and truth of what must seem to them a very strange story indeed.

BOOK II—IN SCOTLAND.

CHAPTER I.
TENTS AND BOATS FOR THE HIGHLANDS.

SINCE writing the last chapter, I have descended from my hermitage on the hill, but not without having brought my picture to a satisfactory conclusion. I am none the worse for the experiment, in any way, and have learned more about camp life in one month of actual apprenticeship than if I had studied it in books of travel for twelve.

I intend to go to the Highlands in the spring, and encamp there several months. I cannot settle down, as Constable did, to paint subjects of inferior interest, when an inexhaustible land of pictures lies to the north at a distance of only three days' journey.

In the midst of mere green fields, the higher artistic faculties, such, for instance, as the sense of colour, must get debilitated from sheer want of exercise. The pleasant green of a good pasture is all very sweet in its way, especially to cockneys who live surrounded by streets of hideous brick, and to whose sight anything green is therefore of itself a wonderful refreshment, but I like green best in the little lawns that Nature puts in the middle of purple heather, and I appreciate the richness of these Lancashire pastures considerably less than the farmer who calculates their annual produce, or the cows that consume it. Everything seems quainter and more formal than ever now after my month amongst the heather, which I got as much attached to as any grouse. An enclosed meadow gives me an uneasy sensation, as if it were a fine drawing-room. I pine for the purple moors.

The shepherd lad who used to bring my milk on the hill is permanently installed here as my servant. He is green and awkward yet, having been so recently caught, but I hope to be able to tame and educate him in time. A more fashionable domestic would not serve my purpose, so I must even accept the trouble of teaching this wild moor-bird. In the course of these papers I shall call him "Thursday," that being the day of his arrival here.

A fine Newfoundland pup I had intended to take with me died during my absence, and the dog I had on the hill is not worth his railway fare, so he must remain in Lancashire. I have bought a magnificent bloodhound-mastiff at a menagerie, where he was exhibited in a cage. He is very young, and of most powerful build, besides being one of the handsomest dogs I ever saw.

The little lawn in the old-fashioned garden here has quite a look of Chobham or Aldershott There is my hut erected upon it, at present, and two tents.

In the neighbouring town they are busy making two life-boats for me. When they are finished I will continue this chapter with a description of the launch, and conclude it with a dissertation on Boats, which may be broadly divided into two classes, *Life-boats* and *Death-boats.*

The largest sheet of water in this neighbourhood is a canal reservoir at Colne, covering rather less than a hundred acres of land. I have been passing a few days very pleasantly in teaching Thursday the mysteries of rowing and steering on my new craft, by way of preparation for the Highland lochs.

The launch came off gaily. Colonel C. very kindly lent me his fishing cottage at the reservoir, and I invited all my friends to see the boats launched, giving them afterwards luncheon in the cottage. Then, after the launch, my good friend the seigneur of that country took me and all my guests up to the Hall to spend the evening, and I have been staying there ever since, leaving Mr. Thursday at the cottage to look after the boats.

Before the launch my crew was a singularly inexperienced one, he never having even floated upon water in his life; but now, after an apprenticeship of less than a week, he can row, and steer, and take in a reef, in a tolerably tidy manner for so green a hand.

The reservoir being no bigger than Rydal Water or Grasmere, there is not much sea-room, nor can we hope for an opportunity of observing how the new boats would behave in a heavy sea, but everything hitherto has been satisfactory enough.

Amongst other voyagers, two young ladies did my boat the honour to go on board of her for a cruise, and, having explored the hundred acres of canal water, returned without accident to port.

My boats are an adaptation of the double canoe, constructed in galvanized iron with water-tight compartments. Each canoe has its rudder, and the two rudders work together by a connecting rod. The deck is roomy and firm in proportion to the draught of water, and the larger of the two double boats carries a lateen-sail with singular steadiness. In adapting the old savage idea to my own use on the Northern lakes I wish to have a craft that will possess the following qualities in combination:—

1. She must never require *baling.* Any water she may ship must discharge itself.

2. She must be incapable of being capsized.

3. She must not draw more than nine inches of water.

4. She must have a large, flat, steady deck, that I can put an easel on, and a chair, and a table in calm weather, just as well as in my painting-room.

No common boat could possibly possess these qualifications. It became therefore necessary to set one's inventive faculties to work.

In the Marine Museum of the Louvre there are some interesting models of South Sea canoes, both double and with the balancer. During a stroll through that Museum I found something which seemed to promise all I required, with a little careful adaptation.

The result is a craft which, though utterly unorthodox, the reverse of nautical, and a piece of open rebellion against all the traditions of old England on the subject of boats from the days when painted Britons paddled about in coracles, down to the last University boat-race, may, nevertheless, be of much utility to me.

I have, then, two boats, each of them double, and I call them the "Britannia" and the "Conway" in honour of the tubular bridges, to which they bear some resemblance, being tubular, double, and of iron.

A little incident which resulted from some mismanagement on the part of the crew, Mr. Thursday, served as an excellent test of the strength of the "Britannia." In order to teach Thursday a little more rapidity in his movements than he had acquired during his years of contemplative pastoral life, I purposely delayed my orders as long as I dared, and then thundered them forth as if I had been commanding a company in the militia. Yesterday, the wind being stronger than usual, and squally, I sailed at the stone embankment of the reservoir, intending to lower sail in the last thirty yards, and make Thursday break the violence of the concussion with an oar, thinking some practice of this sort might be useful in case of meeting suddenly with rocks. So I went at the stone wall very courageously, and when within thirty yards thundered out to Thursday to lower sail. Now, the halyard was fastened to belaying pins, and Thursday had contrived to fasten it in so exceedingly effectual a manner that it would have required at least ten minutes of patient labour to undo his knots. We are now ten yards off. Thursday is too confused to get the oar out in time. If I attempt to turn the boat's head into the wind, I shall damage the rudders or bulge her side against the stones. There is nothing for it but to go straight at the solid embankment. The embankment is strong enough, at all events, and the shareholders of the canal company have less to fear than the owner of the "Britannia".

The wind astern is furious. At it we go!

A shock—enough, as I thought, to shatter the whole boat to pieces—a slight rebound—another, but less violent shock, and the prows rested on the stones of the sloping bank. Two small grooves were neatly chiselled in the stones by the two iron toes of the double boat, but the boat itself was not injured in any way.

My hospitable friends here would have me stay longer, but I think that the rudiments of Thursday's nautical education being already theoretically acquired, the rest will be best learned on a stormy Highland lake.

At the beginning of this chapter I promised to conclude it with a dissertation on life-boats and death-boats. An unexpected accession of material illustrative of that subject has just come to my hands.

A paragraph recounting the launch of the "Britannia" and "Conway" life-boats, having appeared in all the Lancashire papers, an unforeseen consequence has resulted from the extraordinary publicity thus given to our little picnic. Mr. Wilman, the ironmonger, of Burnley, who very innocently made the boats after my drawings, has received an angry epistle from a Manchester agent, demanding royalty upon them as an infringement of some Mr. Richardson's patent. I regret to say that I never heard either of Mr. Richardson or his patent, having found the type of my boat in the Louvre; however, it seemed my wisest plan to put myself into communication with Mr. Richardson himself. An amicable correspondence between us has ended by confirming my views on the subject of life-boats to a degree altogether unexpected, and it is with the greatest pleasure that I find myself obliged to yield any credit of adaptation or invention I might else have claimed in favour of a predecessor in the same path, who has richly earned whatever fame may hereafter reward his exertions. The only fault I find with Mr. Richardson is that he should have patented his improvements. To restrain, for selfish ends, the general adoption of -any invention which, as in this instance, is likely to preserve human lives, is to abandon at once the high ground of humanity. Besides, although Mr. Richardson's practical energy in proving the value of a well-known principle deserves the willing recognition I here accord it, the adaptation of the South Sea model to English materials was so obvious and easy that neither Mr. Richardson nor myself have any ostensible claim to originality.

My correspondent has sent me a most interesting little book published by Pickering, and entitled, ***The Cruise of the "Challenger" Life-boat, and Voyage from Liverpool to London in 1852.*** It is one of the most delightful little narratives I ever read. [Notes *: Not for literary merit, which it does not pretend to, but for manliness, which is better. The frankness of its jealousies and animosities is quite pardonable under the circumstances.]

After a series of experiments, extending over many years, Mr. Richardson had a life-boat constructed for him at Manchester, on the principle I have adopted for my own, but with several minor differences, as, for instance, an open grating instead of my flat deck—differences occasioned by the rougher service to which his boat was destined.

This boat of Mr. Richardson's, the "Challenger," has challenged all the life-boats in England to such a stern trial as no boat-builder ever before imagined. Amongst other startling novelties in this challenge was a proposition that the rival boats should be torn through a tremendous sea, by steamers, and anchored **broadside** to the surf, with the crew on the windward gunwale. It is scarcely necessary to add that this challenge has never once been accepted. Why these life-boats are not adopted, but, on the contrary, resisted and ridiculed, seems sufficiently intelligible.

They are not ***orthodox;*** they are contrary to immemorial usage; they have not the sacred, traditional form of boats. Newspaper writers call them ***rafts.*** People attached to conventionalisms will not even look at them. Such persons, who take all on hearsay, and refer nothing to nature, never can believe it possible that a form of boat which has always been used by the first maritime nation in the world is not the best conceivable form. They do not know that our sailors have, until quite recently, been far better than our ships, which, such as they were, the French taught us how to build; and that ship-building, ***as a science,*** is one of the latest of discoveries. And now everybody admits that the common life-boat is full of danger; and innumerable accidents have proved the very title a mockery, so that "***death***-boat" has been more than once suggested as an amendment: still the old vicious form is not to be abandoned, because it is orthodox, it is conservative, it is nautical, and respects the consecrated tradition of old England.

And is it not better to perish thus respectably in a boat of the true nautical model, than to save one's miserable life at the price of such a violation of established custom, as this revolutionary Mr. Richardson proposes? For what true Englishman would basely save his life on a pair of tin pipes, on a wretched, uncomfortable-looking raft? You would rather drown in dignity, reader—of course you would.

To this, Mr. Richardson may answer with great truth, that the main question is not whether his tin tubes are nautical, nor yet whether they ought more justly to be classified as a boat or as a raft, according to the somewhat arbitrary rules of maritime nomenclature; but simply whether they are efficacious instruments for the saving of shipwrecked men.

Another reason why such inventions as these, which appeal to natural law (being intended for use on a planet where, so far as all experience seems to tend, natural law is omnipotent), cannot be immediately recognized, is the inconceivable ignorance of the commonest facts of science, in which the great body of people who call themselves educated lie as yet like brute beasts. Thus it has constantly happened, both to Mr. Richardson and myself, that our boats have elicited questions indicating a degree of darkness which no intelligent person would suppose possible in any civilized country, and proving that one may be highly educated in the conventional sense, and yet remain plunged in the profoundest intellectual barbarism. [Notes *: Such questions, for example, as this: "How did you put the air into the tubes?" proving absolute ignorance of the nature of all fluids, even of the very atmosphere we breathe. Other people often fancy that the buoyancy of the tubes must be obtained by filling them with *gas,* as if the difference in weight between a few cubic feet of air and a like quantity of hydrogen were of any practical importance whatever, in comparison with water.]

To have a just idea of the real merits of the common open boat, it is only necessary to consider the following facts.

A most important contribution to physical geography has been made by the agency of a very unpretending little vessel. This little vessel has no qualities of water-line to recommend her; she is singularly ill-adapted for sailing—does not sail at all, in fact, but only drifts, for it is her business to drift. She has, however, one very valuable quality, which is, that so long as she does not run foul of anything hard, she is particularly safe. True, she has a great objection to hard things, being in fact herself made of glass—a brittle material for a boat Her market value is twopence, and she will carry her cargo over three or four thousand miles of ocean-waves as cleverly as many a big ship that has cost a fine fortune. This wonderful little vessel is simply a corked bottle.

An open boat that could bear any comparison with a corked bottle would deserve our respect; but open boats with shipwrecked sailors in them are not in the habit of making such long voyages as corked bottles do.

Here is an experiment in nautical science.

Take, on a windy day, to the nearest fish-pond, a tumbler-glass and a corked beer-bottle, both empty. Let these be your vessels. Set them a-floating from the windward shore. Your corked bottle will arrive quite safe on the other side of the fish-pond (ay, or of an Atlantic Ocean), but the tumbler-glass will be swamped by the first ripple.

The tumbler-glass is the common open boat. The corked beer-bottle is the closed tubular life-boat

Again, here is another very simple experiment

Stand on one leg on a ship's deck in a breeze.

Having stood as long as you can on one leg, try two.

Then see which way of standing is the easier,—on one leg, namely, or on two.

You have now the two great principles of a true lifeboat *First,* she must be closed like the corked bottle *Second,* she must have two supports on the water instead of one, exactly as a two-legged sailor has on a ship's deck.

Now, after having got well hold of the principle, let us see how it answers in practice.

On Tuesday, the 15th of February, 1852, Mr. Cuiball, the proprietor of the "Conqueror" steamer of Liverpool, had a carte-blanche to upset, swamp, or tear the "Challenger" life-boat to pieces, if in his power. A northerly gale being then at its height, Mr. Cuiball towed the life-boat four or five miles head to wind. After this, she was towed ***with her crew on board*** through the worst seas up the river.

After all this, no baling of course was necessary; nor was the slightest injury to the fabric of the boat perceptible. No other life-boat in existence has undergone this test.

Again: eighty persons leaped at once on one gunwale of the "Challenger" without upsetting her. No other life-boat in existence has undergone this test.

These two trials prove the validity of the principles laid down above. The first trial, by towing, proves the value of the closed tube or corked bottle principle. The second trial, by fourscore persons leaping together on one gunwale, proves the ***stability*** gained by the double tube or two-legged principle.

As for my boat, she was not built for hard service on the sea-coast, but merely to be safer and steadier on fresh water than the common open boat. Let us compare her in these two respects with the common open boat

First, then, let us examine such a familiar specimen of the common model as we may find at any watering-place on the coast

She reminds one, rather, of half a walnut-shell. She is probably half full of water, if it has rained all night; for she serves not only to float on water like a ship, but to hold it like a cistern. There is a little rusty iron can in the stern, with the handle broken off. This is the instrument with which she is to be emptied; and as the can holds a quart at most, you may calculate how long it will take to empty a hundred gallons, which may be thrown into her at any moment in a rough sea; and this may lead us to reflect further, whether, in every case, the little tin can would quite clear out the hundred gallons before another wave splashed another hundred into the cistern; so that the question of Life and Death reduces itself into a contest between one little tin can, the Protector of Life, against an innumerable army of breakers, the Menacers of Death; for, if the water comes in faster than the tin can empties it out again, you are lost. But there are heavy iron weights in her, you see, as well as the tin can. These weights constitute, to any one in the habit of reflection, a still more damaging confession of dangerous construction. Without them, the boat could not carry sail ten minutes in a breeze, and with them, if once the boat fall on her side and the weights tumble to leeward, nothing can save you; whilst, in case of a big wave dropping into the boat with that clumsiness peculiar to plethoric masses of water, down she goes at once to the bottom, like a dead sailor with cannon-balls to his feet. So the tin can is a confession that water is expected to enter, and the ballast is a confession of instability.

My own double iron tubular boat, the "Britannia," offers a striking contrast to this.

In the first place, there is neither tin can nor ballast to be seen about her; for the sufficient reason that, being closed against the ingress of water, she never requires baling; and again, that being wonderfully steady under canvas, by reason of her double construction, she is wholly independent of ballast

Nay, more. If you choose to send a bullet through one of her tubes under the water-line, so long as the bullet does not pass through her from end to end, still she shall float lightly; for she is divided internally into little water-tight chambers, each of which has a separate life and buoyancy.

With regard to speed, though not built for speed in any way, but for stability, that I may draw from nature on her deck, she is yet not inferior to ordinary boats of her own length, and sails well to the wind, owing to her two keels, which give a double hold on the water.

As to Mr. Richardson's object, the saving of life from shipwreck, it is enough to say, in order to prove that the subject deserves some attention, that the average annual catalogue of wrecks on the coast of Britain alone *exceeds a thousand.*

And as for my own object, which is to render boating a safe recreation, instead of one of the deadliest ever invented, I believe all Europe may be challenged to name any lake or river of importance where fatal accidents have not occurred, in consequence wholly of the unsafe construction of the common open boat.

Good people fancy that the loss of life by drowning is an inscrutable dispensation of Providence. When it happens on Sunday, it is for Sabbath-breaking; when, however, it happens on Tuesday or Wednesday, what then? Are we to be told that it is for Tuesday-breaking or Wednesday-breaking?

It is very convenient to lay the blame of our own imbecility on Providence; yet, as it seems to me, it were not only more prudent, but a great deal more pious, to pay some attention to those laws of nature under which Providence has placed us.

Lastly. If any reader is disposed to be angry with me for getting prosy and argumentative in this chapter, let him reflect a little on the condition of certain widows and orphans, who need never have put on mourning, if the principles here laid down had been generally applied to practice for the last half-century. There have been tragedies enough of the unproductive sort. If there is a superabundance of manly life in England, there may be bloody wars ere long that will quench it in salt water, under clouds of cannon-smoke; and it were wiser to reserve our victims for this nobler sacrifice, than to let them slip unprofitably out of the world by the upsetting of treacherous toy-boats in ditches and fish-ponds.

CHAPTER II.

THE AUTHOR ARRIVES AT LOCH AWE.

A FEW nights since, there rested on the highest point of the Highland road in Glenara, a singular group. It was past midnight. Far down in the valley lay the expanse of Loch Awe, gray and mysterious in the dim twilight. A vast range of mountains rose beyond, whose outlines and summits were confounded with fantastic cloud of exactly the same colour and character. There was just enough light in the sky to show the group of travellers as they halted. Three men, a horse and cart, a great tawny bloodhound, and a shepherd's dog, were easily made out by two graziers who passed that way, but a strange machine on two wheels in the rear baffled them altogether. They passed on, however, without arriving at any satisfactory conclusion.

The three men, the horse and cart, the great bloodhound, and the shepherd's dog, remained where they were; the strange machine in the rear stood by itself. It had no horse nor shafts, yet it went on wheels, and the difficulty was, how to get this queer machine down the hill, for it was huge and unmanageable.

"Will she no come doon the brae?" said one of the men with a pure Highland accent

"Who'll come fast enoo; that's all as I'm feared on," answered another in un-mistakable Yorkshire.

"Hold on, Campbell, and let us think the matter over a little," said a third voice in plain English. "I remember that the road is steep from here to Cladich."

"The warst brae from Inverara to Lochow, sir."

"Then we cannot 'old her fro' runnin' over us, for who's th' 'eaviest consarn as ever I tackled sin' I' ere wick."

"Hold your tongue, and do as you're told, and we'll get her down safely. Get the plank out"

The Yorkshireman found a loose plank in the strange machine.

"Tie one end of the plank to the axle, about a foot from the ground. That'll do. Now go in front and guide her, and I'll keep the plank down for a drag."

Here the speaker took his stand on the plank, and held to the strange machine, which started down the hill, and went tolerably well till it came to a short level.

"Halt! this is all very well here, but when we come to the real hill, it won't answer. Campbell, will the mare holdback?"

"Ay, sir, the beast'll do that."

"Then suppose we tie *her* behind the machine instead of me, and then I can help my man to guide it in front One man isn't enough there."

"The beast would be the better o' the cayrt behind her. Het would keep her back if the wheels were dragged."

Hereupon horse and cart were fastened to the rear of the strange machine.

"And how will you drag the wheels, Campbell?"

Before the Highlander could answer this question, the Yorkshireman, with great alacrity, seized the loose plank and passed it through the wheels between the spokes. "There, sir," said he confidently, "that's the way we drag wheels up i' Widdup."

Off started the whole caravan.

"What are you stopping for now?"

"Marecy upon us! Guid guide us!"

Here the Englishman, finding the body of the cart on the ground, with the wheels and axle considerably in the rear, the horse standing stock still, and the Highlander lost in wonder, burst incontinently into peals of laughter.

The Yorkshireman stared through the dim twilight, and having *felt* the cart, satisfied himself that it was without wheels. Then he scratched his head.

The Highlander became very grave, and solemnly said, "I doot we'll no get hame the nicht." And, in truth, there seemed slight hopes of getting there.

At last, after careful examination by *touch* (it was impossible to see), it turned out that since the Highland wright who built the cart had omitted to put nuts to his bolts, the Yorkshire expedient for dragging the wheels had done it more effectually than was desirable, by lifting the body off them altogether and dropping it down in the road.

After a long delay the cart was lifted upon the axle and reladen; the mare replaced in the shafts, the strange machine tied in front, the cartwheels locked with ropes, and the whole descended the hill.

"Hae ye lost something, sir?"

"Yes, I don't see my dog,"—the great bloodhound was missing. "We must not go on till he is found; he will worry every sheep on the hill."

Here the speaker took a dogwhip from his pocket, and applying the end of it to his mouth, whistled for ten minutes without ceasing.

Then all listened silently. A faint, distant howl came from the moors.

Again the shrill whistle sounded for some minutes. A still pause succeeded, and a great spectre-like bloodhound as large as a wolf cantered up.

At the inn, the inn-keeper came out with a candle in his hand to welcome his expected guest. The light fell on the strange machine. It seemed like four great black tubes of iron—a large pair with a lesser pair upon them.

"What are these, sir?"

"Only my boats."

"Well, sir, if these are boats, the like was never seen on Lochow."

The next day the baggage-waggon came on from Inveraray, where we had left it, and after having stayed a day or two at the inn, that I might choose a good site for the encampment, I decided, finally, to establish it on a large green island in the middle of the most picturesque part of Loch Awe.

Astronomers teach us that if we could visit a heavier globe than ours, we should find everything increased in weight, and that the strength which suffices for all ordinary work on the planet Tellus, would be prostration and debility on Jupiter.

It is not necessary to go to Jupiter for an example of this. A load for one horse in England is more than enough for two in the Highlands. When I left home, my light waggon, full of camp materials, the whole weighing less than a laden cart, was bravely taken to the station by one mare; little, old, and out of condition. She had a terrible hill to descend, but did it quite coolly, without dragging a wheel, the driver walking quietly by her side. To take the same waggon from Cladich to Innistrynich, a shorter distance, ***two horses, six men, and two boys were found necessary, with ropes to hold back, and a shoe to lock the wheel.***

For the first few hundred yards all went well; but when we came to a little descent, the shaft horse stopped, and, on being remonstrated with, lay down very quietly in the ditch on the road-side, twisting the iron-plated shafts out of shape.

"Tonald, Tonald, what gars the beast do the like o' that?"

But Tonald kicked the beast.

Then the beast rose up and groaned, but refused to labour. And there was a wonderful clamour in Gaelic. As for me, notwithstanding the injury to my shafts, I laughed till I was faint. At last, as soon as I could speak, I suggested that the leader be tried in the shafts. But it fell out that this beast was no better than the other, so, since the horses could not draw the waggon, I proposed to draw it myself.

Just then came a little one-eyed man, who shrieked with laughter at my Highlanders and their steeds, and swore roundly that a common railway porter would have carried the whole on his back. He could speak Gaelic too, and so ridiculed the Celts in their own euphonious tongue that at last they sent the horses back and took

the waggon down to the lake without them. Still the horses figured handsomely in
the bill.

CHAPTER III.

THE AUTHOR ENCAMPS ON
AN UNINHABITED ISLAND.

THIS island of Inishail, where I have pitched my tents, is a long green pasture
in the middle of Loch Awe, of a very tame and quiet aspect, broken only by one
rocky eminence, crowned with a few straggling firs. There is a miserable patch of
plantation on the eastern side which adds nothing to its beauty, and a ruin at the
other end surrounded by tombs, but the ruin has no architectural value. The shore
of the island curves beautifully into bays. Between the ruin and the plantation stand
my tents. The island is all one blue field of flowers, as if the sky had fallen; it is always so in spring; in summer it is covered with green fern; and in autumn, when
the fern dies, it reddens the whole island.

This bit of pasture land would be nothing anywhere else, but here it is remarkable for its admirable position. It is placed in the very centre of the most picturesque
part of Loch Awe. From it you can see Kilchurn Castle, and Ben Cruachan, and
Ben Anea, and the Pass of Awe. What Inishail itself lacks of picturesque beauty is
compensated by the close neighbourhood of the Black Islands, as exquisite a pair of
wooded isles as the most fastidious artist could desire. In short, this spot of green
earth is the best head-quarters I could have chosen. It has been inhabited before,
long ago, by a convent of Cistertian nuns. They were turned out at the Reforma-
tion, and their poor little chapel has been left for the winds to sing in ever since.
Not many stones are left of it now, and its foundations lie low amongst the moss-
covered tombs of the old chieftains. But the people bring their dead here yet, and
lay them under the shadow of their broken walls, so that the island is a land of
death, of utter repose and peace. Was it not well in barbarous mountaineers to bury

their dead in lonely isles, where the foot of the marauder trampled not the grass on the grave, and where the living came not, save in sorrow, and reverently? The mainland was for the living to fight upon, to hunt upon, and to dwell upon; but this green isle was the Silent Land, the Island of the Blest. Hither the chieftains came, generation after generation, borne solemnly across the waters from their castled isles: hither they came to this defenceless one, where they still sleep securely, when their strongholds are roofless ruins; their claymores dissolved in rust; their broad lands, that they fought for all their lives, sold and resold; and their descendants sent into exile to make a desert for English grouse-shooters.

On this island, then, inhabited by the dead, stands at length my little hut, cosy as ever. Thursday's hut has a good wooden floor, and wooden walls roofed over by a pyramidal tent, strong and impervious, and heated by a capital little cooking stove in the middle, whose pipe serves for a tent pole. An old Crimean tent stands beyond Thursday's white pyramid, valueless, indeed, for shelter, but useful as a receptacle for fuel, and as a sort of kitchen, being provided with a grate and chimney.

And there, in the beautiful bay, the "Britannia" rides at anchor, and the "Conway" is drawn up on the sandy shore of the island.

And down by that sandy shore, still and cold in his grave, lies my poor hound. An uncontrollable thirst for blood, making him utterly ungovernable where sheep were to be got at, has led to this fatal but foreseen result. I try to console myself for having passed sentence upon him by observing how happily the little flock on the island gathers round the camp, and how the tender lambs graze peacefully even on the shore itself, down by Lion's grave.

CHAPTER IV.

EDUCATIONAL.

A MONGST other labours that I have proposed to myself during my Crusoe life on the island is one worthy of Robinson Crusoe himself—namely, to teach Thursday pure English. Hitherto he has spoken a rich mixture of the Lancashire and Yorkshire dialects, an uncouth and barbarous patois, which, though interesting in a philological point of view, preserving, as it undoubtedly does, many words of Saxon or Danish origin long since lost to refined society, does not possess equivalents for those respectful forms of expression commonly used by servants in speaking to their masters. I therefore told Thursday very decidedly that he must do one of two things—either learn English or leave me; and he preferred learning English. Now, this Thursday was a raw shepherd lad from the moors, ignorant of everything but pastoral life; and pastoral life is not quite so sentimental on the Yorkshire moors as it is in the foolish poems of cockney writers of the last century. Thursday had, however, a strong desire to improve himself, and, as I was willing to help him, soon fell into the position of a private pupil rather than a domestic servant; and, indeed, many private pupils pay dearly for instruction of a much less profitable nature. But old habits are not easily rooted out, and the gradual replacing of words peculiar to a barbarous patois by words belonging to the accepted language of all England was a very slow and very tedious business, and one which cost me an infinity of trouble, and him innumerable blows.

Yes, I thrashed him daily, and that severely, for weeks together; yet he was a voluntary victim. There was one unlucky word of his, which on the Yorkshire hills stands for our words *only, but,* and *except;* I mean the word *naut,* which is much in vogue in that country, where the people are of so cautious a disposition that they can never state anything roundly, but must always qualify every statement with a drawback or an exception. Against this detestable word *naut* my first efforts were vigorously directed; so in exchange for it I gave Thursday the three words, *only, but,* and *except,*—an excellent bargain for Thursday, since in place of his single coin, whose origin was obscure and circulation limited, he received three pieces of royal English, current wherever that language is spoken on earth. But my unhappy pupil, notwithstanding the most hearty and laudable desire to get rid of his word, and the most perfect willingness to replace it with the three I had given him, found that the old word stuck to him like a burr, whilst the new ones were never at hand when wanted, but required to be sought for, and, when found, inserted into the phrase with the utmost neatness and care, like a patch in a garment. One day, therefore, when the obnoxious word had occurred a dozen times in as many minutes, the following conversation took place between myself and my poor pupil:—

THE AUTHOR.—There seems to be only one way left for you, Thursday; and that is, that you consent to be thrashed every time you use that word.

THURSDAY.—Well, sir, I'm sure I'd be rid of it fast enough if I could *naut* cob it away like a stoan.

THE AUTHOR.—There, *naut* again!

THURSDAY.—Confound it! eah, [Note *: Corruption of *yea,* used constantly in Lancashire for *yes.*] its allus [Note †: Always.] comin' when it isn't wanted.— Dang thee (apostrophising the word itself), dang thee, thou's noan wanted; go thee back to Widdup, and dunnot thee come back again *naut* when they send for thee.

THE AUTHOR.—There, Thursday, *naut* again.

THURSDAY.—Bless me, sir, that word's allus comin'! I think it mun [Note ‡: Must.] be the devil hissel as sends it; if I could *naut* be one day bout [Note ¦: Abbreviation of *beout* for *without.* The word *beout,* unabridged, is common in Yorkshire.] sayin' it I s'd be contenter by th'auve. [Note §: More content by half.]

THE AUTHOR.—*Naut* again, Thursday.

THURSDAY.—Well, sir, you may lick me, then, for I see I's never get no larnin' *naut* its licked into me, same as a whelp.

In short, the poor fellow came to me that evening, and said that he had taken the resolution to bear patiently any personal chastisement I might think proper to inflict, if only I could make him learn English. He said he believed seriously that it was the only way he should ever learn, and that he had determined to submit to it as a necessity. The day after, accordingly, this system of instruction was put into practice; and I am really afraid that, when Thursday went to his hammock at night, that heroic martyr to learning scarcely found a bone that was not too sore to rest upon, so often had he been punished during the day. The next day these inflictions were, however, a little less frequent, and at the end of a week a very remarkable diminution was observable. Gradually the obnoxious word fell into disuse; and although, after the commencement of this excellent course of discipline, Thursday got into a rebellious habit of running away from correction, he steeled himself into fortitude when I pointed out how this resistance to correction would defeat his own ends. The truth is, that Thursday ran much better than I did, so I could never come up with him; wherefore I preached him a little sermon, and made an appeal to his feelings of honour and duty, rebuking him in a touching manner for his want of gratitude in thus refusing what was intended solely for his benefit. But on board the boat escape was impossible, and it was there that the most wholesome lessons were given and received—given, not without sorrow, for it is at all times a sad necessity to inflict chastisement; all schoolmasters are agreed upon that—and received, not without occasional murmurs of impatience, such as idle threatenings on Thursday's part to throw himself into the water, threatenings which, as I very well knew, were in no danger of being fulfilled. Then I, on my part, would threaten to abandon my pupil to his ancient ignorance of polite letters, rather than relax for an instant the severity of discipline. And I am happy to be able to add, to Thursday's immortal honour, that he refused not the rod, but gave his back to the smiter!

This system of punishment was never abandoned, nor even relaxed, [Note *: The system remained in force for several years after the above was written. It was not confined long to the word *naut,* but removed successively almost all Thursday's habitual faults in speaking.] but has already become practically obsolete, for the reason that the word against which it was directed has been, by its means, totally banished from Thursday's vocabulary. O all little schoolboys who read this, think how happily you are situated, and what blessings you enjoy! you, my dear and fortunate young friends, who have had the inestimable privilege of being thrashed from your earliest years! this poor boy, Thursday, had not your advantages.

CHAPTER V.

THE ISLE OF INDOLENCE.

IS this a place of toil or a haven of rest? What living thing toils here? Why should I fret myself, and paint under the intolerable glare of this dazzling, cloudless noon? The sheep lie panting round my tents. The white gulls rest on the rocks. My boat sleeps motionless on the still water; she floats on a vast liquid mirror, so perfect everywhere, that the eye can find no flaw. The splendid lake, from shore to shore, lies hushed in a long, deep trance of calm, that has lasted I know not how many burning days. I count the days no more. They have been still, and burning, and blue like to-day, now for I know not how long. Why should I count the days? Somebody else will count them, far away in the stifling towns.

I will float on the lake like the boat, I will rest on the shore like this little flock, I will sit on the dark rocks in the lake like those indolent fowls of the sea; but one thing I will not do—I will not blind my eyes with staring at that sapphire-flaming sky, nor weary my soul with mixing dull imitations of it from the costly dust of the lapis lazuli. All is rest here. The dead rest in their cool, dark graves, out of the heat and glare, there not far from my tents, round the little ruined church. The countless streams of Cruachan have ceased to flow; they too will have their week of rest, and they lie in the cold granite heart of the hills, safe from the fierce god who would change them all into pale white clouds if he could find them.

I begin to have vague impressions of unreality. This life does not seem quite real. I am dreaming, and expect to be awakened some ordinary commonplace morning as usual. But for the present let me at least enjoy my dream. I will eat lotos. Alas, the lotos blooms not here! I will smoke a yet more flagrant plant, and envy those lotos-eating Greeks no more. I will sit with my pipe in the tent's cool shadow.

The tent, I perceive, suffers a degree of lassitude, and is sensible of this Indian heat. It hangs in careless curves, and has lost its tightness and trim. Well, we are none of us very much on the stretch just at present, and I see no reason why the tent should not participate in the general relaxation.

I have only bathed eight times to-day. I live like a seal, in the water and out. But I have an advantage over the seal. I found out this morning that I could smoke very comfortably in the water, whereas the unfortunate seals cannot smoke.

It is pleasant to lie on one's back in the bay, smoking cigars. The combination of sensations is curious and interesting. And there is a certain feeling of triumph in being able to keep that little spark of etherial fire alive above the abyss of waters. I fancy then that the cigar has a finer flavour than on land—at least, I like it better; probably, I unconsciously sympathize with the cigar, when my life, like its little fire, is kept burning on a fearful deep, which could so easily extinguish both.

Thursday tells me that the candles melt in the candlesticks, and fall down when the sun puts forth his strength in the morning. It is an act of becoming humility on the part of the candles. But what is more distressing is, that Thursday and I are in a fair way for being prostrate also before long, and I don't see that we owe the sun any such homage.

This I take to be due only to our diet. I lived very much better on the Lancashire moors. Now, animal food becomes tainted in a day, and the whole country cannot supply vegetables. Neither beef nor mutton are to be had all round these sixty miles of shore. It is true I might purchase lean kine and bony sheep, if I were willing to take them alive; but after the first joint what could we do with them but salt them? and who but a Highlander or a sailor can live long on salt food without suffering from it? I have sent for beef to Inveraray; but the lowland poet gave so damaging a report of that city that I never expected to find good flesh of oxen there, nor have I found it. If I send to Glasgow, what then? the beef will be I rotten before it arrives, this hot weather. There is nothing left for it but patience—and a little bread and butter.

An Englishman out here, accustomed to good keep, is like a corn-fed hunter in a field of thistles. Thursday is getting weak, and complains, in his way, of exhaustion. "I feel quite ***done,*** somehow, sir," he says. And no wonder, for the poor fellow has not had a dinner this month past. Once, by some miraculous good fortune, we had gathered together with infinite pains the materials of a substantial repast. Smiles of contentment shed their lustre on Thursday's countenance on this auspicious occasion. He strutted about rather proudly, I thought, as one well-fed. "You seem very happy today," I said. "Why yes, sir," answered Thursday, "its such a honour to a man to have eaten a ***real dinner.***"

It never answers to slight the laws of our nature, and pretend to be independent of common necessities. The inexorable master of every man is his belly. HUNGER is the most terrible of all besiegers—the strongest fortress in armed Europe cannot contend against ***him;*** and, from the poor tinker under his rag to the emperor in his war-pavilion, no one who undertakes camp life can afford to neglect his warnings.

Day after day the lake has been sinking lower and lower into its bed, and black stony islets lift their sinister-looking heads above its polished surface in a hundred places. And now, when the water is at its lowest, there has come an Egyptian plague of flies. Even the water is full of little poisonous red creatures that bury themselves in the skin, and have to be picked out with a penknife. And we have thousands of big flies on the land, that settle continually on our faces and hands, and send a needle-like proboscis down through the skin, leaving on Thursday an envenomed swelling after every stab, but on my own more happily-constituted cuticle nothing worse than a minute puncture. Water and air are filled with a million foes.

Dim in the upper air rises the red peak of Cruachan. There is a strange patch of white upon it. It is a little field of winter lingering into June. It is pure, cold snow! Oh what a sensation to melt a little of it in this mouth that never tastes anything more refreshing than tepid water! What pleasure ineffable to plunge these hot and feverish hands into its crystalline depths! But that little patch of Paradise is three thousand feet above me! How shall I ever climb those arduous heights? Day after day I look at it with longing eyes, but it descends no lower—comes no nearer; only

I fancy its precious area has somewhat lessened, for it seems not so broad to-day as yesterday, and yesterday it did not seem so broad as the day before. Its shape, too, alters somewhat. It is melting away in the sun's eye; and tiny rills, cold and pure, are draining its dazzling field.

I am on the highest peak of Cruachan. I drink fair water of the rock sublimed with snow; for the snow rests yet in the stone crevices high above the burning valleys, and the air is still fresh and sweet on the mountain, though the vaporous atmosphere that broods on the low lake is heavy with a deadly languor and weariness.

Weak and exhausted as we are by the overpowering heat, we are in poor condition to climb mountains; but to breathe for one hour such a delightful air as this that fans my temples now, and to quench one's thirst with one draught of such divine coolness as that bottle of snow-water at my side, is enough to repay one for any toils such as we have gone through.

When we got into the great desolate valley that lies a thousand feet above the sea, as if the mountain were a colossal statue of granite that held a site for a city in its lap, I realized more distinctly the exquisite truth of John Lewis's Frank Encampment on Mount Sinai; for here, after the burning drought of June, the dry, red precipices far from us stood out with all their peaks clear in stony detail against a shadeless sky.

Having climbed the great shoulder of the hill instead of following the stream in the corrie, we found that a huge chasm still separated us from the peak, but that this chasm might still be in some measure avoided by creeping along the face of a precipice several hundred feet high. Thursday preferred to try the precipice, being an active mountaineer; but I descended patiently into the chasm, and laboriously toiled out of it again up the stony peak. Thursday, however, very nearly lost his life on that precipice.

He had proceeded safely along a narrow ledge of the rock, till he came to one particular point, dangerous enough to frighten a chamois. The path was broken in places by fissures two or three feet wide; and, having crossed one or two of these, Thursday found that the ledge of rock he had hitherto followed either ceased to exist altogether, or was at least interrupted by a massive buttress of granite that projected from the face of the cliff. Now, as it happened, on the buttress itself were two little projecting points; and Thursday, partly in fool-hardiness, partly, I believe, in that healthy unconsciousness of danger, which is a common characteristic of sound nerves and a clear head, thought he should like to look round the corner. But in order to effect this it was necessary for him to put one knee on the lower projection and one hand on the upper; and that accordingly was the position he took. It was not an enviable one. Under him was a depth of above a hundred feet of sheer precipice, and below that a long slope of granite debris; and everybody knows how hard granite is, and what unpleasant-looking edges its fractures offer. Thursday looked round the buttress. There was not a ledge big enough for a sparrow to perch upon; it was one smooth wall of rock. He told me afterwards that he had given himself up for lost, but thought he might as well try to get back again as drop helplessly from fatigue and giddiness. The projection he held on by was a loose broken bit of granite; he knew it might come away at any time, and then there would be no hope. So he *felt back* cautiously with his foot, and in some inexplicable fashion regained gradually, but in going backwards all the time, the narrow ledge he had left, and, so returning, escaped death.

He rejoined me on the great rough pyramid of the peak. The impression of John Lewis's Sinai was so strong upon me that I could have believed we were climbing some great stony mountain of the East; for there was no mist, and the heat was almost insupportable. The stones themselves were warm when we touched them, and yet down in the deep fissures the snow lay white as if in winter.

We rest at last on the summit. The effect of the Highlands of Scotland seen from one of their highest peaks resembles nothing so much as the ocean in a gale of wind fixed for ever in a photograph. It is a sea of mountains, sublime in its vastness and in the huge proportions of its granite waves, yet not satisfactory to the artistic sense. It offers a splendid panorama, but not one picture. The sweetest and even the sublimest pictures are laid in the habitable earth, and we need not go to the snowy summits to seek them. Still, if you would feel the immensity of the world, go to the mountain-tops, and reflect that the vast circumference of your horizon is but a round spot on its mighty sphere.

The great precipices of Ben Cruachan are capital subjects for study. I think they are the sublimest walls of barren rock I have yet seen. One of them, on the Loch Etive side, rises grandly between us and the sea. We see nearly the whole length of Loch Awe, the upper end of Loch Etive, and the great calm ocean in the west, dim with heat and vapour, with mountainous islands rising out of it mysteriously. But to the east are the Highland hills, clear and sharp in their innumerable multitude of peaks,—some brilliant with snow, others pale with inconceivable distance, all various with exquisite changefulness of hue, pale purples, and tender greens, and far away the hues of heaven itself, rose and blue of ineffable delicacy.

The great lake spreads out below us calm like a sea of glass. It stretches far away into the pale haze of the high horizon; and on its whole length, from end to end, not a single breeze dims its exquisite surface. Floating on it, like fallen leaves in a still basin in a garden, lie the green isles; and on one of them, a speck of dazzling white, stands the little lonely camp. The moors are spotted with miniature lochs, set like shining mirrors in the hot heath.

It is time to leave off sketching, and this scribbling. There is a long line of glittering light on the mysterious Atlantic. In half an hour the sun will set.

CHAPTER VI.

THE THREE MAD MEN OF THE ISLAND, AND THE MAD MAN OF THE MOUNTAIN.

THERE dwells by Loch Awe a mysterious personage, concerning whom circulate the strangest rumours. Wherever I go I meet him, for he wanders continually. His face is sunburnt and weather-beaten, and his full, handsome beard has the delicate variety of colour a painter loves; the moustache dark brown, and the beard itself passing into cool dark greys. He wears the Highland costume, with a pair of sabots, such as are common in the provinces of France. His frame is powerful and muscular. No one has ever seen him without a silver-mounted meerschaum, which he smokes leisurely. Like himself, it is brown and well-seasoned.

This mysterious personage is always attended by a young man with long black hair, commonly supposed to be his son. As to the actual relation subsisting between the two, or their purpose in remaining at Loch Awe, no one has any knowledge whatever. It is said that he has before visited the lake under another name, so that the one he now bears is not considered to be his own. In the course of the present narrative we will call him Malcolm.

What has most excited my interest in the rumours concerning Mr. Malcolm is the prevalent opinion of his hardihood. It is commonly believed that he is entirely independent of the comforts so generally sought after by tourists—that all hours and all weathers are alike to him. He has a tiny boat upon the loch rigged with jib and mainsail, and in the stormiest gales she may sometimes be seen, like a little white bird on the great waves, flying before the wind. Often in the dead of the night, when the ferryman carries some belated farmer over the lake, he sees this white sail glide across his path till it fades away in the pale grey of the distant waters; and sometimes, on sunny days, the miniature craft comes gaily with flags and music, and a silver horn wakes the echoing hills.

I determined to seek this man's acquaintance. I felt sure that the secret of his wanderings was less the pretext of sport than the love of nature; and it seemed to me that we should have this at least in common, and, it might be, other feelings also. So I gave chase one day, and took him and his friend prisoners on board my craft, and towed his ship like a prize to the green island where my tent was pitched

He had been fishing all night, and one of his prizes was a fine twelve-pound trout; so, knowing very well that Thursday had never seen a trout weighing above half a pound, the ordinary weight of the great prizes of his piscatorial youth caught in Yorkshire rivulets, I told him to "go to the boat and fetch a trout he would find in it." Off he went, and to see him returning with the trout was exceedingly amusing. He stopped frequently to look at it; then he talked to it, and told it in pure Yorkshire that there were no such fish as it where he came from. At last he arrived at the camp, his astonishment still unabated, and burst forth into enthusiastic admiration of the fish, when Malcolm told him that trout twice the weight had often been taken in the lake, and that once or twice an instance had occurred of a capture reaching above thirty pounds, all which wonderfully enlarged Thursday's views on the subject of trout-fishing, and, I believe, sometime afterwards furnished matter for a letter to his father, a Yorkshire gamekeeper.

Malcolm left half the trout at the camp, and sailed away in the evening. Two days afterwards, I being at work with Thursday repairing the sail and fitting new-stays, a faint bugle-note came with the breeze, and soon a little white sail glided between the wooded islands near Inishail, a red flag flamed against the green foliage, and Malcolm landed.

That night he fished in the Pass all night long without sleeping. I know very well the fascination that held him there. You will not find a scene in all Scotland more impressive than the Brandir Pass, when the black narrowing water moves noiselessly at midnight between its barren precipices, or ripples against them when the wind wails through its gates of war. Malcolm said it seemed fearful and horrible that night, as if inhabited by supernatural powers; and truly, to glide before the invisible breeze into its gloomy mountain-portals at black midnight would take the frivolity out of any one, even, I do believe, out of a holiday tourist. It is no time for levity when you hear before you the roar of the rapid Awe, seeing nothing, gliding as it seems to inevitable destruction, in so frail a bark as Malcolm's. On, on glides the fragile thing, on to the stony river!—on to the gates of death—gates once barred by brave men when the Bruce fought John of Lorn. The bones of the slain lie there yet, under their grey cairns.

In the early heat of the next morning, I went down to the beach of the island,

and found Malcolm and his friend there, lying sunning themselves on the sands; so I addressed them after Robinson Crusoe's fashion, and invited them to my castle, where they breakfasted.

Malcolm's way of eating is peculiar. He has accustomed his appetite to such irregular supplies that it has gradually acquired the power of storing up materials for future nourishment whenever opportunity offers. It is not unusual with little boys, after having eaten as much as they possibly can, to fill their pockets with oranges and cake by way of providing for future necessities. But Malcolm has no occasion for such supplementary magazines, his own natural one being elastic enough to contain provision not only for present use, but future. This vaccine accomplishment of his has proved at times rather inconvenient to his host, when neither meat nor bread would keep, and the stock of both was necessarily limited. The ancient philosophers who objected to the use of the egg as human food on the sufficient ground that it contains the four elements are practically disregarded by him, and the quantity of incipient chicken life sacrificed annually to the support of his would afford matter for calculation. By way of preparing himself for the more serious business of breakfast, it is a custom of his, when eggs are attainable, to beat a dozen of them together in a basin with whisky and sugar, and eat the whole raw mess with a spoon, like soup. That morning's breakfast in the camp was no unworthy proof of Malcolm's valour. We sat very comfortably in my little hut, with the door open, and the great calm lake around us seen from three of its four windows, like three exquisite pictures painted with supernatural splendour on its walls. We had capital trout to begin with, that Malcolm had caught a few hours before, with rosy flesh as firm as salmon. How many of these delicious fish we consumed, I cannot tell. To these succeeded mutton-chops and boiled eggs, and here lay the most serious deficiency. Thursday had only boiled half-a-dozen eggs, he having destined one for me, one for Malcolm's friend, and four for Malcolm. But his calculations availed him nothing. When Malcolm perceived that the dish was empty, after having broken his fourth egg, he inquired politely if I would allow him to ask Thursday for another egg; then called out—

"Thursday, how many eggs did you boil?"

"Why, sir, I boiled *six!*" said Thursday aloud; then muttering to himself, "and plenty too for three people, after all them trouts and mutton-chops."

"Six?" said Malcolm interrogatively.

"Yes, sir, *six*" replied Thursday with firmness.

"Do you mean to tell me you only boiled six eggs, sir?" repeated Malcolm severely.

"I thought you'd had enough mutton-chops and fish beout heggs."

Now this answer, which implied that Mr. Malcolm was, in Thursday's opinion, eating more than was good for him, was not, I admit, characterized by becoming humility; for Thursday, in his position in life, ought not to have presumed to set bounds to the fleshly appetites of his superiors. Neither does the wording of his reply leave nothing to be desired. I know that *beout* is not considered so elegant as the more classic "without," for it is in this latter form that the word is found in our best writers; and I am aware that the aspirate before the word "eggs" is, in fact, superfluous. But on the part of Thursday, I ought to say that he was not yet disciplined into the submissive manners required from servants; and as to any little defect of language that may have crept into his reply, I may observe that, in every case, people in anger speak the language which long habit has rendered most natural to them. Recent refinement is a thin disguise worn only in good humour; put the wearer out of temper, and he doffs it in a moment.

"Go and boil six-and-twenty," said Malcolm.

"Very well, sir; but where am I to find them?"

"You'll find two dozen in the box in my boat."

Then I told Thursday, privately, not to mind Malcolm's order, but to boil him four eggs only; which, with the four he had eaten, the plates of mutton-chops, the plates of trout, the loaf of bread, and the six cups of strong coffee, I considered a sufficient breakfast.

After breakfast Malcolm always smoked several pipes of tobacco; and as we smoked together, he told me a good story of some ladies he had met with on the shore of the lake. They were escorted by gentlemen; and Malcolm exchanged a few words with them about the scenery. "Have you been to the island?" said one; "there are three men there living in tents; each has one tent, and they are all mad." Then, turning towards Ben Loy, the fair speaker continued, "You see that tent up there on the mountain; it belongs to another mad man of the same party."

"Well, but," said Malcolm, "that happens to be snow."

The idea of snow in June afforded them infinite amusement, for snow is not often observed at this season on the Alpine heights of the London hills. Malcolm gravely reiterated the truth about the matter, but drew down upon himself nothing but ridicule, and so left the tourists in disgust.

These people had not learned the use of their eyes. The snow on Ben Loy covers at this moment a larger area than twenty bell-tents; and the outline of the patch indicates so plainly that it fills a concave surface of rock, that even a cockney might see what it is.

The cool, round assertion that three mad men live in this camp tickles my fancy exceedingly. I remember that some days ago a yachting party from Inveraray came to see the island. I was painting in the hut, and at the same time giving Thursday his reading lesson, when we found the camp suddenly surrounded by the enemy. I went on with my work, and took no notice of the invading forces, but heard a male voice say very distinctly and positively, "You see there are three tents, and one man lives in each tent."

"By Jove!" cried Malcolm, who had finished his third pipe, and was amusing himself in the interim with his telescope—"by Jove, there they are again, the Oxonians and their sisters!"

"So much the better. Since we are here, three of us, why not affect madness, to confirm their idea that the camp is a species of lunatic asylum?"

So we rigged ourselves out oddly enough. As for Malcolm, he required little embellishment. He wore a pair of white sailor's trousers and a blue shirt. His long beard looked wild enough to frighten young ladies whose papas, and uncles, and brothers, and lovers were most probably all shaven like dead pigs. By way of a companion, Malcolm said he must have his big pipe. "Thursday," said he, "will you fetch the rosewood box out of my boat, please?" Thursday brought a thing like a large writing-desk. Malcolm found a key, and opened it. There, in a bed of crimson velvet, lay the friend of his bosom, the delight of his eyes, the solace of his soul! It was his favourite pipe. How glorious was its mighty bowl! What soft and mellow tints the strong oil of a thousand replenishings had given it! From the pale yellow of the sea-foam clay it had darkened in its ripening, till you might trace in its exquisite gradations all the intermediate tints, down to a rich brown, like the brown of a deep pool in a Highland torrent. Its broad lid was of massive silver, surmounted by a magnificent cairngorm. By its side, in separate lengths, lay a long tube of the same metal, embossed with rich designs, and the mouthpiece was made from a lump of pure yellow amber.

Malcolm's friend seemed wild enough with his long black hair and red shirt.

For myself I reserved a costume such as never was seen in the Highlands. It happened that, last winter but one, I had enrolled myself amongst the pupils at the celebrated Gymnasium of Monsieur Triat, in the Avenue Montaigne, at Paris. Having fortunately finished my course of instruction at that excellent institution without breaking my neck, I bore away, as a memento of it, the costume used in our exercises. This somewhat gaudy uniform consisted of a pair of tight red drawers, a tight blue jersey, a long red sash, and a pair of yellow boots. It had been slipped, amongst other things, into one of my portmanteaus, and so Thursday found it for me that morning.

So we spread the deck of the boat with a great buffalo skin and carpets, and set sail, not forgetting Malcolm's cornet-à-piston and his big pipe.

As we stepped into the boat Malcolm cried out, "Robin Crusoe! Robin Crusoe! here's a footprint in the sand!"

Yes, there on the beach of my desolate island was indeed visible, with fearful distinctness, a footprint in the sand! Sharply impressed it was, not by the naked foot of some cannibal savage, come to banquet horribly on the shore, but by a pretty Parisian shoe, worn by some delicate lady.

Then we gave chase to the tourists; we, the Three Mad Men of the Island. But the Mad Man of the Mountain rested still in his tent of snow.

Malcolm's pipe was exchanged for the cornet-à-piston, and, with martial music sounding over the water, we were soon in hot pursuit. Alarmed at our possible intentions, (and what evils might not be apprehended from three mad men?) these unhappy tourists, pale with fear, hastened by furious rowing to regain the land. Once landed, they escaped to the woods. Malcolm wished to land also, and continue the pursuit; but being unwilling to bring about a meeting under such circumstances between him and the prettiest of the ladies, I felt it my duty, in his own interest, to oppose that proposition.

Their idea thus confirmed, I have no doubt that these tourists will long embellish their tales of travel with accounts of their courageous conduct in that terrible meeting with the Three Mad Men of the Island.

After this pardonable practical joke, I proposed to Malcolm to have a swim in the loch; but he excused himself at first on the plea of headache. At length he consented, and I plunged in before him, expecting him to follow. Some minutes afterwards I saw a venerable man approaching me in the water. He was bald and majestic, and as he swam towards me—and he swam remarkably well—I saw that his beard swept the ripples, and behold, it was Malcolm's beard; but the head was not Malcolm's, for my friend had a profusion of dark brown hair, whereas this strong swimmer was as bald as a phrenological bust. The riddle was explained, and the apprehensions of headache also, by a handsome wig which lay with Malcolm's clothes in the boat. It turned out that Malcolm was a vigorous man of sixty, with all the strength and buoyancy of youth. How elastic his spirits were, and how hardy his frame, I had an excellent opportunity of observing during a voyage we undertook that evening to the other end of Loch Awe.

This man must have drunk of the fountain of Eternal Youth. After fishing during a long, sleepless night in the Pass of Awe, in a little cockle-shell that a strong salmon could upset in a moment, he had gaily taken part in a boyish frolic, then sported in the water like a young Etonian, and now, finally, at sunset accepted, without any pause or hesitation, my proposal to sail twenty miles and back on a cabinless raft

CHAPTER VII.

A LAKE VOYAGE. LOG OF THE "BRITANNIA."

AFTER having chased the silly tourists, we made rapid preparations for our long voyage. I left Thursday in the camp as garrison, having an able crew in Malcolm and his friend. The following narrative of our voyage is condensed from the log of the "Britannia."

The wind fell at sunset, and during the whole of that calm summer's night we floated so quietly that our motion was utterly imperceptible. It was a delightful voyage; the very slowness of it was a great charm. Slowly the scenery changed, and slowly the dim shores faded away behind us—before lay endless mysteries. It was like a glorious dream; it was like a fair mysterious picture of a great white sail, curved by some faint breath of imaginary wind ever going we know not whither, yet resting there eternally! I lay on the buffalo skin on the deck, warmly clad in fur, and Malcolm sat for hours at the helm. Many a pipe did we smoke that night as we talked over his recollections of forty years—we two watching there together, whilst his friend Campbell slept. At last the dawn came, and we were in another scene; for we had floated into the second of the three reaches of Loch Awe.

When the sun rose we landed in a little rocky bay, and made preparations for breakfast. A foolish trout or two had snatched at our lifeless flies as they floated behind the boat on the calm water; so we gathered a few dry sticks and made a little fire between two stones, to cook the fish and boil our coffee. Then Malcolm, great in culinary science, acted as *chef,* and soon we had a capital breakfast of trout, and eggs, and ham. We had a square stone for a table, and Mr. Campbell, as waiter, covered it with a clean little tablecloth, and laid covers for three. And a merry meal we made of it, we three.

This was just at sunrise, and we enjoyed that spectacle whilst we breakfasted. After a due number of pipes, the sun began to be pleasantly warm, and we resumed our voyage. Reclining on the deck, we attained the marvellous speed of half a mile an hour, and floated lazily into the magnificent bay that lies opposite to the ruined castle of Ardhonnel. It was a glorious morning, and we sailed quite fast enough. There is a time to be swift, and a time to be slow. Across ploughed fields, the express from London to Glasgow may go twice as fast as it does, and welcome,—the faster the better; and over the Atlantic waste the mighty steamers may traverse their twenty knots an hour, without drawing forth any other feeling than our most cordial admiration and good wishes. But the traveller who truly understands the uses of the world, only hurries over the dull desert that he may linger in the fair oasis, and there *are* scenes which excite in us no other desire than to behold them thus for ever.

We three, at least, were determined not to be hurried. It is a notable fact that, on a certain day of June in the year of grace 1857, three Englishmen were travelling in the Highlands at the rate of half a mile an hour, and would not have thanked anybody to get them forward a bit faster: they were not tourists.

We three tortoises, then, or snails, or whatever you like to call us, floated thus lazily into a great bay; and as the sun was by this time hot, we two younger ones refreshed ourselves in the water, whilst Malcolm looked on from the boat, and criticised our bad swimming. After our bath, we resumed our attitude of profound repose, and lay on the deck luxuriously, with our heads on airpillows and our bodies stretched on the buffalo skin. My recollections of the rest of our voyage are strangely confused and indistinct. I remember a ruined castle, ivy-clothed, on a beautiful island. I remember the pale peaks of Cruachan rising far away in the sultry air; and then the castle changed as if by enchantment, and its broken battlement assumed loftier proportions and a more fantastic form: then I heard at intervals the music of ripples on the boat's side, as if she danced before a freshening breeze; and there were intervals of absolute silence, as if I had become suddenly deaf. And at last I heard the ripple no more, and forgot all about the boat and the lake, to dream of a garden at home in England with six old yew trees and a sundial.

"Captain, I'm sorry to awake you, but I wish to know whether we are to enter the harbour at Feord, or to lie out for the night."

It was Malcolm's voice, and I awoke to find myself in a scene quite new to me. During eight miles of our voyage, Campbell and I had slept side by side like two children, and Malcolm had been watching over us all the time, and steering the boat patiently, though he had not so much as dozed for sixty hours. It seemed as if we had sailed into other, and to me unknown, waters; for the third reach of Loch Awe is as distinct from the second and first as if it were another lake. We sailed towards what seemed an ironbound coast with smooth precipices of rock enclosing a little bay. But in the bay, behold a little narrow opening just wide enough to admit the boat; and through this strait between the rocks we glided softly into the sweetest miniature lake I ever saw, guarded all round by most picturesque miniature mountains, and fed by a tiny stream. I should never have suspected the existence of this exquisite natural harbour, if Malcolm had not told me of it before.

We selected, however, another bay for our bath; and as Campbell and I bathed together, the boat rode at anchor, and Malcolm slept at last. After my bath I lay reading on the deck, and fell asleep too. Shortly after, Malcolm awoke me.

"Captain, what's to be done? This is not a good anchorage, and a strong breeze is coming from the east, which will be a gale o' wind at night. Look how the sky is overcast already; there is going to be a great change in the weather."

I jumped to my feet at once, and saw the white waves up already. Even in our sheltered bay the boat dashed and splashed, and tugged at the cable violently. There was a total revolution in the weather. "We must go back to the harbour, Mr. Malcolm, and at once, or we shall not get through the strait without danger."

So we double-reefed the sail, took off our shoes and stockings, rolled up our trousers, packed all the things to secure them from the spray, weighed anchor, and sailed into the white breakers. It was now dusk, and I stood at the bows on the windward tube to act as man on the look-out. Wave after wave came over the tube, and I was often up to my knees in water; but I knew the boat, and trusted her.

Then we rushed forward to the gloomy precipices, and it seemed in the twilight as if the wall of black rock before us could afford no refuge. Any stranger to the place would have thought we were rushing on certain destruction. Our only chance of hitting the entrance to the harbour, for it was already nearly dark, was to keep quite close to the shore on our right, that descended perpendicularly into the deep water, a tremendous wall of solid rock, stained and polished as if it had been built of black marble by an enchanter in the Arabian Nights. So we darted swiftly between the sombre portals, impelled by a howling gust, and in a minute afterwards found ourselves floating on calm water, in a little quiet lake, our speed decreasing as the impetus died away. Then we dropped anchor and arranged ourselves for the night, in some haste, for the big drops were beginning to fall.

Now, the way we arranged matters was most equitable and ingenious. The deck afforded a spacious bed, big enough for three persons, and we gave the middle place to Campbell, he being younger and more delicately constituted than we were. I was enveloped in a huge coat of sheepskin, that descended to the ankles, and I wore on my head a seal-skin cap, with flaps tied down over the ears by way of night-cap, and a pair of sealskin boots to keep my feet warm. I had supplied Campbell with a costume exactly similar. Malcolm had a seal-skin coat of his own, and huge knitted stockings that did just as well as our seal-skin boots. These stockings were a valuable addition to the picturesque of Malcolm's costume, being of a most brilliant red.

So we went to bed, not supperless. Our counterpane was quite waterproof, and we arranged waterproof sheets over our heads in such a manner as to protect both heads and pillows from the rain, without in any way interfering with respiration. Sheltered thus, we lay on the deck as snugly as possible, in a state of comfort really wonderful when you consider that a strong gale was blowing all the while from the east, which entered our harbour in the form of violent gusts from every point of the compass, and that the rain was heavy and incessant the whole night long. As for me, I slept so pleasantly, and felt so delightfully warm and cosy in my seal-skin boots and night-cap and my great sheepskin coat, that I was quite angry with Malcolm when he disturbed me at five o'clock in the morning.

"Captain, I say captain, sorry to disturb you, as you seem so comfortable, but I'll tell you what it is, I must be put ashore."

"Confound you—ah, I beg your pardon, Mr. Malcolm, was it your voice I heard?"

I opened my sleepy eyes, and a more pitiable yet ludicrous sight they never beheld. There stood Malcolm in the cold light of early morning, drenched with rain, and presenting an appearance so utterly forlorn and miserable, that he might have made a guinea in an hour or two as a street beggar, if he could have transported himself in that plight to the metropolis.

He had slept comfortably enough during the night, but, owing to some movement of his, the waterproof counterpane had hollowed itself into a perfect cistern or reservoir of water, and, another unlucky movement having formed a fold in the counterpane which acted admirably as a conduit, the whole contents of the reservoir had been precipitated upon Malcolm's neck, whence its chilly stream penetrated to his body, and even to his innermost apparel. Thus inundated, Malcolm had endeavoured to console himself philosophically with a pipe, but his matches were wet too, and wouldn't burn; so he yielded to his fate, and prayed to be put ashore that he might seek shelter from the bitter rain. I argued that it was very comfortable where we were, and preached resignation, being warm and dry myself, just as Dives says Lazarus ought to be thankful for his lot, and cheerful under it; whereas God knows Dives would be anything but patient if he had to take upon himself the lot of Lazarus. At last we went ashore, and walked on to a little Highland village, where we found an inn.

In ten minutes after our arrival, there was Malcolm all right again, and merry as good-humour could make him. I rather suspected the reason, when a particularly pretty Highland girl came into the room to light a fire for us. She was willing to learn the art of cookery, and our excellent *chef* most kindly undertook to be her instructor. And this it was which produced those beaming smiles of satisfaction on good Mr. Malcolm's face! Such is the power of benevolence, that the mere hope of communicating to a poor fellow-creature instruction of a nature calculated to mitigate the hardships of her lot is sufficient, as we see, to shed a pleasing radiance on the countenance in circumstances the reverse of luxurious!

We had a capital breakfast of ham and eggs; and when Malcolm saw that there were only a dozen eggs in the dish, he requested our fair waiter, in the most polite and charming manner, to fry a few more immediately. I must confess I felt a little ashamed of Malcolm and his appetite, but without reason; for he soon ingratiated himself so well with every inhabitant of the inn that I believe he might have stayed there a week for nothing, notwithstanding his appetite.

It was really delightful to see our friend's happiness; how he enjoyed his mighty breakfast, and his pipe after it, and how he chatted with the inn-keeper and the old mother in the chimney-corner, and the pretty serving-maid.

At last we decided, in spite of the gale, to try to beat against it as far as the next inn, at any rate, which would be eight miles nearer home. We got out of the harbour, and, under a double-reefed sail, **did** beat to windward for a while; but Malcolm was at the helm, and I fancy he regretted the black eyes of his pupil at the inn, for the boat did not sail so near the wind as usual, and we decided to return and wait twenty-four hours for a change of weather.

On our return, the most important question was, what we were to have for dinner. Our experienced **chef** charged himself with the organization of this repast. At the mention of dinner, the Highlanders seemed as usual much astonished; for dining is a habit by no means universal, and, like many other southern usages, has as yet acquired but an uncertain footing in the north. It seemed, however, to Malcolm, very much to be regretted that so excellent a custom should be here comparatively unknown, and he busied himself in the kitchen with the instruction of the beautiful maiden in the elements of culinary science. Two or three unlucky chickens were running about before the door, whose lives he ruthlessly sacrificed, and then proceeded with an unheard-of quantity of eggs to make us a capital pudding. Add to this ham and potatoes, and it will be evident that we had as good a dinner as any traveller need wish for.

After dinner came grog and tobacco; for were we not sailors in an inn? and who shall forbid us the sailor's luxuries? And so we three sat pleasantly by the great peat-fire whilst the tempest howled outside, and were as merry as if we had been staying there of our own freewill. I can't say much for our beds, because, though not proud, I confess to a certain degree of daintiness as to my bedding. I like sheets, for instance, and clean ones, and I don't like dirty blankets wherein Highland drovers have preceded me. Now, there were no sheets whatever on our beds, and as to the blankets—but these are not agreeable reminiscences.

The next morning we quitted the inn, and the landlord, according to the courteous old Highland custom, gave us each a glass of whisky for nothing after the bill was paid, and then walked with us down to the boat. How astonished he was!

"Never was the like seen on this loch; she was a wonderful boat; them that made her was surely clever—they had great schooling."

The wind was dead against us, and quite strong enough to be agreeable. The waves were five feet high, which indicates rough weather on a narrow, land-locked sheet of water. We packed everything with great care in the waterproof sheets, and laid all the luggage in the middle of the deck, binding it down with cords. Then we pulled through the little strait, and ten minutes afterwards were beating to wind-ward. The landlord and a friend of his followed along the shore, watching us with fear and wonder; for a true mountaineer dreads water, and the art of sailing against the wind is ever to him an incomprehensible mystery.

For eight miles we worked thus in the teeth of the wind, and so got to Port Inisherrich. Malcolm looked forlorn as he stepped ashore. He had been sitting bare-footed in the stern of the boat in his white sailor's trousers; and now the trousers, which were wet with rain and spray, clung to his manly limbs, and our friend re-sembled exactly a professional London mendicant in the character of a shipwrecked mariner. Malcolm had but that one pair of trousers on board our craft, so in order to dry them it was necessary that he should submit his person to the process of roasting. There being an excellent fire in the kitchen at Port Inisherrich, he took his station before it, and bore with great courage the inevitable torture. It is, in truth, a most uncomfortable way of procuring oneself the luxury of a dry seat. When the evapo-ration begins, one experiences sensations of an alarming character; yet so mixed, that it would be difficult to analyse them satisfactorily. As to prudence, when the caloric imparted to the person by the fire is in excess of that which is carried off by evaporation, there is not the slightest danger to be apprehended. When Malcolm's trousers ceased to steam, and the fine sculpture of his legs was no longer visible, his spirits rose rapidly to their usual degree of good humour; and having replenished the inevitable pipe, he took his old station at the helm, and we again set sail.

It was now late in the afternoon, and the wind had fallen. Still, a light breeze blew sufficiently in our favour to allow us to hold our course; but at night this also fell, and we passed the whole night on board, steering and sleeping by turns, except when we rowed occasionally to get an offing to catch some transient breath.

In all that night we only made eight miles, for the sun rose as we reached Port Sonachan. And a more magnificent sunrise I never saw. Slowly the dawn came in the east, and gradually the sky brightened; then suddenly a flood of light illumined every crag and mound on the hills, every tree in the forest, every tuft of grass on the sloping pastures.

We floated in a glassy calm. Malcolm lay on the deck with his face turned westwards. I was sitting at the stern looking to the east.

"There is a delightful breeze in our favour," said Malcolm; "it is coming up from the west."

"And there is a tremendous wind against us," I answered; "it is coming down from the east."

We were both right. We looked westwards, and saw a steady ripple advancing towards us; we looked eastwards, and the white waves were foaming under a violent east wind. We ourselves lay becalmed in a neutral sheet of glassy water that separated the hostile winds.

The west wind came up quickly and filled our sail. The east wind came down and met the west wind. Our sail flapped and shivered as the two winds struggled for the mastery, and then strained tight under the pressure of the conqueror.

So it was the old story, and we were again beating against a foul wind. Malcolm lay fast asleep on the deck, weary of watching; and as for Campbell—but to explain the peculiar precariousness of his position, I must revert to the construction of my boat.

She has four rowlocks, two on each side. Commonly, she carries only two oars. The rowlocks revolve in iron sockets which stand on the gunwales. The boat has no bulwark, except a little one three inches high, because bulwarks are an impediment to sailing; but when we are not rowing, the oars rest in these revolving rowlocks, parallel with the keels, and so serve the purpose of- rails. It was on one of these oars that Mr. Campbell took his seat, and I observed with alarm that occasionally, when we fell into the trough of the sea, Mr. Campbell was within a very little of falling backwards into the water. He was fast asleep. So as I did not consider a boat's rail on a rough day the best seat for a sleeper, I made my friend lie down on the deck, and did all the work of the boat.

Malcolm awoke soon after, and we beat up to the green island; and Malcolm was cunning enough to sound the trumpet under pretext of explaining to me the mechanism of the instrument, but in reality to warn Thursday of our arrival, that he might make culinary preparations for our reception. And then we breakfasted in the most copious manner on the grass under the shadow of the tents, and after breakfast fell fast asleep, all three of us, then and there.

As for Thursday, he had lived alone in the island during these days and nights, sleeping with no other neighbours than those silent ones, the dead people in the graves; yet we found him in health and safety, and mental calm, with hair un-blanched by fear.

CHAPTER VIII.

FARTHER EXTRACTS FROM THE LOG OF THE "BRITANNIA."

AS the reader will probably be troubled with a good deal about sailing in the course of the present work, the author has mercifully decided to spare him for the present, when treating of that subject, a minuteness of detail which would be likely to prove monotonous. It is very possible that the reader regards all boats with dis-like or fear—as murderous inventions for the destruction of human life; or with indifference—as things which do not concern him; or with contempt—as toys: and a person who does not look upon them with quite other feelings than these would never hear with patience those endless histories of alternate storm and sunshine, foul and fair wind, which possess so inexhaustible an attraction for better-constituted minds.

So I propose to myself in this chapter to conclude what I have to say of the "Britannia;" to give some farther account of her voyages, and to state fairly the qualities and defects which frequent trials have discovered in her.

I have planned a tent for the deck. This gives more comfortable accommodation on a wet night than Malcolm enjoyed when, as narrated in the preceding chapter, the rain-water ran down his neck. I extract from the log the following account of a night passed under this new tent:—

"In the little basin at Feord, which we entered at nightfall, we cast anchor at once, without landing, and Thursday soon erected his new boat-tent, which I found to be a decided improvement on the former open-air arrangement. There was room in it for two persons in a sitting or recumbent posture; and I rejoiced, on entering this hospitable pavilion, to discover that Thursday had spread the deck with india-rubber cloth, and had laid over that several strata of dry carpet and skins of beasts, so that, propped up by air-pillows at the end of the tent, which lay to the head of the boat, I reclined luxuriously like a Turk, and dined in great state, being waited upon by Thursday on his knees. A regard for veracity compels me, however, to observe that these genuflections are not to be understood as a proof of humility on the part of Thursday, nor of inordinate pride on mine, since they arose simply from the deficient height of the dining apartment, which necessitated this abridgment of my domestic's person. After we had both dined, Thursday, whom I had taught to read, lay at a distance as respectful as the narrow limits of our lodging permitted, and was soon absorbed in the surprising adventures of Robinson Crusoe, which for him, enviable student! still possessed the first charms of novelty. His master, however, less intellectually inclined, lighted his evening pipe, whose incense-cloud crept to the roof of the tent like a wreath of mist, and thus escaped at the open end at the stern. Then, when the last fibre of tobacco in the bowl of my brown meerschaum was turned to pale dust, and the history of Robinson Crusoe had no longer power to keep poor Thursday's eyelids from falling, I told him to make my bed, and turned in and fell asleep at once to a strange lullaby of pattering rain-drops and wailing winds, and so never stirred till Thursday awoke me in the morning, and the bright sunshine streamed in at the open end of the tent."

There is a great advantage in a boat-tent which no land-tent can ever possess. It is possible in any boat-tent to combine narrowness of dimension with an abundant supply of air. This may be done by simply leaving that end of the tent quite open which is at the stern of the boat. No matter how the wind changes during the night, the boat will always keep her head to it, and therefore neither wind nor rain will ever enter the open end; but the foul air is sure to escape as fast as it is generated by running along the roof (just as the tobacco smoke did), and as fast as it escapes, its place is supplied by fresh air from without. Often that evening in one quarter of an hour the wind would come from every point of the compass, but the boat swung round and round, and always kept the closed end of the tent to windward.

Being occupied with my drawing the next morning, it was after one P. M. when I left the bay. I may remind the reader that this bay is at the western extremity of Loch Awe. We left it with a fair wind, sailing through the narrow channel that unites it to the great lake, and then, without a minute's pause or interruption, the same fair wind wafted us up to the river Orchay at the other extremity, a magnificent and memorable voyage on a sunny inland sea as long as Windermere and Ullswater put together.

It was the perfection of freshwater sailing. There I lay, hour after hour, in one long trance of tranquil happiness, two instincts strong in me from childhood, the love of landscape and the love of boating, feasted and gratified to the utmost.

We passed the castle of the Black Knight. We passed the isle of Erreth, the isle of tombs. We passed the castle Ardhonnel, first nest of feudal Argyll. We heard the roar of Blairgower, where the stream plunges into its deep abyss. We watched the magnificent range of Cruachan, forming the background to an infinite succession of wonderful natural pictures. And all this time the sky above was blue and bright, with only a few white clouds sailing majestically before the wind, and the broad waters, of a yet deeper blue, were broken only by such laughing waves of summer as dance about the golden bark and bear the beautiful swimmers, in Etty's poem of Pleasure.

Thus, without haste or effort, but serenely as the white clouds above us, the white sail of the "Britannia," curved by the constant breeze, drew us with a gentle luxurious motion through twenty miles of the fairest scenery in Europe. It was nearly sunset when we passed through the narrow strait that separates the Black Islands, then we glided swiftly along the green coast of Inishail, passed the beautiful Fraoch Elan, famous as the enchanted Hesperides of the Highlands, shrouding in thick growth of wood the remains of a little castle whose lords were most chivalrous gentlemen, and whose guests were anointed kings. Then we sailed where the lake is dark and deep, under the shadow of those frowning hills which had shown so pale from afar in the morning. And so we held our way towards Kilchurn, and then into the stream of the Orchay, where we furled sail and cast anchor.

Thursday erected the boat-tent which had served us so well the preceding night at the other end of the lake, and I was examining the contents of the provision box with a view to supper, when a friendly voice hailed me from the river side, and, looking up, I recognised my friend the doctor, who invited me to land and spend the evening with him. The doctor had rooms in a comfortable farm-house close at hand, so we spent a merry evening together, Thursday all the time being under the boat-tent, absorbed in the study of the provision box and the adventures of Robinson Crusoe. Late at night I went on board to sleep, the doctor having pressed me in vain to accept a bed. What did *I* want with a bed, with so noble a yacht at anchor in the river?

It is singular that, though everybody has been finding fault with the "Britannia" ever since she was built, no one ever finds out her real faults. In kindness to these people I here propose to point them out.

The greatest fault is want of sufficient bulk and buoyancy in the tubes. An enormous reserve of floating power is essential in a double boat. For want of it, the "Britannia," in heavy squalls, submerges her lee tube when there is any burden on her. She is, therefore, not fit to carry heavy luggage in rough weather. This want of buoyancy is a great fault.

Proofs of this have only been too frequent since my arrival here; for instance, in the following extracts from her log:—

"We had to beat against a stormy wind in thick, blinding rain from the river Orchay to the bay of Innistrynich. Though we sailed under double reefs, the wind was yet violent enough to snap a strong sheet like packthread, and if a snug little bay had not been close at hand we should have lost way whilst replacing it. The waves were high and fierce, with white crests that the gale carried off in a fog of spray. The spray and rain together concealed at times the shores of the loch, so that it seemed as if we were out at sea, far from the land. *A heavy squall caught us once, and buried the lee tube entirely. I was up to my knees in water, and the baggage was floating about the deck,* but the good boat rose again immediately, the deck cleared itself of water, and yet we had never to trouble ourselves with baling. In a common open boat, after shipping a sea like that, a desperate contest would have begun immediately between Thursday, armed with the orthodox tin can, and an endless succession of breakers."

Here is another extract. It describes my removal from the island of Inishail:—

"In crossing the lake with the "Britannia" laden to the water's edge, we found ourselves in rather an unpleasant predicament. The walls and floors of the encampment, piled upon the deck, raised us high above it. The sail was double-reefed, and the tiller-ropes exceedingly inconvenient to work. The novelty of finding oneself raised up to so lofty a position above the water had a certain charm, and I was expatiating to Thursday on the desirableness of having a deck at the height of the floor we were standing upon, with a snug little cabin under it, when a tremendous squall, from which there was no escape whatever (for we were in the very middle of the lake), came whitening the waves to the eastward. I tried to get the sail lowered, but there was no way of doing it without cutting the halyard, because the winch was hidden under a quantity of luggage; so I determined to let the squall do its worst, and leave the sail to shiver in the wind. ***It was very soon upon us, and drove the whole of the lee tube deep under water; indeed, the whole boat rushed under water, six feet of her length being invisible under a boiling surge.*** I expected everything to be washed off the deck, ourselves included; but managed to bring her up to the wind, when the bows rose, and shortly afterwards the squall abated. We had passed a cord or two over the cargo, which probably saved it from being washed away. Of course the boat was none the worse for having been under water, as not a drop could ever enter."

Another fault, also due to want of buoyancy and height in the tubes, is the comparative ease with which the "Britannia's "bows may be forced under water when going before the wind. Often, when sailing before a violent wind, I have let it force three or four feet of her length under water. No real harm comes of this, except that it stops speed, and wets the passengers with showers of spray. This is disagreeable, but not dangerous. In common boats, this vice is often the cause of fatal accidents. A yacht on Derwentwater, over-masted, went down head foremost in this way, and those on board were drowned.

As a piece of construction, another glaring fault of the "Britannia" is, that ***she is two whole boats joined together by beams, and not two half boats.*** This defect I owe to the South Sea models in the Louvre, and therefore it is none of mine, though I had no business to imitate it. It is indeed a very great defect, and the usual ingenuity of the savages failed them entirely here, or they would have found this out by experience, and discovered the remedy. In every double boat the inner sides ought to be smooth and straight from end to end. If you choke up the channel with bulging forms inside, your boat can never attain high speed. The "Britannia" only sails six knots an hour at best. When I study the currents and eddies produced between the tubes at five or six miles an hour, I see that her wedge-shaped bows drive two currents of water inwards, which meet each other like the two lines in the capital letter V. Where they meet they have to rise into a wave, because at that point the channel between the tubes is exactly a foot narrower than it is at the cutwater. This wave is maintained nearly at its first height till the tube begins to narrow again towards the stern, and the force expended in raising this weight of water is of course deducted from the speed of the boat.

Again, in the construction of a double boat, as much attention ought to be given to her lines as if she were a single one. We have all gone wrong hitherto in this respect The South Sea savages were wrong with their straight-sided, double canoes, [Note *: In the old quarto edition of ***Captain Cook's Voyages,*** which I have at hand, I find elaborate drawings of the South Sea double canoe, with plans and sections; and in all these drawings, the sides of the canoe are parallel, except at the extremities. In the Louvre, however, the lines of one or two models of double canoes are almost as good as those of a Venetian gondola. The balancing-logs, though, are merely logs of timber pointed at the ends, as one cuts a common lead pencil] and straight balancing-logs. Mr. Richardson was wrong with his straight-sided, round, iron tubes, and I was wrong with my straight-sided boat-shaped pontoons.

Now, when I indicate these faults, I know beforehand that all those kind friends who were always finding imaginary defects, but lacked the wit or discernment to discover the real ones, will cry out together, "We told you so!" Pardon me, good friends, you did ***not*** tell me so. You told me the boat would sink, and it has not sunk; you said the tubes would be torn asunder—they are as stiff and firm as ever, bound tightly to their strong beams; you told me the boat would be capsized, and she has not been capsized; you said she would never sail to windward, and I have sailed against a gale from one end of Loch Awe to the other. Of all your idle predictions, ***not one*** has been verified. And now, when I tell other and more intelligent readers of real faults, in order that future constructors may avail themselves of my experiments, do not pretend you knew them before. You had all the will to discover defects, and all the desire to make predictions of disaster ***which might be fulfilled,*** but you lacked the sense to see the really weak points, and the foresight to prophesy the degree and kind of failure.

As to safety, the object I proposed to myself, I have succeeded completely. The boat is safe to that degree that any one who has been accustomed to her is unfitted for all common boats ever after. I have got so used to carrying canvass in all weathers, that henceforth I feel myself disqualified for all other craft. I have lost that wakeful apprehension of possible danger which is so essential to a yachtsman. Safety breeds carelessness. But are we to place our lives voluntarily in constant jeopardy that we may not grow careless? Is not careless safety better than careful peril? I would rather sing merrily at the helm, when the storm is raging, than count in anxious silence the chances of Life or Death.

CHAPTER IX.

A FRIEND IN THE DESERT.

MALCOLM is not the only person who has visited the camp. Lonely as I am, I have friends and visitors. These visitors are of all sorts, from the peerage down to absolute pauperism.

One day, on the island, an old man of eighty came to see me. I knew him here several years ago. He is not very rich; indeed, some people might find it difficult to live on his income, which does not exceed threepence-halfpenny a day. He is a householder, but his household is limited to himself; and his house is worth, as it stands, from three to five pounds, exclusive of the site. A house worth five pounds, and an income of threepence-halfpenny a day, not a soul to help one, and the burden of eighty-two years on one's back! Somewhat meagre materials for happiness, these.

The people say he seeks me from selfish motives; that because I rendered him a little service years ago, he thinks I may do as much to-day or to-morrow. Well, and if a little self-interest *does* urge his old tottering limbs to the camp, what harm is done? Is poor old Duncan the only person in this world who keeps up an acquaintance which is likely to be advantageous to him? I think I know others who have

not the same excuse of iron necessity, and who yet pay court to more powerful
men, with more of slavish sycophancy than this poor simple old peasant is capable
of. His little wiles are so plain and on the surface, I can read them all beforehand,
so that there is really no deceit. He knows that I know what he wants. It is all quite
straightforward between us. He comes to me, to the camp, and he gets a cup of hot
tea or coffee—beverages rare to him, and precious as the nectar of the gods—and
while he drinks his coffee, he enjoys a conversation in which he finds endless novelty, and a pleasant stimulus to an aged but by no means worn-out brain, which still
retains its appetite for information. And then he knows that when he goes away
there will be a silver shilling in his pocket that was not there when he came. And
with all these inducements, is it not rather a proof of great delicacy in my poor
neighbour not to come ten times oftener? He was with me a few days ago, and I
know he will not come near me again for six weeks, unless I send for him. And what
sort of a life will he have of it in the meantime? In the morning, when he awakes
in that little damp cottage by the stream, who lights the old fellow's fire? who gets
him his breakfast? If you, Mr. Dives, who read this somewhat unsympathetically,—
if you live to fourscore years, you will be petted and nursed like a new-born babe.
Petted and nursed you entered upon life, nursed and petted you will go out from it.
If your lordship's little finger should happen to ache when it shall be venerable with
the wrinkles of four-fifths of a century, respectful envoys will come galloping on
swift steeds from distant castles and halls, to express the deep interest and anxiety of
their several masters in the well-being of that important member of your lordship's
person. A maiden, swift and silent in all her movements, shall light your fire whilst
you are yet in unconscious sleep in the great, curtained, tented bed. Kind eyes of
son or daughter shall watch for your waking, and your wrinkled yellow forehead
shall be kissed, let us hope, with true affection, by children whom poverty does not
detain far away at relentless labours. Then, when the bright fire is burning in the
grate, and the lofty chamber is gay with sunshine, you shall be lifted by strong yet
gentle arms out of that soft recess of sleep, and washed and swathed and brushed
and combed till you revel in that delightful cleanliness which has nothing to do
with godliness, but is the most precious result of wealth. And then your easy chair
shall be wheeled over the velvet floors into another atmosphere, fresh, fragrant,
pure, yet warm and genial as summer; and there shall you be read to, or talked to,

all day long, as you will. And, lest your strength fail, there shall be delicate dishes provided for its continual restoration, and the most precious juices of the grape shall fire your thin blood with their sweet stimulus. O Dives, Dives! not thus is your poor brother attended at *his* levee.

When he wakes, what then? There is not a soul to help him. He is eighty years old, remember; and at that age one may chance to feel a little tired or faint in the morning. And then the fire, is it alive yet under the heap of ashes, or has it gone out? That is a serious question, especially in winter frost. Well, by chance there *is* a smouldering yet in the ashy peats. And now for the breakfast. The old man dresses himself with trembling hands. Perhaps he is not over cleanly. Perhaps he does not take a cold bath from head to foot every morning as you do; but, in truth, his circumstances are not so favourable to that health-giving observance as yours are, my dear sir. He would have to fetch the water from the stream, and then, where is the sponge-bath to come from? Would you have him flood his clay floor, and make a puddle of it? And then, dirt is a garment, and poor folks, when they are prudent, don't like to throw it aside until they can afford to buy another to supply its place. So I dare say, on the whole, my friend dispenses with the rite of ablution. He is not a Mahometan Turk, you see, but a Scot and a Christian, so washing is not amongst his religious duties.

Yet he will say his prayers and read his chapter in the old Bible if, perchance, this time he find his spectacles. And as for the wants of his body, there will at least be none of that hesitation in the choice of dishes which may perplex your old stomach, Mr. Dives; for if you would live on threepence-halfpenny a day in the Highlands of Scotland, there is only one thing for you, and that is oatmeal. Water, of course, you may have (of a brown colour), for the trouble of fetching it; and, as salt is cheap, you may salt your porridge; but to porridge you are bound irrevocably. Porridge three times a day for a year makes a thousand repasts, all porridge! Old Duncan thanks God humbly and sincerely for his eighty thousandth basin of that delectable aliment, and sits down on the untidy bed with his old brown Bible.

Now, porridge, as I take it, is not a bad thing occasionally, with plenty of thick cream; though, for my own individual organization, I find it rather too heating, and not supporting enough to do hard work upon; yet the most fervent believer in the virtues of that over-extolled mess, oatmeal porridge, would, I fancy, demur to eighty thousand repetitions of it. One could smoke eighty thousand good cigars, if one had a long life to do it in; but eighty thousand messes of oatmeal porridge—a southern stomach sickens at the thought!

And if that judicious old Duncan prefers what he gets here to that eternal porridge, little do I blame him. On the contrary, I applaud his taste and discernment. And if I fancy that he may relish my society as much as the society of his clock, I hope I do not flatter myself unwarrantably. My talk may not always be very wise or very good talk, but there is, at any rate, more variety in it than in the monotonous tick-tack of an old cheap clock. But I declare we get positively intellectual together sometimes, Duncan and I. We talk about London, and the electric telegraph, and the Leviathan, and Louis Napoleon, and other vast and mighty subjects. I believe my conversations with my old pauper friend are a great deal more interesting than much of the talk I have had to do at rich men's feasts. Here is a specimen of it. I do not pretend that we, either of us, threw any very bright or novel light on the subjects we touched upon, but we were both in earnest; he entirely interested in the talk, and I in him.

Fancy the Isle of Inishail on a glorious summer's day, the camp upon it, white and brilliant; on the green grass in front of the tent a grey-headed Highlander and a young Englishman sipping their coffee together; Mr. Thursday standing a little way off, astonished and scandalised at so unwarrantable a degree of friendliness towards a ragged old fellow, living on public charity—"a regular common beggar, for he's naut else."

DUNCAN.—Well, sir, and they're sayin' noo that London's an awfu' big toon; noo, is it as big as Glasco'?

THE AUTHOR.—Yes, it's six times as big as Glasgow.

DUNCAN.—Sax times as big as Glasco'; gosh me! what a fearfu' place! And they're sayin' that there's a deal o' money in London, and all these rich English shentlemen come frae London, and I'm thinking it must be a ter'ble rich place. Mr. Cool, and Mr. Smith, and the Capt'n that was with them, came frae London, and I hae the address o' Mr. Smith's hoose, that he gave me, ye see, and I wrote tull him wi' my ain hand, and I'm eighty-two years of age.

THE AUTHOR.—Yes, you write uncommonly well for your age. I've seldom seen a clearer hand.

DUNCAN.—An' please, Mr. Hamerton, can ye tell me noo, if it's true what they're sayin', that the letters are goin' frae Glasco' to London in one nicht. They're sayin' that it's the railway that takes them.

THE AUTHOR.—Yes, it's quite true. I've come from London to Glasgow myself in one night, in the same train with the letters.

DUNCAN.—It's fearfu' fast, gosh me, gosh me! An' is it true that they've a way o' sendin' word by long wires that reach frae Glasco' to London? They're sayin' that they're sending word by wires instead o' letters.

THE AUTHOR.—Yes, you mean the telegraph. It's quite true. But I'm afraid I cannot make you understand it very well; indeed, nobody quite understands it. They know enough about it to make it act, but not enough to give good reasons why it acts. The news is sent, as you know already, by means of wires.

DUNCAN (*with eagerness*)—An' please, Mr. Hamerton, can it go fast, the word that they're sending by the wires?

THE AUTHOR.—Yes, very fast indeed; a great deal faster than your letter to Mr. Smith, and that, you know, went from Glasgow to London in twelve hours.

DUNCAN.—Gosh me, gosh me! they hae great schoolin'. Gosh me! faster than my letter to Mr. Smith, that went frae Glasco' to London in twelve hoors!

THE AUTHOR.—Yes, ten times as fast—twenty times as fast—a hundred times as fast!

DUNCAN (*astounded*).—A hunder times as fast! Gosh me! gosh me! it flies on the wings o' the wind!

THE AUTHOR.—Yes, you may say so; only the wind does not go half as fast. I've sent messages myself that have gone hundreds of miles between two ticks of your clock at home. The messages go so fast that it really takes no time at all.

DUNCAN.—Gosh me! and they didna ken hoo it flies, and it flies sae fast! And does the word come right as ye sent it?

THE AUTHOR.—Yes, yes, just as if you wrote it in a letter.

DUNCAN.—An' please, Mr. Hamerton, is it true what they're sayin', that the Emperor o' France is going to make war against Scotland? And has he as large an army as they're tellin'?

THE AUTHOR.—He has a very large army indeed, but I don't think it likely that we shall be troubled with it over here.

From the Emperor of France, Duncan naturally diverged to the Queen of England; and after various minute inquiries respecting her Majesty's personal appearance, the number of her children, the size of her establishment, and the extent of her revenues, we got somehow to Balmoral, and thence to the subject of English visitors to Scotland in general, when I asked Duncan what he thought of my tents. Duncan, with much tact, replied that he had a great respect for tents and for them who dwelt in them; and when I demanded in some surprise the reason for so unusual a sentiment, he answered, "because the Scriptur' says that Abraham dwelt in a tent."

CHAPTER X.

A LETTER FROM THE AUTHOR IN PARIS TO A FRIEND OF HIS IN LANCASHIRE.

HOTEL DU LOUVRE, PARIS.

MY DEAR——,—Why I should write to you from Paris *apropos* of my camp in the Highlands you will learn in the sequel, if you will have a little patience.

I have an anecdote to tell you of something which amused me very much yesterday. I often dine at the table d'hôte *in the hotel here. Yesterday, during dinner, I thought I recognised a middle-aged bachelor whom I saw at the camp last year under rather peculiar circumstances. He was sitting a long way off, and at another table. You know that immense dining-room, so like one of the big saloons in the French palaces, and you may easily understand that without a telescope it is by no means easy to recognise an acquaintance across a* parquet broader than many a French estate.

After dinner I got into conversation with two or three French gentlemen in the coffee-room, and as we were smoking our cigars, I found out that my middle-aged Englishman was in the same room, looking very hard at me indeed. Then he came quite close to me, that he might listen to my French, and get to know whether I were an Englishman or not. I knew he could not find me out; English people never can unless I choose to let them, and so I went on with some story I was telling without apparently paying the slightest attention to my English friend, being too much amused with the idea that I was puzzling him; but not having any desire whatever to cut his acquaintance, which I meant to resume when it suited me. At last our little knot broke up, and I was left alone with the *Moniteur* and the *Times* on the table, a little porcelain dish of lucifer-matches, and my porcelain cigar tray, in which still lay, temptingly, a fresh cigar. In lighting this I felt that I was very keenly observed, and so took care to choose the *Moniteur,* casting a glance only at the *Times.* My English friend came and took the *Times,* then sat down and looked at me over it, shielding himself from time to time behind his newspaper. At last, after a hearty stare of full five minutes, which I bore like an Emperor without wincing, he laid down his paper and said, "Excuse me, sir, are you an Englishman?" I answered in English, but with a villanous French accent, that "I had not the honour to be the compatriot of Monsieur."

"Anyhow," he said, "you understand English?" I answered, with much embarrassment and hesitation, in English words, but with French idioms and a French accent, that I understood English very well, though I could not speak it. On this my English friend began his story, which was exactly what I wanted him to do.

"Well, sir," he said, "this is the most wonderful instance of an almost perfect resemblance between two people I ever saw in my life. You are the exact duplicate of a young Englishman I once met with in Scotland under very singular circumstances. Come, since you understand English, I may as well tell you the whole story.

"It is as queer an adventure as you ever heard of. I am fifty-seven years old, and what you call rich in France. Nobody was ever less disposed to adventure. I am as quiet and as respectable an old bachelor as any to be found in Cheltenham, where I usually reside. I am particularly careful of my health, at least since my great attack of rheumatism which seized me in December, 1845, and which my own prudence has kept off since then.

"Every year I take a tour. I have been up the Rhine, I have been in Switzerland, and I would have gone to Rome, but I hate Popery. Some friends of mine persuaded me in the year 1857 to go to the Highlands of Scotland, and, having no particular reason for going anywhere else, I went.

"I got safely enough to Inveraray, and thence in a pony-carriage to Dalmally. Dalmally is a very pleasant little place, with a large, comfortable inn, and a church conveniently near. They told me there was good fishing to be had upon Loch Awe, which is at no great distance from the inn, so I resolved to stay at Dalmally some weeks.

"The day of my arrival was a Saturday. Sunday I spent at the inn, with the exception of those hours which I passed in church. On Monday morning I set out for the lake. The hotel-keeper told me there was not a single man at liberty that day, all his men being engaged by a party of tourists who had set out on a pic-nic. But the hotel-keeper said I might take one of his boats, which I should find by the river-side.

"I followed the river Orchay through the fields, till I came to Kilchurn Castle. After spending an hour in exploring the castle, I determined to venture out upon the lake. There was a pleasant breeze from the east. So I let the boat drift quietly before the breeze, and fished from it, but did not catch anything.

"The wind began to freshen, and when I had got fairly out in the greatest breadth of Loch Awe, I began to feel very hungry. So I stopped at a pretty little is-land, where I found a small ruined castle, and ate my lunch in the castle. The wind began to blow very much stronger then, and I found, on looking at my watch, that I had idled away the whole day. It was late to begin with when I left Dalmally, and I had been botanising all the way down to Kilchurn Castle, and then I don't know how much time I had spent at the castle itself, for I am a bit of an antiquarian, but the day was far spent when I had finished my luncheon on the little island.

"I had tied my boat up in a corner very nicely sheltered from the wind, and so I found it safe enough when I sought for it again.

"I got out into the middle of the lake and pulled with all my might, but could not get fast forward on account of the violence of the wind. After rowing like this till I was quite tired, I began to see that I was making very little progress indeed, for the island where I had lunched was still not three hundred yards astern,

"I then thought that if I could get to either shore so as to walk to the inn, and leave the boat wherever I might happen to land, it would be a wise thing to do; but the waves were by this time terribly high, and as soon as ever I tried to turn the boat sideways to the wind, a great wave came splashing into it, wetting me to the skin, and putting a great deal of water into the boat. Talk of the sea being as calm as a lake! the sea would be anything but pleasant if it were always as rough as Loch Awe was that night.

"Though I am a prudent old bachelor for the most part, and little disposed at present for adventurous expeditions, I have a certain amount of courage, and have served in the volunteers when a lad. So I did not lose my presence of mind when the water came into the boat, but tried to think quietly about my position.

"I now saw how needless it was for me to think of getting back to Kilchurn; but what alarmed me more was the impossibility of rowing to the shore across such stormy waves. So with all my prudence I determined to take my chance of an attack of rheumatism, and pass the night on a large island that lay about a mile farther down the lake than the island where I had landed, but in such a position that I could drift down to it without crossing the waves at all.

"So I drifted very carefully with the boat half-full of water, and my clothes drenched, looking forward with bitterness of soul to a miserable night and a long attack of rheumatism to follow. To add to my discomfort, a terrible shower of rain came on, wetting such of my clothes as the spray had left dry, and, thus forlorn and wretched, I drifted on to the shore of the island.

"About twenty yards from the shore the boat gave a tremendous thump against a stone, turned her side to the waves, thumped again twice or three times, and was filled in a minute by the breakers. As for me, I rolled out of her somehow, and stumbled and floundered about, up to my middle in water, till I got ashore.

" 'Well, but the boat,' I said to myself; 'something must be done about the boat.'

" 'Hang the boat!' I answered myself, 'what do *I* care about the boat? a five-pound note will make all right when I get back to the inn.'

" 'Yes; but how ***shall*** I get back to the inn? Here am I, cast ashore on a desolate island, as unhappy a wretch as Robinson Crusoe himself, and I cannot swim ten yards. How ***can*** I get back without the boat?'

"But the boat bumped and thumped against the stones, and knocked a great hole in her side before ten minutes were over, so I tried to think no more about her, and turned my attention to the subject of dinner.

"The subject of dinner was a bitter subject for me. No one enjoys a good dinner more than I do. I have lived six months in Paris, and know all about French dishes except their names, which I never could learn for the life of me. But I am a good judge of a dinner, only I must have a dinner to judge. My dinner that night on the island seemed like one of those wonderful assizes one hears of now and then, where the judge comes gravely to try cases and there are no cases to be tried.

"On examining such materials of comfort as I had about me, I found that I had a flask of brandy half-full, a box containing two sandwiches, wetted, and a cigar-case not badly replenished. But my matches were all thoroughly damped, and would not burn. So I looked at the cigars with a bitter feeling of their uselessness, and took a pull at the brandy-flask by way of consolation. I was not yet sufficiently reduced to eat the wet sandwiches—nor my shoes.

"I found a little wood of fir trees on the island, and lay down in it with such miserable sensations as I hope I may never experience again while I live. I was dreadfully cold. The wind howled through the little wood most dismally, and the rain, which pelted continually against the fir trees over my head, dropped from them upon me in big drops, so that I felt as if I were under the dropping well at Knaresborough, in a fair way of becoming a beautiful specimen of petrifaction.

"I wish I could give a fair notion of my misery. When one is really and truly miserable, as I was then, it would be a comfort to think one had some chance of finding sympathy, but nobody will sympathise with an old bachelor like me. I have told this story twenty times, and people always laughed at me and called me Robinson Crusoe. But I should like to see *them* in such a position. It was no laughing matter for me. It became very serious indeed; and as I got colder and colder in the wood, I began to feel that I might be found there cold and dead in the morning, like the babes in the nursery tale.

"I took another pull at the brandy. I tried once more to light a cigar, but it was no use with my wet matches. Then I tried to get into a better sheltered place, and found a few branches that some one had cut from the fir trees, and with them made myself a sort of a bed. Oh how sadly I thought on the aches and pains I might have to suffer for that night!

"I lay thus covered up with pine branches, and said my prayers. Then I tried to sleep, and I believe I did sleep some time, for when I next opened my eyes all seemed much darker than before; in fact, it was already eleven o'clock. But after this I could sleep no more, for my teeth chattered together with cold, and I was as stiff as a corpse.

"There was nothing for it, then, but to take exercise, so I walked out of the wood weary and stiff as I was, and made my way to the shore. There was light enough to distinguish land from water, and I stumbled along over the stones on the beach till I came to a piece of driftwood, which I did not see, so I fell over it and hurt my knees. When I picked myself up, I walked on but slowly, and soon got into the thick of a wilderness of fern, but I knew that I must walk on and on to keep up the circulation. The rain all this time never ceased at all, but kept hard at it, pelting at me most cruelly.

"Well, I stumbled on till I came to the corner of a precipitous rock, and, on turning this corner, I saw the most unexpected and astonishing sight that ever I saw in my life.

"There were three tents, or rather two tents and a hut, all in a line, as I have seen the tents at Chobham camp. I went up to the first tent; there was nobody there; I looked into it, and saw a good fire burning in an iron grate. The grate had a stove-pipe for a chimney, which went through a hole in the tent. Now I could not have resisted this chance of lighting one of my cigars if I must have been transported for it to Botany Bay the next morning, so I crept into the tent and lighted my cigar at the fire.

"When I had lighted my cigar I sat down to warm my hands, which were fearfully cold. I found the interior of the tent comfortable enough, at least in comparison with the wood, but it did not seem to be inhabited regularly. Some peat and firewood were piled up in it, and a frying-pan left on the ground led me to suppose that it served as a kitchen to the other tents. The tent was comfortably sheltered from the wind, and I enjoyed the good fire. Bright as the fire was, however, I took the liberty of putting another peat or two upon it, and then I believe I fell asleep.

"When I awoke I found myself still in the same place, with the fire very low, and a chill feeling in my limbs, on account of my wet clothes. Just then I heard steps approaching the tent, and a voice singing,—

'In the days we went a-gipsying
A long time ago.'

In a minute afterwards, a sharp, active-looking servant-man came into the tent. On seeing me he stopped short in his song, and started very violently, staring at me without saying a word. So I told him that I had been cast ashore on the island, and begged leave to warm myself at the fire. Then he said he must tell his master, and so left me to myself again.

"I had not long to wait before he returned, and his master with him. His master was a young man of twenty-five, with a beard and moustache, and a pleasant, friendly countenance. He shook my hand as if we had been old friends, and began to scold me for not coming straight to his 'hut,' as he called it, where he said I must have some supper; then, seeing how wet I was, 'But first,' he said, 'you must change everything you have on. Thursday,' he said to the servant, 'put out a suit of my clothes, with flannels, and a clean shirt for this gentleman, in your tent, and let him have a hot foot-bath. Put some water on in the big pan here immediately.' Then, turning to me, 'I must apologise for putting you to dress in my servant's tent, but we must have our supper in mine, and he will prepare it here.' Then he led the way, and I followed him out in the rain to the next tent. I found it a very comfortable place indeed, with a wooden floor, and low wooden walls, and a stove in the middle, the stove-pipe serving as a tent-pole. Here the servant laid me out a complete suit of dry clothes, and, having aired the shirt and flannels at the stove, and put me a clean comb and brush, left me to my reflections.

" 'Well, after all,' I thought, 'this is not a bad ending to my adventure. I'd rather be here than in the wood. I used to think a tent a very poor sort of a house indeed, but, by Jove, I shall know its value for the future.' Then, looking up at the nice striped lining of the servant's tent, I thought, as I heard the rain pelting on it, outside, what a blessing it was to be so well sheltered.

"In a quarter of an hour I was in a dry suit, and sat by the stove waiting for the servant to bring my footbath. I had not long to wait; he came very soon, and gave me a round tin foot-bath, with hot water, and a clean towel. 'Please, sir,' he said, 'master says you had better not eat anything if you can wait a few minutes till supper is ready in his hut; but if you are very faint he will send you some whisky.' I thanked the lad with all my heart, but said I could wait cheerfully enough; and so there I sat, with my feet in the warm bath, and my body in dry garments, with the pleasant prospect of a good supper before me. Then the question presented itself suddenly, why the camp should be on the island at all Hitherto it had seemed to be there merely for my accommodation; but, as my senses recovered themselves gradually, under the pleasant influences of surrounding comforts, I began to speculate about the camp. 'Anyhow,' I thought, 'I shall get to know all in time.'

"The servant-man had laid by my side clean stockings and a pair of seal-skin boots, lined with white down. I had just encased my feet in these delightfully soft and comfortable boots when the servant came again and said, 'Please, sir, supper's ready; will you come this way, sir?' Then I followed him to the hut, or rather walked close to his side, for he held up an enormous white umbrella to shelter me from the rain, and soon I found myself in as snug a little box as one would wish to see. It was something like a yacht's cabin. The walls were painted white and hung with beautiful engravings, except where green curtains concealed four windows, one in each wall. There was a little fireplace, too, with a fire in it, and the floor, which was of wood, and elevated to a considerable height above the ground, was covered with a dark red carpet. A small square table of mahogany stood in the middle of this little apartment, with a cloth laid for supper and a little lamp burning. Two chairs were placed opposite to each other, and my host, having welcomed me afresh, and kindly inquired if I had over-come the effects of the cold, took one of the two chairs and invited me to take the other.

"I believe I never had a merrier supper in my life. The servant brought first a dish of red lake trout, very well cooked indeed, and after that a venison cutlet. Then we had coffee and cigars; my host smoking in preference a seasoned meerschaum, evidently an old friend. Then he would have me narrate the history of my arrival on the island, but when I came to that part about lying down under the trees like the babes in the wood, he became quite grave, and said I might easily have died there if I had slept till I was benumbed; then he would have me take a glass of toddy to keep off the bad consequences of my miserable hours in the wood. And so we got very merry indeed.

"Then I thought it a good opportunity of getting at the purpose of the camp, why it was there at all on the island; but I could not obtain any satisfactory answer whatever, and was left to ascribe it to mere whim, or any better reason that I could find out for myself. There seemed to be a mystery hanging over the camp. Not a word on the subject could be got out of my host 'Never mind,' thought I, 'I will tip the servant to-morrow morning, and so get to know all about it.'

"We talked about all sorts of things; about politics, and Paris, and Louis Napoleon amongst the rest. That led me to think you must be my host, because he seemed familiar with Paris.

"After that we talked about the French and English military camps, and then I began to fancy my host was a military officer, but could not explain to my own satisfaction what so small a military camp could mean.

"When we had smoked, I don't know how long, my host said, 'I beg pardon for my want of hospitality, but you must really go to bed now;' and without farther preface he called for his servant, who removed everything from the table in a jeffey, and unscrewed its legs and stowed it away, putting the lamp and other things on four corner-shelves that seemed made on purpose for such services. Then, in two minutes more, by unrolling a hammock that was strapped up to one end of the hut, and fastening it with straps to staples in the other end, he provided me with a bed. Then, opening a sort of ottoman, he took out several bags of flannel and linen, put them one within another, and laid them on the stretched hammock. My host then explained to me how I was to enter with much circumspection the innermost of these bags, and so said, 'Good night,' and left me. It was not without some difficulty that I introduced myself into the bags, but, once in, I felt wonderfully comfortable, and fell fast asleep in a minute.

"The next morning was gloriously fine, with a brisk breeze from the old quarter. At eight o'clock my host knocked at the hut door, and told me that breakfast was ready. We breakfasted outside the hut in the open air. We had ham and eggs, and mutton-chops, and coffee. After breakfast my host said, 'I have been to look at your boat, but it is quite useless for the present; you must let me put you over in mine:' and so we went down to the beach where my host had two boats, one at anchor in a little bay, the other drawn up on the sand.

"I never saw such queer boats in my life. They were something like flat rafts, being merely tin tubes supporting a wooden deck, but my host assured me they were perfectly safe; and, indeed, we sailed over very pleasantly on the larger one. All this time I could not get a word out of my host as to the nature of his occupations, or his object in living in camp. My last hope was in the rather heavy tip I reserved for the servant-man.

"Watching my opportunity when we had landed on the mainland, I slipped half-a-crown into his hand, and then asked carelessly, 'Who is your master? and why does he live here in camp?' But the servant was a Yorkshireman, and told me such a history about his master and himself as I could neither make head nor tail of; but not one word of direct answer could I get out of the lad.

"When I got to Dalmally, I asked the waiter if *he* knew. My host, it turned out, was a young Englishman already known to me by reputation for about a week before I saw him, as the author of a poem called 'The Isles of Loch Awe,' which I bought at Inveraray, as I was going to see Loch Awe itself, and thought I might as well know something about it, though it was only poetry. I don't think he's much of a poet. He seems to me to take after Wordsworth, and the lakers, and that American poet, Tennyson; now I prefer Lord Byron to the whole lot of them. As to his purpose in encamping, it seems to be the study of landscape-painting. I know nothing about painting, and care as little; but I have learned the value of a tent, and shall never forget the lesson as long as I live."

So he ended his history. "Well," said I in pure English, "I'm very glad you enjoyed such hospitality as I was able to offer you."

"Begad! it's you after all!" exclaimed he like an Irishman. "I could not believe there was such a duplicate in the world, and I couldn't make out how one of those horrid foreigners came to look so like an Englishman; but," added he, checking himself suddenly, and looking rather grave, "you mustn't mind what I said about the poetry, will you? I dare say it's very pretty: I don't know much about poetry; you must excuse me."

"No, I won't excuse you," I answered laughing, "for you have been guilty of a bit of invention yourself, and invention, you know, is the very fountain of poetry."

"Do you mean to say I've been embellishing a bit? Upon my honour, everything happened as I've told it You yourself are a witness."

"It's all correct but the cutlets. You said they were venison; now I remember distinctly that they were nothing but plain Scotch mutton."

On this my friend declared that, mutton or venison, they had saved his life, and he meant to repay them with interest, though he never could give me a supper which would do me as much good as that supper did him. However, next day he made me dine with him at the Trois Frères Provençaux in the Palais Royal, and invited two other Englishmen to meet me, to whom he narrated the whole adventure over again. The dinner was something wonderful, and the bill tremendous, but he paid it without wincing.

CHAPTER XI.

THE ISLAND FARM.

ALL who have read the beautiful story of Undine must remember the opening lines.

"Several hundred years have probably elapsed since a worthy old fisherman sat at the door of his hut on a beautiful evening, mending his nets. The spot of ground on which his dwelling was situated was extremely picturesque. The emerald turf on which it was built extended far into a broad lake, and to an imaginative mind it seemed as though the promontory, enamoured, strove with all its force to penetrate into the beautifully blue limpid stream, while, on the other hand, the water, actuated by mutual passion, endeavoured to encircle in its embrace the lovely spot with its undulating grass and flowers, its waving trees, and cool recesses. The one was impelled towards the other with almost human sympathy, and it was natural, each was so beautiful."

Not less beautiful is the peninsula of Innistrynich, which juts into Loch Awe, joined to the mainland only by a low green meadow, submerged when the waters rise. I have chosen this place as a kind of dépôt and centre of operation, and taken it on a lease of five years.

It is so rich in fair natural pictures that I shall probably travel very little for the next year or two, till I have painted the best of them. The old hut is erected here, and will be moved about from place to place on the island as its services may be needed.

The island rises into rounded knolls of fair pasture, with green park-like glades, and great stones of a marvellous colour, rich in wonderful lichens and mosses. There is one noble stone in particular for which I have the friendliest love and admiration, and which I visit every day. It stands about twelve feet high, and overhangs like a leaning tower. It is covered with a perfect mosaic of silver and purple and green. The broad spots of lichen upon it seem like a map of some unknown archipelago. How many thousand years has it stood there whilst those silver spots have spread!

And not only have I excellent studies of stones quite close at hand, but also most noble studies of trees. There is no better place on Loch Awe than this peninsula for rich and picturesque foliage. There are some magnificent groups of oaks, not very large, it is true, but not the less grand artistically. These little oaks of Innistrynich, rooted in the hollows of the rock, and nurtured by a rude climate, are as magnificent in their grey, knotted, ancient, long-suffering hardihood, as a Highland bull, though short in stature, is mighty in his bold bearing, and massive build, and black, terrible mane. And there are old hollies, centuries old, not pitiful garden shrubs, but strong trees, whose twisted trunks are washed by storm-waves in the winter, and there are venerable thorn trees that stand in the spring like tall hillocks covered with the thick snow of their sweet blossom. Then there is the mountain ash, clothed with scarlet in the season, when his million berries glow like heaped-up beads of red coral. And there are delicate little birches with silver stems, and young aspens with little leaves fluttering like the wings of butterflies in the faint breeze. But high above the oak and the birch tower the stately sycamores and firs, and there are two or three great ash trees fit for a king's demesne.

And between and beyond these fair and stately trees, and through the intricate trellises of their leaves, there are yet lovely sights to be seen. You cannot walk twenty yards on this island without coming upon some new and striking picture. The lake, in fine weather intensely blue, shines through the lower branches, and through the girdle of little shrubs round the shore its tiny waves gleam like sapphires, and the fair mountains rise beyond it with green, soft, mysterious surfaces, and delicate untraceable edges against the soft blue sky.

And then, in front of the island, at the extremity which juts the farthest into the lake, there is a little square whitewashed cottage, with a verandah. I made it a condition when I agreed to take the island that four of the windows of this cottage, those belonging to the principal rooms, should be removed, and replaced with fair sheets of perfect plate-glass. They had little lozenge-shaped panes before, which no student of nature could tolerate in such scenery. The invention of plate-glass is one for which we landscape-painters can never be sufficiently grateful. I heard of a man the other day who put a thousand pounds' worth of plate-glass windows into his house all at once, and not only that, but paid the bill without a murmur. I sympathise with that man—I honour him! On the other hand, I hate little lozenge-shaped panes, no bigger than a visiting card, that cut up a splendid scene into meaningless fragments. They are fit only for churches and schools where nobody ought ever to think of looking out of the window.

My cottage, however, is a complete artistic observatory. I have a reach of lake before me five or six miles long to the westward visible through two of my plate-glass windows, and to the north there is Ben Cruachan, himself visible through another. So long as I remain in the house, not a single effect of importance on those broad waters and mighty mountain-side will escape me, and I shall obtain a comprehensive series of memoranda, including effects of every season of the year, and every hour of the day, and every state of the atmosphere. By this means, watching continually the changes of aspect produced in a few familiar scenes by every change of effect, and taking careful notes of such changes, I shall solve the most perplexing of those difficulties which baffled me last year, and, I confidently hope, after five years of such constant observation, winter and summer, here and in the camp, come at last to realize my ideal of fidelity in landscape-painting.

This little cottage is a considerable addition to my accommodation. It contains twelve habitable rooms, each about ten feet square. I shall, however, require an increase in my establishment, for poor Thursday, ingenious as he is, cannot do everything.

And there is a farm, too, to be looked after. The island contains twenty-eight acres of land, which will keep me a horse, and a couple of cows, and a few sheep. I shall make a good garden on the southern slope of the island, from the house to the shore; there is nothing but a little square kailyard now.

I have put a Scotch farm-servant into a cottage on the island. He will be my gardener, and go to Inveraray with a cart for supplies.

With the garden, and easy communication with Inveraray, I hope to live considerably better than I did last year. No one knows the utility of green vegetables till he has been deprived of them. I got quite out of health last year for want of such common things as any market gardener near London would supply for a shilling or two, rarities utterly unattainable in this famous county of Argyll, except by actually sowing them in the ground, and waiting patiently till they grow.

A little re-arrangement has wonderfully increased the utility of the camp. Hitherto it has not been sufficiently portable to be easily removed from place to place, and so I have lost, in a great measure, the advantages of a nomadic life. But the whole camp is now quite portable. The hut is erected on two large wheels, and presents a striking resemblance to a bathing-machine, with the door at the back: if there were a good beach here I should certainly employ it in that character, as well as for artistic purposes. To the old waggon is now added a convenient box or body, composed of the wooden walls of Thursday's hut, and capable of containing all the materials necessary to a gipsy expedition—tents, boxes, provisions, &c. Outside this body, and on the top of it, are seats for four persons, like those in a dog cart; and the interior being lighted by two small windows, affords, when empty, an excellent berth for Thursday. My travelling camp will consist of two of Edgington's best travelling tents, with strong waterproof floor-cloths. With this I hope to make several extended expeditions, but for the present shall probably confine myself to the work immediately around me, of which there is a bewildering abundance.

The greatest inconvenience I foresee here is a want of out-buildings. I have only two or three thatched constructions—they look like old cottages. Lancashire people have a passion for spacious farm-buildings, which I share to the full, because space is always necessary to a high degree of order and cleanliness. It is quite beneath the dignity of my mare to be lodged with cows, and yet there is no other place for her. However, both she and I will have to bear with little inconveniences, and I am happy to have secured so desirable a centre for the execution of my future plans. I shall begin first by working near home, and paint perhaps a dozen pictures of scenes within five minutes' walk of my house, then I shall gradually enlarge the circle of my labour, till it reaches a diameter of about a hundred miles, with my house for a centre. It is probable, therefore, that for some time to come there will be no matter of interest to narrate in these pages, unless it be an occasional excursion to a distance in order to keep up our efficiency in the practice of encamping, and to prepare us for the last two years of my lease, which will in all probability be exceedingly active, as the circle of my work will by that time have enormously expanded.

For such a purpose as mine it would indeed be impossible to find a better position than this island of Innistrynich, and it is pleasant to feel myself established here securely for five years of uninterrupted observation, during which the proprietors, in the elegant diction of the lease, "have bound and obliged their respective constituents, and their heirs, to warrant it to the said Philip Gilbert Hamerton and his foresaids, at all hands and against all mortals." These, cautious Scots dare not warrant the island to me against the immortals, that is, the ghosts. And they are especially precise and explicit in the form of words by which they make me bind myself to leave at my end of the lease:—

"And the said Philip Gilbert Hamerton bound and obliged himself and his fore-saids to flit and remove himself, his wife, bairns, family, servants, goods, and gear, forth and from the said possession at the expiry of this tack, and to leave the same void and redd to the effect that the said First parties or their foresaids, or others in their name, may then enter thereto, and enjoy the same in all time thereafter."

CHAPTER XII.

A GIPSY JOURNEY TO GLEN COE.

WE have had a wild summer here this year. In England, I hear it has been glorious and golden, like the climate of Egypt. In France, the beautiful sun, like a generous host, has given, without stint or limit, the rich juice of a vintage unparalleled in its abundance, so that the labourers in the vineyards knew not where to stow the overflow of wine, and put it in washing-tubs and cattle-troughs, because their casks would contain no more. This very year, in the unfavoured mountains of Scotland, the peasant could not get his peat for the winter hearth, nor the farmer his little crop of hay, nor his poor harvest of oats. The peats were cut, but never dried; there they lay, in little miserable mounds, on the black moor, and soaked and rotted, day by day, till all the virtue was soaked out of them. The thin blades of corn have been levelled by the wind, as though cavalry had charged over them; and farmers have deferred their hay harvest, in the bare hope of a little sunshine, till the dead leaves lie upon it now, in this dreary month of November. I suppose they will cut it soon, and the feeble sun will look upon it languidly, from the southern hills, a few short hours by day, hardly long enough to melt the hoar frost from it

As for me, my farm is such a miniature affair that I made my hay in a tolerably fine week we had in the summer, and got it all safely housed in my little barn. In the month of September, one fine morning, I issued marching orders, and set forth on a campaign.

The whole of my insular kingdom was instantly thrown into unwonted commotion by the promulgation of these commands. Seven fires were lighted, and provisions for several days cooked in an hour or two. A terrible sentence thinned the poultry-yard, and many a fine cock that crowed that morning in the vigour and pride of youth, lay cooked and cold in a provision-box far away on the morrow! My gardener (an excellent butcher, by the bye, a very desirable qualification in a Highland servant) had killed a sheep the day before, so we had plenty of mutton.

We started with the waggon at sunset and encamped that night in Glen Urchay. I occupied one of Edgington's tents, and Thursday slept in the waggon. As we were pitching the tent two friends of mine came from the hotel at Dalmally to see me. We sat talking and smoking till two in the morning, when my friends left me, and I laced the tent door, having first looked at Thursday through the window of his waggon, where he seemed marvellously comfortable, and at poor Meg, the mare, who stood tethered hard by with an air of perfect resignation.

And yet the only member of the expedition who was dissatisfied with the arrangements for the night was this mare, Meg, whose resigned expression had probably been assumed to mask her sinister intentions. No sooner were we asleep than she got entangled with her tether, and, struggling violently, awoke Thursday, who went to her assistance with his lantern, and then returned as fast as possible to his cosy berth in the waggon, anticipating no further interruption to his slumbers. Delusive hope of rest! an hour later Meg was wandering over the wild moor, and Thursday stumbling after her in the dark, cursing her in his heart.

Now, by good luck, Thursday caught the beast after a long chase; but he had no rope to make a halter of, and the mare had left hers behind her. So poor Thursday was obliged to take Meg by the forelock (as in the days of our youth we were metaphorically recommended to catch a venerable personification of Time), and endeavour to persuade her to return quietly to her post. Wandering thus, the mare led Thursday, who, of course, had no control over her whatever, to a little Highland farmstead; and then Thursday called out to the farmer, and pretended he had led the mare, just as an unhappy king or prime minister, who is dragged by a perverse nation into all manner of difficulties, always pretends to act of his own royal will and pleasure.

"Have you a bit of rope?" cries Thursday.

"Na, na! there's nae rope about the hoose."

"Have you a bit of rope *for sixpence?*" cries Thursday, with a profound knowledge of human nature.

"Weel, weel, maybe there's a bit o' rope; but ye'll no be wanting a lang ane."

So the farmer gave Thursday the shabbiest sixpenny-worth of old rotten cord that ever was bought and sold, and Thursday paid for it, there and then, the sum of sixpence, on his own responsibility.

Then Meg, believing herself effectually haltered (though that was a delusion), followed Thursday very submissively to the camp. And, during the rest of the night, he got a quarter of an hour's sleep out of every half-hour, like the man who walked a thousand miles in a thousand half-hours. But Meg, the mare, slept not, neither did she slumber; but entangled herself continually.

The next morning I breakfasted luxuriously in the tent, and after breakfast one or two carriages passed with tourists. I may observe here that Thursday is very sensitive, and hates tourists on account of their impertinent manners, so he never misses an opportunity of irritating himself by watching these contemptuous travellers. As for me, I calmly proceed with whatever business I may have in hand, whether eating or smoking, or even the low and degrading occupation of studying from nature, without particularly troubling myself about the giggling companies of snobs who infest the Highland roads at a certain season of the year. For is it not in the nature of the true British snob on his travels to stare at all things? I should as soon think of being angry with the owls in the Zoological Gardens, because *they* stared, or at the monkeys because they chattered, as at the noble animal first classified by the celebrated naturalist, Mr. Thackeray, for acting after *its* nature, which combines the observation of the owlet and the eloquence of the ape.

But Thursday, not being acquainted with the writings of Mr. Thackeray, has not learned to see the snob on his amusing side, and on this occasion he remarked to me, with much irritation, in what a very contemptuous way these tourists had stared at the camp and how exceedingly high and mighty and majestic they seemed. Why, of course they did. It's a fine thing to ride in a carriage occasionally, and, when people aren't used to it, that lofty kind of locomotion has a certain elevating influence on their sense of dignity; and I am sure I should be sorry to say a word against the innocent gratification of this proper pride, especially since it is not expensive, but may be freely indulged in for ninepence a mile.

During the day's journey we had a good opportunity of admiring that wisdom of our ancestors which, instead of carrying roads through valleys, as is our more modern custom, did formerly, in order to give exercise to horses, compel these animals to climb and descend the sides of the surrounding hills. It would have been quite possible to construct a road in the level tract at the foot of Ben Loy, but the engineer preferred to display his activity by leading all future travellers a very fatiguing race over the inequalities of the mountain opposite. The labour wasted in the course of one century by a little bad civil engineering at the first planning of a road is rather startling when we think of it.

We were descending a very steep declivity, and the mist was thick in the valley. Through the mist came a great stream down from the opposite mountain, and we saw it gleaming below us, grey and dim, like a silent stream in Ossian. Then we looked up, and the mist broke away for one minute, and, lo! toppling over our very heads, up, up, in the air, like an eagle, hung a shapely mass of something we knew not, something purple and grey, mysteriously marked with a thousand scars, and spotted with a thousand shadows, hanging in the full sunshine, as if a fragment of another planet were hovering over the world; for it seemed of solid rock, and yet shapely in its magnificence; and it was wet, and glistening as with recent rain, and coloured with fair hues, like the mosaics of a marble dome!

It was the crest of Ben Loy. I have seen Ben Loy a hundred times, but never like that. The mist had exaggerated it, so that it seemed as if no mortal foot could ever wander there. It did not belong to the world. It seemed unearthly, supernatural, terrible.

The illusion was easily accounted for. The base seemed remote in the mist, but we saw the stony crest without any mist whatever, in the full, clear sunshine, so that it seemed quite close to us—far nearer than the stream at the base. It came upon us, too, unexpectedly. Lord Dufferin has recorded a similar effect. [Note *: "Hour after hour passed by, and brought no change. Fitz and Sigurdr—who had begun quite to disbelieve in the existence of the island—went to bed, while I remained pacing up and down the deck, anxiously questioning each quarter of the grey canopy that enveloped us. At last, about four in the morning, I fancied some change was going to take place: the heavy wreaths of vapour seemed to be imperceptibly separating, and in a few minutes more the solid roof of grey suddenly split asunder, and I beheld through the gap, thousands of feet overhead, as if suspended in the crystal sky, a cone of illuminated snow."—*Letters from High Latitudes.*

This effect did not, however, contain the ***contradiction*** that astonished me before Ben Loy. Lord Dufferin did not see the base of Jan Mayen at all. Now, I ***did*** see the base of Ben Loy, removed far away by the mist; and this discrepancy between the apparent distance of the base and the nearness of the summit made the effect almost incredible.]

Then we drove through a long dreary valley, till we came to Tyndrum, where I had hoped to increase my stock of provisions; but there were none in the place, not even a morsel of bread nor an egg. I saw a Highland boy, however, whose admirable beauty would have done credit to any palace in England where beef and other tissue-forming materials are most abundant. His face was of the very richest colouring, rather dark in complexion, with carnation glowing through the brown. He was a precious study of colour. I think I shall invite him to spend a week at Innistrynich, and then paint a few oil-studies of him from nature. How rich was that dirty tartan of his, with its vivid, soft colours and picturesque texture; and how well formed his bare legs below the kilt, with their early promise of manly strength, and the lithe suppleness of their boyish grace! Graceful indeed he was, as a young stag, with a certain shy waywardness in his attitude, as he leaned against the rude walls of his father's hut and gazed at us when we passed by.

As we approached the Black Forest the lines of the hills changed their character. They fell in grand concave curves, drawn with the utmost force from the summits to the stream down in the glen—mighty and majestic curves, so simple that any amateur would think he could draw them, and yet so subtle, that the genius never lived who could have rendered them with absolute accuracy. On our left was a frightful precipice, and as Meg trotted down the steep road I often congratulated myself on her steadiness and discretion. In the valley below there was a vast desolation of grey stones, rolled and rounded in a thousand floods, and spread broadcast over the barren vale, with a pure stream picking its way amongst them.

I encamped that night in as lonely a place as I could find; and, having backed the waggon down on the moorland, tied the mare to it, with a sheet on her back to keep her warm, and a little haycock to afford her occupation and amusement. An hour afterwards we were as comfortable as possible. Thursday had got his supper, and lay asleep on the waggon, Meg was busy with her hay, and I was sitting with my pipe after dinner, in an elysium of repose. It is with especial pleasure that I recall those evenings in the tent. When the fatigues of the day were over, and my house built for the night, with the buffalo-skins spread over the thick carpet, candles burning, and smoke curling gracefully in long wreaths from my brown old pipe up to the gabled roof, with no sound but the babbling of a brook, or the pattering of the rain, I felt as thoroughly happy as our poor querulous human nature will admit of.

There is the finest wood of Scotch firs at Loch Tulla that I have yet seen. Near Lord Breadalbane's kennels I found a good subject for Landseer—an invalid deerhound that had been gored by a stag at bay.

A great advantage about the waggon in comparison with the public coach is, that I can stop whenever I want to take a sketch. Thus, during the whole of this pleasant journey, I had a box containing sketching materials close to me on the roof of the waggon; and whenever a fine mountain outline or good natural composition struck me, I pulled up Meg, who soon accustomed herself to these intervals of repose, and drew very much at my ease, where I sat, on the box. On a coach I should have been whirled through the country without a chance of sketching. I enjoy this sort of pilgrimage, especially on account of the facility of sleeping wherever I will, without having to consider the distance from the inns. In ten minutes from the time I pull up, I can have a house ready to receive me on the wildest heath; and a good, serviceable house too, weather-proof and warm. This is delightful for a painter, to whom nothing is more tormenting than prudential considerations about eating and sleeping. As for me, I may take a drawing of any subject I choose, and have my house at hand when it is done; and whilst I am busy with *my* work, Thursday, an artist no less earnest in his own line, is organizing a repast to refresh me after my labours. In the meantime, envious artists pass me on the tops of coaches, or on foot, compelled by absolute necessity to dine at an inn ten miles off, and very likely when they get there they will have to post on another ten miles to sleep. The coach passed us in the Black Forest, when I was too busy to look at the passengers, but Thursday suffered much annoyance from their uncivil behaviour. He was highly indignant, and declared the travellers to be "no gentlefolks;" but they were a fair sample of the common tourist class, no worse than the average; and I have no doubt the most of them would have treated me with great respect under other circumstances, but on this occasion the sketch-book excited their contempt, as a sketch-book always does, when they believe the holder of it to be an artist.

In trying to analyse this question, so as to find out why silly people invariably behave impertinently whenever they see a painter at work, I came to the conclusion that, independently of the social contempt for the artist, which the best modern novelists have recognised as a characteristic of our age, there is another reason, less obvious, and still not to be overlooked. On those occasions, when a painter is annoyed by the flippancy of pleasure-seekers, he is almost invariably the only person present who has at the time any serious thought or occupation whatever. This sense of non-conformity on the part of the painter to the humour of the hour excites instantaneously in the spectators a disposition to combine against him. I believe any seriously-occupied student would have to put up with similar interruptions; but it is fortunate for students in other pursuits that they can study in the retirement of the closet. Besides, there are certain things which, however innocent in themselves, appear odd and incongruous whenever a third party comes upon the scene; and, as Emerson has very well shown, the study of nature is one of these things. No one but a landscape-painter ever dares to enjoy nature without some mask or apology. Other people seek this enjoyment also, but they always pretend to have other business on foot, either shooting, or a necessary journey, or their health, or some other prosaic every-day excuse. But the painter avows his object frankly; he is, indeed, forced into this exceptional frankness by the circumstances of his position; for if he were only to glance at nature furtively when out on other business, like the rest of the world, he would never come to produce good pictures.

When the coach passed me I was hard at work trying to analyse and make a note of an effect of rich, soft, misty moorland colour, which Linnell has rendered with wonderful veracity, and which no other man, so far as I remember, has ever yet been able to interpret at all. But it is no use talking about it here. I used to delude myself with the belief that words recalling scenes vividly to *myself* which I had studied intensely in nature were capable of producing the same effect on others. I forgot that to render vivid an impression once made, as the developing solution does in photography, is quite an easy thing in comparison with the object I proposed to myself; namely, to *create* the same impression in minds where it had no previous existence. I waste very little time in description now, because I find words quite incapable of conveying any idea of effects of colour and light to persons who have not seen them, and have come to discover that written language, however justly chosen and carefully fitted, must always, for purposes of landscape-painting be a very clumsy and unmanageable medium.

So we will say no more about this effect, though in truth I look upon it as by far the most important event of the whole expedition.

And now to Glen Coe. Meg had three miles to trot down hill, which is the only trotting Meg ever does. Whenever I came to a certain angle of declivity, without putting on the break, Meg began to show symptoms of uneasiness, going first to one side and then to another, till at last, when she found that I neither wanted her to go over the precipice on the one hand nor to break her neck against the rock on the other, Meg prudently decided to submit to the pressure from behind, and even trot a little, like an unprogressive government with public opinion at its heels. Then, when the waggon pressed hard, and seemed to get heavier and heavier, what a flurry Meg would get into, till, for safety's sake, I tightened the break on the hind wheels, and so relieved her.

I fancy the scenery of Glen Coe approaches nearer to the stony Arabian landscape than any other scenery in Scotland, for the mountains have a barren strength and steepness which remind one continually of the stone buttresses of Sinai, as we have seen Sinai in photographs and the drawings of John Lewis. Glen Coe, being not only one of the grandest scenes in Britain, but the most terrible of all in its associations, deserves a closer record than water-colour sketches of misty weather, or studio pictures done from hasty pencil memoranda. It is an excellent subject for photography, but no photograph can give its colour, which is delightful.

I was fortunate in seeing Glen Coe for the first time under a noble and mysterious effect, for the whole air was full of mystery. Far below us stretched a valley that seemed of supernatural vastness, whose entrance was guarded on the one hand by a wall of precipices, and on the other by a domed tower of solid granite, huge and pale in the misty air. This dome gleamed all over with purple and green, changing continually. It was covered with a network of irregular, fantastic decoration, a wild arabesque of faint rose colour, paler than the pale green ground it was laid upon. This enchanted dome was a solid rock far higher than St Paul's, and its mosaic of purple and green and rose colour was only the little patches of short grass, and red, dry channels of a thousand streams, and purple steps of precipice.

But in the vastness of the valley, over the dim, silver stream that flowed away into its infinite distance, brooded a heavy cloud, stained with a crimson hue, as if the innocent blood shed there rose from the earth even yet, to bear witness against the assassins who gave the name of Glen Coe such power over the hearts of men. For so long as history shall be read, and treachery hated, that name, Glen Coe, shall thrill mankind with undiminished horror! The story is a century old now; the human race has heard it talked over for a hundred years. But the tale is as fresh in its fearful interest as the latest murder in the newspapers. Kind hospitality was never so cruelly requited; British soldiers were never at once so cowardly and so ferocious. That massacre was not warfare; it was not the execution of justice; it was assassination on a great scale, and under circumstances every detail of which adds to the inexpressible painfulness of the fact. It is lamentable that the character of William, on the whole respectable, should be blackened by so foul a stain.

When we got to the King's House, I stopped to drink a glass of beer, not in honour of his majesty, but for my private refreshment. The landlady and hangers-on evidently expected me to descend from the box, send Meg to the stable, and order dinner and two bed-rooms. They never were more mistaken. Their representations of the distance from King's House to the next inn were quite thrown away upon a wandering gipsy like me, with a snug tent packed up inside his waggon. I thanked them for the information, paid for the two glasses of beer, and trotted on, leaving the astonished landlady and her staff to meditate on my cruelty to animals, and on my unaccountable repugnance to a night's rest in the royal precincts. Half an hour later I was dining comfortably in my own private hotel, and Meg, unconscious of the landlady's tender sentiments on her behalf, was dining very comfortably too.

I pitched my tent by the side of a little stream, and under the shadow of the great dome of rock I mentioned before, the relative position of my tent and the dome being like that of a shop in St. Paul's Churchyard and the dome of the cathedral. The moon rose behind it, and one or two splintered pinnacles of rock came sharply against her light in a black silhouette. The whole scene was exceedingly impressive, from its indescribable desolation. As I have observed before, it is of course in such desolate situations that a tent or hut seems by contrast most snug and cosy. That night the rain fell in torrents, and I was busy until very late, sensitizing waxed paper for photographic negatives—a tiresome process.

The next day was very windy and wild, but I got a study in pencil and two photographs. This expedition being in part a photographic experiment, I mention these negatives here. In another chapter I mean to consider the whole question of the relation between photography and painting, and the ways in which photography may serve a painter who employs it for especial purposes, at greater length than I can here, in a parenthesis. Having had occasion to spend some time in Paris last winter, I had profited by the opportunity of learning the waxed paper process, from a pupil and assistant of Gustave le Gray, who invented it; and during my journey to Glen Coe I determined to try whether its convenience in travelling was as ample a compensation for the comparative imperfection of its results as some photographers consider it to be.

The second night in Glen Coe was wilder and wetter than ever; and as on the following morning the weather seemed to have settled for rain, it seemed wiser, under the circumstances, to retreat to the granite stream in the Black Forest, where I had some drawings and photographs to take, as that position would be nearer home, and we were only provisioned for a week. To start on an expedition in the Highlands one ought to be provisioned beforehand, like a ship leaving port. In order to lessen the consumption of my own provisions I sometimes stop and feed at an inn, when it happens to be convenient; but it is not often so, on account of my work. Innkeepers, I find, will not let you have provisions, except in the shape of orthodox repasts, unless you know them; and as the innkeepers are the only people in the country who have either fresh meat or common bread, one may be temporarily reduced to considerable inconvenience for supplies. In future I shall act upon the experience acquired during this gipsy expedition, and pay greater attention to the commissariat.

I find, too, that Meg is not strong enough for the work she has to do, so on a future expedition I must have two horses. For this once I hired a leader at the King's House, to climb the hill.

I pitched my tent, then, by the granite stream. It was the finest study of granite I had yet found. The clear water ran swiftly in its smoothly-polished channels, down at the bottom of its deep and narrow crevices. And the colour of the rock! how exquisite! Stern, and hard, and cold as it was, older a hundred times than the pyramids or the sphynx, it had the hues of the dawn and the rose. And down in its hollowed basins the water lay clear as the pale green sea, and the granite seemed to glow with a ruddier hue when it rose to the air out of the cold waters, as if those flames lingered in its substance yet that made it fluid as the sea, an infinite ocean of fire, far back in the immeasurable past But the pale grey lichen spreads on it now, and the sweet waters flow over it, and the naked foot of the shepherd treads it, and the snows of winter rest upon it perennially in the mountains, and the water does not fly off in hissing clouds of steam, but lies still in the polished basins; and the bare sole of the shepherd's foot presses it unscathed, and the snow melts not from its hollows on the hills, for the great globe has cooled, like a cannon-ball from the casting.

In the evening the weather had improved, and I got a few photographs on the papers already sensitized at Glen Coe. It was a beautiful moonlight night, with a sharp frost. During the night I got up very often to look after my negatives, which were developing slowly. The waxed-paper process is tedious and unsatisfactory. In the morning I was up very early photographing, and getting colour memoranda. I developed my negatives afterwards on my road home. I found that one was really valuable, and the rest nearly worthless.

The waxed-paper process is in one respect more striking than the wet collodion. I mean in its property of retaining the undeveloped image. When, at the end of my day's march, far from the scene where I had exposed the papers in the camera, I took them from my portfolio at night, I often gazed long and wonderingly on the white waxed paper, paper as blank and void as when it came fresh from the mill. Then I laid each in the bath, ignorant of what image would come there, and slowly a faint chocolate tinge appeared here and there on the white surface, and then, amongst the strange patches of brown, a pale, ghostly image became dimly visible, the phantom of some scene I had passed that day, and this pale phantom-scene grew more and more defined, but with all the natural conditions reversed, the most brilliant light represented by the intensest black, and the deepest points of shade left in perfectly stainless paper, over which the acid brooded powerless; and the objects at the right hand were changed to the left, and still, with all this reversal of natural order, how marvellously truthful those images were as they seemed to rise out of the paper, and fix themselves upon it, like the magic pictures of an enchanter! It is a wonderful quality, indeed, of this sensitized waxed paper that it shall retain so long an accurate image, utterly invisible! There is a strange analogy between this and the action of the memory. The image is impressed on the leaves in the brain, but is laid aside quite blank in the portfolio. Years hence some circumstance shall arise that shall flood that forgotten sheet with a magical developing fluid, and the images shall come forth, as those wonderful waters flow over it, clear in every detail, till we shall be startled and frightened at its fidelity!

My habit of stopping to sketch on the road produced quite a little collection of memoranda—things of no use whatever to paint from, being far too slight for that, yet excellent practice in their way, as a preparation for sterner mountain-drawing. The photographs I find to be practically of no use. I might have known this before, if I would have condescended to try to copy one; but though I saw no harm in getting a photographic memorandum of something I had myself seen and studied in nature, I had determined in my own mind that no artist could wisely copy photographs taken by other people of places he had never seen. [Note *: I leave this just as it was written. Subsequent investigation has convinced me that no artist should ever *copy* a photograph at all, though most artists do, more or less. But as memoranda of *isolated* natural facts, photographs are invaluable. By seeking only for one fact in each photograph, you may get, in a large collection, a rich encyclopædia of facts of form. In this way the photograph is very useful to all students of nature; not otherwise. It can never replace good drawing, and is valueless for pictorial purposes, on account of its defective scale of light, and its false translation of colour into shade. I will explain this at length hereafter.] This distinction always appeared to me very clear indeed, not so much as regarding the interest of the purchaser of the picture as the painter's own interest. Whoever buys a picture buys it with his eyes open, and it is his own fault if he cannot tell whether it is good or worthless without being told the history of its construction. But I considered that a painter who painted from *bought* photographs, instead of studying nature for himself, would cheat, himself out of the study he so missed, and thus be by far the greater loser of the two.

As to other matters, I came to the conclusion that a camp, to be kept in the highest degree of efficiency, ought to be systematically provisioned, because the physical work of everybody out in camp is exceedingly heavy, and Englishmen are quite worthless without good keep. There was Thursday, for instance, as strong and hearty a fellow as you would wish to see on a Lancashire moor, quite knocked up at the end of our journey, as soon as the cold chicken and mutton-chops ran short; and, as to a painter, his work from nature is in itself exceedingly fatiguing, and the slightest derangement of health is fatal to all such labour as that. After a little more experience, when my plans are definitively arranged, I think it probable that I shall reach a high degree of efficiency in the art of camp-life, and conduct successfully extended expeditions. Already we are far sharper and livelier than we used to be.

We got home at last, quite ravenous. A week's gipsying is good for the appetite.

CHAPTER XIII.

CONCERNING MOONLIGHT AND OLD CASTLES.

SOME of the prettiest and most popular lines in the "Lay of the Last Minstrel" are the well-known ones in which the tourist who would see fair Melrose right is counselled to

"visit it by the pale moonlight;
For the gay beams of lightsome day
Gild, but to flout, the ruins grey."

I knew all Scott's best poetry by heart when I was a boy, and these lines had, I remember, an especial charm for me in those days. I did not perceive then, what I know now, that this is one of the few passages in the writings of Scott in which the colour is false and the sentiment affected. The ivory and silver were very pretty in the poetry, when I did not know that Melrose was red, and the preference of moon-shine to sunshine highly poetical and just, before I knew that the Minstrel was so little in earnest on the subject as never to have once taken the trouble to drive over from Abbotsford and see Melrose for himself, as he had so warmly recommended everybody else to see it; whereas I, poor enthusiast as I was, befooled by the North-ern Wizard, had put myself to considerable inconvenience to do his bidding. Still, as everything has its use, this disappointment led me to study colour in moon-light far more attentively than I had ever thought of doing before. Formerly I had accepted, without question, the popular conception of moonlight—the colourless ivory and ebony ideal. But Melrose taught me much. I got into the ruins furtively, one moonlight night, clambering the wall with a schoolboy's eagerness, my head full of an endless music of melodious rhyme, expecting to see before me, in mag-nificent reality, a vast abbey, whose imagery was edged as with silver, and whose buttresses were alternately built as of ebon and ivory—a fair white fane standing in the moonlight like a poet's vision.

Well, it was very beautiful, certainly, but not in that way. I have since seen the sculptured pavilions of the new Louvre, white as alabaster in the full moon, whilst the long row of lighted windows in the dark old Tuileries told of an impe-rial festival in the hall of the Ambassadors. Silver or ivory would be a permissible material wherewith to construct a simile if one were describing this moonlit palace of new white stone, fresh from French quarries, just carved all over by sculptors yet alive. [Note *: And yet, even already, this is no longer true. At the time I speak of, the stone was only just carved, the scaffolding only just removed. But now, when I copy out this manuscript for the press, the new Louvre is already grey, and no moon that will ever shine on that palace henceforth will have the power of again realizing Scott's ideal of moonlight.] But Melrose never looked like ivory at its newest, still less so many centuries after the death of its builders. The local colour of Melrose bears a closer resemblance to common London brick than to ivory. So I, poor simple youth, saw my illusion destroyed by a single glance, and have remembered ever since that the moon respects local colour, and does not translate everything into black and white, like an engraver.

The moon respects local colour, yet modifies it. Other changes are also produced by the transient colour and condition of the atmosphere; so that, as in all artcriticism, it is a difficult task to arrive at any positive laws which can be stated definitively in words. For instance, one of the most commonly known laws about reflection is, that the reflection of any object in water is darker than the object itself; but an ignorant person who had found this law in some critical work would inevitably commit himself if he attempted to apply it indiscriminately, for it often happens that reflections are very much paler than the objects reflected, merely because there is a thin stratum of mist on the surface of the water; *and this mist may be so thin, and lie so level on a calm lake, as to be utterly imperceptible in itself and only recognisable by an experienced landscape-painter, on account of the reflection being somewhat paler than usual.*

Moonlight on ruined castles and glittering lakes is the favourite subject of the very worst painters. They paint it by recipe. I have seen pictures of moonlight which were executed in a London picture manufactory on that recognised commercial principle of division of labour which is so scientifically applied to the production of a pin. I was informed by a person in the secret that these works of art were, each of them, produced by a series of workmen—a draughtsman, a dead-colourer, a man for details, a glazer, a scumbler, and a finisher. The result of their successive labours had that skilful hardness and decision peculiar to pure handicraft. The question occurred to me how many of these mechanics had ever *seen* a ruined castle by moonlight. Theirs was the ivory and ebony ideal—the pianoforte fingerboard ideal, as one may say—where buttress and buttress alternately seem framed of ebon and ivory. The moon shed a flood of light on the rippling water, broad at the spectator's feet, and narrowing itself gradually as it receded to a vanishing point in the distance, according to the orthodox laws of perspective, and in direct reversal of the facts of nature. I am afraid that this great modern principle of the division of labour is, after all, better applied to the production of pins than pictures.

Not being myself willing to wreck any reputation I might hereafter have to acquire on those mysterious moonlit waters which so few have sailed with success, I determined long ago to let no amount of personal inconvenience prevent me from studying moonlight thoroughly from nature; and when sober people are gone to bed, and the moon high in heaven silvers the broad waters, I often take Thursday with me, and a solitary white sail flies all night long from island to island, a lonely wanderer of the waves.

I always take a note-book with me on these occasions, and, when the moonlight is not strong enough to write by, have a little lamp on deck to illumine its pages whilst I cover them with hasty memoranda. Then the next day I try to approach in oil colour the hues I have studied in nature, and, after many ignominious failures, am just now beginning to see why so few painters can manage moonshine. Grave gentlemen of a practical turn of mind may think these midnight voyages very silly and enthusiastic enterprises, and maids who love the moon may think them very romantic. They were undertaken, perhaps, with an artist's enthusiasm at first, and since pursued not without some feelings of romance. For art cannot be attempted successfully without strong enthusiasm, nor what is best in nature felt without some sense of her deep and intense romance; but neither the one nor the other is an ***illusion.*** My work from nature is no more the result of illusion than the work of any other naturalist. The art of landscape-painting is not to be learned within brick walls. When I am out with my memorandum-books amongst these islands at two o'clock in the morning, I am working just as hard at my profession as a London lawyer at his, who at the same hour is immersed in the details of a case before a lamplighted ocean of law papers. Few people can understand this now, so that I always expect such voyages to be attributed to freak, which, as I am aware, is the explanation that most readily presents itself to others, and is, indeed, very generally adopted by my friends and neighbours. But people will understand these things one day, when they shall come to perceive that true art is not a school-girl's pastime, as they think now, but a man's pursuit, which, like any other worthy and noble occupation, requires the sternest devotion of all his energies.

One bright evening late in September, I set out, after dinner, for Kilchurn, to get a series of observations on moonlight colour; for I had studied Kilchurn closely enough to remember the ordinary daylight colour of every part of it. Dugald and Thursday rowed, for the water was like glass. Gradually the exquisite little island of Fraoch Elan grew larger and larger, and then detached itself from its twin sister island, and the two dropped gently astern like islands in a panorama. Then companies of white mists in pillar-like shapes, about as tall as human beings, glided over the smooth floor of water like a procession of ghosts. When we got to Kilchurn, and had safely passed the bar at the entrance of the bay, we floated quietly out into the midst, and Kilchurn stood before us in the full, mellow light of the moon.

A shallow mist had flooded the broad pastures by the Orchay. Gradually it crept across the bay. It was not above a foot deep, but *all the reflections turned pale suddenly.* Even the stars themselves became ruefully wan down there in the water, and the mountains were mere ghosts of mountains.

The stones of the masonry were all distinctly visible in the keep of Kilchurn, and the colour just as various as in daylight, only every tint was mixed with moon-grey. The grass at the foot was of a greyish green, glistening with dew. There was very little purple or blue of a positive kind, though a true picture of that scene might appear bluish by contrast with pictures of sunshine if hung near to such pictures in a gallery, or by contrast with the sunshine itself, as it plays on the warm furniture of a dining-room; but as I saw Kilchurn then, purple or blue were by no means its pervading colours. The sky, which was intensely deep and clear, was of a blue-grey, but the castle was all subdued pale greens and grey gold. The shadows were without detail, and soft in outline; the detail, where visible, seemed more mysterious and unintelligible than in daylight, *but not less abundant.* Every observation I find in the notebook I took with me, and every sentence scribbled on the sketches I made that night, seem like hostile criticisms on popular pictures—not, however, on such works as Turner's little study of warm moonlight at Millbank, done as far back as 1797; nor the Eve of St. Agnes by Mr. Hughes; least of all on Landseer's illustration of the Midsummer Night's Dream.

Landing under the keep, I walked to a little distance from the north-east angle, and sat down there to watch the changes in the aspect of the castle, as a pure, white mist from the river Orchay became gradually denser. A little aspen near me came with fairy-like delicacy against the sky, and contrasted well with the massive breadth of the keep. No detail whatever of masonry was visible now—only a sort of grey roughness. The moon shone through all the barrack windows (from the *inside,* for there was no roof), and corresponding spots of light lay in their places in the great shadow under the north side. Some trees at the west end receded like phantoms into vacancy. The whole castle now became a pale, mighty phantom, and certainly I never saw it under a more poetic aspect. Londoners are familiar enough with effects of fog; but rows of hideous brick houses seen through a filthy Thames miasma do not take that hold on the imagination which I confess Kilchurn conquered over mine when I saw her silent towers fading away like a dream in the moonlight, as the pure exhalations of the Orchay gathered in a great white cloud around her.

The legend of Kilchurn is very beautiful and affecting; I have told it already in verse (in "The Isles of Loch Awe"), and cannot repeat it here in prose. Legends of that sort are scarcely fit for prose, which lets the sweet essence escape.

The old castle, like most old buildings, has been ruined by man, and not by time. Henry the Eighth, Oliver Cromwell, blundering stewards, and apathetic proprietors, are the real authors of most of the ruins in Britain. With a little friendly care and attention a strong building will last a thousand years, but a fool will demolish it in a day. Kilchurn is a ruin merely because an economical steward thought the roof-timber would come in very well for the new castle at Taymouth, and so carried it thither. But he had omitted to measure the beams, which turned out to be too short, and therefore, of course, useless. Then, when the roof was off, the old castle became a general stone quarry, and furnished stones ready cut to all the farmers who chose to steal them. And the new inn at Dalmally, and the queer little sham Gothic church over the bridge, being erected some time afterwards, the now ruined castle furnished hewn stones to both those edifices. There is not a fragment of wood in all Kilchurn; there is not one step left there of all its winding stairs. Yet, in the forty-five, the building was garrisoned against the Prince; and in the latter end of the last century there were tapestry on the walls, and wine in the cellar, and a casque and shirt of mail still hung on the walls of the armoury. Alone with these relics lingered one old servant as housekeeper. She was the last inhabitant. Some domestics might have objected to the situation. Fancy a London housekeeper shut up alone in a great ghostly feudal castle on a narrow island rock, with waves roaring round it in the long northern winter nights, and the sobbing wind flapping the figured tapestry, and rattling the armour in the armoury! Not an attractive place, certainly, and scarcely likely to suit one of those numerous applicants whose advertisements crowd the columns of the *Times.* I think, if I had been the old housekeeper, I should have paid frequent visits to the wine cellar.

Fifteen miles from Kilchurn is the little island of Ardhonnel, with its sturdy little castle, where the great Campbells lived long ago. A gentle breeze had dispersed the vapour that gathered round Kilchurn, and its faithful reflections were effaced by the ripple that gained strength every minute under the increasing wind. It was only half-past ten o'clock, and the temptation to sail to Ardhonnel was irresistible. I took a little boat in tow at Innistrynich, filled with camp necessaries, and soon sped with a full sail before a vigorous breeze. It was pleasant to lie on deck in a buffalo-skin, and smoke a meditative pipe, as I watched the moonlight dancing on the waves, and the changing forms of the mountains. The shores were so vague and mysterious that I could scarcely see a recognisable detail, and yet so infinitely full and rich that, except in the shadows, there was nothing like vacancy. What baffles bad painters when they attempt moonlight is this mystery both of colour and form. Colour is subdued in moonlight, so men whose senses are dull think there is no colour at all; detail is confused in moonlight, so they think there is no detail. But a moonlight picture requires just as much *painting* as to colour, and drawing as to form, as a sunlight one. The hues are as various as in sunlight, and the detail as infinite, only the hues are under a magic spell, and the detail thrown into an inextricable confusion. But so far from moonlight being easier to paint than sunlight, it is, if possible, more difficult; for ten men can paint a positive, visible fact that the eye can lay hold of, for one man who can render the subtlety of that mystery which the imagination alone is qualified to apprehend.

I think never lover doted on a mistress as I on these landscapes. I am never tired of watching them; I can never have enough. Never yet have I been able to go to bed on a bright moonlight night without a secret pang, as if it were a sin not to sit for ever at the divine spectacle; and even then I open my shutters, that the moon may look into my room, and I on her white clouds. How intense and deep the sky is around her! how soft are the white exhalations! And as one is passing before her, see how its edge burns with pale crimson and violet! Oh, who shall penetrate the eternal mystery of the night? what poet shall ever exhaust, what painter worthily imitate, its splendours?

Soon after midnight we found ourselves off Port Sonachan, but it was three in the morning when the boat glided under the shadow of Ardhonnel, between the castled island and the shore. The men immediately pitched the tents, and I busied myself with writing observations in my note-book, intending at some future period to paint the castle as I saw it then. The moon was golden now, and near her setting; she hung over the opposite shore of the lake, and laid a long, unquiet path of light across it. Her warm, low light glanced across the thick ivy on the castle wall.

Ardhonnel is an exquisite little island. There is just room enough upon it for the narrow stronghold and no more. A few trees, stately in form and heavy with foliage, stand to the east of the building, and the building itself is covered all over with ivy. In the trees there dwells a colony of rooks, and in the ivy an owl. These are the only garrison of the ancient fortress of Argyll.

My tent was soon ready, so when the moon had set I shut up my memorandum-book and went to bed; that is, rolled myself up in a buffalo-skin. I was busy again at sunrise, making a study of colour and taking photographs. Ardhonnel is magnificent at sunrise; its light-and-shade is so powerful, and its colour so rich. When the massive towers are relieved thus vigorously, and reflected in every detail down in the calm water, it is one of the most effective studies in the Highlands.

Long ago, when Ardhonnel was a strong fortress full of warlike men, like a ship of war anchored for ever in an inland sea, the sentinel pacing the battlement at sunset fancied he heard a faint cry from the mountains. Very likely he paused a minute and looked in the direction of Loch Avich, then, hearing nothing more, resumed his measured beat.

An hour has elapsed and the sun has set. The sentinel stops again suddenly; this time, too, he has heard a cry, but nearer and clearer than before, and so piteous, that he is thoroughly interested now.

A boat leaves the island. The rowers pull vigorously across the lake. Just as they reach the mouth of the little river Avich, which flows from Loch Avich down to Loch Awe, there is a rush of men in the green copse as of hunters after their prey.

The boat scrapes the pebbles. Out of the copse rushes a beautiful woman, clad like a chieftain's wife. She leaps into the boat and falls down exhausted. The rowers push off instantly; the pursuers reach the shore too late. The lady is saved.

"'Tis a far cry to Loch Awe!" said the sentinel who had saved her.

And they told the story in the country round about, how the wife of Mac Dougal of Lorn had fled from her husband who threatened her life, and how, when she came to the hill above Loch Avich, whence her father's castle of Ardhonnel first became visible in the far distance, she had cried for help in her agony, fleeing before her pursuers. Then all the people wondered, and thinking that no earthly power had brought her cry so far, they said one to another, "Far is the cry to Loch Awe!"

And the lady's brother went out to the Holy War, and, being in Egypt on his way, was surrounded by Saracens, so he cried for help. But one of his companions sarcastically quoted the common saying, "Far is the cry to Loch Awe!"

And another chief of the Campbells, in battle in the north of Scotland, told his men how they had to rely on themselves alone, for, said he, "'Tis a far cry to Loch Awe, and far help from Cruachan!"

So the saying passed into a proverb, and became the watchword of the clan

Campbell.

CHAPTER XIV.

1859.

I WILL not trouble the reader with details of studies always pursued in scenes with which he is already familiar. It cannot interest anybody to know the insignificant details of an uneventful life. I have had many difficulties to contend against, which may lead, ultimately, to conclusions of some value to others who pursue the same objects; but these conclusions cannot be fully stated as yet, nor in this place. For instance, with regard to photography in its relation to landscape-painting. Nobody has ever yet answered the often-suggested question how far photography may be useful to the landscape-painter; and whether, under certain limitations, he can wisely practise it himself. Nor can I answer this question yet, in any decisive way. I have hitherto only practised the waxed-paper process, and cannot speak authoritatively of the limitations of the wet collodion. Besides, I perceive that photographs taken for especial purposes, as memoranda, may be useful to a degree which as yet nobody has any idea of, for such photographs are not to be had in the market, where they would be unsaleable, except to artists.

Again, with reference to the study of nature, I dare not as yet advance definite opinions, because my object is so new, that the experience of my predecessors is of little assistance, except in merely technical matters. For instance, Turner's way of study, good for an imaginative painter, is not exact enough for a topographic one; just as in literature, the degree of accuracy in historical facts which suffices for the poet or the novelist is quite unsatisfactory to the historian. On the other hand, what is known as the pre-Raphaelite system of doing all from nature is obviously inapplicable to transient effects. Between these two some other system will have to be ultimately traced out, and I am making experiments to that end, which include the painting of a good many pictures, so that it is not likely I shall be able for some time to offer any definite conclusions on this subject either. In the meantime, my journeys are limited to twenty miles from home.

In my private note-books for this year I find only two passages likely to interest anybody but myself; the first is a description of a beautiful pool where two young men were drowned when bathing, and the other an account of the coming of the first rain-clouds across the Atlantic after the long drought, which I was fortunate enough to witness from the summit of Ben Cruachan.

THE POOL OF DEATH.

The weather here is terribly hot still. I have explored all the streams in the neighbourhood in search of a good bath, and have at last found one. It is five miles from here, but I ride that distance willingly to enjoy a swim in its clear sweet waters.

I found the pool out by accident. Not very far from Dalmally a little stream glides under the road, as it slips away noiselessly by the thick hedgerows till it buries itself finally in the broad Orchay. A few hundred yards higher this stream passes through some of the very richest rock scenery I know anywhere. The dell is dark and narrow. The slender stream runs under and over huge masses of rock, but there are marks on those masses which prove the force of mightier floods—holes, broad, deep, and regular, bored as smoothly as a cannon's mouth, by the whirlpools of ten thousand winters. After studying these exquisite subjects with the delight of a painter who has loved streams since childhood, I continued to climb higher, and came at last quite suddenly on the most delicious natural bath I ever saw in my life. It was surrounded on three sides by walls of perpendicular rock. Over one of these walls fell the whole stream in one narrow waterfall of intense and silvery whiteness. The pool itself was deep under the waterfall, and the bottom rose gradually to within five or six feet from the surface, but the water was so clear that every pebble was distinctly visible.

One of my neighbours, who followed a little behind, now joined me. He had never seen the pool before, but immediately recollected that two young men had been drowned there. No one ever died in a more lovely place. One could easily fancy their fair young bodies, pale and cold as marble, lying deep under the crystalline waters like sunken statues, motionless, when their bereaved friends found them, some bright afternoon in summer. The stream fell into the quiet pool with the same sweet music the day of their death, no doubt. The blue sky canopied them with a colour as bright and gay, the merle sang over them in the silver birch, and nothing in Nature mourned for them. But down in the village one or two dark huts were darker and sadder that night, and for many a day from that date the murmur of the unthinking rivulet must have sounded in the ear of the mourner like the confused mutterings of a remorseful murderer.

THE COMING OF THE CLOUDS.

The summer of 1859 will long be remembered in the Highlands for its African drought. Towards the middle of June, the thin soil was parched like the desert all over the country; the grass was baked brown in the pastures, the cattle were dying of thirst, water was carried in boats from the mainland to the islands in the western sea, for all their springs were dry. Dunoon was supplied with water from Greenock. The crops would not grow. Day after day the blazing sun stared with his hot eye unveiled upon us. One afternoon, as I was painting from nature, I had the curiosity to ascertain the actual heat of the sun's rays where I was sitting at work, and found it to be a hundred and ten degrees. And this heat lasted for months. Most of the streams were dried up entirely, and remained mere stony beds, giving geological evidence of aqueous action at some indefinite period of the earth's history. The lake receded from its shores, and shrank daily within a space that grew narrower and narrower, till the inhabitants of Loch-Awe-side began to wonder whether their loch was not going to evaporate altogether.

At last a day came, the 17th of June, so ineffably clear and brilliant that you might see every stone on the crests of the highest mountains, as if one could have touched them by stretching out a hand. Aerial perspective was annihilated. The eye, accustomed to the broad, well-defined spaces of misty weather, was utterly at fault in judging of distance. Seen from Innistrynich island, the peak of Cruachan seemed to belong to Ben Vorich, yet there is a chasm between them two thousand feet deep and two miles across, as a bird flies. I could not resist the temptation to climb the mountain on such a day.

When we got into the corrie, I was more and more confirmed in the hope of seeing all that magnificent panorama which, on rare occasions, is visible from the summit of Ben Cruachan. The rugged outlines of the mountain stood clear and sharp against the deep azure of the sky; and in the pastures near the summit of Ben Vorich every stone and every tuft of grass were visible.

At last we gained the summit, and as Thursday was arranging a few provisions he had brought in his havresack, I adjusted my telescope and looked round me. In the south, far beyond the remotest hills, the blue lowland plain lifted itself to the sky. I saw the great expanse of Loch Awe glittering in the bright sunshine. There was not a detail hidden. The whole valley was burning and parching as it had done for three terrible months, except where the narrow lake lay wasting in its stony bed, day by day.

But the hour of deliverance was at hand. The isles of the sea were darkened by a gloom of vapour that came heavily over the Atlantic. Shining clouds of silver brilliance were built like glittering domes on the peaks of the thirsting islands, ready to melt themselves into numberless streams. The black masses of rain-cloud behind came fast over the sea-encircled mountains, summit after summit was hidden, island after island was engulphed in the advancing vapours. At last a shred of white mist came whirling over our heads within six feet of us, and was gone with the speed of an eagle in wild flight over the abyss. It was the pioneer of a great army of clouds that invaded the shores of Scotland beneficently that day.

Five minutes afterwards came two other shreds of mist, whirling and tumbling till they dashed fairly against the sharp peak of the mountain, and then, gathering themselves together, rushed on to the south. And then the glittering sea became dim, and the sun himself was shorn of his dazzling rays, and looked through the mist with a round, white face like the moon's, and that was the last glimpse we had of him; for in a few seconds the whole ocean of Atlantic vapour was upon us, tumbling and wreathing itself, and tearing and surging with mad velocity, till it overwhelmed the whole chain of the Grampians in one deluge of grey mist.

The view by this time being strictly confined to half a dozen grey stones, a few broken bottles (relics of tourists who, not having the fear of Ruskin before their eyes, had eaten lunch on the mountains instead of saying their prayers), and other matters of familiar detail of a like interesting nature, I determined to descend, which we could still do with perfect safety, as we could see at least six feet before us; which, as Thursday observed, "is plenty for somebody' at isn't reight gaumless."

CHAPTER XV.

I.

BEN CRUACHAN ON A DECEMBER EVENING.

ALL the hills are thickly covered with snow, delicately finished by the wind as a sculptor finishes a statue. Every now and then I can see a little wreath of what looks like intensely white smoke rising into the thin evening air from the edge of the great precipice near the summit of Cruachan; it leaves the slope of the mountain outline rather slowly at first, then curls itself suddenly and vanishes; it flickers like a white flame. It is snow carried by contending whirlwinds; if we were in it we should be blinded by it, and think it rather a terrible phenomenon. From this island it looks like a little silver flame cresting the mountain with its feathery wreathing.

The sun is setting on the opposite side of the lake. Every boss on the mountain casts its sharp azure shadow on the snow. The great shoulder of the hill throws a broad shadow into the deep corrie. It would take a week for a hard-working artist to draw all these shadows with tolerable accuracy. I am obliged to content myself with a hasty sketch, for the sun is descending.

At this moment the picture is perfect. The sky has become an exquisite pearly green, full of gradation. There is only one lonely cloud, and that has come exactly where it ought. It has risen just behind the summit of Cruachan, and pauses there like the golden disc behind a saint's white head. But this cloud is rose-colour, with a swift gradation to dark purple-grey. Its under edge is sharply smoothed into a clearly cut curve by the wind, the upper edge floats and melts away gradually in the pale green air. The cloud is shaped rather like a dolphin with its tail hidden behind the hill.

The sunlight on all the hill, but especially towards the summit, has turned from mere warm light to a delicate definite rose-colour, the shadows are more intensely azure, the sky of a deeper green. The lake, which is perfectly calm, reflects and reverberates all this magnificence. The islands, however, are below the level of sunshine, and lie dark and cold, the deep green Scotch firs on the Black Isles telling strongly against the snows of Craiganunie. The island between here and Ben Cruachan is so thinly covered with snow that the dead rusty fern shows through.

All the forest on the steep slopes of Cruachan is dark purple-grey.

The lake shivers here and there where the cold north wind descends upon it. Sheltered by the mountains, the rest of its vast floor is tranced in glassy calm.

II.

LOCH AWE ON A MISTY MORNING.

All the lake excessively pale, and nearly the same colour as the sky, which is one sheet of tender grey. Two promontories stand opposite each other, one terminated by a domed hill, the other by two wooded islands.

All this land is reflected quite accurately in the quiet water, the only difference being, that the double image is harder in the air above than in the water beneath.

The reflections are **not** darker than the reality, because the thin mist coming between has paled them.

Between the two promontories there is an open space of water; nothing is visible beyond it. There is a range of hills in reality, whose base is only two miles beyond the promontory, but they are totally invisible. The lake, therefore, looks **infinite** and very sublime.

III.

LOCH AWE AFTER SUNSET, OCTOBER 10, 1859, LOOKING TO WHERE THE SUN HAD GONE DOWN.

The lake shore is all massed in rich, intense, indescribable, deep brownish blackish purplish obscurity. There is not one detail to be seen in it.

The distant hills on the left, however, rise in flat grey.

Behind all this there is a great dim ash-coloured cloud, rising very high. In this ashy cloud is a great rent showing golden-yellow through it, like the dress of a disguised princess gleaming through a beggar's rags.

Far above this yellow rent is a great opening, showing a pale green sky, and, above this, barred rain-cloud of a dun colour, illumined by soft warm light reverberated from the hidden gold of the sky below.

The water is quite calm for the most part, but about a thousand acres of it are just now slightly rippled by a soft inaudible breeze. Wherever this breeze is breathing, the reflections are of course effaced; in its stead there is a great field of a pale ash-colour reflected from the cloud, except the **edges** of the field under the golden rent in the cloud, which take a narrow border of bright yellow.

But in the middle of these thousand acres of breeze there is one spot, perhaps in reality about a hundred yards across, which the breeze has not touched at all—it is a little isle of enchanted calm, set in a rippling sea.

There is also a promontory of calm about three hundred yards long, ***entering boldly into the midst of the breeze,*** yet resting there in charmed peace, for the moving zephyr leaps over it, and leaves it, as if it were protected by some super-natural spell.

What the reason of this phenomenon may be I leave to men of science. I should be glad to hear of a satisfactory solution, but could scarcely offer one. What becomes of the lost breeze? Does it die, or does it rise? It certainly leaves the water quite untouched. It is, however, enough for me as an artist that ***the fact is so.*** If I were to paint no facts but such as I could explain, I should not advance far. And these mirrors of perfect calm inlaid in great fields of ripple, are one of the most beautiful of all the phenomena of water, so that I cannot help painting them. It is quite incomprehensible to me that other painters never attempt this effect at all. It occurs at least fifty days in every year on all our great lakes.

Of course each square yard of calm surface, however isolated, reflects its own portion of the landscape, just as if all the rest of the lake were calm. I have met with people who could not, for the lives of them, make out how this should be. It is for the same reason, I suppose, which makes one human being sensitive to natural truth, and all the crowd round him quite incapable of receiving it. The isolated human soul receives nature truly, in spite of the opacity of the great multitude that hems him in on every side, but cannot disturb his guarded calm; the isolated mirror of protected water reflects the land quite faithfully, though the millions of ripples round it look dull and opaque as lead.

I have often gone in my boat on purpose to examine these isolated calms. I have found them sometimes no bigger than the floor of a good dining-room. I have crossed ***lines*** of calm as narrow as the lobbies in the House of Commons, and apparently quite as well protected against the wind. The fishermen on Loch Fyne, who have observed the phenomenon, account for it by a theory that it is produced by oil rising from fishes. It is certain that the thinnest film of oil will prevent the wind from ***rubbing*** water into ripple, but this explanation seems to me quite insufficient I believe the true reason is to be sought in the peculiar movements of light breezes, about which very little is known.

When I put these things in my pictures, many people, I find, will not believe me, as if a painter who had planted himself for five years on an island in Loch Awe, for the express purpose of studying the phenomena of water, might not be supposed to know enough of the subject to entitle him to common credence.

IV.

LOCH AWE AFTER SUNSET, SEPT. 23, 1860, LOOKING TO WHERE THE SUN HAD SET.

A line of low hills, with great woods of larch and fir. Behind these, purple heather hills, ridge behind ridge. All the local colour, which is very rich, is subdued and modified by grey.

Above the hills a pale green aquamarine sky graduated to pale yellow at the horizon. A cumulus rises behind the hill, and the cumulus is warm grey, edged all round with burning but pale gold. Two clouds above lie in level golden lines, full of light.

The water is most of it rippled pretty strongly, and this ripple is all of a cold slaty grey, which seems to bear no relation to the sky, nor to anything else.

But in the midst of this strong ripple there are spaces of an acre or two each, which are ***just dulled*** by a very faint breeze, which seems independent of the other and stronger breeze that causes the slate-grey ripple.

Now, these little dull calms reflect the *sky* perfectly, and they are so placed that if they were glassy calms they would reflect the dark hills.

These little dull calms reflect, as I said, the *sky,* consequently they are paler than the surrounding slate-grey ripple.

To complete the picture, we have a space, which in reality is about a hundred yards by fifty, of **perfect, glassy** calm, unruffled by the lightest breath of air, **yet surrounded entirely by a breeze.**

This streak reflects a portion of the heather hills, and is consequently very dark and very rich in colour. What is very curious about it is the exquisitely beautiful golden edging, quite narrow, that runs nearly round it like a delicate golden binding round a piece of dark brown velvet, only the edging here is softly gradated. This golden edging comes from the bright *clouds.*

Why all this should be I cannot quite positively explain. What makes the very narrow line between a glassy calm and a breeze reflect the intensest colour it can find in the sky, so as to border the dark calm so artistically, is more than I undertake to find reasons for. But I paint this truth without hesitation, because I have seen it.

V.

CRAIGANUNIE AFTER SUNSET, JULY 15, 1858.

The mountain is green-grey, colder and greener towards the summit. All details of field and wood are dimly visible. Two islands nearer me are distinct against the hill, but their foliage seems black, and no details are visible in them.

The sky is all clouded over. From the horizon to the zenith it is one veil of formless vapour.

At the zenith it is of a cold grey-slate colour; but lower down it becomes violet, dashed all over with soft wavy plumes of glowing crimson flame, as if it had really taken fire and were burning underneath like the rafters of a burning hall.

The water is wonderfully elaborate. There is one streak of dead calm, which reflects the green mountain perfectly from edge to edge of it. There is another calm shaped like a great river, which is all green, touched with crimson. Besides these there are delicate half calms, just dulled over with faint breathings of the evening air; these, for the most part, being violet (from the sky), except at a distance, where they take a deep crimson; and there is one piece of crimson calm near me set between a faint violet breeze and a calm of a different violet. There are one or two breezes sufficiently strong to cause ripple, and these rippled spaces take the dull grey slate of the upper sky.

Realise this picture as well as you may be able, and then put in the final touch. Between the dull calms and the glassy calms ***there are drawn thin threads of division burning with scarlet fire.***

This fire is of course got from the lower sky. I know whence it comes, but how or why it lies in those thin scarlet threads ***there,*** where it is most wanted, and not elsewhere, I cannot satisfactorily explain. I offer the following, however, as a solution:—

A miniature swell is produced at the edge of the calm water by the neighbouring ripple. This swell consists of low, long wavelets, whose surfaces, not being really touched by any wind, retain as perfect a polish as the calm itself. On the summits of these shining little waves the most brilliant light in the lower sky, whatever its colour, is sure to be reflected like a low moon on the sea ripple. Thus these wavelets select the brightest edging of the clouds, and reflect it a million-fold. These millions of reflections, which in reality are spread over a considerable surface of gently undulating water, say five or six yards broad, and some hundreds of yards long, as the case may be, are to the remote spectator massed together in one thin line of intense light and colour between the glassy calm and the surface actually touched by the breeze.

The half calms, or dulled calms, already described, appear to take their colour nearly always from the sky towards the horizon. The strong breezes, on the other hand, take it from the zenith, owing, of course, to the angle of the wavelets. What I call a dulled calm is, I am inclined to believe, a surface of water which has been visited by a breeze, and rippled, then suddenly abandoned by it. The ripples take a long time to settle away altogether into the glassy calm; in the interval they leave a very low, long swell, which takes, when seen from a distance, the character I call a dull calm. When a very soft breeze is ***just beginning*** to agitate a surface of glassy calm, it will produce nearly the same effect upon it.

The reader, however, is only bound to rely upon my facts, not my explanations. I never state anything in ***paint*** without having the fullest authority for it, because paint only ***states*** facts, and does not pretend to account for them. But when I write, and try to find reasons for the phenomena I describe, it is probable that I may often be in error.

VI.

A FINE DAY IN JUNE, 1860.

In perfectly serene weather, with a refreshing breeze, the phenomena produced are extremely simple. The atmosphere in sunny weather is rarely quite clear in damp countries; and a fine day in the Highlands generally produces vapour enough to make the hills very soft and tender in outline. The type of the most enjoyable Highland weather is this:—The mountains in their own local colour, not much altered by the effect; green for the most part, and scarred with reddish, or purplish, or grey rocks, all outlines soft and tender and vague, still perfectly well denned even in their softness. The sky, a very pale lovely blue, delicately gradated; the water, if under a pleasant sailing-breeze, as intensely blue as ultramarine can get it, yet a very deep colour, not to be got out of ultramarine alone, because there are purplish browns in it produced by the play of the dark brown water with the azure sky-reflections. Lastly, if the wind freshens, all this dark blue will be flecked with snowy crests of breakers.

Highland scenery is never so *lovely* as under this aspect. It has, of course, much more power over the mind when the effects are succeeding each other in their strength. There are effects which are enough to make one weep, and others that fill one with active excitement; but this soft and tender purity of the wandering air, the light music of the waters as they break in tiny waves all round the quiet isles, the velvet texture of all the earth's covering, the pale azure of the cloudless sky, the deep blue of the lonely inland sea, all these things lull us into dreams of another life and world; as if these were the sapphire floors of heaven, and these its isles of rest!

The loveliness of the colouring in such weather is due to the exquisite harmony of three great fields of colour. First, the blue of the sky, tender and pale; then the rich olive-green of the mountains, pale also, yet full in colour; lastly, the deep, intense blue of the water.

Nature will sometimes heighten this picture with brilliant white. She will put pure white clouds in the sky, and whiten her dark blue waves with foam. Man does no wrong to her picture when he cleaves those waves under a cloud of white canvass, scarcely less lovely upon the water than Nature's own clouds in the air above.

VII.

AFTER RAIN, JULY 1, 1861—9.30 P.M.

The summits of the Cruachan range are all hidden in mist. The lake is not dead calm, but just subsiding into it. All the breezes have died away.

There is a huge cloud at the base of Cruachan, of a pale bluish grey. It is all quite clearly defined against the dark hill. Its base is about sixty feet above the lake at the lowest point. Its summit rises to a height of sixteen or eighteen hundred feet. It is exactly seven miles long. All its outline is sharp and hard, except towards Kilchurn.

VIII.

CALM AFTER RAIN, MAY 21, 1861—8 P.M.

The sky is blue at the zenith, greenish towards the horizon. Great lake clouds are rising fast, and one peak is perfectly islanded by them. This summit is dark purple, and as hard and definite in outline as it would be possible to draw it. An enormous cloud is engulphing this mountain all round in vast billows of opaque, luminium-coloured grey.

A mountain on the left has a sort of peruke, more like cotton wool than I ever saw any cloud before; the crown of the hill piercing the peruke as a priest's skull seems to pierce his natural head of hair when he is tonsured. This mountain-top, however, is intensely dark and deep in tone.

All the local colouring of the land is uncommonly full and rich, on account of the recent rain. Under the cloud in the far distance the hills run into an azure, quite like Titian's distances. The whole light is Titianesque in its solemn evening gloom. Titian, however, would not have valued the pearly grey of the cloud at its true worth, it would have been too cold for his feeling. Veronese would have liked it better. Neither would have painted it as it is. I wonder how David Cox would have interpreted it.

IX.

OCTOBER 10, 1859—9 P.M.

At this season, Ben Cruachan is patched with blood-red fields of fern. To-night it is belted with a narrow girdle of white cloud, which is carried in the front of Ben

Vorich too, thin and light as a girl's sash. In the corrie, the upper part of the mountain is intensely and darkly blue. The summit is hidden in pale grey rain-cloud. The lake is calm and reflects everything.

X.

OCTOBER 10, 1859—4.30 P.M.

The mountains are all extremely full in colour after rain, and this *autumnal* colour. The distant ones mingle an intense blue with all their purples. Far off rises one pale grey crest, neither purple nor blue.

On the right, a thick, opaque whitish-grey cloud lies low in the valley; the mountains rising far above it clearly and sharply. The cloud looks as heavy as if it had been cut out of white marble.

The hills to the left have, as it were, thin *scarves* of white semi-transparent mist floating in graceful curves about their feet.

There is a great promontory jutting into the lake which receives the full splendour of the setting sun, and is all in one flame of red and gold autumn colour, made intense by late rain, and relieved against the dark mountains behind it which lie in the shadow of Cruachan. This burning promontory is all reflected in the calm lake.

The sunshine catches the side of Ben Vorich. The anatomy of Ben Vorich comes out wonderfully under slanting light, it is so muscular and complex. Its full golden colour in the lights is very fine to-night.

The little group of islands about Fraoch Elan is in full light.

All the details of cloud and mountain are reproduced in the calm lake, but slightly brushed together by an invisible ripple.

The foreground consists of trees with foliage of burning gold.

Over all this splendour the sky is one roof of leaden grey, elaborately carved into a thousand beams of wavy cloud one behind another. In all this vast roof there is only one little narrow opening, and the sky seen through it is of a yellowish grey. Towards the horizon the cloud itself becomes bluer, and then finally gradates also to a yellowish grey.

XI.

THE BLUE HAZE.

A landscape-painter once asked me if I had ever seen the blue haze in Wales. I knew what he meant, and said "Yes;" for it is a very common effect there, but a very beautiful one, and not easily forgotten. It has the advantage of marking the recession of distances better than any other; and, as the colour is extremely lovely, this effect is a great favourite with artists.

It comes on here in the Highlands very often in the afternoon, when the weather is calm. The sky about the sun is generally very warm in tone.

Out of the blue haze all the minor hills on the flank of a great mountain rise sharply one behind another, paler and paler as they recede, with every interval marked with a precision no other effect admits of.

I see no reason why this effect should not be generally intelligible. Mr. Wyld, the painter to whom this work is dedicated, has rendered it often, and with complete success, and buyers appear to like it in his works. It is an effect admirably suited to Mr. Wyld's feeling for tender passages of pale colour, and his general love for softness of outline, which is here essential to truth. It suited Turner, too, who attempted it often, and Claude aimed at it in some of his most delicate distances. But I cannot, at this moment, call to mind any work by either Turner or Claude, nor, indeed, by any other master, which has interpreted this particular effect with such unquestionable success as Wyld's large picture of Conway.

I cannot at present refer the reader to any work of my own in which this blue haze is seriously attempted, except a large picture on which I shall be occupied in the autumn of the present year (1862), to be entitled "The Upper Gates of Glen Etive."

XII.

A BIT OF LAKE SHORE.

It rises in three distances, one behind another.

The first consists of woods and fields, till we reach a grey precipice with a velvety green bank on the top of it. This part of the subject is full of various greens and yellows. There are pale greens and dark greens, bluish greens and yellowish greens. In this lie golden fields of corn, and other fields where the gold and the green contend together. These different greens and golds, though they gleam as if they were strewn all over with emeralds and nuggets, would be worth little, comparatively, if there were not that great curtain of hill just behind it, a curtain of deep purple heather, more intense, more precious, and more lovely, than the purple of a king's mantle.

Behind it rises the third ridge, much paler, yet still richly purple, only streaked and variegated with greens and greys.

I am speaking quite soberly when I say that, if all the velvet weavers of Lyons, and all the goldsmiths in London, were set to clothe a model hill with velvet and jewels, they could never match the glory of this wild Highland shore.

In this miserable art of word-painting, when we would convey an idea of depth and softness of lustreless colour, we talk of velvet, when of brilliant colour, we talk of gems. Less than a month ago I held in my hand the purple velvet mantle of a crowned king, good velvet enough, good as ever came from the looms of Lyons. It was a handsome cloak, no doubt; but these hills are more royally clad than he who wore it. *Their* purple is subtle and varied, and modulated over every inch of it; the royal mantle was monotonously dyed. And as to emeralds, one dewy gleam of soft short grass in a damp spot is better, so far as colour goes, than a whole basketful of them.

XIII.

SUNRISE IN AUTUMN. MIST RISING.

The sky is perfectly clear, quite blue, but as pale as possible.

All the upper part of the hills beyond Cladich is intensely clear, so that the outline seems quite hard against the sky. For about a thousand feet downwards this clearness continues. All this is already in full early sunshine, the colour in the light being a mixture of greens and reddish browns, very rich in its way; but all the shadows are very pale, and have a great deal of blue in them.

A wood comes down to the shore, on the left, which is quite free from mist; but between this wood and the mountain a white cloud is rising. It is about a thousand feet high, and cuts quite sharply against the hill-side, where the top of it looks so solid and so level that an imaginative person might fancy it would be agreeable to ride along it on horseback.

The most beautiful and peculiar feature of this picture remains to be described. The mountain-crest, which is in reality seven miles off as the crow flies, looks quite close at hand, because it is in the clear upper air. The shore of the lake, which lies in the mist, seems to recede into infinite space, tree behind tree, each paler and paler in the grey veil of cloud. *So here we have a hill whose base actually appears much farther from us than its summit;* and yet the effect is a strangely attractive one for a painter, for there is the contrast of silvery mist on the lake and ineffable clearness in the upper air.

I intend to paint a picture of this effect, and shall get it as true as I can; but only for my own private collection. It is quite useless to exhibit such effects, because they are not understood—a most lamentable impediment, for they are exquisitely beautiful, and ought by all means to be recorded.

XIV.

A MORNING IN MARCH.

Against a sky of pale pure green stand out the snow-covered mountains. They are **plated** with thin snow this time as a bronze statue might be plated with silver. No form is lost, every detail of the mountain's muscle is so well defined that it looks as if it were all carved out of supernaturally white marble.

Across a thousand hillocks, streams, ravines, bosses, and buttresses, the bright early sun is shining. Every shadow has its own sharp, clear, exquisite outline; and as for their colour! it is to pale ultramarine what fresh mountain-snow in strong sunshine is to white-lead in a garret.

Under this the lake lies grey and cold, rippled by a light breeze; and its tiny waves break on the snow-covered islands with a low, monotonous music. And behold! on the high and dazzling brow of Ben Cruachan a cloud has wreathed itself suddenly, like a white turban; and, as I look, I hardly know which is the whiter, the mountain or the mist.

XV.

LOCH AWE ON AN EVENING IN MARCH.

The shores and islands are all covered with snow, yet thinly, so as to let the dark moorland appear through it in a thousand fantastic streaks. The sky is like lead, the lake of a dull, monotonous grey; and the cold wind comes across it from the northern mountains in fitful, melancholy gusts. The island I live upon is the foreground of the picture; it is covered thinly with snow, and dotted with heaps of dead fern. The stunted oaks look sad and grey. Ben Cruachan rises in the north, pale against the leaden sky, covered from head to foot with half-melted snow, arrested in its thawing by the night cold.

The shades deepen, the hills and islands grow stranger and stranger. They are truly ghastly now, like corpses of hills laid out in solemn state around a desolate mere.

Has my island floated away into the northern sea; and are these the hills of the dark ice-world?

It is a landscape to make one weep for mere mournfulness—so lonely and sad it is, so utterly chilling and cheerless.

XVI.

A CLACHAN.

A genuine Highland clachan (hamlet) is one of the most picturesque things in the world, especially just after rain, when the colour comes out. The houses, as everybody knows, of one story only, are built of great rough stones, and thatched in a rude way with rushes. Considered as artificial things, they do no honour to their artificers, for all their beauty is due to nature, and to the poverty of the builders, who were not rich enough to contend with nature. Whenever Highlanders are well off they cease to build picturesquely altogether, the inns, and farm-houses, and kirks, being uniformly square and hideous, whilst the castles of the nobility are usually, if of recent date, devoid of all interest, except as enduring examples of the lowest bathos of the "Gothic" renaissance. If the Highlanders could build churches and castles as grandly as they build poor men's huts, their country would be as great in architecture as it is in scenery.

The poor men's huts have the sublimity of rocks and hillocks. The colouring of the walls is so exquisite that it would take a noble colourist to imitate it at all. Gold of lichen, rose of granite, green of moss, make the rude stones of the poor man's house glorious with such colour as no palace in all England rivals. And, as if it were especially intended by nature that full justice should be done to her fair colouring by the most desirable foil and contrast, she has given the Highlanders peat, which they build into stacks close to their habitations, and whose intense depth of mingled purples and browns makes their walls gleam like jewellery. And when some cottage in the clachan lies empty and deserted, and the woodwork of the roof rises, a grim skeleton, above the abandoned walls, blacker than black, yet full of deep purples in its blackness, arrangements of colour become possible to the painter such as the strongest colourists desire.

And all the adjuncts are so perfect. The landscape about a clachan is nearly always lovely. There is sure to be a grey precipice or purple hill within sight, or a rocky stream, or, at any rate, a picturesque group of trees. Then the people who live in it are so picturesque. I have never in my life seen finer figure-subjects than some noble groups of strong, hardy children, playing about the doors of the huts, and clad in all manner of admirable rags. And the very cows are clothed in lovelier fur than any other cows. Nothing in animal life is grander than a little Highland bull, black as coal, and majestic as a king, marching heavily, with a strong sense of his own personal dignity and might. No wonder Rosa Bonheur likes the Highland cattle. It is enough to drive a painter half crazy with delight to see the sunshine in their fur! Then what *variety* of colour there is in them. You have them of all colours—black, cream, tawny, red, and brown, grouping with each other exactly as if they were artistic cows composing grand living pictures for our especial pleasure.

Nor is any painter likely to forget the sheep with their twisted horns, that the travelling tinker will make spoons of some day for the cottagers' wives. And now and then he will find a goat, or even a young roe-fawn from the mountains, as I have seen cherished and petted by children as lovely and graceful and active as itself.

These things shall you see about the cottages of our poor peasantry; these, and commonly also a little field of corn, all green and gold in its partial ripening, and laid, perhaps, by thoughtless gales. There will be a little kail-yard too—that is, a miniature garden for cabbages—and a plot for potatoes.

And out of these little huts there come as fine women as eyes can behold. Mighty and robust is the typical Highland beauty. Her eyes are brown, like the pool of a stream in the heather; her cheeks are full and florid as red apples; her hair is of deepest brown or black. Strong arms has she for labour, stout legs for travel, full breasts to feed her babes. Her structure is more for use than grace; her feet are large, her ankles thick, yet she is a glorious creature.

XVII.

A LAKE STORM, OCTOBER, 1860.

The wind is tearing the trees up by the roots. There are breakers in front of my house as large as those on the sea-shore in a fresh breeze. I think the waves out on the loch are about five feet high, measuring from the bottom of the hollows to the crests, but I doubt if they are higher, though when you are amongst them they look so.

I tried to get my "Britannia" (double tubular life-boat) out in it, but found it impossible for Thursday and me to make way against the wind, which was perfectly furious. We could not have pulled out of the bay to save our lives. I had the boat broadside on for some time, and she bore it well. I was as comfortable as if I had been in the house.

The shores of the lake are all dim monotonous grey. The water looks fearfully black at times, all flecked with white yeast, that flies from crest to crest when caught in the air. Terrible rain-squalls cover the lake from shore to shore with a sharp line of ghastly grey, that advances in all its breadth over the great black cauldron of waters as fast as charging cavalry.

The hills are streaked with white streams; there is a torrent in every ravine. The distant roar of a thousand waterfalls mingles with the loud noises of the wind and waves.

XVIII.

A CALM DAY, MARCH 29, 1859.

We have had several weeks of continual storms. They have come from the Atlantic, like the march of an infinite army. It seemed as if they would never end, never have passed over us.

The last of their tumultuous host is gone. A morning has dawned at last, the Sabbath of the winds and waves.

The lake lies stilled in sleep, reflecting every isle and every tree along the shore, its bright plain dimmed here and there by faint breezes, that remain each in its place with singular constancy, as if invisible angels hovered over the waters and breathed upon them here and there. And under the great mountain what a dark, unfathomable calm! What utter repose and peace! It is incredible that ever wind blew there, and though but yesterday this shining liquid plain was covered with ten thousand crested waves, and countless squalls struck it all over like swooping eagles flying from every quarter of the heavens, it lies so calmly to-day in its deep bed, that one cannot help believing, in spite of all evidence, that thus it has been from the foundation of the world, and thus it shall be for ever and for ever!

The hills are clothed with purple, slashed with green. The sky is not cloudless, but the clouds move so languidly that their slowness of movement is more expressive of indolence than the uttermost stony stillness. Like great ships on a rippling sea, with all their white sails spread, they float imperceptibly westwards, as though they had eternity to voyage in. And just under them, in blinding light, behold the shining crests of snow!

XIX.

A STREAM IN ACTION.

If the reader happens to possess "The Isles of Loch Awe," he will find a vignette entitled the "Bridge of Cladich." Its subject is a single picturesque arch thrown high over a rocky stream, with waterfalls.

The stream, as I said, is rocky, and the rocks are very bold and high. Yet sometimes the volume of water is so tremendous as to hide every rock in it, even that great central mass under the bridge in the vignette.

On such occasions it is worth while to stand upon the bridge and look over. The water is very wild and very fierce, and very strong, yet not lawless, for it follows certain forms with wonderful fidelity. The rocks under it dictate the form of its flowing, and the water steadily obeys. Yet there appear to be little periodical pulsations and variations from the law, caused by subtle minor laws. Thus, I perceive that a certain jet of spray is thrown up every quarter of a minute or so, at a particular spot, as regularly as the action of a steam engine, and at certain stateable intervals a wave on the shore rises three inches higher, then subsides to its old level. The end of an alder bough is dipped in the current and thrown out by the force of the water; but the spring of the wood forces it back again, and the contention of the two produces an alternate movement as regular as that of a pendulum.

In spite of the rapidity of this torrent's flowing, there are parts of it nearly at rest, except their own ceaseless circling in deep holes at the side. There are great lumps of thick yellow yeast in these places, whirling round and round.

The colouring of the water is full of fine browns and yellows, good tawny rich colouring with creamy white at one end of the scale and something like fire-opal at the other.

Anything like realisation of water in such furious action is perhaps impossible; but I see no reason to despair of a fair interpretation of its principal forms and hues *under a gloomy sky.* The moment the sun comes out on white water we are checkmated, of course, because we have nothing in the colour-box bright enough to match it.

The enormous force of a stream like this in full action may be best illustrated by an anecdote.

Not long ago I was rowing home from Port Sonachan at midnight, in a little open punt. The night was intensely dark and very wet. I kept near the shore, and was very much astonished to find myself suddenly in white water, for there was just light enough to distinguish white foam from the black lake. Once in this white water, I was caught and tossed and driven about like a cork, but luckily escaped being capsized, and rowed with all my might till I got safely out of it. It was the river Cladich, which happened to be in flood, and came out far into the lake before its force was spent.

XX.

A STREAM AT REST.

Brown pools, very deep, very smooth, and very quiet; pale golden-yellow at the shallow side, where not an inch of water covers the smooth pebbles, then darkening as the water deepens through all the shades of gold and brown to something darker and more terrible than mere blackness. Out of this, and all round it, rise grey rocks almost white now in the dazzling weather. A thin trickling thread of water still creeps on from pool to pool. Its low music is the only sound I hear, except the hum of the wild bee's wings as he flies down the summer stream between its banks of flowers.

I had decided to limit myself to twenty sketches when I began this chapter, and

I will give no more, as I know very well they are very tiresome to read. But I stop short only out of consideration for the reader. I could easily fill a volume as large as this with such studies of Highland landscape, and a whole volume of them would be needed to give any idea of its immense range and variety. In this chapter I have only just been able to touch upon the subject slightly. I have not even analysed the most ordinary effects of rain, but these have been often painted, and the public is familiar with them. I have not mentioned a castle, because descriptions of one or two of them occur in other parts of the work, and for the same reason I have said nothing about moonlight.

It would have been well to mention a fine chord of colour, found perhaps oftener in the Highlands than anywhere else.

In the twilight, after sunset, before the greens of the lower hills have lost any of their intensity, you will constantly find, after rain, a picture arranged thus:—

Upper Sky—Filled with *grey* rain-clouds.

Lower Sky—A band of ***deep golden yellow*** near the horizon.

Upper Hills—***Intense purple*** (against gold in the sky).

Lower Hills— ***Deep greens*** (against purple of upper hills).

Water—All *grey,* with ripple.

This chord of gold, purple, and green, enclosed between two cold greys, is always magnificent, and the lowness of the light makes it available for a painter's use.

How far the Highlands may be generally useful to our landscape-painters as a school of study, and what effect the country is likely to have on them if they study in it long, remain to be considered.

It is unfavourable to the severe study of *form.* The forms are as beautiful as need be; but it is difficult to get a fair opportunity of drawing a mountain delicately from head to foot, in such a cloudy climate as this, unless one lives here, as I have done.

Then it needs such cumbrous defences against the weather. It is unnecessary to explain this here, because it has been explained already in this volume.

I confess that I would not now, after five years' experience of the country, come here for the hard, scientific study of mountain anatomy, though I hope often to revisit the country to refresh my recollection of it.

But for the discipline of steady work from nature I shall henceforth keep to the drier climates of the Continent.

This in common prudence. Hard drawing of mountain-form is very difficult in continual mist and rain, and a week of such work in a bad climate carries you no farther than two days' work in a good one, whilst it fatigues you more, and is incomparably more unpleasant

This country is a wonderfully great and noble school for landscape *effect.* Two or three years' residence in it for the express purpose of studying effect would be desirable for any landscape-painter with memory enough to paint effects. He ought, during his residence here, to paint very rapidly, say about one small picture a week, for the purpose of rendering as many effects as possible in the time. I have lost a great deal of valuable time here in trying too obstinately after accuracy in *form.* A prudent artist would study form thoroughly in France, and then come to the Highlands to acquire a knowledge of effect, accepting such form as he could easily come by, but taking no trouble about it.

Local colour is here less easily studied than in less changeable climates, because it is nearly always altered and interfered with by transient effects.

Transient colour here is to be had in the utmost conceivable splendour and power.

The scenery here is full of magnificent natural composition, but that is not at all like the common composition **patterns,** and is so unconventional as to be disliked by shallow artists. It is a good country wherein to study nature's art of composition.

But I doubt whether it is prudent even for the strongest men to work much from nature in this climate without the protection of a tent, and even then the dampness of the ground may bring on rheumatism.

All these considerations drive painters inevitably to make hasty memoranda when they come here, rather than careful studies. The swift and apparently rude execution of Cox was, I have no doubt, brought about by similar influences in Wales. Hence it is wiser in pre-Raphaelite painters to select those continental climates where simple sunshine is the ordinary weather, and the grand effects are rare.

For artists, on the other hand, who are strong enough to work entirely on the Turnerian system, and for whom a hasty sketch is all that is necessary, the Highlands offer as noble a field as could possibly be desired. It does not in the least matter to them that the weather makes the accurate portraiture of mountains difficult, because they do not attempt portraiture. The form of a hill or a castle is to them of just the same importance as the form of a cloud—no more; and as they walk or drive through the country an occasional rest for half an hour by the way is all they need for sketching.

CHAPTER XVI.

A LONG DRIVE IN THE GLENS.

I THINK I understand now the philosophy of carriage-keeping.

Suppose I have a precious little collection of pictures and engravings, the interest on which represents about £200 a year.

Suppose my neighbour has a handsome carriage, costing him altogether about the same annual sum.

My pictures can be seen only by my friends and servants. My friends, probably, think me a fool for spending my money in paintings, and my servants think the pictures, frames included, worth from five to thirty shillings apiece, and respect me and them accordingly.

But everybody sees my neighbour Thomson's carriage. Brilliant with silver and varnished leather, his proud steeds clatter over the pavement, dazzling the eyes of thousands. Every peasant knows that Thomson keeps his carriage; every shopkeeper bows Thomson's wife into that splendid vehicle. Robed in state, she goeth forth like a queen to the festivals of the rich, whither my wife, let us suppose, is conveyed in a hired fly. All the world knows that carriages are costly. Money spent in a carriage is like a beacon set on a hill that all eyes behold. It is an advertisement of wealth far more public in your own neighbourhood than if you printed a daily advertisement in the *Times,* announcing your receipts, like a public company. So, if you want to be respected, pinch as much as you will in other things, but keep, oh keep, a carriage! Let its lining be silken and soft; let its lamps be brighter than stars; let your armorial bearings (inherited or stolen as the case may be) be blazoned on its delicately-hung doors! Let its handles be of silver and its ornaments of embossed silver. Let its caparisoned steeds shake your shining crest on every strap of their trappings. Then rush through the sylvan lane and the crowded city, everywhere shall the respect of multitudes await you! Gentlemen shall lift their hats and ladies bow and smile; rustics shall pull their unkempt locks, and tradesmen bend low with reverence.

Now, my carriage commanded no man's respect. I wonder why? I am sure it was a very tolerable sort of carriage. And it really was very disappointing to be despised after all, when I had bought Thursday a pair of handsome boots, and made him sew a bit of gold band round his cap (to say nothing of his green jacket and beautiful brass buttons that all shone like mirrors), for the express purpose of inspiring the minds of the multitude with respectful awe and fear.

I am sure that it was a very capital carriage. It is true that it grew like a tree, or Mr. Ruskin's great book, or a Gothic cathedral, and was not designed and executed all at once, like a wheelbarrow. And if it could not command respect, it shall at least have fame; like many a great soul whom the neighbours scorned and the nations remember.

First of all it existed in the shape of a platform with four wheels of equal size, like a Lancashire stone waggon. The platform was intended to carry a boat. It was, in fact, a boat carriage.

Then the two fore-wheels were replaced by smaller ones for facility of turning.

So it remained for a long time. Then, when Thursday's hut was taken to pieces, its walls were turned to other uses. One of them became a kitchen table, and the remaining three formed, with the already existing platform of the waggon, a great box, measuring eight feet long by three feet wide, and more than three feet high—the very thing to carry camp materials in, but more useful than elegant.

Then, after being jolted a few hundred miles, I decided to add springs, being luxuriously desirous of personal ease. It was also a question of safety. I had been nearly jolted off my high seat several times, and on a stony road had only one hand for whip and reins, being obliged to stick to the waggon with the other with all my might and main.

At the same time that I added the springs I got a pole, so that I might drive a pair, and so get on faster, for poor Meg went but slowly when the waggon was full.

Now, the colour of the carriage was peculiar. The wheels were a dark green—very respectable indeed, I am sure. But the body, being made up of Thursday's hut, was a cool and delicate grey. Thursday's hut had been originally lead colour, but as that turned out too hot in the hot weather, Thursday, with his own artist hand, had superposed a coat of white. For facility of working he had put too much turpentine in his white, and the rain had washed it partly off, showing the lead colour underneath, as great artists often leave visible the dead-colouring of a fine picture through all the subsequent processes. I could compare this effect on the waggon to very noble things indeed, if I thought the reader would appreciate it. It looked like a grey Highland mountain at twilight, on a gloomy winter's evening, when the snow is scattered thinly over it and shows its lead-like substance through.

But the public does not appreciate variety and gradation in carriage-painting, so I ordered the whole waggon to be painted according to a tint I mixed myself, which the colourman praised extremely, and called "a most beautiful wine colour."

I intended to glaze it with crimson-lake when dry, and rule pretty lines of vermilion all over it, but I thought it did very well as it was, and so left it the plain unvarnished "wine colour." It was a great error. It should have been all glazed and varnished, and ruled with red lines, and I ought to have had my arms with all my quarterings delicately emblazoned on each side; but then, if I had had all these delightful splendours, I should have required a new set of double harness with shining scraps of electroplate upon it, and there was an expense I could not bring myself to incur. So this piece of economy consigned me to the condemnation of unrespectability.

For the harness was of the plainest. Plain black leather, not varnished, with plain black metal-work and common iron bits; not one jot of electro-plate about it. The cut of it was massive and strong, like light cart harness, and in the same homely fashion; the whole turn-out looking something like a military ambulance waggon, not in anywise like a gentleman's carriage. To have transformed such an equipage into a gentlemanly one would have been a costly and very unsatisfactory folly. So, although the waggon was certainly not respectable, I determined to be contented with it such as it was, and abandoned the sweet dream of neatly-ruled red lines, bright varnish, and glittering electro-plate.

As to the horses, I still kept our old friend Meg, and hired another called Kitty, from the inn at Dalmally. The first time they made their acquaintance Meg and Kitty were put together into my stable. Now, my stable was separated from the hen-house by a thin wooden partition, and as both Meg and Kitty did nothing but kick all night through, they entirely demolished the partition, slew some old hens, broke numberless eggs, and made a pretty job for the joiner. Only imagine the state of the cock-and-hen community during that awful night, with a ceaseless battery of four armed heels beating their poor defences down!

Meg was safe in single harness, but in double she had a fault or two. She would kick and dance all the way down every steep hill, an accomplishment more amusing to the bystander than to the driver, who, perched on the dangerous pre-eminence of the box, had to keep his horses well together on the narrow roads, and prevent them, if possible, from throwing him over dizzy precipices or into stony streams. These tendencies of Meg's led me to be rather cautious with her, and Thursday, I suspect, considered me a coward; but as Thursday could not drive a pair at all, I never trusted the reins in his hands, and went on in my own cautious safe way, letting Meg kick elegantly down the hills, and bearing with equal patience Mr. Thursday's murmurings of discontent.

Kitty had only two faults. She was extremely uncertain, and shirked her collar whenever she could. Poor Meg, on the contrary, threw herself into hers with all her might, and so drew for two. The consequence, of course, in such cases, as in rowing, is that when one side pulls and the other does not, the vehicle or boat has a strong tendency to turn, which tendency may on the water be counteracted by a rudder, and on the land by letting the pulling horse pull out to his own side if you cannot whip the other up to his work. Such faults are of less importance on level roads, where a good driver will force an ill-assorted team to work together at least endurably well; but on such roads as that from Inveraray to Ballahulish, if horses are to do their duty to each other and their master, there must be some natural compatibility of disposition between them.

In this particular journey that I record here I drove through Glen Urchay to the Black Mount. Glen Urchay is full of thoroughly Highland scenery, with its broad salmon stream, and the rich low land that it bounds with such beautiful great curves—land so green and soft and level, so sweet a contrast to the brown barrenness of the rugged hills—broad pleasant pastures, where the picturesque cattle feed, and whither the wild deer descend in the early morning, going to the hills again like the mist when the sun shines down in the glen.

And there is a fine rocky landscape at the falls, as good as those our landscape-painters bring us from Norway. The falls of the Urchay are not deep, but they are grandly composed, and the brown water turning to yellowish white, as it creams up into foam from the deep pool, or dashes itself over the edge of the rocky barrier, is well contrasted by rocks of a cold, pure grey like the grey of a heavy rain-cloud that the sun has left at night. The water-*sculpture* on the rock is also singularly fine at these falls, the eddy holes so smoothly and delicately bored, and in such numbers. Every true painter has an intense perception of some fragment of natural truth that nobody else seems to care for; but it is really astonishing that the exquisite beauty of water-sculpture should have been so little felt by the most celebrated men. Turner only cared for it occasionally, and never enough to paint it in full and perfect detail. Of all our living landscape-painters there is only one seems really to enjoy the kind of sculpture which such a stream as the Urchay can accomplish in innumerable years. Mr. Pettitt paints it faithfully.

There are, too, some grand Turnerian streams from the hills in Glen Urchay, leaving when dry, as they generally are in summer, immense areas entirely covered with nothing but grey stones, such as Turner loved so dearly, and, as it seems to me, with such good reason.

With good reason I mean in the artistic sense, not the carriage-driving sense. For it so happened that in driving precisely across the most delightful of those stony streams, I broke one of my springs, and, there being no blacksmith in those parts, had to content myself with a piece of wood fitted to the shape of the spring, and bound to it with a bit of rope. This elegant and ingenious device did not add to the brilliance of my appearance, nor tend to increase that popular respect which, as I have already hinted, was with difficulty brought to attach itself to my equipage.

These repairs were executed at the Black Mount. The inn had one guest, and I found him at tea, or dinner, or breakfast number two, or by whatever other name you please to call that ever-recurring meal. He had been living ten days in the inn, and had enjoyed tea, and ham, and eggs exactly twenty times—that is every morning at nine o'clock, and every evening at six, with no dinner between. Such a régime would make an Englishman ill, and drive a Frenchman mad. In the case of this unhappy gentleman it was tempered by moderate toddy and immoderate tobacco, or else I suppose he would have died of it.

The next day nothing was to be seen or done on account of the rain, so I stayed quietly in the inn eating ham and eggs, drinking tea, smoking tobacco, and chatting pleasantly with my new friend.

At Bagdad, I suppose, in the golden days of good Haroun Alraschid, the people talked about the Caliph; at Paris, in these days, I have observed that the English who crowd the hotels under the mighty shadow of the great palace, talk with most pleasure about the Emperor; at the Black Mount the travellers dwell with delight on the greatness of Lord Breadalbane. Deny it who pleases, great power has an intense fascination for us all. The proprietorship of land on so vast a scale as the

Breadalbane estate has something in it of imperial greatness, which awes and excites the imagination. The secret of the eager curiosity which all men feel concerning such personages is that they would like to be in their position, and wonder what it feels like to be there. Every properly-constituted and well-cultivated man has infinite desires. Ignorant people when they get money are miserable, because they do not know what to do with it, and so either save it without an object or throw it away in mere follies, the most ignorant of all sometimes actually putting bank-notes between slices of bread and butter and eating them, others eating them only metaphorically, but with equally slight satisfaction. But to a cultivated man the revenues of an empire would only be a welcome power of realising his views on a great scale, and the income from a great estate no more than a moderate and very limited power of expressing his ideas in ***things*** rather than in mere words. The one thing which would please me in great wealth would be the possession of noble works of art. A poor man only gets the art which cheap processes may reproduce. Architecture and painting are both hopelessly beyond his means; a little wood-carving, a plaster cast or two, and a few engravings and photographs, are all he can give himself. With the profoundest feeling for great architecture, he is forced to live in some abominably ugly house that he rents, or buys, or inherits, because he cannot afford an artistic one; with a passionate love for exquisite colour, he cannot purchase the work of a single good colourist. It therefore happens that the artistic instinct, though not usually found in avaricious, nor even in quite prudent natures, has a great need of vast wealth for its full satisfaction. And as the Marquis of Breadalbane is an interesting person to sportsmen, because he possesses an enormous deer-forest, so he is not less interesting to lovers of art, because he is rich enough to buy fine Landseers. To so hearty a lover of Highland scenery as I am he has another very unusual object of envy,—he possesses thousands of most glorious natural landscapes. His estate being so rich in scenery has, to a true painter, a magic far beyond the magic of mere wealth. An estate of equal value at Manchester would not magnetise a painter's imagination at all. But this wonderful proprietor, who really ***owns*** such mountains as Ben Lawers, such castles as Kilchurn, such lakes as Loch Tay and Loch Tulla, is to our minds associated with all their splendours, and it foolishly seems to us that every free wreath of mist, and every steadfast granite crest, must know, as we know, that it has for its legal master the courtly chief of Breadalbane.

What interests most Englishmen in the empire of Breadalbane is not, however, the landscapes, but the deer. Their number—a good deal exaggerated by popular rumour—is, in reality, perhaps about seven thousand, five thousand having been counted at the last census. The deer census in the forest is taken, of course, all in one day, like the census of the human population. When the country is all covered over with snow, a day is fixed, and the foresters go out, each alone on his appointed route, bringing in their returns at night.

A wonderful sight at the Black Mount is a grand drive of the deer. One of the grandest took place a little time ago for the pleasure of a foreign prince, then staying at Balmoral, to whom the marquis wished to show some lordly Highland sport. The head-forester, Robinson, had only forty-eight hours to gather the deer from all their wild fastnesses in the mountains, but himself fixed the hour when the prince should see them pass. The time fixed was two o'clock in the afternoon. The prince arrived at Loch Tulla at two minutes after twelve. When the royal carriages stopped at the lodge Robinson took a white pocket-handkerchief from his pocket and fluttered it for a few seconds in the air. From far distant points on the hills twelve invisible foresters were all levelling their telescopes at the lodge, and all saw Peter's signal; then they knew that the prince had come, and the drive began. Peter was sure that the deer would pass the point he had reserved for the prince at two o'clock precisely, so conducting him to the pass he waited quietly, looking perfectly cool and satisfied.

At five minutes before two an officer in waiting on the prince looked at his watch and said, "The deer cannot be here in time," for not a horn was in sight. Robinson answered quietly, "Please look there, sir," pointing to the entrance to the pass. Something dark was agitating itself in the distance: a forest of antlers came tumultuously over the brow of the hill, mingling their dark branches like the branches of a forest when a hurricane tears over it; and at two o'clock precisely, nearly a thousand deer were bounding and rushing before the astonished count, every head of them coming within range of his rifle.

The same Peter Robinson showed me a fine brood of young peregrine falcons that he was keeping for the use of a great Indian maharajah who passes some time every year in the Highlands. These peregrines were all fine young birds, with soft white down, and dark eyes, and a very ferocious expression, as if, with the precocity of cruelty, they had all the desire to tear one's eyes out; and only regretted that they had no wings yet.

This Indian maharajah is passionately fond of falconry, and a very interesting sport it would be, I dare say, only the hawks often fly away and despise all the allurements of the lure. A great foreign prince came to witness the sport of falconry as practised by this Indian magnate. This being a state occasion, gosshawks of a wonderful breed were to be exhibited. The first gosshawk, it is said, being launched at the flying game, paid no attention to it, but sat down quietly on a stone.

It is said that this prince gives such quantities of physic to his hawks that he seriously inconvenienced the unfortunate inhabitants of Killin by exhausting the doctor's medicinal stores; and the doctor found that, instead of purging good Christians, he had to keep in a state of healthy digestive activity the ferocious stomachs of innumerable birds of prey.

And, if the birds wanted physic, the Arab falconers wanted opium. By the bye, apropos of Arab falconers, a stranger coming to witness the sport spoke to one of those mysterious and romantic Orientals, doubtful whether his English would be understood; but was delightfully disappointed when the Arab answered him in a pleasant Irish brogue of the fullest flavour. Some of these Arabs are of the genuine race, and eat opium (so they say) as we eat bread and butter. Two of them, ignorant of English, went to the doctor to buy a bit of opium, and employed to that intent all the eloquence of signs. But the doctor, being an Orientalist, and having travelled in the East, spoke to them in Arabic, and even gave them a big lump of opium, on which they loaded him with expressions of boundless love and veneration.

Of course, the gamekeepers think this falconry very unsportsmen-like, and class all the finest peregrines, gosshawks, or jerfalcons, together, as wretched vermin, fit only to be shot and nailed up on a rail. However, as the maharajah gives ten shillings a piece for all young falcons, the keepers suppress their feelings of contempt for the donor and pocket the ten shillings. It is curious to reflect on the different estimation in which a peregrine falcon is held by a keeper of our day and a nobleman's forester in the middle ages. In those days a man would as soon have shot a good hunter as a peregrine.

The maharajah is said to be an excellent Christian, and leads the life of a true English gentleman, sporting on week-days and going regularly to church on Sundays, on which occasions he appears in various costumes as fancy dictates. I have heard of an amusing combination of brilliant Indian diamonds with homely Scottish trews.

The consequence of his visits to the Highlands is, that everybody is after peregrines. Since the young birds are now worth ten shillings a head a nest is a great prize. Seeking the nests is, however, rather a perilous employment; and the maharajah's own falconer being on one occasion suspended over a rocky abyss, it was found quite impossible to pull him up again. So he climbed up the rope, hand over hand, with his peregrines in his pocket.

On quitting the inn at the Black Mount, an unforeseen accident compelled me to return to its tea and ham and eggs for twenty-four hours longer.

It occurred to me that, as the waggon was rather heavily laden, I would leave one or two articles of camp furniture behind me in charge of the innkeeper; and to that intent I turned the vehicle. Meg, however, being impatient of the stoppage, gave a sudden twist, and damaged the connecting rod of the break, so as to render it utterly unsafe. The frightful idea of this connecting rod breaking as we were going down Glen Coe, decided me to have it welded again. On taking it off, I broke it easily at the damaged place; and Thursday rode off with it to Tyndrum, a distance of ten miles, where he got it solidly welded. Whilst Thursday was at the smith's I made a study of Loch Tulla.

I began to hanker after a dinner, and thought of opening my provision boxes; but, remembering that I had lonely glens to explore and illustrate, where no dinners were to be found, I reserved these and tried what was to be done with the landlord. When you ask the landlord of a Highland inn for a dinner, any time out of the regular tourist season, he always seems astonished at so extraordinary a proposition. His senses do not readily receive it; a painful vacuity spreads over his otherwise intelligent countenance. When, at last, the idea comes home to him, that the traveller really desires so exceptional a meal, a melancholy sadness and embarrassment settle there; and you hear faint inarticulate murmurs on his lips, which invariably end in an ignominious and precipitate flight, whose poor pretext is to see what the house contains. If you persecute the man no more, he will certainly not reappear, only too delighted to be rid of your importunities at so easy a cost of invention; but if, on the contrary, you pursue him into his own fastnesses, he puts a bold front on the matter, stands his ground like a stag at bay, and tells you that there is "mutton ham, and pork ham, and eggs, and—and—cheese—and—and—and—"

At last, the traveller loses all patience; and, if a man of experience and wisdom, says he won't have any dinner; but only some tea, with ham and eggs to it, which is, in fact, the one meal the house contains. On this announcement, the visage of the host shines with sudden satisfaction and relief, and the simple repast is prepared with alacrity.

The next morning we got away from Loch Tulla, and drove to the King's House Inn. The highest point of the road from the Black Mount to the King's House is said to be the highest public road in Great Britain. The descent from that point to King's House afforded Meg a delightful opportunity for the display of her agility; and she capered and kicked from the top to the bottom, to the imminent danger of our lives. On coming to one little bridge, she started aside suddenly, and nearly upset us over the little parapet, which the wheels grazed as we passed.

At King's House I got an uncommonly good dinner for the time of the year, with real bread to it, and fresh meat, and other dainties all unknown at the Black Mount. As for Thursday, he got a wonderful feed, and received such a degree of attention as fairly overwhelmed him. He was altogether comblé. He could not do justice to all the good things set before him. As for the horses, they fed abundantly on corn and hay in the stable; and the bill for all this amounted to the moderate sum of four shillings and sevenpence.

I pitched my tent in Glen Coe, and got a careful study before night. The sunset in the glen was truly magnificent, and the rocky hills opposite the sunset glowed with crimson light. The scenery of Glen Coe is very like that of the corrie of Ben Cruachan, and nearly, I imagine, on a level with it. The truth is, that the road here carries a stream of tourists through the **upper** mountain scenery. At Loch Awe you may climb up into such scenery; but the roads do not carry you there. The landscape in Glen Coe is therefore good for the study of upper mountain-form, seen quite near at hand; especially good for granite **precipices,** which exist here in perfection. For colour, the reddish rock, heightened to crimson by the sunset light, and contrasted against a pure green sky, as I saw it that evening, is as fine as anything in mountain colour can be. There is a striking grandeur of line in the mountain forms at Glen Coe, and this quality, together with the infinity of detail and the intense clearness of the mountain air, kept John Lewis continually in my thoughts.

There are times in our lives which we look back upon with infinite pleasure not unmingled with melancholy: times, as it seems to us, of almost perfect happiness, full of calm and peace, sweet halting-places in the weary pilgrimage of life. These days I passed in Glen Coe are, to me, one of those ever-remembered times. I remember all I did and all I thought so vividly that it seems to me as if I could narrate the minutest details of every hour that passed. Splendid weather, long hard days of happy and successful labour, perfect peace all day and quiet rest in the lonely tent at night;—all this, too, in the very finest scenery in Great Britain; was it not glorious? Solitary and laborious as my simple existence was, with nothing to do but draw till eye and hand were weary, and no one to talk to but one poor faithful servant, I would not have exchanged it, day against day, for the life of the wealthiest noble in Belgravia!

Whilst I was busy with my work that evening, Thursday set up my tent on a beautiful green natural lawn, bounded by a little crystalline stream. There the tethered horses fed, and Thursday prepared my tea, and spread it luxuriously on a white tablecloth, the table being my great box for studies.

After tea, of course it was necessary to smoke the inevitable pipe. The seductions of tobacco, easily resisted in a house, are absolutely irresistible in a tent. I think it is the fresh air that gives me such a mighty appetite for a pipe; but the certain fact is, that when in camp I cannot help smoking, nor do I think anybody else could—unless it made him sick.

I find the following observations on the subject of smoking in my note-book, and as they were really written in my tent on this particular excursion, they will not be out of place if I insert them here.

People who don't smoke—especially ladies—are exceedingly unfair and unjust to those who do. The reader has, I dare say, amongst his acquaintance, ladies who, on hearing any habitual cigar-smoker spoken of, are always ready to exclaim against the enormity of such an expensive and useless indulgence, and the cost of tobacco-smoking is generally cited by its enemies as one of the strongest reasons for its general discontinuance. One would imagine, to hear these people talk, that smoking was the only selfish indulgence in the world. When people argue in this strain, I immediately assume the offensive. I roll back the tide of war right into the enemy's entrenched camp of comfortable customs; I attack the expensive and unnecessary indulgences of ladies and gentlemen who do **not** smoke. I take cigar-smoking as an expense of, say half-a-crown a day, and pipe-smoking at threepence. I then compare the cost of these indulgences with the cost of other indulgences, not a whit more necessary, which no one ever questions a man's right to if he can pay for them. There is luxurious eating, for instance. A woman who has got the habit of delicate eating will easily consume dainties to the amount of half-a-crown a day, which cannot possibly do her any good beyond the mere gratification of the palate. And there is the luxury of carriage-keeping, in many instances very detrimental to the health of women, by entirely depriving them of the use of their legs. Now, you cannot keep a carriage a-going quite as cheaply as a pipe.

Many a fine meerschaum keeps up its cheerful fire on a shilling a week. I am not advocating a sumptuary law to put down carriages and cookery; I desire only to say that people who indulge in these expensive and wholly superfluous luxuries have no right to be so very hard on smokers for *their* indulgence. Then there is wine. Nearly every gentleman who drinks good wine at all will drink the value of half-a-crown a day. The ladies do not blame him for this. Half-a-dozen glasses of good wine are not thought an extravagance in any man of fair means; but women exclaim when a man spends the same amount in smoking cigars. The French habit of coffee-drinking and the English habit of tea-drinking are also cases in point. They are quite as expensive as ordinary tobacco-smoking, and, like it, defensible only on the ground of the pleasurable sensation they communicate to the nervous system. But these habits are so universal that no one thinks of attacking them, un-less now and then some persecuted smoker in self-defence. Tea and tobacco are alike seductive, delicious, and—deleterious. The two indulgences will, perhaps, become equally necessary to the English world. It is high treason to the English national feeling to say a word against tea, which is now so universally recognized as a national beverage that people forget that it comes from China, and is both alien and heathen. Still, I mean no offence when I put tea in the same category with to-bacco. Now, who thinks of lecturing us on the costliness of tea? And yet it is a mere superfluity. The habit of taking it as we do is unknown across the Channel, and was quite unknown amongst ourselves a very little time ago, when English people were no less proud of themselves and their customs than they are now, and perhaps with equally good reason.

A friend of mine tells me that he smokes every day at a cost of about sixpence a week. Now, I should like to know in what other way so much enjoyment is to be bought for sixpence. Fancy the satisfaction of spending sixpence a week in wine! It is well enough to preach about the selfishness of this expenditure; but we all spend money selfishly, and we all love pleasure, and I should very much like to see that cynic whose pleasures cost less than sixpence a week. [Note *: It is needless to allude to field sports and luxurious dress, whose enormous cost bears no more proportion to the cost of smoking than Château Margaux to small beer, or turtle soup to Scotch broth.]

Besides, tobacco is good for the wits, and makes us moralize. All the above sagacious observations came out of a single pipe of tobacco (Duncan's mixture, Buchanan Street, Glasgow—famous tobacco to smoke); and the cleverest parts of many clever books and review articles are all tobacco.

Next morning I got up very early and was hard at work drawing before breakfast. When the sun became warmer, I began to "feel more jolly," as Cambridge men have it Thursday served me a very comfortable and even elegant breakfast outside the tent. He has one great merit as a domestic—he keeps his silver remarkably clean. Not a nobleman in England has brighter spoons and forks than I had out in the wilderness. I cannot say as much for Thursday's management of horses: he hates the trouble of them; he is always muttering to himself all manner of dreadful imprecations against the poor brutes. When he is about them he never ceases talking to them, telling them they are going to have a hard day's work, and making other observations of an equally pleasing character. Towards night, when in camp, Thursday becomes very anxious about the horses, foreseeing a good deal of trouble with them: this anxiety escapes in murmurings, addressed alternately to himself and to them. If we could have conducted the expedition without the aid of horses, Thursday would have been much happier and in a far better temper.

That day, when I had done my study, Thursday and I led the horses all down the worst part of the glen, and I resumed the reins only when Meg's ways were not likely to be very dangerous. It would have been perfect madness to drive her down Glen Coe without a break of sufficient strength to stop the waggon altogether, considering how heavily it was laden, and how steep the road was. The weather continued splendid, and extremely hot, and my impression of the central scene in Glen Coe was so powerful, that as I drove forward to Ballahulish, I did nothing but regret not having stayed there.

The truth is, that in noble scenery, five miles a day is as much as any painter ought to travel. The right thing for a painter is to go on *foot* in a good climate (this, of course, excludes the Highlands altogether); and if the country is lonely, let him take a tent and a stock of provisions in a strong common cart, with one strong horse to draw it.

I stayed at the inn at Ballahulish. When I asked for bedrooms there was no alacrity to receive me, not the slightest attempt at politeness, not even common civility. It was all the waggon (Thursday said), that unlucky, plain, wine-coloured waggon. If it had had varnish and red lines, and a bit of electro-plate about the harness, the waiters would probably have been civil; if instead of the waggon I had brought a pretty pony carriage with me, the waiters would have fawned like little dogs and the hostess welcomed me with humble but warm-hearted hospitality. So that a philosopher who despises frippery in itself may philosophically adopt it in order to command civility. No one cares less for unmeaning finish in ugly things than I do, no one has less enjoyment in vulgar splendours, no one contents himself more easily with plain, rude things for common service, and yet the next turn-out I set up shall have neat red lines and varnish, aye, and electro-plate too; for the respect of the people is convenient, though contemptible, and it is, on the whole, pleasanter to be treated with servility, though it be base, than scorn however groundless.

The next day rose so clear and splendid that I could think of nothing but Glen Coe, and long to be back again in the very heart of it. Loch Leven from Ballahulish is lovely enough, very grand both up and down, and the mountains rise nobly out of the sea. Still, though the water was so blue and lovely, and the hills covered with such rich greens, and such delicate greys and purples, and in the far distance such a perfectly exquisite azure, and though the white sails of a stately yacht shone out against the mountain that rose out of the sea, suggesting pleasant possibilities of sailing, in spite of all these attractions, and in spite of the hope of getting a good study of Ben Nevis, I found that all the time I was making my study of Loch Leven I could think of Glen Coe only. I wished especially to make two studies there, and would willingly have paid five pounds an hour for fine weather to do them in. I had been longing for those studies for years, and now a fair chance of obtaining them seemed to lie before me. So after working all day at Loch Leven I trotted quietly back in the evening to the banks of the black lake in Glen Coe, and there under the shadow of its dark precipices my tent was pitched at night.

As the reader probably knows, there is a great slate quarry at Ballahulish, and this slate quarry produced phenomena so entirely new to my horses that they were anything but pleasant to drive. Fortunately the hours of blasting were over for that day, but Meg and Kitty found much material for wonder and excitement in passing through the quarry and its village, and the only way of crossing the little tramway which these foolish horses could discover was to leap over it If they had leaped both together it would not have mattered, but Kitty hesitated whilst Meg jumped, and between them they nearly upset us.

Thursday's great anxiety being as usual to get rid of the horses as soon as possible, he took them to a lonely shepherd's house in the glen, and then devoted his undisturbed attention to the preparation of my supper. By the time I had finished it the moon looked down on the little tent across the stony summits of the mountain, and a glorious night began, so grand and solemn and lonely that I could have stayed out in it, and sauntered by the shore of the gloomy lake till dawn. As this pleasure, however, would probably have cost me several hours of good daylight on the following day, and consequently so much work, I renounced it, and only stayed out in the moonlight long enough to let myself get thoroughly impressed by the effect, and to ascertain such facts as were necessary to its future realisation on canvass.

I was at work early in the morning, and kept at it till evening. About noon, as it seemed to me, the subject reached its highest perfection as an effect of serene summer weather. The sun was extremely hot, and the day brilliant to the utmost possible degree. The subject is a very noble one, and I intend it for a great picture. Here is a word-picture of it, accurate as far as it goes but necessarily very imperfect, as word-pictures always are.

The lake is a small one, and probably very deep; the colour of the water, stained by the moss-land, becomes intensely gloomy in the lake. Contrasting vividly with this dark colour are the hues of the flat alluvial land near the lake. These consist of perfectly white sand passing into greyish and pinkish sand in subtle gradations. This sand lies broad on the river's banks. Beyond the river and immediately under the mountain, is rich green meadow grass; and nearer to the spectator, on his own side of the stream, there are patches of pale bright emerald grass; nearer still, great fields of small stones, chiefly of a pale purple colour, and in the immediate foreground dark green grass again but this time rough and poor.

Imagine all these colours infinitely heightened by the intensest sunshine, and opposed to a lake that ***looked*** about the colour of Vandyke brown as it is squeezed out of a tube, and you may have some vague idea of the vivid splendours of the foreground.

Then immediately out of the lake, and out of the alluvial land to the left of the spectator, land just as flat as the lake itself, rose, almost perpendicularly, a tremendous precipice, and behind this precipice, looking over it as a man looks over a low garden wall, rose a great rough stony peak, all its rich rock-detail clearly visible, and its barren edges cutting out sharply on the sky, with little fields of snow in its cool granite hollows dying away imperceptibly day by day in the hot sun, and trickling down to their low grave in the black lake by silent invisible streamlets.

And the great precipice, how glorious in strength of structural form and painted delicacy of exquisite colour! In structure like the side of a cathedral, alternately vertical wall and steep sloping roof; only that here the alternation is repeated ***seven*** times instead of twice. In colour thus:—the steep slopes all delicate green or pale purple as they are clothed with thin grass or covered with purple débris of the cliff, and then the vertical walls full of infinite variety of yellowish, reddish, and bluish grey, shining here and there with silvery mica, as if powdered with millions of minute diamonds.

And the great broad shadows upon its mighty front, how they veiled it with cool depth of solemn gloom, last lingering fragments of the night clinging to the sheltering cliffs! For night lingers under their shadowy walls as winter in their fields of snow.

I drew it line for line, and fissure for fissure, till the last red light of the sunset had faded from its clear and silent heights. Then, in the twilight, we drove on to the great central scene in Glen Coe, the noblest and grandest of the whole glen. Never hunter was more keenly eager after an antlered king of stags than I for that glorious scene. The night became cloudy and dull, and I passed it in almost sleepless anxiety. I would have given a hundred pounds for three fine days, and strength to labour every daylight hour.

Poor Thursday had gone on to King's House in the dark with the horses, leading Kitty and riding Meg. They took him off the road several times, and, I imagine, played him some unpleasant tricks. However, he got back to the camp about one o'clock in the morning, in a state of great weariness, but sound of limb.

The next morning at six o'clock, when I looked out on my subject, it seemed probable that the day would turn out well, probable, but by no means certain. At eight, however, it was clearer, and at nine perfectly cloudless, clear, and splendid, and so it continued the whole of that day and the day after.

When I am in camp in fine weather the morning bath is the luxury I most enjoy. How different to dabbling in one's shallow sponge-bath in a chilly dressing-room, is a plunge in the clear pale green depths of a sunlighted granite pool! Those morning baths in Glen Coe I shall never forget whilst I live. Water clearer than crystal, and pure as the mountain air, contained in great natural basins of smooth granite rock, rose-coloured, or pale tender grey, and so lonely that no living thing can see you, except the falcon that flies in the blue air above, or the fishes that dart through the transparent water.

And here is the central scene, the noblest picture in Glen Coe.

A sharply curving road, with a bridge spanning a torrent in the foreground, the road sustained by great walls on the side of the precipice, but without parapet, except a low one on the bridge itself. The curves of the road are extremely beautiful and complex. In the space of a hundred yards there is a sharp curve to the right, then a slight one to the left, and after that another gentler curve to the right again. In the same space the road ascends and descends and ascends again, the complication of the two sets of curves being as beautiful as anything well can be in mere road curvature.

The foreground is made very rich with the rocky ravine containing the stream which the bridge crosses. A second stream of less importance runs side by side with this, but still nearer to the spectator, and falls into it soon after passing under the road. Several hundred feet below, down in the valley, a third very beautiful stream with precipitous granite banks joins these, coming into the picture at the spectator's left hand. A fourth stream, in a succession of waterfalls, descends a great mountain exactly opposite the spectator, and this fourth stream is richly bordered by beautiful trees. These four streams meet together in a spot some hundred feet below the one where my tent was pitched, and then run together down the glen in one fine falling torrent, which afterwards becomes a winding river in the valley, feeds the black lake Treachtan, and then runs on to the sea. This river is the Cona of Ossian.

The mountain-forms which fill the rest of the picture are three buttresses belonging to the great mountain on your left, as you descend the glen from King's House to Ballahulish. In the openings between these buttresses appears the upper structure of the mountain, exactly as the spires and roof of a Gothic building appear above and between the projections of its lower walls when the spectator is standing near.

In this case a curious and very impressive illusion is produced by the perspective of the buttresses. They seem to be *towers* of rock, and this is especially true of the central one, which is one of the most astonishing things in the Highlands. The truth is, that the apparent summit of this tower is in reality a good deal lower than a spot far down on its side—a fact I suspected from the first, and subsequently ascertained. I intend to paint a large picture of this subject; and I know beforehand that most readers of this book, on looking at the picture, will have great difficulty in believing that the summit of the central tower-like buttress is much lower than the lump on its side, and hundreds of feet lower than the peak to the left of it and the ragged edge of rock to the right.

The colour of the mountains in this part of Glen Coe is, in fine weather, so bright and delicate, that on my own side of the glen their rocky summits told against the blue sky *as a vigorous lights* every detail distinctly visible in the clear air. The relief of the illuminated rock, with its burning reds and purples, and dazzling variety of silvery and golden greys against the intense depth of the blue sky can, it is true, only be attained at all on a scale of light far lower than nature's, but to sacrifice *such* colour altogether is downright sacrilege; and strange as it looks to the uninformed spectator when painted honestly and in earnest, this, which is one of the most glorious as well as one of the most frequent aspects of mountainous landscape, ought to be frankly painted in colour as true as may be, even at the cost of some unpopularity. It is no digression to speak here of this aspect of mountain scenery, for during two whole days in the middle of Glen Coe I could think of nothing else. I consider this simple fine-weather aspect doomed beforehand to unpopularity, because it is clear enough to let you see the minutest details of mountain-form; and a public which for centuries has been content to admire Claude's way of filling up a feeble and unmeaning outline with a uniform patch of bluish grey as the ideal of mountain-painting is not likely to endure, and will not easily be brought to tolerate, works full of most elaborate detail and intense and various colour, yet almost entirely devoid of any appearance of aerial perspective. For the harsh fact is, that the dimness of objects does not express their measurable distance, but only the humidity or impurity of the atmosphere; and therefore the common theory of aërial perspective is of no use as a test of artistic truth. The houses on the opposite side of any London street are, in a November fog, a good deal less visible than the detail of a precipice seen in clear weather across an Alpine valley several leagues broad; and the summits of mountains miles away always seem so near to inexperienced climbers in clear weather, that they invariably expect to get to the top of them in a ludicrously impossible space of time. In spite of these facts, however, people *will* have what they call "aërial perspective" in pictures, and the consequence is that painters, if they have to live by their art, must confine themselves to those conditions of the atmosphere where there is haze enough to produce it. [Note *: Not too much haze, however. The ordinary public is as intolerant of true mist-painting in Turner, as it is of true clear weather-painting in John Lewis. The happy and popular medium is the quiet afternoon haziness of Claude and Cuyp.] When the world knows a little more about nature, and will tolerate artistic interpretations of other natural phenomena than the three or four which it understands at present, we may hope for full and faithful renderings of mountain-form in cloudless light and truth unveiled.

Having worked all day long at my study, I stretched my legs by climbing the mountain on my own side of the glen, with a view to ascertain the real structure of the opposite buttresses. As I suspected, they turned out to be mere spurs or projections of the mountain's lower structure, not independent rock-towers. I also ascertained, what astonished me more, something about the actual position of the peak which had seemed to overlook Loch Treachtan. The *travelling* of great peaks is an astonishing result of perspective. They seem to march along the horizon like moving spectres. They are everywhere. A single crest is the centre of interest for a thousand landscapes. Travel as fast as you will, they travel with you, like a haunting spirit; like your own memory—your own conscience—your own sins. [Note *: Very lofty cathedral towers do the same in lowland landscape.]

It was a grand sight to see the great lonely glen under the rising moon, with its silvery winding stream, and its distant lake, and all the stony crests that guard it.

After another very hard day's work at the same study, I went to King's House in the evening.

I had broken my labours in the middle of the day by a walk to a lonely deserted cottage, a mile or two from my tent. No one lives there now, but it is one of the most exquisite dwellings, artistically considered, that I have yet seen. It is curious to think how many thousand pounds are continually spent by rich people in the creation of houses so abominably ugly that no true artist can look at them without pain; and yet the poor deserted dwelling of a lonely Highland shepherd contained interest enough and beauty enough to occupy and delight the most fastidious and cultivated artist for a whole month at least. There are only two kinds of architecture which a true artist can endure—the one which, as in the case of the Highland cottage, is full of ***natural*** beauty, which the builder, from sheer poverty, has been forced to let alone, because to efface it effectually costs money; and the other, as in a Venetian palace or Gothic cathedral, which is full of ***artistic*** beauty, produced by splendid human invention, based on the study of nature, and expressing itself by the aid of boundless wealth. The intermediate kinds of building produced by money without mind, and devoid alike of natural and artistic beauty, are, to all persons endowed with any true artistic feeling, utterly repulsive and uninteresting.

The beauty of this Highland cottage was all of it natural beauty, associated with, and no doubt heightened by, the melancholy human interest of the deserted roof and desolate hearth. The spectator could not but feel that this solitary house in the desert had been some one's home, stricken with poverty it is true, and lost in isolation, yet still a home, perhaps all the dearer for its very loneliness. But beyond this interest, man's work had little to do with the attractiveness of the place. The arrangement of the colour on the stones was purely natural—as much so as that on the surrounding rocks. The smooth, short, soft lawn in front had been shaven by no gardener, the little stream directed by no designer; yet the lawn was fit for the feet of a princess, and the little pools of the stream that lay cool, and deep, and clear between tiny perpendicular cliffs of granite, were pure enough for the bath of a water-nymph. By way of a bridge, the trunk of a single tree was thrown across the narrow gorge; and under it slept a pool, long, narrow, and very deep. The grey thatched cottage, the soft natural lawn, and the little stream, so humble in themselves, but surrounded with so much magnificence, so peaceful, so lonely, and so desolate, gave me far purer pleasure than Versailles, with its soulless architecture, its formal fountains, and its acres of preposterous paintings.

Near King's House I examined a moveable hut used by the men who mend the road. It contains berths, if I remember rightly, for about a dozen men, but of course they are narrowly lodged. A hut about the same size would be a useful possession for a painter, who, if a bachelor, might live in it permanently with quite as much comfort as people ever get in a small yacht I was told that this one had been temporarily occupied by a landscape-painter who wished to study in Glen Coe during the winter season. I could pass a winter in it very merrily myself, if I might cut a hole for one of my plate-glass windows, so as to be able to work from nature without going out of doors.

Having determined to go down Glen Etive, I remained at Kings House only long enough to get a good study of the head of Glen Etive as it is seen from there. As this is certainly one of the grandest scenes in the Highlands I shall attempt a description of it in this place.

A foreground of wild moorland, with a picturesque cottage. A magnificent peaked mountain on the right, like a dome; on the left, a tall steep mountain like a Gothic roof; between the two another mountain, low on the horizon and blue with distance.

Such is the rude sketch. Now let us fill it up with a little colour and detail.

In the first place, the foreground is very rich in colour. As so frequently happens in Highland scenery, there are patches of short grass of the most intense, incredible emerald; and this emerald is rendered infinitely more brilliant by dark purple peat. The greater part of the more distant moorland is olive-green; here and there the bare earth shows itself, and that is reddish, which intensifies the olive. Then the whole is scattered very plentifully with grey stones, very often bluish.

Close to the spectator the foreground is rich in dark purple peat, and millions of golden flowers, and rushes whose green blades are tipped with red. In the midst stands the grey cottage, with the open end of its cart shed turned to the spectator; and this open end contains such a depth of gloom as delighteth the soul of an artist.

The mountain on the right is in local colour most delicately decorated. It is covered with courses of innumerable streams, many of them of quite a tender rose colour, and the grass between them has such a delicate green, and there are *such* greys, and *such* purples, and all mingled in sweetest mystery, enough to break one's heart.

Very beautiful, and in the same manner, are the granite forms and hues in the mountain on the left. The distant one in the middle, as I saw it, was merely a blue film against the sky, tender as air.

As soon as I had driven a hundred yards on the road down to Glen Etive, I knew what to expect: I had fourteen miles of wild, rough, Highland bridle track before me, along precipices and hills, and through innumerable streams—not a pleasant prospect with horses that required incessant attention. The first specimen of a bridge was not unfavourable. It was of rough planks certainly, and hung over a rocky torrent at a dizzy height; but then there were some pretensions to a rail; and the bridge was broad enough to enable me to drive over it without being accurate to an inch. After this the road kept on the side of a precipitous declivity on the right bank of the River Etive; but there was breadth enough for the wheels, and the turns were not unusually dangerous, the great fault of the road being that it inclined to the side of the precipice instead of to the side of the hill. Still, a careful driver may do very well for the first eight miles in Glen Etive.

I encamped in the middle of the glen for two nights, and afterwards continued my journey to the head of the loch.

Though the road for the first eight miles was bad, it became infinitely worse afterwards. I should think a pair of horses were never driven over a more unlikely track. I had exactly wheel breadth, with scarcely an inch to spare; and one or two wooden bridges over rocky streams had no parapets whatever. I admired Thursday's courage extremely, as he sat next me on the box. I think it requires far less pluck to drive on a dangerous road than to sit tranquilly beside the coachman, knowing that your life hangs on the nerve and skill of the man at your side. No doubt the necessity for thought and care lulls the nerves; but to be in considerable danger, ***and do absolutely nothing,*** is enough to try the strongest of us. Thursday's coolness, however, was more apparent than real He told me afterwards that he never felt so uncomfortable in his life, and that he always held himself in readiness for a leap.

And now about the scenery of Glen Etive.

Immediately after visiting Glen Coe, the traveller may not think it very astonishing; but it is really exceedingly fine; and, in my opinion, **one of the very grandest Highland glens I have ever seen.** That noble granite stream, the Etive, is to me full of interest, for it abounds in admirable pictures. I have never seen finer water-sculpture anywhere than on the rose-coloured rocks of the Etive, nor more picturesque Scotch firs than those which in some places shade it with their dark foliage. There are terribly black pools, too; one especially, where the deep water winds in a narrow channel that a stag would leap over, between two precipitous banks of massive granite.

The mountain scenery is throughout magnificent, and grandly terminated, when you reach Loch Etive, by a line distant view of Ben Cruachan. There is a noble domed tower of rock seven or eight miles from King's House, which *is* a tower and not a buttress; and a few miles nearer the sea the outlines, as you look up the glen, have a wonderful vigour and energy, one great festooned line especially, as graceful as a loose chain suspended unequally from its two ends. [Note *: If the reader really cares about fine Highland glens, I counsel him by all means, if he can possibly spare the time, to stay two nights at the King's House Inn, where Mrs. Christie will make him as comfortable as any tourist ought to desire, and whence he can conveniently make an excursion to Glen Etive in one of Mrs. Christie's conveyances on the intervening day. No tourist that I have ever met seemed to think of exploring Glen Etive, all their attention being concentrated on Glen Coe; but I think it a great pity that they should pass so near to such a noble glen without giving a day to it at least. Since it is desirable to vary the Highland routes as much as possible, I beg to suggest to those interested in such matters, that a magnificent and entirely new route might be opened from Oban to King's House by having a steamer from Oban to the head of Glen Etive in communication with a coach running all through the glen from the shore of Loch Etive to the King's House Inn, where it would meet the Glen Coe coaches. Loch Etive and Glen Etive would thus be both of them conveniently opened to tourists, and they are as fine in their way as anything in the whole range of Highland scenery. The road in Glen Etive would, of course, have to be improved, but it might be made fit for coach traffic at a moderate cost.]

We got to the head of Loch Etive without having capsized the waggon, and encamped on the river's brink, where it mingles itself with the faintly saline waters of the loch. There we remained during sixty hours of incessant rain. By sitting in the door of the tent I contrived, however, to obtain a careful study, and I got one precious sketch of Ben Cruachan, with all the blue evening shadows on him. After that I saw him no more. The head of Loch Etive is a very wild and lonely, but by no means uninteresting place. There are one or two cottages there, strangely isolated. A rowing boat comes up occasionally from Buna we with supplies, and this is the most frequent communication with the outer world. In such a place as that a tent is indispensable to a painter. I could not have got ray study at all if I had been obliged to return to King's House to sleep.

As the rain poured quite pitilessly on the third day of my encampment at the head of Loch Etive, and as there seemed to be no prospect whatever of an improvement in the weather; considering, moreover, that the hills were all hidden in the mist, and the provision-box nearly empty; I drove back to King's House, and thence the next day to Loch Awe, where I and Thursday arrived, weary and hungry, and wet to the skin.

I desire to add here a few observations closely connected with the subject of the present chapter, on the habit of travelling as conducive to progress in art.

The love of travel which characterises modern landscape-painters is a peculiarity worth consideration. The reader will, perhaps, scarcely believe me when I tell him that it is precisely my artistic tendencies which make me *dislike* travelling more and more. When I cared less for my art I had a strong turn for travel, and planned explorations of all the most interesting regions of the globe. None of these plans did I ever put into execution, because, as I knew more of art, I came to perceive that much wandering was not good for it. I can scarcely understand how a painter can ever be a tourist. Nothing torments me like a tour. To pass so much admirable material and not have time to make good studies of it, is to me the torture of Tantalus. My first impulse when I come to a noble subject is to pitch my tent straight in front of it, and stay there twelve months; but since that cannot always be, let me at least stay long enough to draw it carefully, and watch it with the light of seven or eight sunsets and sunrises upon it; and, if possible, also under the tender mystery of moonlight. To look at Loch Awe day by day under all its aspects for four years exactly suited me, and I could have stayed twenty years longer in great contentment, with no other variety than the changes of the forms as my boat moved, and the changes of effects as the weather and the seasons altered. I was once dragged past Loch Awe in a coach at ten miles an hour, in perfect misery; and when I had lately to go down the valley of the Rhone in a railway-train, I did nothing but wish that I could give several years to the journey. But life is not long enough for such travelling as would quite suit me, and so I made a compromise with necessity; and yet I know that, after all, at this rate Death will certainly catch me before I have seen the tenth part of what I want to see, and so put a stop to my wanderings, in this world at least, for ever. But, let the tourist be in ever such a hurry, he will see no more, probably even less, wasting his time in travel. And if he saw a new scene every day of his life, how near would he have come at the end of it to exhausting the glories of one planet? I think my appetite for natural beauty is, to say the least of it, as vigorous as his—probably even keener, since it needs far less the stimulus of change. And I think that I do not enjoy a less quantity of beauty in the long run than the most indefatigable of tourists.

But it is certain that the common practice of modern landscape-painters is against me. They most of them combine the occupation of the artist with the amusement of the tourist. Turner was a great tourist, especially on foot; and much in the habit of slight and rapid sketching, as is most convenient for travelling artists. Now, for the tourist sketcher who travels rapidly, a tent at all heavier than the colourman's sketching tent is a useless incumbrance. A mere sketcher can generally contrive to get to an inn at night, and I should never recommend him to adopt the tent as a habitation. What is best and pleasantest for him is a light dog-cart, with a sketching tent and a portmanteau inside it. And let him live at the inns. Or if he' is a good walker, a knapsack, sketching-block, and stout stick, with two good pairs of boots, and a little money in his pocket, are all he needs.

In my-opinion, a snail is the perfect type of what an artist upon his travels ought to be. The snail goes alone and slowly, at quite a rational pace; stops wherever he feels inclined, and ***carries his house with him.*** Only I fear that the snail does not give that active attention to the aspects of nature which ought to be the constant habit of the artist.

BOOK III.—IN FRANCE.

CHAPTER I.

FIRST HEAD QUARTERS.—A LITTLE FRENCH CITY.

ON a narrow flat ledge, near the top of a very steep French coteau, stands my painting tent. Before me, spread to an infinite distance, on my right hand, Burgundy, in front of me, Champagne. The river Yonne comes winding down the broad valley, with long reaches and sharp curves; miles away a little isolated gleam shines alone like a tarn. Below my feet runs the river, at the foot of this steep bank of chalk. A little farther down it passes by a city, whose magnificent cathedral rises, a towering height of pale golden grey, infinite with dimly perceived ornament, out of green dense masses of the richest foliage. All round the town, but especially on this side of it, are stately groves of lofty poplars, standing like disciplined troops in line and hollow square, curving also here and there into crescents, and casting their dark shadows on spaces of grass that springs greener for their friendly shade.

Before we go down to the city, let us look around us here upon the hill. We are amongst the vineyards.

They are not celebrated vineyards; for although we are in Burgundy, the pro-

duce here is not to be compared to the precious gift of the hills of gold. Yet the innumerable proprietors of this little hill watch with keen interest the gradual filling
of its millions of green clusters, and you or I may admire the grapes or eat of them
with pleasure when they shall be fully ripe, yet not care to drink of the wine they
yield. It is pleasant to sit here in the sun, outside the tent, and watch the labourers
in the vineyards, for the mind of man always experiences a certain satisfaction in
being itself idle and watching others work. The labourers are of both sexes, men
with brown arms and breasts, and broad straw hats; and women, the rich glow of
whose sun-burnt faces tells even at a distance, when they rise occasionally out of
the green sea of vine leaves wherein they stoop and are hidden.

Between the foot of the hill and the river runs the railway from Paris to Mar-
seilles. We have been so long accustomed to be told that railways are prosaic things
that I count on little sympathy when I confess that those four thin lines of iron
have, for me, an irresistible fascination, and excite reflections quite as absorbing
as any which that towered town suggests. On those two rails nearest the river,
there, just there, borne, on a thousand wheels, rolled the mighty hosts of France
that met the Austrians at Solferino. There also passed their calm and terrible Captain swiftly, like Fate, yet with-nothing of military ostentation, in whose ears still
rang the acclamations, on that occasion loud and genuine, of the warlike people of
Paris. All Italy awaited him then, thrilling with the hope of liberty; Italy believed
in him, Austria feared him, all Europe thought of him only. And perhaps the other
line nearer us is, to an Englishman, awful with still more affecting associations.
On many a dark night a very few years ago a locomotive rushed furiously along
it, dragging two post-carriages at a wild and reckless speed; fire glowing under its
thundering wheels. It came from the Mediterranean Sea, carrying our Indian mail,
carrying sorrow and mourning to many an English home; cruel letters packed carefully together in sealed bags, to be scattered abroad in England, every one of them
too sure to hit some tender anxious breast. Railways are as rivers, flowing, not with
water, but human life and intelligence, and all of them acquire a kind of sublimity even in a very few years. But most of all is this line sublime. It is the one great
highway of Europe. Sovereigns, princes, ambassadors, travel by it continually, and
scarcely a single express train passes over it which does not carry some powerful or

famous personage.

In looking at a French landscape like this lovely one before us, an Englishman is struck by the sense of space gained by the absence of walls and hedges. This is, artistically, a great advantage. The eye ranges with a sense of liberty to which the presence of any visible obstacle is an insuperable impediment. A broad French plain has the sublimity of a great lake or the sea. The mean ideas of property, and farms, and petty quarrels about boundaries, never suggest themselves in the presence of such a broad expanse as this. The land seems infinite and immeasurable, as if it belonged to God alone. The only divisions are those of colour; it is like a vast floor of many-coloured mosaic.

This little flat ledge where the tent stands is, geologically, unaccountable. It interrupts a strong natural curve for no conceivable reason. It is artificial. It was the beginning of an intended terrace, begun some years ago by a gentleman now dead, who built himself a pleasure-house on the crest of the hill. This pleasure-house remains a monument of the vanity of human wishes. It seems that its owner enjoyed the view so much that he must needs pass much of his time here, and to that end erected a convenient summer-house, consisting of a pleasant well-finished octagonal room, with a kitchen and other offices behind it. Above the room rises a belfry, where a man may stand and enjoy the view, and toil the bell for his pleasure, and to the bewilderment of the dwellers in the plain. To the left of the house is a delightful *bosquet* or bower of linden trees, forming regular and almost impervious walls of greenery, which inclose a space as large as a good dining-room. To the right is another bower, but smaller, with sweet glimpses of the scenery through the leaves; and behind the house is an avenue of linden trees and a vineyard, also a remnant of an old rubble-built Gothic chapel, with tiny round arched windows, and one bearded statue canopied by a luxuriant mass of ivy. All this is highly delightful, but there are things yet more marvellous to be seen here on the hill. Near my tent there is a hole in the chalk leading to the very bowels of the earth. A long passage, connecting cells far apart, winds till it arrives under the house, and it is said that the late owner intended to cut other passages and cells, but wherefore, no man knows. [Note *: Perhaps as a refuge from the heat, which is often intense here when there is no breeze. It is also likely that one of the cells may have been simply intended for a wine cellar.] One thing is certain; he loved the place, and spent money there for the love of it Night and day he came up here from the little city in the plain, and sat in his pleasant octagon room, and mounted his belfry, and descended into his winding subterranean passages, and, hermit-like, visited his hollow cells. But at last he fell ill, and gave his beloved little place, with its bowers of linden trees and its fruitful vineyard, to the holy Archbishop of Sens, that the archbishop might say masses for his soul; and he died, and whether the archbishop said any masses or not I have never accurately ascertained. But it is evident that the archbishop cares not for the little summer-house, for the hill is steep and high, and the good prelate loves better his quiet garden under the shadow of the cathedral, where the ripening apricots redden in the sun, and the fattening pheasants cackle in their aviary.

We are often told how barbarous English people are, so that nothing can be left accessible to them which they will not savagely deface; and many pleasant places in England are now closed to the public because some disgraceful wretches have formerly done mischief there. But even here, in civilized France, I observe the same unaccountable tendencies. The little summer-house had several windows daintily bordered with narrow lines of stained glass, probably for the amusement of those curiously-constituted minds which experience a strange satisfaction in looking at a landscape through a discolouring medium. The walls of the octagonal room were also daintily panelled, and everything was finished with much care and some degree of taste. But barbarians came hither from Sens, and removed bricks that they might get at the bolts of the door, and unbolted it, and entered in, and smashed every pane of glass in the windows—stained or colourless, they left not one remaining; and they damaged the delicate panelling, and scrawled inscriptions on the walls, and left everywhere the marks of their stupid destructiveness.

So much for the last hermitage of St. Bond. The first was erected in consequence of a vow, as legends tell. The saint who dwelt there descended every day to the river Yonne with his water-jug, but every day as he climbed the hill the devil came and broke the jug, and spilled the water. This he did for seven years, at the end of which time even the saint's patience began to be a little wearied, and he vowed that if the devil might be kept from plaguing him he would build a hermitage on the hill; and thenceforth Satan, who must have broken exactly two thousand five hundred and fifty-five water-jugs—which Dr. Colenso, I suppose, would consider an improbable number—desisted from that somewhat monotonous amusement.

Sens is seated on the right bank of the river Yonne, opposite a large island with many houses upon it. There are two bridges going to the railway station, and a picturesque straggling street The city itself is entirely belted by magnificent avenues, chiefly elms, which here in France grow to a wonderful height, with astonishing freedom and grace. I remember a still finer avenue of old chestnut trees, now removed, which never recovered the ill-usage they got from the Cossacks, who encamped here during the invasion, and wore the bark away from the trees by the friction of horse-tethers. An incautious mayor finished the ailing trees by raising the level of the road, and so burying some portion of their trunks. These avenues follow the course of the old walls, now nearly all removed, but there are picturesque bits left here and there. Instead of the grand old Gothic gateways, they have put an absurd triumphal arch in one place and still more stupid columns in another. Still there is a fine postern left, hidden behind the trees. The avenues are double—I mean there are four lines of trees, and in the middle large green lawns, one of which is watered by a rivulet In their love of public walks the French give us a good example. Sens, with a population of ten thousand, has far better and more extensive public walks than either Manchester or Glasgow. I know that in England some watering-places have walks to attract visitors, but Sens is not a watering-place; strangers seldom stay there more than an hour or two, and the walks are simply for the health and recreation of the inhabitants themselves.

Avenues which *encircle* a town, with large green spaces in them for exercise, are much better than some isolated spot inaccessible to half the population. And if the town grows *beyond* the avenues, what matter? are they not accessible to the outsiders also? Fancy what a boon it would be to the inhabitants of a large English manufacturing town to have such avenues and lawns as those of Sens circling it, and held for ever inviolable as municipal property sacred to the public health! The lawn in the middle, like the *tapis vert* at Sens, ought to be wide enough all along for cricket, and everybody should be allowed to play there under certain slight restrictions necessary for the preservation of order. Spaces might also be set apart for gymnastic exercises, and furnished with such simple apparatus as common gymnastics require. It may be said that the English people do not care about trees, and lawns, and exercise, and "that sort of thing"—that they prefer beer and gin. I wish you would try them. I feel convinced that, if such public walks belted our northern towns, the inhabitants would all take to them as ducks take to water.

The avenues look best when some procession is passing along them. The Senonese are rather fond of getting up what they call a "cavalcade," ostensibly for some charitable purpose, but in reality because it amuses them. The last cavalcade of this kind I happened to witness—a charming sight for a child, and highly suggestive to a painter, but not perfect enough to produce the degree of illusion necessary to keep one quite serious. However, there is compensation in everything, and if the spectacle had been quite unexceptionable, it would not have been half such good fun. The subject represented was a return from hunting during the Regency, the charitable object was the relief of the cotton operatives about Rouen, and the date of the festival was the first Sunday after Easter in the present year (1863).

I saw the procession first from the upper windows of a house near the palace of justice, the next but one from a sharp corner. In the same street, but a good way round the corner, stands the sous-préfecture, whence the procession started; so we heard the strains of martial music and the trampling of many steeds some time before we saw anything.

Suddenly a number of boys and young men rushed round the corner, and came under the windows where we stood. They were dressed in loose scarlet tunics, not unlike the tabards of heralds, embroidered with green, yellow, and white flowers. They had white sleeves, and blue knickerbockers, and red stockings. Their caps were of divers colours, bordered with fur. They all carried long blue poles with trumpet mouths at the tops, but these were not musical instruments. The use of them we very soon learned If we had flattered ourselves that by being stationed at a good height above the street we had cunningly escaped contributing anything to the relief of the people at Rouen, we had deceived ourselves. The long blue trumpets were presented to us; they touched our very hands. On putting a piece of money into the trumpet's mouth it entered with surprising facility, and slid down a tube of blue cotton, by means of which it safely arrived in a box at the lower end of the pole. In spite of their disguise I recognized one or two of the lads who carried the poles; and I, not being disguised, was of course only too easily recognized by them. But I was a fool for putting too much money into the first trumpet, for others came after, and then I was reduced to coppers, which looked shabby; whereas if I had wisely limited myself to a franc at once from the beginning, I might have met all demands respectably.

The blue trumpets, to our great relief, passed by at last, and were presented to other windows. Then four gendarmes came round the comer on well-groomed horses, with their usual rather solid and heavy aspect, terrible to all disturbers of the peace. Then came the band of the 65th regiment of the line, playing martial music. And now for the grand cavalcade!

For my part I made up my mind to believe it all if I could; but it seemed more as if I were in a picture gallery or a theatre than really witnessing a return from hunting. Still it was well got up. The dresses, made in Paris on purpose for such occasions, were costly and good, and carefully studied from actual costumes of the period; and if the wearers of them were not exactly princes, they looked even yet more princely than real princes do.

Three huntsmen on horseback. Their coats were striped with narrow bands of blue and silver and gold. They wore cocked hats and red breeches, and blue saddle-cloths.

A company of foot guards, wearing black hats edged with red, blue coats with white stripes, and scarlet breeches. They bore halberds.

Four trumpeters, with loose surcoats of blue, powdered with golden fleurs de lis, black cocked hats edged with gold, white breeches faced with yellow, and high boots. They sounded their trumpets continually, two at a time. These trumpets were of the old French hunting pattern, winding round the body of the trumpeter, passing over his left shoulder and under his right arm.

Rabatteurs, wearing long curls, grey felt hats, and white plumes. Their coats red, with black velvet cuirasses, each with a huge silver star in the middle of the breast.

Breeches white, faced with red. Boots high, with mighty gilded spurs.

As these stately personages were riding proudly past with drawn swords, just under our windows, the horse in the middle, a heavy grey beast, took it into its head to make a violent attack on its right-hand neighbour.

The first two kicks missed, but the third was only too well planted, for it sent horse and man rolling over in the gutter. This, however, was partly due to the anxiety of the attacked horse to get out of the way of the aggressor. The riders both kept their seats, and did not look alarmed. I particularly admired the one whose horse came down. He had received a kick on his left foot, hard enough to break his great gilded spur, part of which was picked up afterwards; yet he held his drawn sword steadily in the air, and resumed his place in the procession, just as I have seen an English life-guardsman do under like circumstances. A little delay was occasioned by this accident; and when the procession moved forward, the gentlemen composing it kept at a respectful distance from the heavy grey horse in the middle.

The Grand Huntsman, all in crimson velvet and gold, with a bâton like a field-marshal's, and an air of infinite importance.

Piqueurs de la Meute. I cannot remember how these were dressed, but have a dim impression of some absurd costume like that worn by the army in *Faust,* as played at the Théâtre Lyrique.

La Meute. At any rate I remember the doggies, which were *au naturel.* Little is to be said in their favour. There had been a rumour that the emperor would lend us a pack of hounds from Fontainebleau; but surely these sorry little dogs were not a deputation from the imperial kennels. They were decidedly the worst part of the procession; but they trotted along contentedly, glad to be out for an airing, and happily ignorant of the expressions of contempt that hailed them on every side.

Mousquetaires à pied. Exactly like a regiment in an opera.

Trumpeters on foot Not much better than the poor doggies. Wretched little fellows, totally destitute of calves, and yet endowed with blue breeches and red stockings. The tallest was put in the middle. They wore black cocked hats with white edges, powdered wigs with tails, and scarlet coats with silver facings. They had a mournful look, as though inwardly conscious of being absurd.

THE WOLF. An unlucky beast probably killed in some neighbouring wood, [Note *: My next door neighbour killed a very fine wolf in the woods near Sens, and keeps his skin as a trophy.] and now borne triumphantly, having his legs tied together, and a long pole thrust between them, which pole rested on the shoulders of two lads with blue coats and red breeches. The victim was painful to behold. His open mouth showed savage teeth, and his tail hung inversely, beating time with a regular cadence to the steps of the bearers.

To the wolf succeeded a stag between two foxes, the three borne upon a litter. It was impossible to believe that the little dogs we had just seen could have had anything to do with the death of that stag.

Two youthful pages followed. They had a feminine look, and were probably girls. They wore long red coats, black velvet breeches, and white stockings. They had long brown curls under black cocked hats.

THE REGENT. His Highness wore a black hat, a coat of sky-blue moire, embroidered with silver and gold, and sky-blue breeches. This august personage had a most splendid appearance; and I am credibly informed by Monsieur le Maire that

that sky-blue coat and those sky-blue breeches had cost no less a sum than twenty pounds sterling.

To the Regent succeeded two princes; and here I proudly record a personal incident. One of their Highnesses deigned to speak to me. It is true that under the royal wig I recognized the familiar features of a baker of respectable standing in the town; but he looked a prince, every inch of him.

Indeed, all these personages bore themselves with a regal air. It may have occurred to the reader to feel some slight disappointment on seeing the faces of real kings, for they do not always come up to one's lofty ideal; but these men did. That baker was just as good a gentleman and prince (to look at) as any that ever I saw; and if he had been a real prince, he would have won all hearts by the grace of his condescension. Men would have said of him," See how easy it is to recognize princely blood," there being a strong tendency in mankind to call qualities princely when they belong to princes; though, when precisely the same graces adorn common folks, they excite nobody's admiration.

And my bell-hanger, who passed as a great lord, and deigned to give me a lordly smile and bow, what peer of France ever bowed better? The next time my bells won't ring, he will come with his tools in his hand, in his plain workman's dress, and humbly toil for me. But can I forget that he rode behind the Regent with that noble air of pride?

There were many lords of the court, some on horseback in velvet coats of various colours, others in a huge gilded chariot, drawn by four fat horses.

At last the procession passed us. It traversed all the quaint old streets. It circumnavigated the great square in front of the cathedral. It emerged from the little city, and wandered into the faubourgs beyond. It passed gleaming and glittering under the green old elms in the avenues. It crossed the bridge and penetrated into the faubourg on the island in the river. After having dazzled the eyes of the islanders, it returned to the avenues without the walls, and there many good-natured householders, sitting on the terraces of their gardens, handed glasses of ale or wine to the thirsty riders.

The proceeds of the collection, chiefly, I suspect, in sous, quite filled a large box, which followed the procession in a carriage. I am afraid, after the expenses, not much was left for the poor folks at Rouen, and one cannot help regretting that the charitable people who poured money into the blue trumpets which were applied to the windows, and into the tin boxes carried by those who begged amongst the crowd, did not rather give the same amount directly to some of the many committees, which hand it over, without deduction, to those who really have need of it.

I saw no more of the procession. In the evening there was a grand military concert on the public lawn. A large circle was brilliantly illuminated with festoons of lamps hanging from tall masts crowned with banners. The music was good, and about two thousand people heard it.

In other parts of the promenades there were the usual amusements of a fête day, and some little boys of my acquaintance were rendered extremely happy by a ride on the wooden horses; and, hard by, other equestrians in a circus rode on horses of real flesh and blood, which galloped round and round. Spangled ladies in short petticoats stood on the platform before the circus, crying mightily, "Come and see;" some were fat and some were lean, but only one was pretty. Then there were boxers boxing, powerful athletes with thick muscular arms and dreadfully brutal looks. And whilst the sunshine lasted, there was a balloon man, with a cluster of red india-rubber balloons hanging like a bunch of shining cherries high in the blue air; and he let one of them go to attract the attention of the crowd, and it rose and rose till it passed far above the cathedral towers, and gradually became a tiny speck up in the blinding light about the sun, when the strongest eyes lost it.

These Senonese cavalcades may be seen from two points of view. Are they an indication of childishness or of culture? I incline to the latter view. I like the attempt to keep the past in our memories by these reminders. Here was a little lesson in history brought home to ten thousand people. Who was the Regent? Those who did not know, asked; those who did, replied. There was much conversation on historical topics in Sens that day, much criticism of the costumes, some discussion as to the acts and character of the Regent. The present writer, whose knowledge of history is unfortunately somewhat general, and even vague, learned several facts which he did not know before. But the strongest impression was made upon the boys; and a juvenile from the Lycée, who sometimes dines with me on a Sunday, talked of nothing but history over his nuts and almonds, and asked me many questions which, I am ashamed to say, I was utterly unable to answer.

As machinery for collecting money for charitable purposes, a cavalcade is a cunning device. It passes through every street and before every house. It excites so much curiosity that the people are all sure to be at their windows; then there are so many collectors, that those who refuse to the first, give to the third, or sixth, or tenth.

The Senonese have a terrible custom of marching about with drums. There is a tradition that, many ages ago, the Saracens penetrated hitherto, and so dismayed the inhabitants that they were on the point of abandoning the city, when a virgin of Sens, whose name history has failed to preserve, took a drum and marched about the streets drumming. Then all the other young women in the town took drums, and drummed; and the Saracens, hearing this tremendous and universal drumming, concluded that there must be a mighty force within the walls, and abandoned the siege. And so, because the Saracens threatened Sens, nobody knows how many hundreds of years ago, and because a virgin, whose name nobody knows, excited all the others to drum with drums, all modern citizens of Sens who may happen to have a constitutional antipathy to noise are to have their nervous system horribly tortured and put out of order by a mob of drummers parading the streets by torchlight. It is incredible what an uproar they make. It shakes the houses from top to bottom; the very stones in the paved streets dance under the drums. There they go with their infernal rattle, torches flaring, and a mob of children after them, who love noise as much as I hate it.

To finish the festivities of the cavalcade, of course I knew that the drummers would gather themselves together. And if any sick were lying in their beds that night in anything like that state for which straw is laid down before people's houses, depend upon it, those drums were the death of them.

Of the usual festivities of the place, it is not my lot to see very much. I am not addicted to dancing in the open air, as Mr. Pinchbold did when cruising on wheels in this part of the world. Sometimes, as I walk round the promenades on a Sunday evening, I perceive gleaming through the thick foliage in front of me festoons of coloured lamps, on approaching which I hear strains of music, and discover the postman who brings me letters sitting on high, divested of his official uniform, and playing energetically on the clarionette. Around him are violinists, and performers on all kinds of instruments; before him, on a large wooden floor, laid down for the occasion and defended by railing, whirl a hundred couples in the mazes of a waltz. Hard by the ball are stalls for refreshment, and in the distance the inevitable rotatory machine with the wooden horses, whereon tall young fellows gravely sit, their feet touching the ground, their coat-tails hiding the tail of the horse, as they calmly await the motion which is to them so full of charm.

One of the first questions usually asked of an Englishman who lives in France is, whether he likes French cookery. A prudent man, when the question is put to him at an English dinner-table, tells a lie, and says that English cookery is far superior. Taken broadly, the difference between the two nations in this matter is, that the French *can* cook, and the English *can't;* but dishes which are so extremely simple as not to require any scientific cooking at all are generally better in England.

To borrow an illustration from my own craft. I very often admire, with humble wonder, the astonishing perfection with which carriages are painted. We painters of pictures could not paint carriages so well as men bred peculiarly to that trade. Very few of us could lay the colour quite evenly enough, or, if we did, it would only be by great effort; whereas a simple carriage-painter, who has never troubled himself about gradation and what we call texture, lays on his paint with a masterly perfection of method. So a French cook is too artistic to succeed where art is superfluous; and *there* we beat him.

"Do you mean to say that you like frogs?" asks the indignant reader. Yes, I do. And here allow me to remark, that if you are ignorant of the taste of frogs, you are, gastronomically speaking, sunk in the depths of barbarism, and an object of pity, even as some wretch who has never swallowed an oyster. Fancy chickens from Lilliput, as much more delicate than common chickens as they would be smaller, and you have some notion of what frogs are like. One of the most galling disappointments I ever had to bear was to leave untouched a plate of frogs, because I had to go off by the train. For the first forty miles my soul was a prey to vain regrets; and even now, though I have eaten many a plate of frogs since then, I have not quite got over it.

But the common English notion, that the French are fed on frogs habitually, is a mistake. Frogs are much too dear to be anything but a luxury; and you might as well say that the English population is brought up on woodcocks.

The Burgundians are fond of their great big vine snails; but, in my opinion, the principal merit of snails is, that they are good, strong, nourishing food. The way that snails are generally served in good houses is this:—Seven or eight of them are brought on a little hot silver plate, with a tiny silver two-pronged fork, made on purpose. The seven snails are by no means unpleasant to look at, their shells being beautifully white and clean. The entrance to every shell is stopped with a sort of paste, pleasant to the taste. You insert the fork and pull out the inhabitant. He is a huge animal, and of a dark brown colour graduating to black. The black is the best. The beast is not pleasant to look at; so you should transfer him rapidly from his shell to your mouth, and, when there, you find him very like an enormous morsel of tough beefsteak. Masticate him if you can! If you are successful, and go boldly on till you have emptied the seventh shell, you must be a hungry man indeed, if you have not sufficiently dined;—and this, not because you are made sick, but really because these big snails are strong meat.

Next to good eating, the French love good wine, and, better than either, witty and intellectual conversation. The wines, as I said, grown at this particular place are not to be recommended; but all the best produce of Upper Burgundy is to be got here. The variety of wines grown in Burgundy is much greater than Englishmen generally are aware of. White burgundy with soda-water rivals Byron's hock and soda-water. The sparkling burgundies of the better sort are as good as the best champagne; and the precious red wines which Englishmen used to appreciate so highly in Esmond's time are sold here, and even at Dijon, at the rate of ten francs a bottle.

In saying that the French are fond of good conversation, an exception must be made. French girls, whom Mr. Ruskin, perhaps not unjustly, defined as the sweetest-tempered living creatures in the world, might also be characterised as the most silent. A French maiden properly brought up is a miracle of modesty; her dress, her manners, are the extreme of an ideal simplicity. Admirers crowd respectfully about her; and she never seems to suppose it possible that she can excite any admiration: if utterly neglected, she seems just as happy in her own quiet way; nobody can tell what she is thinking. Always calm, contented, placid, and yet lifted so far above us by never condescending to seek our homage, she wins it as her natural right. Men talk to each other in her tranquil presence with an uneasy feeling that she is criticising them inwardly. She is that

Mystery of mysteries,
Faintly smiling Adeline.

She is clear, and yet inscrutable, like the blue depths of a Swiss lake in a calm. This is the secret of her inexhaustible interest. Who knows whether she is shallow or deep? Sometimes one fancies there are faint gleams of subdued sarcasm in her gentle eyes. She seems a serene Intelligence dwelling apart from the world.

Is she in thought as absolutely innocent as she looks? Of course, charitable Englishwomen, calling themselves Christians, say she is a sham, and that they would not let *their* daughters be educated in her company. It is easy to gain credit for penetration by slandering simple girls who are foreigners; but every one who knows respectable French society, knows very well that there is no foundation whatever for slander of that kind. The young French girl in the higher classes is, unfortunately for her, only *too* innocent for this world, of which she is almost as ignorant as a newborn baby. Some day her papa will say to her, "My daughter, thou art going to be married," and she, in simple filial obedience, will yield herself up to the chosen son-in-law. There is something sad and touching in that simple history, so often repeated. Whether French parents will ever have a higher ideal for their daughters than mere purity, and simplicity, and ignorance, it is difficult to say; but at present, although some girls are bred as English ones, knowing good and evil, it is always a great disadvantage to them in France, though a rational Englishman would probably like them all the better for it

Conversation amongst men is more entertaining; and married women, especially when oldish, talk cleverly, and are often keen politicians. The French are at their ease in the region of ideas, and so their conversation has the charm of speculative interest Besides, they cultivate conversation as an art. They read less than we do, and talk more and better. They become eager and excited in the elucidation of their thoughts, which seems to produce a sort of electrical flashing, seen in England only in rare instances. They have the fault of interrupting each other very unceremoniously, and in that respect lack politeness; but this is an affair of temperament. They do not hesitate in speaking, as our upper classes do. Probably in the last century the English hesitated less; at present we hesitate most painfully, and, if we go on, perhaps the next generation will not be able to express itself verbally at all, but will carry on conversation by writing.

After knowing the French intimately for a few years, it is easy to see what ideas are dearest to their mind. The leading ideas are the key to all national character. The English national ideas are religion, and wealth, and political liberty. The French national ideas are religious liberty, political equality, and national strength. The difference between a love of religion and a love of religious liberty is obvious: the bare conception of religious liberty only awakens in nations which are internally divided on religious questions. If a powerful majority, say nine-tenths of the population of a country, heartily accepts a particular form of faith, it will compel the remaining tenth to conformity, and at the same time assert that there is perfect religious liberty in the country, because there is really no desire on the part of any one to disobey the governing church. Thus it has been recently asserted in a Spanish newspaper that in Spain there is perfect religious liberty, because every one has really the liberty to do what he desires—that is, to be a good Catholic, for no true Spaniard could desire anything else. The English conception of religious liberty is, on one or two points, of a like character, especially with reference to the observance of Sunday, on which day every Englishman has perfect liberty to do what he desires—that is, to observe it in the Anglican manner, for no true Englishman could desire anything else. When a majority becomes sufficiently strong to call itself universal unanimity, it soon loses the power of intellectually apprehending the nature of individual liberty. The French conception of religious liberty is, therefore, unintelligible to many other nations. It amounts to this, that on the grounds of religious dogma no government has the right to impose *any* observance on the whole nation, because, whatever the observance may be, there will be some persons in the nation who do not mentally believe in the dogma on which it is grounded; and to compel these to conformity would be an act of religious tyranny. The arguments advanced by Mr. John Stuart Mill in his Essay on Liberty were already familiar in their essence to the popular French mind; and that exquisitely-written treatise, though full of what to the English may seem new and daring speculation, fell with the effect of truism on our neighbours.

The French are not nearly so sensitive about political liberty. Louis Napoleon has made himself a secular despot; but he would never dare to enforce the observance of the most sacred and essential ordinances of the Romish Church as the English Parliament enforces the observance of Sunday. The utmost efforts have been made by the clergy to induce him to make a religious ceremony essential to marriage; but, in spite of his strong desire to conciliate the Church, he cannot and dare not yield that point. And so much do national feelings differ, that the French often assert that, little as they love Louis Napoleon, they would rather be governed by him seven days in the week than by an English Act of Parliament on the first day only.

The idea of political equality, in the French sense, is perhaps even less intelligible to us than the French conception of religious liberty. No Frenchman that ever I have talked with has advocated the crude conception of equality which our writers amuse themselves by refuting. No Frenchman ever, in my hearing, denied the natural inequalities inevitable amongst men; but between these natural inequalities and the attempt to represent them politically, there is, they argue, a step of such difficulty that it is wiser never to attempt it. They say that our political inequalities are purely artificial—are as far from representing the natural inequalities as their own system of theoretical equality. On the question of the suffrage, they freely admit the inconveniences of giving every man a vote; but our system of boroughs, by which one small town elects a member, and another larger one is unrepresented, does not seem to the French in any way an accurate imitation of the natural inequality. In all discussion they are mercilessly logical; and the Englishman's argument for many abuses, that they work well practically, seems to the French mind an ignoble concession to the basest sort of expediency.

There is also a moral root for the idea of equality in the French mind which is entirely wanting to the English. They have a kind of self-respect quite different from ours. The sort of rudeness from persons of superior rank which Englishmen accept as quite natural and right, the French resent as impertinence. A friend of mine was taking a drive with a rich French countess in a country where the rank and position of the countess were known to every one. She wanted to know where some peasant lived, and, seeing a man working in a field by the road-side, stopped the carriage and called out, "Good man, where does such a one live?" The man replied simply, "Good woman, he lives at such a place;" he being a Frenchman, with the idea of equality in his head. Once, in Scotland, I heard an English visitor call out to a labourer, "Man, whose boat is that on the lake?" but the Scotchman replied with deference. It seems intensely absurd to the English to have to be polite to poor people; yet every French peasant exacts courtesy. A thoughtful Frenchman would tell you that by this courtesy he has no idea of denying natural inequality; on the contrary, he thereby recognises its profoundly mysterious nature. An Englishman, meeting a man evidently much poorer than himself, has not the least hesitation about treating him as his inferior; but a Frenchman is courteous to his possible superiority on many points quite as important as money. And, as we come to know mankind better, does not the French view acquire graver claims to consideration? You may be rich and famous, and you may meet in the street some poor unknown operative, and that man in the street may be, for anything you know, at that very time exercising a self-denial so heroic, that no moral effort you ever made in all your life is to be compared to it. Or he may be endowed with natural faculties in comparison with which yours, though everybody has heard of you, are commonplace. Let us be courteous to his possible superiority; and, even if he were certainly our inferior in all things, surely our superiority is not so god-like that we are entitled to be rude to him.

These ideas go so far in France that I could relate many astonishing anecdotes in proof of them. A French lady told me that she had never been presented to the Queen of England, because she thought it possible that the Queen would not treat her on a footing of equality. Now, to interpret this sentiment coarsely as a pretension on the lady's part to equal position with Her Majesty, would be merely to misunderstand her. The Frenchwoman's next observation explained her meaning. "A formal recognition of such wide difference of rank is a complete bar to the interchange of ideas, so that conversations with people too exalted to be contradicted have no intellectual interest." And French princes, both of the House of Orleans and the present dynasty, know this so well that they always meet cultivated Frenchmen on intellectual grounds common to all, recognising a certain philosophical equality in human beings beyond the distinctions of rank.

The next idea, that of national strength, is more powerful in France than with us, as is proved by the willing consent of all Frenchmen to the conscription, and their unfailing support of any ruler, no matter how tyrannical at home, who will make the name of France great and terrible abroad. The one unpardonable sin of Louis Philippe was that France under him ceased to hold that supreme position in European politics which all Frenchmen look upon as her natural right. The open secret of Louis Napoleon's success is that, whatever may be his crimes, he has undeniably put France into the proud place of leader in the councils of Europe.

A striking contrast between the French and the English is the faith of the

French in intellectual conclusions, and their readiness to carry them into practice; whilst the English are sceptical, and, in secular matters, believe in nothing which they have not seen actually at work. The French take the keenest interest in suggestions, possibilities, and theories of all sorts; but only a very few English minds are much interested in mere speculation. But not only are the French speculative, they are above all things ardent to make speculations realities. In France there is but one step between the reception of an idea and its realization—a realization often so premature as to justify British sneers at French mobility, but often also in the highest degree valuable as an experiment.

The difference between the two nations in this respect was never more curiously exemplified than in the way they have dealt with one of the inevitable questions of modern times—the adoption of a uniform decimal system of weights and measures and money. Every intelligent Englishman has been well aware for many years that the English confusion in these things was irrational and absurd; but, partly from hatred to the French, and partly from his peculiar unwillingness to put intellectual conclusions into practice, he has gone on without making any reform, on the plea—by no means complimentary to the intelligence of his countrymen— that the people of England could not learn a system so simple that any schoolboy above ten years old could master it in half an hour.

The Lycée deserves attention as a specimen of a French public school. It is a very long, narrow, and lofty building, on the site of the old wall of the town, with great court-yards and a chapel. The side facing the promenade still bears many marks of musket-balls, a reminiscence of the invasion. As the stranger walks along the promenades, under those lofty walls, he might excusably infer that the principal occupation of the students within was the production of horrible discords on all kinds of instruments. This impression, though natural, would, however, be erroneous. A system of education is carried on there which, if not in every respect exactly what one might desire, has, nevertheless, the qualities of steadiness, regularity, and discipline.

A striking difference between English and French education is, that in England the education of the upper classes is almost entirely in the hands of the clergy, whilst in France the national education is laic. How far this may seem an advantage or not, depends upon the point of view from which we look at it. If it is good for a nation to be governed by its priesthood, the English system is unquestionably the better of the two, for it gives the priesthood absolute power over a very important part of the nation. If, on the other hand, clerical authority is, as some assert, a kind of power naturally hostile to intellectual liberty, it need not surprise us that many politicians should be anxious to place national education in the hands of laymen.

The functionaries in a French Lycée are divisible into three classes,—Administrators, Professors, and Masters.

The *Administration* consists first of the *Proviseur,* who is the head of the establishment, and directs everything; next, the *Censeur,* whose business it is to attend to the discipline of the Lycée, and who, therefore, is also a powerful personage; then the *Treasurer* and his clerk, who are called the Économe *and the* Commis d' Économat. *The* Économe *is master of all money matters, and is alone responsible for them, not to the* Proviseur but directly to the Court of Accounts. He has an office where he and his clerk keep an open account between the Lycée and every pupil in it, and between the Lycée and all the tradespeople who supply it. Even the *Proviseur,* master absolute in everything else, cannot spend one centime, nor receive one, except his own personal salary. Lastly there is the chaplain (Aumônier), whose office is purely ecclesiastical, and who exercises little or no power but that of persuasion.

The *Professors,* fifteen in number, hear and examine the pupils, but are not present when they prepare their work. There are five professors of sciences and ten of letters. Of the former, three are mathematical, and two teach physics and chemistry. Amongst the professors of letters there is one for English and another for German literature.

The eight *Masters* are the most to be pitied. It is their business to be with the pupils at all hours of the day and night, except during class hours, which are from 8 A.M. to 10 A.M., and from 2 P.M. to 4 P.M. These unlucky masters have to help and direct the pupils whilst they learn their lessons, on which account they are called "maîtres repétiteurs." They sleep in the dormitories with the pupils, they walk out with them when they take exercise, they watch them even in the play-grounds. To my mind, the existence of one of these masters seems absolutely insup-portable. Surely the calm and peace of the grave must have a great attraction for men who are hardly ever alone, whose days and nights are passed amongst scores of schoolboys! I wonder whether they envy the quiet folk in the cemetery.

High up in the Lycée there is an infirmary, and near it dwell three Sisters of Charity, one of whom manages the infirmary, and the other two the linen-room, where all the boys' linen is kept, nicely folded and clean, on pretty oak shelves, which exhale a pleasant perfume of lavender. These two Sisters have to take care that every one of the thousands of things under their charge is kept in good order and repair. Sisters of Charity have no choice where they will go, or what they will do. The Superior of this little sisterhood of three, she who attends to the infirmary, was sent here quite suddenly, and, for anything she knows, may be sent to some other place, and quite a different sort of work, any day. As it generally happens to these good women, she is regarded by everybody with the utmost respect and af-fection. She is a very fat, good-tempered person, extremely kind and obliging to every one, and like a tender mother to the boys in the infirmary. She is very sharp, nevertheless, and soon finds out small patients who sham illness to escape work. For these, as the good Superior revealed to me in confidence, she has a simple treatment which effects a rapid cure. She reduces their food to famine allowance and admin-isters a nauseous purgative. The boys, of course, very soon become ravenously hun-gry, and can stand it no longer, when they profess themselves quite recovered, that they may return to the flesh-pots of the refectory. [Note *: Since this was written, the good lady is dead.]

In a French city the Lycée is the embodiment of modern tendencies and aspi-rations, and the cathedral of mediæval ones. The Lycée is prosaic, scientific, ugly, a place of hard labour for young brains, preparing them for the work of this world by stern discipline of actual acquisition, leaving no time for dreaming about lofty ideas. The cathedral, on the other hand, is from end to end, from base to pinnacle, a great world of ideal aspirations; a place to which, century after century, men and women have gone purposely to get rid of the wearisome pressure of the actual, in meditations on the past histories of idealised personages, in sweet brooding over, and eager longing for, the bliss of a far Paradise. The temper of the Lycée is submission to discipline for the sake of knowledge, the temper of the Church is obedience for the sake of heavenly protection. In the first, men seek to correct their weakness ***by getting to know,*** for they attribute it to mere ignorance; in the second, they seek strength by prayer, and penance, and confession. The Lycée and the cathedral are in more ways than one typical of the modern and mediæval ages. Modem education is acquisitive and critical; the legends of the Church of Rome were endlessly inventive, full of deep feeling, and passion, and power. The Lycée is as prosaic as a Lancashire factory; it ***is,*** indeed, a sort of factory for turning raw boy-material into bachelors. The cathedral is all poetry; I mean that every part of it affects our emotional nature either by its own grandeur or beauty, or by its allusion to histories of bright virtue or brave fortitude. And this emotional result is independent of belief in the historical truth of these great legends: it would be stronger, no doubt, if we believed them, but we are still capable of feeling their solemn poetry and large significance as we feel the poetry and significance of "Sir Galahad," or "The Idylls of the King."

Some persons are so constituted that it is necessary to their happiness to live near some noble work of art or nature. A mountain is satisfactory to them because it is great and ever new, presenting itself every hour under aspects so unforeseen that one can gaze at it for years with unflagging interest. To some minds, to mine amongst others, human life is scarcely supportable far from some stately and magnificent object, worthy of endless study and admiration. But what of life in the plains? Truly, most plains are dreary enough, but still they may have fine trees, or a cathedral. And in the cathedral, here, I find no despicable compensation for the loss of dear old Ben Cruachan. The effects of light on Cruachan were far more wonderful and interesting, but still it is something to see the cathedral front dark in the early morning when the sun has risen behind it, and golden in the glow of the evening when he lights all its carven imagery. Better than either when the sun has set long ago, and the slenderly columned arcades lift themselves story above story, pale in the clear calm air, and the white statues of the mitred old archbishops stand ghostly in their lofty tower. And then is the time to enter in, and feel the true power of the place. Just before the Suisse locks all the doors, go in, and yield to all the influences that await you. Silent worshippers are lingering at twenty altars yet [Note *: There are twenty-five altars in the cathedral at Sens.]—women, all of them, gathering strength to bear their sorrows. They are praying for dear friends, dead and living; they are praying to be sustained in their daily trials. You find them in little groups of two or three, quite silent and absorbed; and here and there one kneels alone in some dim old vaulted chapel, before an altar decked with flowers, almost invisible now. And above the altar a little lamp is burning, one little speck of yellow fire shining faintly, yet for ever. And all the painted windows gleam with a strange intensity, for their tracery is quite black now, and every scrap of glass tells with tenfold power. Thousands of figures are still mysteriously visible—angels and demons, prelates and warriors, and all the saints and heroes of the faith. The flames of hell are still visibly crimson; still visibly writhe in torture the companies of the damned! But the Suisse gathers us all together—us, lovers of fine art, who came on purpose to be pleasantly thrilled by a poetic effect; and those others, the poor women, who came to pray at the altars of the Blessed Saints. I wonder whether he does not miss one now and then, lost in a dream of paradise, or passionate prayer for the dead, far in some lonely chapel before her favoured shrine.

A Gothic cathedral, being intended originally for the great ceremonies of the Roman Church, can only be properly seen and understood when one of those ceremonies is going forward in it. The extreme discrepancy between the splendour of our old English cathedrals, with their obvious adaptation to the Roman ritual, and the simple costume and observances of the English Church, strikes every artist irresistibly. The natural completion of a Gothic cathedral is a visible bishop, with cope and mitre and crozier, surrounded by a crowd of inferior priests, all glowing with gold and embroidery. With those living and moving figures, the painted windows and illuminated vault have a natural and intelligible relationship; but the wig and lawn sleeves (though objects of ambition to the clergy, and of veneration to the la-ity) are in artistic harmony with no English cathedral except St. Paul's. Of course, I speak here only of the æsthetic aspect of this question, and do not meddle with the theological. No doubt, in separating herself from Rome, England did wisely to display the outward and visible sign of her separation by rejecting the sacerdotal vestments. But thence came a discord between the old temples and the new priests.

Let us see how the old cathedral here looks on a great day, and let us try to understand what sort of ceremonies these Gothic cathedrals were built for.

The choir is enclosed by railings, and the priests do not seem to care very much whether we see them or not. The bishops, in the middle ages, performed their solemn offices in a kind of isolation from the crowd, utterly regardless of its convenience in every way. This makes us understand the purpose of the processions. Without processions, as a Gothic cathedral is constructed, not one person in a hundred would ever see the bishop at all; so he and his priests walk round the aisles, blessing the kneeling people.

This time it is the consecration of a bishop—a great event. The archbishop has allowed carpenters to erect seats in the aisles near the choir, to let us get a peep at the ceremony. Of course, many spectators find themselves precisely opposite a huge pillar, impervious to the sight, and there they sit, seeing nothing, and asking their neighbours what is going on. As for me, I see tolerably well through the iron grating. There are three prelates with stiff golden copes and tall mitres. One is our archbishop, who is to consecrate the new bishop. There are also two other bishops seated, in their simple violet dress.

The archbishop is seated in an arm-chair, with his back to the altar. The elected is seated in front of him, with the assistant bishops. This lasts for some time in perfect silence. One of the bishops then rises, and begs the archbishop, in Latin, to raise the elected to the ***onus Episcopatus.*** The archbishop asks for the Apostolic mandate. It is read by a secretary, and then the archbishop administers the oath, which is long and highly curious. After that comes a remarkable catechism, to which the elected has to answer; and every time he answers he rises slightly from his seat. The catechism over, the elected is conducted between the bishops to the archbishop, whose hand he kisses, kneeling. The archbishop turns to the altar with the bishops, and confesses; then kisses the altar and incenses it; after which he returns to his seat.

There is another altar, lower down, for the elected, and there he says mass, but before that he is invested with some pontifical ornaments. Then all chant the great Litany of the Saints, the archbishop on his knees with all the bishops, and the elected, this time, prostrate on his face. It is strange to see that figure, habited so splendidly, stretched motionless on the ground whilst the slow, monotonous chant goes forward, and one wonders whether it will ever have an end.

It does end, however, at last, and then the archbishop stands erect before his chair, and the elected falls on his knees before him. Then they open a great copy of the Gospels, and put the open book on the head and shoulders of the elected, clothing him with it as it were. A chaplain behind him keeps the book from falling.

The archbishop and the assistant-bishops touch the head of the elected, saying, "Receive thou the Holy Ghost." And the archbishop, first taking the mitre off, prays, standing. Towards the close of the long prayer comes an allusion to the splendour of the Hebrew sacerdotal costume, which the Roman Church loves to recall in justification of her own magnificence.

Then they tie a white napkin round the head of the elected, who is now anointed by the archbishop. After unction, the archbishop prays for the new prelate; and then come an anthem and psalm, both recalling the anointing of Aaron. They tie a long white napkin round the new bishop's neck, and his hands are next anointed. Now that the hands are anointed, they are fit to hold the crozier, which, being blessed, is given to the elected; then the consecrated ring is placed upon his finger. All this time the elected has been under the book of the Gospels, which is now removed. Then the archbishop kisses the elected, and so do the other bishops, and the new bishop returns to his own altar, where his head is wiped with bread and linen, and his hair combed with a curious antique comb, which has served that purpose for ever so many centuries. Then he washes his hands; and the archbishop, seated in his arm-chair, also washes his. The archbishop takes the sacrament, and administers it to the elected, at the high altar. Then he blesses the new bishop's mitre, and then comes the great moment when the mitre is finally placed by the three prelates on the new prelate's head. Lastly, the Episcopal gloves are blessed, and the ring is taken off, and the gloves put on, and the ring put on again outside the glove. And now a hymn is sung, and the new bishop walks in procession all through the church, splendid with jewelled mitre and silver crozier, blessing the people as he goes.

Such is a bare and naked outline of the ceremony. But how shall I paint it in words?—how tell of the gleaming of the golden vestments, and the coloured light that fell upon them from the lofty windows of the apse? A group of bishops in full pontificals, close to the high altar in one of the noblest cathedrals the Gothic ages have left us, is a rare and wonderful sight—a sight never to be seen in England, and marvellous to our eyes. Yet one thing still was wanting. The splendid bishops and the Gothic architecture agreed quite well together; but what of the people? I longed for the costumes of the middle ages—for the knights with silken robes over their armour, and ladies dressed in rich embroideries, sitting gorgeous, like illumined queens in missals, or like Esther on the tapestry in the Treasury here, where she is innocently represented as a magnificent Burgundian dame of the thirteenth century.

So much for the artistic impressions; philosophical reflections the reader may not particularly care to hear. But one thing struck me as curious. In the middle of the choir sat Monsieur Leverrier, the astronomer—a person who holds, I believe, the heretical doctrine of the revolution of the earth, and who has presumed to add a planet to the discoveries of a profane science. Leverrier and the bishops seemed incongruous elements; and I looked at his sharp, intelligent face, to see whether it indicated a devout or a critical spirit. It seemed lively and interested, but not devout. Well for you, Monsieur Leverrier, that you live now, rather than in the days of Galileo, or you might not only have beheld pontifical splendour, but felt pontifical power! There are dungeons under the Synodal Hall here, good for heterodox teachers!

Another spectator was more affected. There was a woman at a little distance from me, and exactly opposite a thick pillar, so that for most of what passed she had to trust the accounts of her neighbours; and, indeed, except for the emotions excited by feeling herself physically present at the ceremony, she, poor thing, might just as well have been at home. She kept up a perpetual stream of the most eager inquiries as to what was going on, which she directed to everybody who would pay any attention to her. "What is he doing now? Is he really anointed? What is the archbishop saying now—is he praying for him? Are his hands anointed now? and have they given him the crozier? Ah! to think—to think that he holds the crozier! Ah me! I have confessed to him many and many a time! And what are they doing now?—the ring—ah yes, the ring!—have they put it on? and,—what do you say?— have they taken the Gospels off his back? Ah me! and the archbishop has kissed him—and the other bishops, have they kissed him too? Ah, to think that he is really a bishop now! O God, I thank Thee that I have lived to see this day!"

To this woman, you may be sure, the pageant was anything but tedious or overdone. To an uneducated Protestant it would seem absurd, if not sinful. To a spectator who thinks, it is merely an anachronism. We must remember that the Roman Church holds the principle that splendid public worship is a sacrifice of wealth highly acceptable to God—a principle which, whether right or wrong, has been held by all religions except the Protestant. Now, once admit this principle, and where are you to stop? Even Protestants dress well to go to church; and, as Protestant ladies consider handsome bonnets and fine shawls a fit expression of respect for the house of God, so, I imagine, might a pure-minded prelate don his glittering mitre and golden cope on entering the presence of his Master. As for our archbishop, splendid as he is when on duty before the altar, he is as simple as Wellington at home. His income, to begin with, is less than the tenth part of the income of an English archbishop; yet this income, moderate as it is, might procure him luxuries which he denies himself. For instance, he does not even keep a carriage, but (though always ill and infirm), whenever he has to go into the country, *Monseigneur* goes in a hired fly. One day I called upon him, and found him at work, in the intervals of suffering, in a room altogether destitute of luxury, and with no comfort except a fire, a plain arm-chair or two, and perfect cleanliness. The servant who opened the door was as simple as his master, and quietly tucked his blue apron round his waist before conducting me into the presence of **Monseigneur**, It is true that the Archbishop of Canterbury does not wear such gorgeous pontificals as his brother of Sens, but in all the splendour of *this* world he outshines him infinitely.

As to the effect of religious pageantry on the mind, I suppose our age has outlived it, and it is only artists and poets, or very devout women, who feel it occasionally still. Even royalty has all but abandoned its costume, and kings make little use of their regalia, preferring for public occasions some military uniform, and for private ones the ordinary dress of a gentleman. But in the preceding ages the visible splendour of high office was an effectual strengthening of the hands of rulers, both civil and ecclesiastical, and therefore they wisely paid great attention to it.

It was a fine sight when the procession left the cathedral, and the great doors, eight hundred years old, were opened before the new bishop. There were real monks, with shaven heads and bare feet, such as we see in pictures, and the four prelates, in full pontificals, with all their attendant priests, followed by hundreds of chanting seminarists. A good many women were waiting about the door to have their babies blest by the new bishop; but in one respect the scene differed strangely from what it would have been in the middle ages. *The men did not kneel.* The men are not Catholics.

Some modern writer has complained bitterly of the separation of the sexes by their different systems of thought and education. In France the separation is very wide. The women, generally, are Catholics—the men, generally, Deists. [Note *: Within a radius of one hundred miles round Paris. In the mountainous and southern districts, and generally in places not having much communication with Paris, Catholicism is still a great power, even over men.] I have often tried to get accurately at the real state of opinion, but it is not very easy. This much, however, is certain, that most educated Frenchmen are Deists of a type not unfairly represented by M. Renan, and that nearly all Frenchwomen in good society observe the rites of the Church of Rome. The boys are Catholics when in petticoats, but turn Deists generally between fifteen and seventeen, and remain so all their lives. This difference is, of course, a cause of much estrangement in families, because a Catholic lady finds on certain subjects a companionship in her confessor which she lacks in her husband.

These facts may serve to account for what may seem such strange contradictions in modern France. The position of the Church, for instance, is both very weak and very strong. The direct power of the Church of Rome in France is infinitely smaller than that of the English Church in England, because the men are openly against it; but its indirect power, through the confessional, is still very considerable. For instance, the English Church in England is strong enough to repress the utterance of heterodox opinions in general society, but in French society such opinions are discussed with perfect freedom. On the other hand, such is the influence of the Roman Church in France over the women, that fathers who hate the priests find themselves nevertheless compelled to let their daughters confess themselves to priests, because a girl who should omit the premiére communion *would find her position amongst women perfectly unendurable. And, as Catholicism in women is* comme il faut, many men in France like girls for being Catholics, the more bigoted the better, though it is difficult to see how any union can be intellectually complete between persons who differ so widely on such an important subject as religion.

As to morality, I think there can be no doubt that France, on the whole, is a more immoral country than England; but it is an interesting fact that French mothers dread sending their boys to London, for fear of the dear innocent youths being contaminated by our bad example. The more ignorant French, too, have a horror of the shocking conduct of English girls, whom they look upon as lost to all sense of decency and propriety. Our institution of divorce, though really intended to work in the interests of morality itself, is looked upon by all well-bred Frenchwomen as abominably wrong and immoral; and they say it is hypocritical to affect to consider marriage divine and eternal, when, by our Divorce Court, we have virtually reduced it to a connection binding only during good behaviour. I think an unprejudiced observer would come to the conclusion that between young Englishmen and young Frenchmen there is really very little difference, but that (in spite of our divorce scandals) marriage is less generally respected by our neighbours than by us. That is about a fair statement of the case.

Frenchwomen are generally very active in their houses, giving the whole of the morning to busy superintendence of their servants. French ladies, even rich ones, are often excellent cooks. Their kitchens are pretty laboratories, with tiny charcoal fires sunk in tables of clean porcelain, and rows of many-sized copper-pans, shining like gold. The question as to whether a lady can cook, and still be conventionally a lady, is beyond my depth; but that a woman may be accomplished in all household duties, and still be both cultivated in mind and noble in feeling, is proved by many examples. Eugénie de Guérin is a good instance; but the French provinces abound with such. Charles Dickens had a very telling bit once about the De Quelquechoses, the great point of which was that Madame was to be seen in a morning in a plain dress, hard at work with her servants, to the astonishment of some English ladies, who visited her. And quite right too. Probably she was far too sensible a dame to run the risk of soiling a handsome dress; so she wore a plain print (often washed) when she was busy in the house, and reserved her better things for the drawing-room. [Note *: Ten to one, too, she wore a clean white cap, to keep the dust from her hair; which, to English eyes, completes the resemblance to a servant.]

The Church has survived the *noblesse,* and the bishops are the only *noblesse* which still, in ordinary conversation, receives the title of *seigneur.* This is perhaps due to the fact that episcopal rank is official and not hereditary, the natural tendency of democracy being to elevate official rank by making it the only distinction. It is difficult for an Englishman to realize how exceedingly unimportant in France are even the most ancient and authentic titles of nobility. Whether you are Count de B. or Marquis de B., you are always spoken of as Monsieur de B. Let the reader imagine how much title would be cheapened in England if our peers were always spoken of as *Mister* so-and-so, and if the public knew *and cared* as little about their titles of nobility as it does at present about their coats of arms.

The Café, an institution so dear to Frenchmen, flourishes even in this little city.

One night I went with a friend to a café here, and heard something new. We had hardly been there five minutes when our talk was interrupted by a shrill sound, so strange as to startle us all, and break at once the varied threads of at least twenty conversations. What could it be? It continued, like the warbling of a nightingale, and then burst into a wild, sad melody, softly and tenderly executed, as if on a flute. Still we felt that it was not a flute, nor yet a bird. It came, apparently, from a youth seated at a little table by himself in the middle of the café. He was playing ***upon his hands,*** using no other instrument He went on, and executed several airs from well-known operas—at first with taste and truth; then, afterwards, when he got tired, he began to play out of tune. Still it is very wonderful to be able to make so efficient a musical instrument out of one's two hands. The young man turned out to be a Portuguese, called Ferreira. [Note *: He does not ***whistle*** at all; it is pure flute-playing. The notes are produced *on* the left hand, and he plays upon it with his right. The four fingers of the left hand are opened like the letter V; two fingers on each side. The mouth is inserted in the opening, so that the tips of the fingers come near the eyes. The thumb of the right hand is placed on the palm of the left, and the fingers play freely, as it seems, in the air; but they affect every note. If the reader attempts to produce a musical sound that way he will probably fail, but Ferreira produces two octaves and a half. His ***fortissimo*** is tremendously strong, and his ***pianissimo*** as faint as the distant warbling of a lark. His musical art is very unequal; he soon tires himself, and, when tired, loses precision.]

Besides a great many cafés, and a funny little theatre, Sens supports two establishments of baths. At any hour of the day or night you may have a bath brought to your house, with water ready heated, and carried up into your bedroom, for the moderate price of sevenpence halfpenny before 10 P.M., and a shilling and a halfpenny after. The little old French wash hand basons and cream jugs are of course detestable, but the big cheap warm bath is a capital cleanser.

The French are wonderfully fond of bathing. All the ladies and gentlemen here meet early on the fine summer mornings (between five and eight o'clock) to bathe in the river—in full costumes, of course. The ladies who happen to be well made, look graceful enough in their pretty bathing dresses, but the meagre ones and the corpulent ones do not appear to advantage. The gentlemen teach their wives and sisters to swim, and there is an old sailor who gives regular lessons all the summer through. They stay in the water very long, and try to swim very energetically. Their perseverance is often rewarded by considerable proficiency in that accomplishment.

Enormous rafts of wood come down the river, and it is curious to see how two men can manage them. One stands at the bow and another at the stern. The man in front has a thick pole that he puts into the water, so that one end rests on the river's bed and the other is caught under a ledge contrived for it in the side of the raft. The end of the raft then takes a leap, exactly as a man does with a leaping pole. It is raised out of the water, and at the same time pushed aside. By repeating this operation at the four corners of the raft, whenever necessary, it is easily guided. These rafts, sometimes several hundred feet long, are picturesque objects, with their little huts and the smoke of their fires rising from a vast flow of half submerged wood. At night the rafts are moored by the river shore, and then their bright fires are highly desirable as warnings to belated *canotiers.* One very dark night, when I was rowing homewards down the stream at speed, my boat (a delicate one, by Picot of Asniéres), came into collision with one of these rafts whose fires were out. Luckily, the boat rose *upon* the raft, and received no injury; but I had a Frenchman with me whose nervous system experienced such a shock that he has never stepped into it since.

The great Pear boats are a wonderful sight. I have seen as many pears at once, in the boats, and on the quay, as would cover the floor of Westminster Hall a foot deep; and all these pears were gathered in a little circle round Sens. Indeed, I never saw a place with a market so abundantly supplied in proportion to the population. M. Déligand, the *maire,* having been struck by the same idea, took the trouble to get some statistics, which he gave me. The population is now about 11,000. On the Monday market *twenty thousand dozens* of eggs are sold, and six thousand strangers came into the town, bringing with them fifteen hundred carts. Fancy a proportionate influx of strangers into London once a week! and imagine, if you can, a proportionate quantity of eggs! And not only for its boundless abundance, but its delightful variety, is this market astonishing to an Englishman. You find so many good things that the wonder is how such a little town can eat them up. The secret is, that Sens is one of the feeders of Paris, whose provision merchants and fruiterers buy largely.

The name of our maire, M. Déligand, reminds me of one of his chief functions, that of marrying people; and this brings me to the marriage of the Rosiére. The Rosiére is a girl who bears a rose awarded to her by the authorities for her good character. Amongst the blameless virgins of the place they try to choose the most deserving. She gets a little dowry of twenty-four pounds, left by will for the purpose, and is married publicly with great éclat *by the maire on the feast of the Assumption. I was present at the last marriage of the kind in the Hotel de Ville. The court-yard was lined by a corps of* Sapeurs Pompiers (the Fire Brigade), in full military uniform, with a band. The maire and sous-préfét came in splendid ceremonial costume. All the municipal council and official persons were present. We waited some time for the fair bearer of the rose. At last she came, with her betrothed—a quiet girl, not particularly good-looking, and evidently rather bothered by the publicity of the ceremony. It must indeed have been very trying for her, the centre of all eyes, the subject of innumerable comments. I think she earned her little dowry. Not every maiden would face that ordeal for the sum of four-and-twenty pounds.

At the Hotel de Ville, where the marriage took place, is a library and little museum, whose chief treasures are some relics of Napoleon's life at St. Helena. One is a copy of Beatson's map of St. Helena, on which Napoleon had traced some plan of escape in red lines. He was hesitating, perhaps, between Europe and Brazil, for both words occur in his handwriting. A still more interesting object is an atlas, with a map of a part of Asia in it, on which Napoleon's red line *runs from Cairo to the Indus.* On the margin at the right hand are a good many figures in his handwriting:—

30,000
22,000 infanterie.
4,700 caval.
3—artil.

On the left is a rough calculation of time required. There is also Fleury de Chaboulon's book of Memoirs, with Napoleon's critical notes. His writing, at first sight apparently rather neat, is in reality very difficult to read. Though well used to French scribblings of all sorts, I never met with a more illegible hand.

I mentioned my painting-tent in the beginning of this chapter. I have had a camp on the heights for the autumnal months, guarded by a promising youth, who had just come out of prison when I engaged him, and enlisted for a soldier when I wanted him no longer. One morning, on going to my work, it struck me that Jacob looked unusually grave; and, indeed, he had a long story ready about somebody who had fired upon the painting-tent. Surely enough the tent was riddled with shot; but I felt inclined to believe that Jacob himself, who had a gun for his protection, had been, by accident or carelessness, the real author of the injury. A much more serious annoyance was the number of spectators, who thronged from all parts to see the tent; and they all made exactly the same remarks that the Lancashire peasants used to make. The Lancastrians said, "He's makin' a map;" the Burgundians say, *"Il tire un plan."* The Lancastrians said, "Isn't it cold of a neet?" the Burgundians say, *"Il doit faire froid la nuit."* The Lancastrians said, *"It's tinkers;"* the Burgundians, *"Ce sont des chaudronniers."* In the course of two months and a half thousands of people came to see the tent, and, as they all said exactly the same things and asked exactly the same questions, their visits were less amusing to me than to them. One day came mounted gendarmes, armed and terrible. Feeling perfectly guiltless, I paid no attention to their cries; so one of them, forced to dismount, came heavily on foot, ascending the steep against his will. When he got to the tent at last, he was very much out of breath, and out of temper too. It appeared that my imprudent Jacob had been amusing himself with shooting in the air, and that the shot had fallen on a gentleman on horseback (riding leisurely on the public road below), and that the horse, unaccustomed to that sort of rain, had been unpleasantly restive in consequence. So the gentleman had lodged a complaint, and Jacob got severely reprimanded, which didn't seem to affect his serenity. Indeed, I never saw a youth endowed with such enviable serenity of mind. Scolding had no effect upon him; and he had a little, jaunty, self-satisfied manner which never failed him under the most trying circumstances. It was capital to hear him tell the story of his imprisonment, and the fight which led to it. He had been dancing at an open-air ball, and some *bourgeois* in tailcoats had resented the intrusion of Jacob and one or two other blouses. On this the blouses maintained their rights; and, when the police came to see what was the matter, the gallant blouses fought both the tailcoats and the police. Who would not fight bravely in such a position, inflamed with wine, and under the very eyes of beauty? But the blouses were vanquished and marched off to prison, and the hated bourgeois danced in triumph.

CHAPTER II.

THE SLOPES OF GOLD.

A SMALL piece of orchard and vineyard ground on the heights of the Côte d'Or came into the present writer's possession by events which it is not necessary to recount here. The land in itself is of little value, but the position of it is so fine that it is the very place for an encampment. The reader is requested to picture to himself the three tents in this delightful situation. There is no use in describing camp life in itself; we have already had enough of that, down to very minute details. Let us rather see what can interest us in the country round about the camp.

First, the great plain at our feet, stretching away to the Jura. It seems infinitely vast; and as the cloud shadows fall on its remote villages, and creep from farm to farm, from castle to castle, darkening a thousand groves in turn, innumerable details come forth and are brought into momentary prominence. At the first glance it seems as if a flat plain like this would soon have told its story; but after gazing at it for an hour, we begin to perceive that it has not one story to reveal, but rather an infinite succession of revelations. Day after day we may come to it, and every day find a fresh reading. Like those magic Eastern inscriptions which changed from hour to hour, this prodigious sheet of land changes from minute to minute.

We are on the stony height, a little above the best vine land; but just below us runs that wonderful line of vineyards which extends, with little interruption, to the banks of the Yonne in the north, and southwards by those of the Rhone. And here we are in the richest vineyards of them all. It is a land of wine; they say there is more wine in it than water; the people all drink wine, and talk wine, and *think* wine. From the wealthy proprietor, or successful wine merchant, down to the poorest working vinedresser, the whole soul of the population is steeped in vintages.

An old friend of mine being a wine merchant in these regions, I have seen all the principal cellars. It was agreed between us that I should accompany him for two or three days on a purchasing tour. We started early one morning in a carriage, and set about our business systematically. Wine merchants have little shallow silver cups, with shining bosses at the bottom to see the colour and clearness of the wine. One of these cups my Mend gave me.

I foresee some difficulty if I am to go on calling this wine merchant "my friend," "my companion," and so on, all through this chapter. Why not call him by his name?—it can do him no possible harm; it involves no breach of confidence. His name is Charles Rasse. [Note *: Of course, I have M. Rasse's permission to mention his name.]

Rasse gave me one of those little shallow silver cups, and it was my luck in the course of that tour to see the bright little bosses coloured by the ruby of all the famous vineyards in Burgundy. Our days were dedicated to business, and yet passed in an unremitting sacrifice to Bacchus. We began tasting almost as soon as the carriage started on its road, and we continued, with short intervals employed in driving rapidly from cellar to cellar, village to village, until nearly noon, when we had déjeuner, *prepared by a cook of local celebrity. Now, for a cook to be at all eminent in Burgundy is as difficult as it is for a surgeon to make himself famous in Paris; for Burgundy is the land of good living, and all Burgundians are professed* gourmets. *My impression about that* déjeuner was that, as I had to drink of all the wines in the country, so I was doomed to eat of all its dishes; and the worst of it was, that the repast in question, instead of being a relief from the wine-tasting, was, if possible, an intensification of it. We had now not merely to taste, but to drink. Rasse, being experienced in such work, had always taken the precaution, in the wine cellars, of expectorating every drop that passed his lips; but I had not yet been able to bring myself to that sinful wastefulness, and had honestly swallowed every sample. So we did not start fair; and then Rasse is a Burgundian by birth, and good wine is just as natural to him as water to a Scotch Highlander.

After déjeuner arrived a neighbouring gentleman with bottles of white wine from his own cellar, of whose extraordinary virtues we were to judge experimentally. So we drank these with him, and then continued our tour. How many cellars we visited I really cannot tell, but they cannot have been fewer than fifty, and on the average we tasted say eight casks in each cellar, that would give four hundred tastings, which is probably about the mark. By the time the work was done, I was utterly weary of Burgundy, and the more that we had it at every meal. Of course, I soon got over my scruples against spitting the wine out, and tried to imitate Rasse not only in that, but also in the brook-like gurgling sound that wine merchants make, and which they seem to consider essential to a right appreciation of different vintages. Hearing so much wine-talk too, I amused myself occasionally by pretending to know something about the subject, and by mere accident made remarks which caused me to be looked upon as a judge. The great point is to give yourself the requisite airs. If you can do the gurgling neatly and melodiously, expectorate vigorously and far, and then look very grave and wise for a few seconds without saying anything, you are sure to be respected, and your opinion will be listened to with deference.

The quantities of wine kept in those cellars in Burgundy are prodigious. It is not my business to give statistical information, as I only talk about what strikes me; but some of the larger wine-growers have whole armies of casks, and cellars like railway tunnels. The wealth of the peasant growers is often very considerable. You may frequently meet a rough-looking man in a blue blouse and wooden shoes who has three or four thousand pounds' worth of wine in cask, besides valuable landed property and buildings. One such at Volnay, living in the simplest manner, made us drink some bottled wine that he had kept fourteen years; but I prefer it seven years younger. The union of easy fortune with the habits and education of the poor is a social phenomenon which I have never seen so frequently as in Burgundy, except in the Lancashire cotton district, especially the neighbourhood of Oldham. In one sense the rich peasant is the richest of men, in the proportion of his large means to his little wants; but in another sense is he not just as poor as the common labourer? His money opens for him no new fields of intellectual advancement; it does not improve him as a human being. He has leisure at command, but can make no use of it; he might buy books, but he could not read them; he might travel, but he does not know where to go, or what to go anywhere for. The benefit and enjoyment which he has are the peace of security and the pride of possession. These are no doubt sweet, and he sucks their sweetness all day long.

The Clos Vougeot, as most readers will already know, is a small property inclosed with a wall, and yielding the best wine in Burgundy. It is not so generally known that this inclosure contains a very fine old building, like a château, where the business of the wine making and that of its preservation have been carried on for six hundred years. The exterior of this structure is imposing but plain; the courtyard is picturesque in the highest degree. The cellars are of course immense, and exceedingly well kept As to the quality of the wine, it is, in my humble opinion, exactly on the same level as two or three other of the very best Burgundies, and does not deserve that isolated pre-eminence which fame has given it There is no *better* wine in France, however. Drink of this quality is lost on Englishmen (except exceptions) and it is a sin to throw it away on them. Thinking I could take no more acceptable present to some English friends than a few bottles of Clos Vougeot, I found that the gentlemen (sherry drinkers) considered it a variety of "Gladstone," and the ladies (lovers of sugary champagne) compared it to red ink; and that *was* Clos Vougeot, perfectly authentic and pure. It is certain that English palates are generally quite incapable of *tasting the taste* on which the fame of such wine is founded. We are not prepared for it as the inhabitants of the country are, by drinking nothing but inferior wines of the same species: *they* recognise the superiority at once, and feel the value of the quality which constitutes it. The consequence of this incapacity to taste, is that Englishmen dare not buy wine on their own judgment, but must put confidence in their wine merchant I know a wine-merchant in Burgundy who does a large business in England, and I know another who, ***with the very same*** *wines,* could hardly get any customers at all, the difference being entirely due to a difference of confidence. They say in Burgundy that when the English believe in you they buy blindly, whereas, until you get them to that point, they are most difficult to deal with, because they have no judgment of their own to which you may appeal. The Belgians, on the contrary, are able judges; and a young merchant going amongst them with good wine at a fair price is recognised at once. The Swiss are sometimes good judges also, but the Parisians are nearly as bad as the English.

The same laws which govern the trade in art govern that in wine. When there is little knowledge to appeal to, the name is more than the thing. "This is Clos Vougeot, and I got it of—," is equivalent to "This is a Claude; it belonged to—." If judgment were perfect, there would be no need of names, and no advantage in them; things would then be sold for their qualities.

The landscape of the Côte d'Or may be very briefly described as to its chief characteristics. It is the first rising of the highlands of the Morvan out of the great plain; and as the plain is so vast that no shadow, except that of a cloud, falls on this steep bank, and as the soil is excellent for the vine, the slope is exactly fitted by nature for the production of grapes. The côte is occasionally interrupted by a rocky ravine and is itself often rugged. The buildings are not generally picturesque, because the people are too well off; but the churches are often interesting, and the town of Beaune, with its glorious Gothic hospital, and walls, and towers, is a capital place for an etcher. How I wish Méryon could be induced to spend a year there! The château of Savigny is very grand in its way, and has a good staircase inside, which the owner kindly showed me. I particularly admired the massiveness of its round *tourelles.*

There was another château far up in the hills that Rasse took me to see—a picturesque one also, but incredibly rough, and bearing about the same relation to an ordinary gentleman's house that the piece of agate you pick up on the sea-shore does to a piece which has passed through the hands of the lapidary. In the grand staircase the steps looked as if they had been hewn with an axe. This château, however, was probably only built for a hunting seat.

After leaving this wild place amongst the upper forests, we followed a narrow country road which led us into a remote valley—a valley which seemed to me so exquisitely peaceful and beautiful that I wanted very much to live there; and as this desire was perfectly serious, Rasse took me to see a large mansion which was for sale—a charming place, with pleasant gardens and fountains, and a delightful view down all the little valley. The only fault of this place was that it seemed likely to be beyond my purse—a consideration which often arrests the inquirer after desirable places of residence. I mention this hankering of mine, because the reader is going to make the acquaintance of the capitalist who did eventually purchase that mansion.

We entered a straggling village, and Rasse asked if I were hungry. I pleaded guilty to the soft impeachment. The reader thinks it absurd to call an implied accusation of hunger a "soft impeachment." He does not know the story which the expression recalls to the initiated, and so, whilst Rasse is going on with the carriage, I will tell it him.

A country lad in Lancashire took to reading, and became so fond of that deleterious occupation that he got to be fit for nothing but a schoolmaster. So his friends sent him to Liverpool to be taught that trade, and as he had walked more than thirty miles, his master's wife asked if he were not hungry. After seeking a moment for a phrase of suitable elegance fitted for urbane society, he replied that he "pleaded guilty to the soft impeachment."

Being in the same condition as this polite youth, I was not ill pleased when my friend said to me, "I know a peasant here who will be glad to see us, and give us déjeuner," and we stopped at the bottom of a picturesque external stair, at the top of which appeared a peasant with a red face, gold earrings, blue blouse, and sabots—a jolly, friendly-looking man.

He took the horse to the stable, and in a minute ascended the stair with us. It was a clean simple room with beds in it, a stove, a table in the middle, covered with a tablecloth so coarse that it seemed as if one looked at it through a microscope, knives and forks, and tumbler-glasses. On the stove were many plates heating, and at two sides of the stove sat two sable priests, warming themselves like the plates.

Now, as a priest, when not in the presence of his bishop, or of some pious lady who has a lofty ideal of the priestly character, is usually the joiliest of festive companions, I was by no means sorry to make the acquaintance of these two comfortable *cures.* It is said by profound philosophers that, in order to enjoy thoroughly a good thing that we possess, it is necessary to have some still better and more desirable enjoyment in prospect. That explains why these priests looked so extremely happy by the stove; the heat of it was agreeable, but a still more agreeable pleasure awaited them—the long delight of an elaborate déjeuner.

Some readers may not have had the advantage of taking breakfast with a rich Burgundian peasant the day he entertains his spiritual pastors, and such can have little idea of what a breakfast of that sort consists of. It is not a simple meal of coffee and eggs, but rather a dinner, or two dinners, three dinners, four dinners, served in rapid succession. Rasse whispered to me that we could not have been more fortunate; for where priests fed the pasture was sure to be good.

"Approach yourselves then of the fire," said the old grey-haired priest; "it makes cold to-day. Come you from far?"

In five minutes we were engaged in a conversation on the one wearisome Burgundian topic, the vintage. This lasted till the mistress of the house entered from the inner regions, followed by her daughter and heiress, a fresh-looking girl of fifteen. She welcomed us cordially, and shortly announced that we might sit down to table.

On this the master and the priests sat down, and Rasse and I sat down; but the mistress and her daughter sat not down neither then nor during all the hours that the repast lasted. They served us, and we ate and ate.

Knowing well what to expect, I reserved myself as much as possible. We had soup, of course;—a peasant begins his déjeuner **with soup, which, in the upper classes, no one would dare to serve or venture to like before five in the evening. After the soup came, as usual, beef boiled to rags, and divested of every particle of nutriment. This it is wisest to leave to Frenchmen, who can digest anything. But I knew that better food would come, according to the emperor's sagacious maxim,** "Tout vient à celui qui sait attendre," and I adopted the policy of a masterly inactivity.

We had countless dishes of meat and poultry and game, and at last an elaborate dessert. By the time we had done we had been sitting four hours, and the table was covered with emptied or half-emptied bottles. And during all those hours our host never uttered two consecutive sentences, but only asked us briefly to eat and drink, for the two priests talked so fast and so loudly, and so energetically, that nobody could get a word in. The more they drank the louder they talked; and at last came a moment when they could no longer continue their controversy on their chairs, but rose up to their feet and argued standing for more than an hour, with fierce and violent gesticulation.

And what was all this fiery controversy about? It was about a pinch of snuff. Here it is, epitomised:—

First, how it began—When we had well drunk, the grey priest offered a pinch of snuff to the company, our host accepted, Rasse accepted, I accepted, and sneezed for five minutes without intermission, but the young black-haired priest stoutly refused. He never took snuff, he said It was just one of those opportunities which any one who has the spirit of persecution, the instinct which compels others to conformity, will not allow to pass unimproved. The moment had arrived for the assertion and maintenance of a great principle. "I take snuff, the majority takes snuff, you, a contemptible minority, dare to assume the right not to take snuff, then I say you *shall* take snuff."—"I will not" "But you ought."—"No, I oughtn't" "But you ought, and you shall."—"There is no moral obligation on me to put any snuff up my nose." "But I say there is, under the circumstances." [Note *: As the reader is sure to think that all this is pure fiction, I give him my word of honour that the whole scene, from beginning to end, is as near literal truth as I can possibly get it. It loses a great deal by translation and abridgment; but if I had written it in French, as I thought of doing at first, many readers would have skipped it; and if I had not abridged it, the dialogue would have occupied a hundred pages of this impression. Of course, I do not give the name of the place where it occurred, for fear of injuring the younger priest; the elder is since dead.]

When this had gone on for a minute or two, the grey priest got exasperated and stood up, giving a sweep with his arm which knocked over a bottle and broke our hostess's handsomest glass water-jug—an accident that threw a cloud over her face for the rest of that day, and I have no doubt to this hour embitters her recollection of it.

OLD PRIEST—(with the greatest gravity and in full oratorical style)—You have violated the rules of courtesy. I offered you my box: that box contained a powder which, for the moment, represented my friendly feelings towards all to whom I offered it. Are you aware, sir, that it was not a simple material powder that I tendered you, and that you scornfully refused, but the feelings which produce good companionship? No, no, interrupt me not. It is in vain for you to deny the fact; you have been guilty of a gross breach of good manners. Have you never, when a child, read a small treatise from which you still, in mature years, might learn much that would be profitable to you—"Of Civility, Puerile and Polite?" Therein you would have found a principle laid down which might have guided you in your present difficulty, and saved you from a solecism which, I venture to assert, has lowered you in the opinion of all present. Gentlemen, your generosity prompts you to intervene to shield this offender from my just indignation, but you well know that his conduct is utterly indefensible. Every boy knows that when any thing is offered him out of good fellowship, he cannot refuse it without hurting and injuring the person who offers it. I feel hurt—I have a right to complain; I have been wounded in my feelings; I—

During the last dozen lines the young priest had been on his legs too, and talking just as loudly as the other.

YOUNG PRIEST—I never intended to hurt your feelings—I don't want to hurt anybody's feelings; but I have a right to my own nose. You like snuff; well, then, take it. If these gentlemen like snuff, they do right to take it; but I don't like it at all—it is positively disagreeable to me, so I decline it. I don't decline your fellowship; I eat with you, I drink with you—

THE AUTHOR (thinking that probably the old priest could not smoke and the young one could)—And most likely you would smoke with him, would you not?

YOUNG PRIEST—My dear, good, kind gentleman, nothing would please me better just now than to smoke with you, and him too, if he will.

THE AUTHOR (handing his cigar-case to the old priest first)—Will you accept a cigar? (then to the younger)—And you?

Young priest accepts with avidity, and seizes the author's hand, which he holds long and presses warmly; old priest declines firmly.

THE AUTHOR *to Old Priest*—Sir, you are now guilty of the offence you impute to your brother across the table, and that to its fullest extent. I offer you a cigar: that cigar is not a miserable roll of dried tobacco leaves; it is a portion of my heart—an expression of good-will and kindly convivial feeling. You refuse me, you reject me, you scorn my friendly advances; I consider myself aggrieved, I am hurt, I am wounded.

OLD PRIEST—But I can't smoke, and I can't bear to be where people smoke; and if you smoke here, I protest against it—it is most offensive to me.

THE AUTHOR—Is a miserable consideration for your own ease to make you forget the rules of courtesy? Is it not all the more your duty to smoke, that it makes you ill? Is not this precisely one of those cases where a man is called upon to sacrifice his own ease to the happiness of others? It is necessary that you should smoke, merely to conform to the custom of the people you are with. We all smoke; you must and shall consume this cigar.

OLD PRIEST—The two cases are entirely different.

YOUNG PRIEST—I have as much right to my nose as you have to the tranquillity of your stomach.

OLD PRIEST—What would you do if your bishop offered you a pinch of snuff? would you refuse it? I say you wouldn't.

YOUNG PRIEST—Well, if I didn't, I should only pretend to value it, but really dribble it away quietly on the floor.

OLD PRIEST—That was precisely your duty in the present instance. If you could not take the snuff, you should have accepted it nevertheless, and then allowed the powder to fall gently upon your clothes in imitating the action of taking a pinch.

YOUNG PRIEST—I believe you are a Jesuit.

OLD PRIEST—And you're another.

YOUNG PRIEST—I want to smoke. Our host permits: these gentlemen are waiting your leave to light their cigars. Can you selfishly refuse it?

OLD PRIEST—I decidedly object to smoking.

OUR HOST—If you will let us smoke, I will bring you some more wine.

Exit host. Re-enter host with six bottles of white Burgundy of different growths—two under each arm, one in each hand. General murmurs of applause.

Old priest relents. We are all reconciled. Young priest gets very polite to our hosts pretty daughter, who now enters the room.

Our hospitable entertainer in the blouse bought the mansion, with its gardens, and fountains, and woods; and he left the little cottage where we feasted that day, and went to live in the great house. He was one of that numerous class of steady savers which exists in France. They save quietly every year, and nobody notices them; but at last they suddenly astonish us by making some wonderful purchase. When we left the two priests at the top of the little stair, they returned to table to finish the white wine, and after that they had dinner, and after that more wine, till it was quite late, and then they got home somehow to bed.

The elder of them told us that he had lately knocked down the doctor under the following circumstances:—The doctor was very deaf, and came one night late to see the priest "Who goes there?" no answer, so he knocked him down. This reminded me of what had very nearly been a tragic incident. A relation of mine heard one night a noise down stairs, so he jumped out of bed, took his loaded fowling-piece, and made his way in the dark to the place the noise seemed to come from. He distinctly heard stealthy footsteps on the carpet. "Who are you?" No answer. "Answer me, or I will fire upon you!" No answer. He lifted the gun to his shoulder, and had the finger on the trigger, when the intruder coughed. He knew the cough at once: it was a deaf old lady who lived with him, and had come down stairs to seek for something.

It is probable that my ecclesiastical companions would have been rather better on their guard if they had suspected me of being an Englishman; but they took me for a Frenchman all the time, and it seemed better not to undeceive them. Peculiar circumstances in my life have made me what is called a bilingual, and I enjoy easy access to all country people in France, because they never take me for a foreigner. In Paris it is different The English abound there, and my English face betrays me; besides, when people *see* you are an Englishman, they **hear** your English accent, when it would else be imperceptible. A very amusing instance of this occurred to a lady I know intimately. She came to settle in a country town, where, for some reason, a rumour went abroad that she was an American. Several ladies went to call upon her, and complimented her on speaking French so well for an American, though of course, they always added, the foreign accent was still very perceptible. Now, the fact is, that the lady in question not only was not an American, but was a genuine Frenchwoman, born of French parents, bred in France, and never out of it in her life except once for a month at Brussels. Her husband, too, was a Frenchman; and neither he nor she had any foreign accent whatever, nor any peculiarity of accent, except a slight Burgundian twang, which, as the little town in question was situated in Burgundy, ought not to have sounded American. ***Moral:*** If people can hear an accent which does not exist, when they wrongly believe the person to be a foreigner, by so much the more will they hear it when it ***does*** exist, if they ***know*** the person to be avowedly a foreigner. To escape suspicion altogether, an Englishman perfectly master of French may say that he comes from another part of France, or that he is a Frenchman who has lived a year or two in England.

In parting with these two jolly priests, let me cite an anecdote which is narrated of one of them. Being one day at the table of his bishop, ***monseigneur*** deigned to ask his opinion of the wine. "Bonus vinum," said the priest. The bishop was rather surprised at such an exhibition of weak latinity, but kindly said nothing. Later in the evening he again asked the priest's opinion on wine, but this time of far superior quality. "Bonum vinum," answered the priest. "May I ask," said the bishop, "why, when I last referred to your judgment, you made ***vinum*** masculine, whereas now you conform to the more common practice, and make it neuter?"

*"**A petit vin, petit Latin,**"* said the ***cure.***

CHAPTER III.

SECOND HEAD QUARTERS.—A FARM IN THE AUTUNOIS.

IT being understood that there is no further necessity for dwelling on the details of camp life, I still continue the policy adopted throughout this third book; and, looking round me attentively, but never purposely seeking literary material, briefly note down anything that seems likely to amuse or interest the reader.

On leaving the "little French city" I found a country house which suited me, in the basin of Autun. It has a good deal of land attached to it, which is not in my occupation. The farmer lives near me, and the only land I am troubled with is a large garden and a little wood, both bounded by a clear and rapid stream.

As to the camp, I have it yet in good working condition, and use it occasionally still; but in this beautiful climate a painting tent is scarcely necessary, except for winter studies. And the summers are so long and so splendid that it is possible to accumulate, in the fine weather, abundant materials for studio work when it rains. It is nevertheless the fact that the tents are still pitched from time to time in these regions, which gives me a fair excuse for including these chapters in the narrative of the Camp.

The natural configuration of the country is curious and interesting. As the traveller passes from Dijon to Lyons by the railway, he sees upon his left hand the heights of the Côte d'Or. That is the beginning of an elevated tract of country which culminates in the Beuvray, a hill of rather fine form, but not a mountain, and then descends to the Nivernais and the Loire. Round about the Beuvray lies a region of hilly land, densely covered with wood. This is the Morvan. French people generally have a most exaggerated idea of these Morvan highlands; they tell you it is Switzer-

land over again, which is nonsense. The plain truth is, that the Morvan is a highly
picturesque and salubrious region, enjoying a climate as fine as that of the Burgundy
wine country, but cooler, and with hills just high enough to give very varied and
agreeable distances whichever way you look. Though not so grand as Switzerland,
it is, as a place of residence, preferable to it. It seemed more prudent, too, in my
own case, to study landscape of a comparatively humble kind, and I found here
the two conditions of good climate and available material united in perfection. I
was anxious to be in a neighbourhood where the work of agriculture was done by
oxen, and here they universally employ them. The oxen used here are of a very fine
race, the **Charolaise:** there is also an inferior, but still picturesque, native race, the
Morvandelle. The Charolais ox is usually large, and of a cream white or tawny; the
Morvandeau is small, and often quite black, or black and white. Another great point
with me was that there should be picturesque buildings within an easy drive of my
house, and these I have in great abundance, for Autun is full of them, and most of
the farms and villages round are good subjects for an artist. In water we are tolerably well off also, having a good many tarns, or large fish-ponds, several beautiful
streams, and a river. There are plenty of magnificent trees, especially some very
ancient chestnuts, and the whole series of plants from the land of the vine to the
land of heather and furze.

The people who inhabit these highlands differ in race, language, and manners from those in the plain. This country has always been a poorer country than
the Côte d'Or, and consequently the people are more frugal. No contrast could be
greater than the ways of living on the hills and in the lowlands. The *Morvandeau*
is as sober as the true Burgundian is given to good eating and drinking. It is only
quite recently that the Morvandeau has begun to drink wine at all; a generation
back, many of them did not know the taste of it, and nobody but the rich drank it
habitually. Beer, too, was unknown, and coffee and tea never so much as thought
of, the only drinks being water, milk, and a kind of mead. To this day much of this
extreme sobriety is retained in ordinary life, and only laid aside from time to time at
festivals and fairs. The peasants drink little else than water; the rude labours of the
harvest are carried through without other refreshment than the contents of a water
jug; and the only animal food commonly used is what can be got out of the wearers

of silken attire, by which elegant periphrase they are accustomed to designate their pigs.

The Morvandeaux being an isolated and peculiar people, they are, of course, disliked by the inhabitants of the lowlands, who impute to them many odious faults, especially ferocity and ill-nature. No doubt, if you come amongst the Morvandeaux, or amongst any race of men whatever, with the preconceived notion that they are not to be trusted, and then treat them in such manner as to let them clearly see that you despise and suspect them,—no doubt, if you act so, you act in the very best manner to bring about such usage of yourself as will justify your strongest prejudice. But if, on the other hand, you treat the people with kindness and confidence, you are likely to see quite a different aspect of their character. The Morvandeau may be, if you use him ill, all that his enemies say to his disadvantage, but I have always found him exceedingly civil and disposed to render service. I may mention one little trait of character here, which seems to me to speak in the people's favour. If they have a vacant seat in a conveyance, and pass a traveller on foot, they very seldom omit to offer it to him. This has occurred to me certainly scores of times, and I believe I might truly say hundreds of times. And it is done by people of all ranks, and so habitually as to be thought quite simple and natural. It is the custom of the country, and a custom, in my opinion, which goes far to disprove any general accusation of sullenness against its inhabitants.

Of course, the poor hill-peasant is considered avaricious, as all people are who, having small means, attempt to save for their children; but this is really only what, when practised by richer people in exactly the same proportion to their means, we are accustomed to praise as a wise foresight. The peasant of the Morvan has a fixed notion about his duty to his children which is exceedingly onerous to him. He does not say, "I got a thousand pounds from my father, therefore my five children must have two hundred pounds a piece;" but he says, "I got a thousand pounds from my father, therefore my five children must have a thousand pounds a piece." Imagine the consequences of such a theory in the excesses of frugality to which it leads. The theory cannot always be put into practice to its full extent, but it is the accepted idea of what is right, and an attempt—often a very long and arduous effort—is made to realise it. Again, I find that the peasants here have all the capitalist's way of thinking, rather than the way current amongst those classes whose earnings are large and capital small These peasants do not estimate each others importance by the way they live, but by the amount they are able to give to their children in marriage. Imagine consideration wholly detached from current expenditure, and fixed exclusively on capital, and think what an effect that would have on the society of great cities! It is not too much to say that if such a revolution in opinion were to occur in Paris, half the expenditure there would cease at once. And the peasant of the Morvan is just as independent of outlay for the improvement of his mind as he is of outlay for the sake of appearance. His idea of duty to his children is severe and onerous, as we have seen, but it does not include the most elementary conception of any necessity for educating them. He does not buy newspapers or books, and of course he never travels to amuse himself. His recreation, when he is young, is to dance at marriage feasts and on minor occasions, and, when old, to get tipsy now and then with old fellows like himself when they meet at the market town.

It would be easy to sketch characters from the life in classes superior to the peasantry, but several reasons forbid it. I have a few intimate friends in the neighbourhood, but scarcely any acquaintances; and the idea of serving up one's friends, even though they be Frenchmen, in order that their little peculiarities may afford amusement to the public, and help to sell one's book, is not to be entertained for a moment. Besides, I am far too well acquainted with the French people to write those dashing sketches which require, for their success, the raw foreigner's point of view, his sense of novelty in everything, and his rooted belief that everything which is not exactly what he is accustomed to at home is an infringement, either ridiculous or sinful, of the fundamental laws of the universe. To illustrate this by a real example, I may mention a Frenchman who travelled the whole length of England, and returned to France with one predominant idea about us, which idea was this—"What huge pieces of cheese are served on English tables!" It had happened that at the very first hotel he stayed at there was a gigantic wedge of Cheshire, not yet much cut into, and this so astonished the Frenchman, whose first thought had been, "I can *never* eat all that!" that he never got over it, and to this day tells me of it every time I see him. Now, that is exactly the state of mind in which the amusing traveller lives and writes; and Englishmen who publish books about the French do so for the most part whilst yet in that early stage of amazement at trifles of no consequence. On the one hand they see luxuries they are not accustomed to, and then they cry out how extravagant the French are; then they are shocked by the absence of other luxuries which habit has rendered indispensable to themselves, and they exclaim against French parsimony. But suppose that my friend of the big cheese had lived in England a few years, is it not probable that he would have become accustomed to the sight of a few pounds of Cheshire, and in time even indifferent to it, whilst gradually ideas about us might have formed themselves in his mind above and beyond this first conception of us as eaters of big cheeses?

The French are exceedingly fond of a country life in fine summer weather, but they prefer to winter in towns; and every landowner of any consequence has a town house, or at least a few rooms in some provincial centre, where he meets his own set. What always surprises me in these arrangements is the contentment with which the inhabitants of some spacious château migrate to narrow lodgings, just at the very time of the year when people stay most in doors, and consequently when space is most valuable. It seems, however, a convenient plan to make the nearest town the capital of its own district, as the people all know each other, and the annual removals cause little expense or trouble. There is not a single country gentleman in this neighbourhood who has not a town house either in Autun, or Châlon, or Dijon, sometimes very dismal ones in comparison with their pleasant summer residences. I know an old bachelor who, being uncommonly good-natured, makes his annual migration to Autun for no other reason than because, if he gave it up, his servants, who enjoy the sociability of the little city, would be too much disappointed. Married men often go to please their wives, and I know an instance where the lady, who likes the country all the year round, goes to the town to please her husband. It may generally be observed that whoever in a household has the common custom on his side, will easily carry his point, even against the tastes of a majority.

A practical objection to this system is that the country houses, not being inhabited at the season of the year when they most want it, are liable to deterioration by damp. Anywhere north of Lyons the French winter is just as bad as the English, and as the French are not in the habit of keeping good fires in rooms they do not actually use, they often find their country houses unpleasantly damp when they come back to them in April. The woodwork decays, the papers fall off, the bedding is unfit for immediate use, and you hear of bad colds and attacks of rheumatism. Where there are libraries and collections of prints, the owners, of course, learn that constant fires are indispensable; but small proprietors keep their few books in their town dwelling, which is in every way the more luxurious of the two; and the ***maison de campagne*** is so simple that it would be dreary and wretched without the glory of sunshine, which is indeed so great and splendid a luxury that it supplies the want of all others.

Perhaps a brief description of three châteaux, of very different degrees of pretension, may not be without interest. The most splendid of the three, Sully, is the principal seat of the MacMahons. An Irish surgeon, towards the end of the last century, settled in this part of the world with a view to professional occupation, and married a very great heiress of noble family, to whom Sully and other estates belonged. From this marriage descends the present famous Field-Marshal the Duke of Magenta. The château is a magnificent quadrangle with corner towers outside, the court of quite palatial architecture, as good as the best bits of the Tuileries. There are some noble rooms, one great hall especially, with stately chimney-pieces and baronial furniture. One or two of the old bed-rooms, with tapestry and quaint beds, are very tempting subjects for an artist. Some modern "improvements "have much injured the building as seen from the outside, though happily the noble court is quite well preserved. It is especially regretable that the new chapel should be of bad Gothic, entirely out of harmony with the rest of the building, which is Renaissance.

Another very good specimen of the true French château, though not nearly so magnificent as Sully, is Monjeu. It is situated on the crown of the hills above Autun, and buried in great woods of fine timber, with an opening in front through which the eye ranges, first over a great garden, by Lenôtre, between terraced avenues, and then from crest to crest of far-waving hills to a remote horizon. The place is all but abandoned by its owner, and the stiff courtly garden, so perfect a background for scenes of high life in the time of Louis Quinze, has gained from neglect a melancholy in the highest degree poetical. Vast were the labours that filled the ravine with earth, and held it there with a gigantic wall of masonry fit for a modern fortress; and delicate the art and care with which the costly level had been laid out with walks and beds, with fountain and with lawn. Broad flights of stairs, whose stones were separated by slow forces of vegetation, mighty as levers of iron; statues lichen-spotted, ivy-garlanded; vase and baluster tottering together over the silent terraces;—all these have expression, and expression of the kind to which every true artist is most sensitive. And in the château itself are a score of high tapestried chambers all deserted, and a great hall with carved and painted wainscoting fading in the suns of summer after summer.

In a very retired situation amongst the hills on the other side of the valley stands a little château of the most humble pretensions. As it is to let, and I once had some notion of becoming its inhabitant, I took care to visit every nook and corner in the place. It has the essentials of a real château—round corner towers, a chapel, and a spacious garden; but the roughness of it is such that it would take ten years' rent to make it comfortable. There is, however, something very delightful in the quaint arrangement of these houses; the numerous round towers give many little cell-like closets,—tiny rooms, often of great use to an inhabitant with various occupations; and it seems as if one would get strongly attached to a house with so marked a character of its own; whereas the usual London house, or middle-class country villa, has scarcely more individuality than a cab or an omnibus. Of all the faults of a house, the most hateful is that total want of interest which results from uninventiveness in the planning of it. When you pass a manufacturer's box with five windows in the front and a door in the middle, you know the distribution of the interior as well as if the outer walls were of plate-glass. The habitation which the mind itself may dwell in with contentment must have some variety to interest and amuse the mind. This variety the quaint little château possessed, and therefore, rough as it is, I would more willingly live in it than in many a better-built and more convenient mansion.

Close to this château is a hill which is the scene of fairy legends. People lived on the top of the hill, and lamented the hardness of their lot in having to fetch water from the little river in the valley. So two fairies came to their aid and carried the water up the hill-side. But before they had reached the top, one of them said to the other, "With the help of God, we shall get there at last;" and the other impiously answered, "With or WITHOUT the help of God!" on which the water immediately spilled itself, and now flows from that very spot in a perpetual spring.

When the fairies died out of the land, one of them was transformed into a serpent, and set to guard an immense treasure in a cave in the hill. Before the mouth of this cave was rolled a great stone; but on Sundays, during divine service, the stone rolled back and left the cave open. Now a village woman who had heard of the treasure went to the cave the day of the Fête Dieu. *And, behold, the cave was open, and its floor was all covered with scattered gold and gems. And the woman took her little child with her into the cave, and set it on a table in the middle, and gave it an apple to amuse it whilst she gathered the fairy treasure. And she filled her pockets, and her apron, and the folds of her skirts with gold. Then, suddenly remembering that the service would shortly end, she rushed out of the cave with her booty. A minute afterwards she thought about the child, and looked back, but, lo, the cave was shut, and the child shut up in it. Then she flung the gold and the gems away, scattering them like rain in the mountain grass, and she ran down to the village and told all to the priest. The priest came, and all the villagers with him, to the spot where the woman had scattered the treasure, and they picked it all up, every piece of gold and every precious jewel. Then the priest kept the treasure carefully for one year, and on the next* Fête Dieu he sent the woman with it to the fairy's cave. And she found the cave open as before, and saw her little child still sitting on the table, still playing with the apple she had given him, but the serpent lay coiled round the foot of the table. Then the woman restored all that she had taken, and took away her child, and returned to the village glad at heart.

The Morvan is a region where superstitions have a surprising vitality. Miracles are of quite frequent occurrence, and testified by a thousand witnesses. The incumbent of a village called Ars, a man of saintly character and great benevolence, proved his divine mission by repeating in the present generation many of the miracles of Jesus. It is only a few years since he died, yet the popular faith has magnified him into a mythic personage. Critics who feel any embarrassment about the origin of legends should live a year or two in a country like this, learn its **patois,** and make acquaintances amongst the devout peasantry. They would see legends grow vigorously from little seeds, and would familiarise themselves with a very curious and interesting fact in human nature, which it is absolutely necessary to take into account if we would rightly understand the past.

When any one is ill, they take his shirt and dip it in St Michael's spring; if that fails, and the patient can bear travel, he may go on pilgrimage to a saint's shrine on the mountain. Every year a great crowd passes the whole night there, and beholds a miracle.

This saint is quite modern, of the present century, and consequently not yet even canonized. She was married to a soldier of Napoleon, who, the very day of the wedding, was called away to the wars. For seven years she waited (in legends, absences are always of seven years), when another lover persuaded her to marry him. But the day of the second marriage the first husband returned. Both claimed her, so she announced her resolution to live with neither, but devote herself to religious meditation. With this view she ascended the hills behind Autun, and being very weary needed refreshment, when, lo! a spring gushed for her from the dry rock. She fixed her hermitage near the spot, and, after living a holy life, died there. The spring became a resort of pilgrims from villages far and near. They came with bottles, and filled them with the miraculous water, and carried it home to sick friends, who found health in the blessed draught. Then the priests, who in Catholic countries willingly consecrate all popular superstitions not absolutely incompatible with Christian dogma, saw vitality enough in this to induce them to take it under their patronage. So they built a chapel by the well and placed an image of the saint therein; and now the image, which is usually highly coloured, grows pale and perspires hot sweat on the saint's night, and then the gift of miracle belongs to it, and they who touch it are made whole.

There is a wild legend about a carriage with four galloping phantom horses, coal black, and a phantom lady in it, dressed in bridal white and pale as a corpse, seated by the side of a grim ghost-husband. This apparition is seen at a place where four roads meet, and is attributed to the fact that this gentleman, when in life and driving out with his bride, at that spot blasphemously invoked the Evil One.

Passing from fiction to fact, here is a curious little story. Twenty or thirty years ago (my informant did not remember the precise date) there came to Autun a holy bishop from the far east. He had been cruelly tortured in some perilous mission among the heathen, and his face bore fearful evidence of the sufferings he had endured. His credentials were pronounced perfectly satisfactory, and the then bishop of Autun, with his clergy, lent him support and assistance towards the object of his visit to France, which was the collecting of money in aid of the mission of which he was the chief. The interest excited by the disfigured visage of the good prelate helped him powerfully with the female inhabitants, who contributed liberally. Whenever he walked the streets a crowd attended him. At length he took leave of the faithful city, and proceeded on his way. As he passed through the picturesque village of Couches, a labouring man endeavoured to catch a glimpse of the scarred and wounded face of which everybody talked, and which had so deeply moved the whole population. The labourer was a convict on leave, and he recognized in the bishop a brother convict who had escaped from prison a little time before, and was now turning his wounds to good account in the edification of the devout, and his own private enrichment. This discovery, which the bishop's old friend did not feel bound to keep secret, brought the episcopal mission to a sudden termination.

This reminds me of an event which occurred at Sens during my own residence there. Two sisters of charity made the tour of the town to collect money in order to bring up poor Catholic children in the bosom of heretical England. Amongst other houses they visited mine, and Mrs. Hamerton in my absence received them, and had the benefit of listening to a full explanation of their plans. The taller of the two sisters was a stranger, travelling for the above-mentioned laudable purpose; the other was merely a sister then resident at Sens, who accompanied and presented the stranger. Now this tall sister ***was a man,*** and he might have left the town undetected in his disguise, had not an unfeminine gesture, at a moment when he believed himself alone, betrayed him. He must have acted his part on the whole very cleverly, and it needed immense audacity, for he ate at the same table with the genuine sisters, and slept, it is said, in the same dormitory. The discovery and apprehension of this swindler created some sensation in the little town, and every one, ***after the event,*** remembered some masculine peculiarity. As I have said, I was out at the time he came to my house, and so missed him. Mrs. Hamerton observed nothing unusual except the extreme smallness and beauty of his hands, which were very white and well kept, and which he held before him with a certain ostentation. As the beauty of the hands struck Mrs. Hamerton, even when she supposed their owner to be a woman, it is not unlikely that the possession of them may have suggested the disguise.

One day a young peasant whom I knew very well came to me with a look of evident embarrassment,—a particularly sheepish look, as we say in England. It came out that he was going to be married, and, finally, that he had a great desire that I should officiate as a witness. I have a distaste for ceremonies in general, and have managed on the whole to keep well out of them, but this time no excuse would serve me, since any pretext would be set down to pride, and my peasant friend would feel hurt. So one cold winter's morning I got up long before light, and set off to the bride's house in a distant village. Peasants have no notion about time in anything, and their arrangements are usually such as to leave here and there a hiatus of an hour or two. There was not the least necessity for making me undertake a chilly journey before the dawn; for on our arrival we waited three hours in a state of total inaction, during which I had nothing better to do than watch the opening and shutting of the gigantic cavernous brick oven as the countless dishes were introduced, examined whilst in progress, or withdrawn. So far as I could guess its dimensions, the oven seemed to be three yards deep, or rather more, a yard and a half wide, and a yard high. To heat an oven of this kind wood is burned ***in*** it, not under it, till the bricks all round are thoroughly heated; they retain their heat long after the fire is removed, and cook a prodigious quantity of meat.

Gradually the company arrived, all of them farmers and their families, the older generation in clean blue blouses, their sons, for the most part, in broadcloth. The feminine costumes were generally very handsome and good, and I have no doubt costly, but do not pretend to be a judge in such matters. Peasant women in this part of France live lives of extreme simplicity and even roughness, but on great occasions they dress expensively, without abandoning the costume of their class. A little anecdote will prove to what an extent this goes. Mrs. Hamerton happened to be in a shop in Autun, one day last winter, when a peasant and his daughter came to buy a shawl for her wedding. The old man was very poorly dressed, and the girl seemed as if she had never been in a shop in her life before. So the shopman offered a shawl of moderate value, about ten pounds. The father rather admired this till he heard the price, when he utterly scorned it, and the same process was repeated till a sixty pound shawl was produced, on which the father declared himself satisfied, as the price seemed sufficiently high. A gold chain is also necessary, and peasant girls choose the best they can get.

At length the procession was formed; first marched the father of the bride with the bride on his arm, then the bridegroom and myself, arm in arm, then a great number of couples duly marshalled. Before us marched a fiddler. We had not gone ten yards before we had to stop and give money to a man by the wayside with a thing like a chandelier of many branches, all covered with flaunting scraps of coloured paper, and studded with paper flowers. These things occurred at every twenty or thirty yards, and every time I noticed that the bride's father gave two francs. We all had to give according to our means, and the paper chandeliers, so dearly purchased, were all carried in the procession, which thus assumed an appearance of ever-increasing gaiety. Many guns were fired, and we reached the mairie under an almost royal yet irregular salute. The *maire's* deputy did all the work, the functionary himself being perfectly at sea, or wool-gathering, or whatever else may best express that condition of the mind in which it is totally unfit for the work lying immediately before it. At last he tied the official scarf round his waist, and somehow got through the little bit of business that the *adjoint* could not possibly do for him. Having signed the papers as witness, I had to give the bridegroom to his bride, and made her a small speech on the occasion, of a very simple character, but which, as it turned out, gave great pleasure to the parents, who spoke of it often afterwards. The procession being now re-formed, continued its march to the church—a delightfully picturesque church, very venerable, and wholly guiltless of restoration. The wedding party almost filled the seats, but some disorder was occasioned at first by a peremptory command from the priest that all the paper chandeliers, which had cost so much money, should be carried outside, or else he would not begin the service. They distracted attention, he thought.

The priest went through the usual Catholic marriage service, and I felt rather nervous from the idea that a part of my duty would be to hold a piece of embroidered silk over the heads of the kneeling couple; but it seems that previous young men in my situation had misbehaved when doing this; so the priest had resolved to confide the trust henceforth always to the devouter sex. The bride's sister held my end with the utmost self-possession, as if quite accustomed to it, and the bride herself was happy under the shadow of it; for we were late at church, and there had been a threat that this ceremony should be omitted, which threat had cost her great anxiety and many tears. A marriage is always a solemn affair, and a church is not the right place to laugh in; but the sense of the ludicrous is active wherever anything occurs to stimulate it, and I could not help feeling rather tickled by the clerk in blouse and sabots, clumsily going through the prescribed ceremonial, and producing, by the side of the splendid vestments of the priest, an effect as incongruous as a Somersetshire labourer in working dress, if he could be presented at court. After the ceremony the priest turned his back to the altar, and made a long address on the subject of marriage. He did not put the matter in any new light, but his manner and style were very carefully suited to the understanding of his audience; and as he had known the parish long, and been acquainted with the bridegroom's family for generations, he took the opportunity of recalling at great length the virtues of his deceased grandfather, with an exhortation to imitate them. All this is no doubt strictly within the province of the priest, and yet there seems to be something inconsistent in the idea that a gentleman who, by the necessity of his position, is an old bachelor, should be called upon, also by the same necessity of position, to talk about a state of life of which he had had no experience. No talking about marriage is of much value, however, for every marriage is an entirely new experiment; and when an old married man advises a young one about his dealings with his wife, the counsel in very many cases is not less inapplicable than the empty generalities of an old bachelor.

We all adjourned to the priest's house for the signature of his marriage registers. It was comfortable enough; but most houses of the middle class in Burgundy have a repellent aspect, on account of the general notion that paper and paint need not be renewed more than once in forty years. The people are not a dirty people, the quantities of linen they possess are quite fabulous, they are cleanly in their cookery, they take frequent warm baths in winter and river baths in summer, they rub and polish their oaken floors, and apply as much friction to their furniture as if they hoped to cure it of some rheumatic complaint; but an Englishman entering their houses is immediately struck by an overpowering impression of ancient dirt and long neglect, which impression, if he tries to account for it, will be found to be wholly due to the want of paper, paint, and whitewash. Perhaps this may result from a feeling of despair. The flies are very numerous here, and after two summers a room looks dirty. To look like a well-kept house in a northern climate, a Burgundian habitation would have to be painted and papered every spring, or else decorated with something that would bear frequent washing.

Signing anything is always a nervous business for the unlettered, and not every one present had the courage or the power to attempt it. The bride professed herself entirely ignorant of the art of writing, on which her father informed us all, that in her youth he had provided instruction for her, but that she had never been willing to learn. Ornaments of the body she possessed, chains of gold, shawl of many colours, robe of stiff and glistening silk, head-dress of delicate lace; but the ornaments of the mind, nay, even its most plain and ordinary furniture, had been absolutely omitted. How much more learned was her venerable parent, who, when asked to sign, came forward with a confident air, and wrote his name quite steadily, with some attempt at a flourish! The spectators were evidently impressed by this contrast, by the decline in scholarship apparent in the family, when, unfortunately, the priest said, "Very well; now you must put a *p* for pére. " *The father was now obliged to confess that he did not know how to make a* p, on which everybody laughed outright, to his confusion. He was a member of that numerous class between writers and non-writers who have acquired, by diligent practice, the art of signing their own names, but do not consider it necessary to push their education farther.

From the priest's house the procession went to the village inn, the fiddler fiddling very diligently in front. Here we found tables spread with clean cloths, but nothing on them except a number of white soup tureens full of Burgundy wine, and plates piled high with little sweet biscuits. The wine was liberally sugared,— peasants on great occasions always sugar their wine. After drinking a few goblets of this, we formed the procession once more, and marched through the village to the sound of the fiddle, interrupted by frequent discharges of fowling-pieces. On our return to the house of the bride's father a singular custom was observed. An air of total stillness and abandonment reigned over the whole place. There was nobody to welcome us, nobody to say a kind word to the new bride. The door was shut and bolted, and not even a cat looked at us from the window. The leaders of the procession knocked at the door,—no one answered; again and again they knocked, the whole procession standing in patient expectation. As there was no answer from the inside, the fiddler was placed before the door, and he fiddled for admittance,—still no answer. Then the uncle of the bridegroom took the fiddle and performed. At length a grumbling voice was heard.

"Who are ye?"

"We are your daughter and her husband and their friends."

"I know ye not."

"Open unto us."

"I will not open; I know ye not."

The bride, "I am thy daughter."

A long pause.

The door opens; suddenly a violent hail-storm of wheat flies in the faces of all near it. It is called the *sowing,* and it means, "Be fruitful."

Then a huge loaf is held out in the doorway, and the bride and the bridegroom must bite of it, without cutting it. This accomplished, (it means, "May you have plenty!") the pair stand in the doorway, and all the procession kiss *both* of them, offering congratulations.

Dancing now began, and as everybody present, except myself, was very skilful and active in that exercise, it went on very vigorously. A quadrille, as danced by the peasantry, does not resemble the cold performance which bears the same name in polite society. They add many graces and flourishes, often quite indescribable. They bend and lean on air; they dance as much with their arms as with their legs; they leap and bound like lambs or kids; they are very amiable to their partners, and keep their arms round their waists quite affectionately for hours together; and what is more, from the air of happiness visible on the faces of the girls, there can be no manner of doubt that they like it.

Before our departure for the *mairie,* we had most of us taken a little light refreshment, consisting of four or five dishes of meat and a few tumblers of wine; but in spite of that and the subsequent draughts and sweet biscuits at the inn, we had not danced above two hours before we began to think about dinner. How shall I describe the magnitude of that feast?

The daily life of the peasant is one of the very strictest sobriety. He very seldom tastes meat, and only occasionally drinks wine; sugar is a rarity almost unknown. A festival, to him, is the saturnalia of long-repressed desires. A rich gentleman does not eat much more at a banquet than at his ordinary dinner; animal food is not in itself an exciting delight; sugar has no charms for him; but put the rich gentleman on the peasant's diet for twelve months, and *then* give him for one day the full range of all his appetites, and he would understand the rare excesses of the peasantry.

I regret not to have made a list of the dishes of meat presented to me at table, but I counted eighteen and missed several. No kind of flesh known to be in season was omitted, and the cooks of the village had exhausted all their science. The dinner was really excellent in its way, but I longed for something else than perpetual meat. Vegetables there were none, There was some dessert, however, because our host was of rather a superior class; but the ordinary peasant's great feast consists of nothing but between twenty and thirty different dishes of meat succeeding each other, during long hours of laborious mastication.

I should have been glad to give some idea of the conversation and characters at table, for both were amusing in their way; but I despair of doing them any justice in any language except their own patois, which I do not write for two reasons; first, though I understand it when spoken, I can neither speak nor spell it; secondly, if I could, no English reader would appreciate it. In a general way, I may say, however, that my peasant friends were very shrewd and humorous, but always perfectly polite.

As I was a good way from home I left very early, but the wedding guests danced late out of doors by the light of the moon. The next day there was a great flesh feast at the house of the bridegroom, and many minor repasts at intervals. The bridegroom's younger brother calculated that in the two days he had eaten fifteen meals and danced fifteen hours.

CHAPTER IV.

A RIVER VOYAGE IN A BASKET.

I HAVE said that the boundary of my garden is a stream. Beyond this is a broad meadow, and on the other side of the meadow a larger stream, called the Ternin, from which mine has been artificially detached. The Ternin is a great happiness to me, because full of picturesque subjects along its whole course, and also because there are some deep pools where I take a daily swim in summer. These two pleasures, swimming and the study of nature, were both very great; but the question suggested itself whether it would not be also possible to make the little river yield a third delight. How if I could navigate it? Of course all my neighbours said that was totally impossible, that there were shallows, and snags, and turns, and tree trunks, and branches, and all manner of obstacles. My boat would be caught and engulphed in whirlpools; my head would be smashed against tree boughs; my feet, after I was upset, would be caught in roots and weeds; and I should be both killed and drowned, as the Irishman said.

The Ternin runs about four miles from my house to Autun, where it discharges itself into the Arroux. The Arroux descends in its turn to the Loire, which it meets at Digoin. The idea of connecting myself with the great system of river navigation, of having access by water to the Loire, the Rhone, the Seine, was something inspiriting and magnificent.

I have a good boat, but after trying her on the Ternin, found that she was too long for such intricate navigation, and also that the usual process of rowing was not possible on a rapid little stream where it was always necessary to see well in advance. So I devised a small flat-bottomed coracle, short and buoyant, made of wickerwork, covered with canvas. This cost me altogether about twelve shillings. It has one wooden seat, three narrow wooden keels, and a double-bladed paddle for propulsion. Seated with my face in the direction of the stream's course, I can detect at some distance anything likely to offer an impediment, and take measures to avoid it. The loose paddle is infinitely better than a pair of sculls for such rough work as this. A paddle is equal to two things, and yet it is only one thing; it does not get embarrassed in rowlocks as oars will in a very narrow place; you can push with it on either side in a moment, and it occupies no breadth of water; above all, you can sit with your face to your work.

With this little coracle I found that I could easily perform the whole voyage on the river, and anything more amusing and exciting it is not possible to imagine. The water rushes over the shallows with great swiftness, and swirls heavily in the deep pools; there are hundreds of roots, and sometimes massive trunks lie half athwart the stream; the turns are extremely sharp, and there are violent eddies and counter currents on which the coracle bobs about like a cork. Such boating as this needs incessant attention, but that is the very charm of it. An amusement ought to occupy the mind as well as the body, and not leave it free to continue its labours or recur to its anxieties. Simple rowing on smooth water is, I have always thought, one of the most mechanical of all diversions. Sailing is good, because it occupies one, and needs constant watchfulness. Descending a wild stream in a coracle is quite as good as even sailing in rough weather. You see before you, a hundred yards off, five or six awkward snags all across the stream; you select what seems the best passage, and with a few strong strokes of the paddle get your coracle into such a position that it will rush straight through the narrow channel. In an instant the obstacles are behind you, and you are borne along swiftly, perhaps over rippling rapids, or tossed on leaping waves, or on a deep calm pool a moment's respite is allowed you, and you may light your pipe and meditate on the delightfulness of your position. When you descend in this manner some rapid trout stream like the Ternin, nothing is more amusing than to watch the astonished anglers on the bank. You appear to them as unexpectedly as if you were a porpoise—they open their mouths in amazement—you glide past them in a moment, and are gone.

Work of this kind, I warn the sympathetic reader, is, when you first attempt it, in a high degree alarming. It seems absolutely impossible that you should get out of such an endless succession of difficulties. The first snags, with water rushing between them like a mill-race, have something of horror in their aspect—gaunt arms rising from the swift stream to catch you and rend you. With a little experience these alarms give place to a feeling of perfect self-possession. You learn the art of discovering in time where the best passage lies, and of so placing your coracle that it will be driven through it by the current. You become aware of certain laws or customs of rapid streams, by which you know beforehand how and where they have hollowed water enough to carry your light craft. You acquire such mastery over your paddle that, with a powerful stroke or two, you avert easily what seems certain destruction.

People who live near streams usually pronounced not navigable do not know what they miss. To any such I say get a coracle or a little canoe, and try to navigate your stream. A little wading now and then does no harm, though in the winter and spring I do my voyage to Autun without once quitting the coracle. It might be possible in a sharp little canoe to ascend the stream also, but this seems very doubtful; my plan is to walk home and send the coracle back in a cart. I have not yet read the history of the "Rob Roy Canoe," but can well believe that a boat so carefully built would have advantages over a coracle. I think, however, that for rough work of this kind it is well not to be afraid for your boat, so it is better to have it very cheap and easily repaired. I intend to build one this summer of paper, which seems to be the best of all materials. I shall begin by making a solid mound on the earth the exact shape and size of the canoe, bottom upwards. On this I shall place slips of paper in every direction, dipped in Jeffrey's Marine Glue, till they reach a thickness sufficient to resist hard usage, yet not enough to be heavy. The elasticity of such a boat would be great, and it would be absolutely impermeable; besides, it is quite easy to give it a most beautiful form, favourable to speed. Again, a paper boat would be repaired at once, and the voyager might take a little marine glue as part of his stores.

It is scarcely necessary to observe that nobody ought to have playthings of this kind who is not a good swimmer.

These general observations relieve me from the necessity of describing the voyage to Autun. It is very beautiful. We pass an old château with a picturesque wooden bridge; but the great charm is in the windings of the river, and the glimpses of the towers of the lofty city looking grander and grander, nearer and nearer, as we glide rapidly towards it. At length we pass on the right a great massive Roman ruin, like two sides of a strong tower or keep, which the people call the Temple of Janus. On the left is a picturesque group of houses, a bridge, and a fine Roman gateway, with its arches still entire. Then the coracle passes into the Arroux, and floats, slowly and soberly now, down to the other bridge, under the shadow of the massive Roman walls, whose good masonry has been so pillaged for house building that only a few square yards of the facing remain, yet these fragments perfect as if built yesterday. There is another Roman gateway at Autun, and other walls with many towers built in the middle ages. All these are crowned by the spire of the cathedral, and better subjects for etching it is not possible to imagine. The way the towers group on the side towards the hills is quite glorious, and the more I draw and etch about Autun the richer it seems. The courtyards too, into which no casual tourist penetrates, are full of interest, from the noble one of the Hôtel de Beauchamp, once the residence of a Chancellor of Burgundy, down to little neglected places inhabited by quite poor people, and which one only finds out by the most impudent prying. To describe such things as these the etching needle is a better instrument than the pen, and since I have began to use it, I am no longer tempted to elaborate written descriptions till they become tedious.

EPILOGUE.

NINE years have elapsed since the first experiment in hut life in the Lancashire moors. Looking back across these nine years, the author believes that he can judge of what he then did with as much impartiality as another critic, and with far more intimate knowledge of the circumstances to be taken into consideration.

Ten years ago, when P. G. H. planned his encampment, the direction of English landscape study was almost entirely towards accuracy and detail. P. G. H. never called himself, or desired to be called, a Pre-Raphaelite, but he had warm sympathy with the earnestness in study of which that school set the worthy example. Art may be attacked by two opposite methods, either by trying always from the very beginning for power and unity of effect, gradually acquiring better knowledge of detail by observation and practice; or detail itself may be made the first object, and unity and power of effect looked to as the crown of the edifice. These two methods are simply those of synthesis and analysis; both are necessary in all study, but one or the other is usually the chief aim of the student, and the intellectual habits of the age may determine which of the two shall for the moment enjoy the advantages of being fashionable. P. G. H. would not have been human, he would certainly not have been artistic, if he had not felt the influences and shared the enthusiasms of his age and generation. His idea of study was, therefore, almost entirely analytic; to render the true form and colour of the plants and rocks; the true structure of the mountain and the cloud, seemed to him an aim worthy of all labour, and for the achievement of which any amount of trouble or inconvenience might be cheerfully gone through and endured. This was the state of his mind during his hut life in Lancashire. An old project for the rich illustration of the Loire, from its source to the sea, was abandoned, perhaps unfortunately, for a residence on a well-beloved lake in Scotland. An artist whose training and ideas were almost exclusively analytical might have pursued his studies, in the climate of central France, in life-long unconsciousness of the insufficiency of his method. Happily industrious, producing always work of undeniable interest and value as a record, he might have escaped the reflections on the nature of art which lead to dissatisfaction with mere detail, however accurate. It seems probable that if P. G. H. had gone to the Loire instead of to Argyllshire, he would have done far more work with the brush, and so acquired far greater manual skill, but that the purely analytic habit would have remained with him.

The Highlands taught another lesson, and a very severe lesson it was. The great characteristic of the Highlands is their magnificent unity of effect, and it became evident that the analytic method was here incompetent After a year of constant observation and many practical failures, P. G. H., who could not abandon his desire for analysis, determined to try for a kind of art which should be at the same time minutely analytic, and yet a true painting of effect. It is obvious that such an ambition involved prodigious technical difficulties. The artist who frankly abandons effect, as many English painters seem to have done, may, by patience and hard work, carry analysis very far. The artist who is content to sacrifice detail altogether, as many French painters do, may reach great power and unity. But to combine on one canvas the detail of Brett and the effect of Troyon, is so immensely difficult that it may safely be pronounced to be impossible. And it is impossible for the profoundest reasons—reasons deduced from the eternal laws of the human mind. We are so constituted that art only affects us in so far as it is the expression of some predominant idea, some overpowering emotion. The power of the painter is in his originality of *selection,* by which he emphatically calls our attention to some especial quality or aspect of nature. When P. G. H. aimed at the union of the whole of visible detail with as much as possible of visible effect, he erred in ignoring altogether the artistic right—we may even go farther, and call it the artistic *duty*—of selection.

Art in this is an epitome of life. The man who cannot choose between one thing and another is the helpless victim of the situation in which he finds himself: his friends, his books, his profession, his wife, all tumble upon him, because he happens to be in that place; but men who succeed greatly take their own everywhere, and leave the rest. Unless an artist finds in nature something with which he himself has a peculiar affinity, something belonging to him, he will never do any good; but if, having found this, he is too timid to claim his rights and cultivate his own property, failure equally attends him.

If P. G. H. had had the courage to set aside, once for all, the idea that mere fidelity to the outward form was a sort of duty to the public, he would probably have done much more and much better. Every young man lives under the influence of some one whose authority he respects; and P. G. H. lived under the influence of Mr. Ruskin, which accounts for his tendencies to pure topography. That influence might have lasted longer if Mr. Ruskin himself had not weakened and finally destroyed it by publications whose startling unreason was enough to shake the faith of all but the most devoted disciples. In 1856 it seemed to P. G. H. that Mr. Ruskin was *the* writer on art, as Mahomet, to a son of Islam, is the Prophet. In 1866 it seems rather that Mr. Ruskin is one of the most distinguished critics, as Mahomet, to a philosopher, is one of the greatest religious leaders. The transition from the position of a believer to that of an observant but not hostile onlooker, is in this instance fully accomplished; and whatever critics may still say of me, they cannot any longer accuse me of Ruskinism.

All these remarks about analysis and selection are quite pertinent to the subject of this book, the Camp. Much analysis and little selection lead naturally to tent-work, which offers great conveniences for close analytic study. Artists who work from memory mainly, have no occasion for painting-tents, as I have always said. Hence it happened that when P. G. H. gave up the habit of analysis, and painted large pictures from sketches and studies, he almost abandoned for a time the use of the camp. Now, however, he uses the tents again, but with different aims.

First, he did slow analytic work from nature with the camp.

Next he tried work from memoranda in the studio.

Thirdly, he returned to the camp, but with a view to rapid work, whose chief aim was synthetic.

In the future there seems every probability that the tents will be of frequent service. When these pages appear, the writer will be voyaging in his boat, pitching his camp every night. These voyages, as they occur, may be recorded in some magazine or review, and illustrated in a separate issue of etchings, or the etchings may be accompanied with a brief account of the journey. An artist's excursions ought not to be elaborated into heavy books of travel, but told briefly, without too much effort, and, above all, very liberally illustrated. In these respects the "Painter's Camp" has not yet quite fulfilled my notion of an artist's book of travel; but as the present edition brings it into briefer compass, so some future arrangement may supply the illustrations which, to my regret, are still wanting to its completion.

In conclusion, I take the opportunity of saying a few words on a subject which occupied in the first edition more space than it deserved. Many critics, reflecting no doubt quite faithfully the general opinion, were rather angry with me for opening what seemed an unprofitable discussion about the position of art and artists in the world. They saw in it simply an expression of personal irritation or professional soreness; but this view, I venture to observe, was not entirely just to me. Of all questions in social philosophy not one interested me so much, or on grounds so broadly general, as that of the social estimation of the various occupations of men; and I may add that, to this day, no social subject has for me an interest so deep and inexhaustible. The current estimation of occupations is the key to the state of civilization. Accident led me to direct, for the time, my attention more especially to the rank assigned to my own pursuit; but that of the pursuits of others was not less suggestive, nor less interesting or valuable, in my view, as evidence of our social condition. The solution which I then proposed, ***that the social rank of an occupation is the accurate measure of its governmental power,*** seems to me still the only possible explanation. If this is, as I do believe, a fundamental law of human nature, it is both foolish and useless to quarrel with it; but though it may be useless to quarrel with it, it is not useless to state it. The benefit to be derived from such discussions is the clear separation of the two ideas of nobleness and power. Painting is, if rightly followed, one of the very noblest of human pursuits, but it is not a powerful one; hence its social rank is dubious. The social rank of a perfectly unscrupulous prime minister (*e.g.,* Bismark) is very high; the social rank of a perfectly upright domestic servant is very humble. The real difference is a difference of power, which society must recognize. Nor does it seem difficult to understand why this instinct of deference to the powerful has been implanted in the human mind. Men were intended to be ***governable*** creatures, and deference is a predisposition to obedience. There is, however, a compensation which some years ago I had not known by experience, and so valued less than I do now. That compensation is human sympathy. Authors and artists may possess this to an extent which is really wonderful. Our social rank may not be quite so firm as that of lawyers and statesmen; but honest work may win for us a kindly personal interest in the hearts of thousands, and the respect of intelligent and cultivated men in the remotest parts of the earth. Only the other day a letter came to me from a stranger beyond the Mississippi, full of the warmest encouragement. The knowledge that there are many who care for us, and desire our success, may fortify us against the insolence of snobs.

The Codes Of Hammurabi And Moses
W. W. Davies

QTY

The discovery of the Hammurabi Code is one of the greatest achievements of archaeology, and is of paramount interest, not only to the student of the Bible, but also to all those interested in ancient history...

Religion   **ISBN:** *1-59462-338-4*   **Pages:132**
MSRP $12.95

The Theory of Moral Sentiments
Adam Smith

QTY

This work from 1749. contains original theories of conscience amd moral judgment and it is the foundation for systemof morals.

Philosophy   **ISBN:** *1-59462-777-0*   **Pages:536**
MSRP $19.95

Jessica's First Prayer
Hesba Stretton

QTY

In a screened and secluded corner of one of the many railway-bridges which span the streets of London there could be seen a few years ago, from five o'clock every morning until half past eight, a tidily set-out coffee-stall, consisting of a trestle and board, upon which stood two large tin cans, with a small fire of charcoal burning under each so as to keep the coffee boiling during the early hours of the morning when the work-people were thronging into the city on their way to their daily toil...

Childrens   **ISBN:** *1-59462-373-2*   **Pages:84**
MSRP $9.95

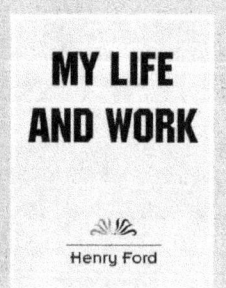

My Life and Work
Henry Ford

QTY

Henry Ford revolutionized the world with his implementation of mass production for the Model T automobile. Gain valuable business insight into his life and work with his own auto-biography... "We have only started on our development of our country we have not as yet, with all our talk of wonderful progress, done more than scratch the surface. The progress has been wonderful enough but..."

Biographies/   **ISBN:** *1-59462-198-5*   **Pages:300**
MSRP $21.95

The Art of Cross-Examination
Francis Wellman

QTY

I presume it is the experience of every author, after his first book is published upon an important subject, to be almost overwhelmed with a wealth of ideas and illustrations which could readily have been included in his book, and which to his own mind, at least, seem to make a second edition inevitable. Such certainly was the case with me; and when the first edition had reached its sixth impression in five months, I rejoiced to learn that it seemed to my publishers that the book had met with a sufficiently favorable reception to justify a second and considerably enlarged edition. ..

Pages:412

Reference   ISBN: *1-59462-647-2*   *MSRP $19.95*

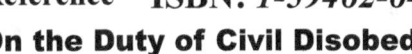

On the Duty of Civil Disobedience
Henry David Thoreau

QTY

Thoreau wrote his famous essay, On the Duty of Civil Disobedience, as a protest against an unjust but popular war and the immoral but popular institution of slave-owning. He did more than write—he declined to pay his taxes,   and was hauled off to gaol in consequence. Who can say how much this refusal of his hastened the end of the war and of slavery ?

Law   ISBN: *1-59462-747-9*   **Pages:48**
MSRP $7.45

Dream Psychology Psychoanalysis for Beginners
Sigmund Freud

QTY

Sigmund Freud, born Sigismund Schlomo Freud (May 6, 1856 - September 23, 1939), was a Jewish-Austrian neurologist and psychiatrist who co-founded the psychoanalytic school of psychology. Freud is best known for his theories of the unconscious mind, especially involving the mechanism of repression; his redefinition of sexual desire as mobile and directed towards a wide variety of objects; and his therapeutic techniques, especially his understanding of transference in the therapeutic relationship and the presumed value of dreams as sources of insight into unconscious desires.

Pages:196

Psychology   ISBN: *1-59462-905-6*   *MSRP $15.45*

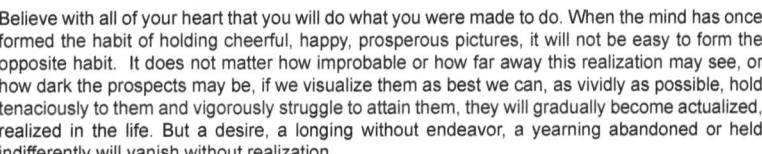

The Miracle of Right Thought
Orison Swett Marden

QTY

Believe with all of your heart that you will do what you were made to do. When the mind has once formed the habit of holding cheerful, happy, prosperous pictures, it will not be easy to form the opposite habit. It does not matter how improbable or how far away this realization may see, or how dark the prospects may be, if we visualize them as best we can, as vividly as possible, hold tenaciously to them and vigorously struggle to attain them, they will gradually become actualized, realized in the life. But a desire, a longing without endeavor, a yearning abandoned or held indifferently will vanish without realization.

Pages:360

Self Help   ISBN: *1-59462-644-8*   *MSRP $25.45*

The Rosicrucian Cosmo-Conception Mystic Christianity *by Max Heindel* ISBN: 1-59462-188-8 **$38.95**
The Rosicrucian Cosmo-conception is not dogmatic, neither does it appeal to any other authority than the reason of the student. It is: not controversial, but is: sent forth in the, hope that it may help to clear... New Age/Religion Pages 646

Abandonment To Divine Providence *by Jean-Pierre de Caussade* ISBN: 1-59462-228-0 **$25.95**
"The Rev. Jean Pierre de Caussade was one of the most remarkable spiritual writers of the Society of Jesus in France in the 18th Century. His death took place at Toulouse in 1751. His works have gone through many editions and have been republished... Inspirational/Religion Pages 400

Mental Chemistry *by Charles Haanel* ISBN: 1-59462-192-6 **$23.95**
Mental Chemistry allows the change of material conditions by combining and appropriately utilizing the power of the mind. Much like applied chemistry creates something new and unique out of careful combinations of chemicals the mastery of mental chemistry... New Age Pages 354

The Letters of Robert Browning and Elizabeth Barret Barrett 1845-1846 vol II ISBN: 1-59462-193-4 **$35.95**
by Robert Browning and Elizabeth Barrett Biographies Pages 596

Gleanings In Genesis (volume I) *by Arthur W. Pink* ISBN: 1-59462-130-6 **$27.45**
Appropriately has Genesis been termed "the seed plot of the Bible" for in it we have, in germ form, almost all of the great doctrines which are afterwards fully developed in the books of Scripture which follow... Religion/Inspirational Pages 420

The Master Key *by L. W. de Laurence* ISBN: 1-59462-001-6 **$30.95**
In no branch of human knowledge has there been a more lively increase of the spirit of research during the past few years than in the study of Psychology, Concentration and Mental Discipline. The requests for authentic lessons in Thought Control, Mental Discipline and... New Age/Business Pages 422

The Lesser Key Of Solomon Goetia *by L. W. de Laurence* ISBN: 1-59462-092-X **$9.95**
This translation of the first book of the "Lernegton" which is now for the first time made accessible to students of Talismanic Magic was done, after careful collation and edition, from numerous Ancient Manuscripts in Hebrew, Latin, and French... New Age/Occult Pages 92

Rubaiyat Of Omar Khayyam *by Edward Fitzgerald* ISBN:1-59462-332-5 **$13.95**
Edward Fitzgerald, whom the world has already learned, in spite of his own efforts to remain within the shadow of anonymity, to look upon as one of the rarest poets of the century, was born at Bredfield, in Suffolk, on the 31st of March, 1809. He was the third son of John Purcell... Music Pages 172

Ancient Law *by Henry Maine* ISBN: 1-59462-128-4 **$29.95**
The chief object of the following pages is to indicate some of the earliest ideas of mankind, as they are reflected in Ancient Law, and to point out the relation of those ideas to modern thought. Religiom/History Pages 452

Far-Away Stories *by William J. Locke* ISBN: 1-59462-129-2 **$19.45**
"Good wine needs no bush, but a collection of mixed vintages does. And this book is just such a collection. Some of the stories I do not want to remain buried for ever in the museum files of dead magazine-numbers an author's not unpardonable vanity..." Fiction Pages 272

Life of David Crockett *by David Crockett* ISBN: 1-59462-250-7 **$27.45**
"Colonel David Crockett was one of the most remarkable men of the times in which he lived. Born in humble life, but gifted with a strong will, an indomitable courage, and unremitting perseverance... Biographies/New Age Pages 424

Lip-Reading *by Edward Nitchie* ISBN: 1-59462-206-X **$25.95**
Edward B. Nitchie, founder of the New York School for the Hard of Hearing, now the Nitchie School of Lip-Reading, Inc, wrote "LIP-READING Principles and Practice". The development and perfecting of this meritorious work on lip-reading was an undertaking... How-to Pages 400

A Handbook of Suggestive Therapeutics, Applied Hypnotism, Psychic Science ISBN: 1-59462-214-0 **$24.95**
by Henry Munro Health/New Age/Health/Self-help Pages 376

A Doll's House: and Two Other Plays *by Henrik Ibsen* ISBN: 1-59462-112-8 **$19.95**
Henrik Ibsen created this classic when in revolutionary 1848 Rome. Introducing some striking concepts in playwriting for the realist genre, this play has been studied the world over. Fiction/Classics/Plays 308

The Light of Asia *by sir Edwin Arnold* ISBN: 1-59462-204-3 **$13.95**
In this poetic masterpiece, Edwin Arnold describes the life and teachings of Buddha. The man who was to become known as Buddha to the world was born as Prince Gautama of India but he rejected the worldly riches and abandoned the reigns of power when... Religion/History/Biographies Pages 170

The Complete Works of Guy de Maupassant *by Guy de Maupassant* ISBN: 1-59462-157-8 **$16.95**
"For days and days, nights and nights, I had dreamed of that first kiss which was to consecrate our engagement, and I knew not on what spot I should put my lips..." Fiction/Classics Pages 240

The Art of Cross-Examination *by Francis L. Wellman* ISBN: 1-59462-309-0 **$26.95**
Written by a renowned trial lawyer, Wellman imparts his experience and uses case studies to explain how to use psychology to extract desired information through questioning. How-to/Science/Reference Pages 408

Answered or Unanswered? *by Louisa Vaughan* ISBN: 1-59462-248-5 **$10.95**
Miracles of Faith in China Religion Pages 112

The Edinburgh Lectures on Mental Science (1909) *by Thomas* ISBN: 1-59462-008-3 **$11.95**
This book contains the substance of a course of lectures recently given by the writer in the Queen Street Hall, Edinburgh. Its purpose is to indicate the Natural Principles governing the relation between Mental Action and Material Conditions... New Age/Psychology Pages 148

Ayesha *by H. Rider Haggard* ISBN: 1-59462-301-5 **$24.95**
Verily and indeed it is the unexpected that happens! Probably if there was one person upon the earth from whom the Editor of this, and of a certain previous history, did not expect to hear again... Classics Pages 380

Ayala's Angel *by Anthony Trollope* ISBN: 1-59462-352-X **$29.95**
The two girls were both pretty, but Lucy who was twenty-one who supposed to be simple and comparatively unattractive, whereas Ayala was credited, as her Bombwhat romantic name might show, with poetic charm and a taste for romance. Ayala when her father died was nineteen... Fiction Pages 484

The American Commonwealth *by James Bryce* ISBN: 1-59462-286-8 **$34.45**
An interpretation of American democratic political theory. It examines political mechanics and society from the perspective of Scotsman James Bryce Politics Pages 572

Stories of the Pilgrims *by Margaret P. Pumphrey* ISBN: 1-59462-116-0 **$17.95**
This book explores pilgrims religious oppression in England as well as their escape to Holland and eventual crossing to America on the Mayflower, and their early days in New England... History Pages 268

QTY

The Fasting Cure *by Sinclair Upton*   ISBN: *1-59462-222-1*   **$13.95**
In the Cosmopolitan Magazine for May, 1910, and in the Contemporary Review (London) for April, 1910, I published an article dealing with my experiences in fasting. I have written a great many magazine articles, but never one which attracted so much attention... New Age/Self Help/Health Pages 164

Hebrew Astrology *by Sepharial*   ISBN: *1-59462-308-2*   **$13.45**
In these days of advanced thinking it is a matter of common observation that we have left many of the old landmarks behind and that we are now pressing forward to greater heights and to a wider horizon than that which represented the mind-content of our progenitors...   Astrology Pages 144

Thought Vibration or The Law of Attraction in the Thought World   ISBN: *1-59462-127-6*   **$12.95**

by William Walker Atkinson   *Psychology/Religion Pages 144*

Optimism *by Helen Keller*   ISBN: *1-59462-108-X*   **$15.95**
Helen Keller was blind, deaf, and mute since 19 months old, yet famously learned how to overcome these handicaps, communicate with the world, and spread her lectures promoting optimism. An inspiring read for everyone...   Biographies/Inspirational Pages 84

Sara Crewe *by Frances Burnett*   ISBN: *1-59462-360-0*   **$9.45**
In the first place, Miss Minchin lived in London. Her home was a large, dull, tall one, in a large, dull square, where all the houses were alike, and all the sparrows were alike, and where all the door-knockers made the same heavy sound...   Childrens/Classic Pages 88

The Autobiography of Benjamin Franklin *by Benjamin Franklin*   ISBN: *1-59462-135-7*   **$24.95**
The Autobiography of Benjamin Franklin has probably been more extensively read than any other American historical work, and no other book of its kind has had such ups and downs of fortune. Franklin lived for many years in England, where he was agent...   Biographies/History Pages 332

Name	
Email	
Telephone	
Address	
City, State ZIP	

☐ **Credit Card**   ☐ **Check / Money Order**

Credit Card Number	
Expiration Date	
Signature	

Please Mail to: Book Jungle
PO Box 2226
Champaign, IL 61825
or Fax to: 630-214-0564

ORDERING INFORMATION

web: *www.bookjungle.com*
email: *sales@bookjungle.com*
fax: *630-214-0564*
mail: *Book Jungle PO Box 2226 Champaign, IL 61825*
or PayPal *to sales@bookjungle.com*

Please contact us for bulk discounts

DIRECT-ORDER TERMS

**20% Discount if You Order
Two or More Books**
Free Domestic Shipping!
Accepted: Master Card, Visa,
Discover, American Express

www.ingramcontent.com/pod-product-compliance
Lightning Source LLC
Chambersburg PA
CBHW080955020726
47505CB00009B/2212